S0-BSD-848

WAYNE PUBLIC LIBRARY

MAR 2 9 2002

THE JOHN FANTE READER

written by STEPHEN COOPER

Full of Life: A Biography of John Fante

edited by STEPHEN COOPER

The Big Hunger: Stories 1932–1959 by John Fante

John Fante: A Critical Gathering

Perspectives on John Huston

THE JOHN FANTE READER

EDITED BY STEPHEN COOPER

WILLIAM MORROW

An Imprint of HarperCollins*Publishers*

THE JOHN FANTE READER. Copyright © 2002 by Joyce Fante. All rights reserved.
Printed in the United States of America. No part of this book may be used or
reproduced in any manner whatsoever without written permission except in the case of
brief quotations embodied in critical articles and reviews.
For information address HarperCollins Publishers Inc.,
10 East 53rd Street, New York, NY 10022.

HarperCollins books may be purchased for educational,
business, or sales promotional use. For information please write:
Special Markets Department, HarperCollins Publishers Inc.,
10 East 53rd Street, New York, NY 10022.

FIRST EDITION

Designed by Fearn Cutler de Vicq

Printed on acid-free paper

Library of Congress Cataloging-in-Publication Data

Fante, John.
The John Fante reader / edited by Stephen Cooper.—1st ed.
p. cm.
Includes bibliographical references.
ISBN 0-06-018496-5
1. United States—Social life and customs—20th century—Fiction. 2. Authors, American—
20th century—Correspondence. 3. Screenwriters—United States—Correspondence. 4.
Fante, John, 1909—Correspondence. I. Cooper, Stephen, 1949– II. Title.

PS3511.A594 A6 2002
813'.52—dc21
2001044182

02 03 04 05 06 QW 10 9 8 7 6 5 4 3 2 1

For Joyce Fante

Contents

Acknowledgments

The material in this reader is reprinted from the following books published by Black Sparrow Press: *Ask the Dust* (1939, 1980), *Dreams from Bunker Hill* (1982), *Wait Until Spring, Bandini* (1938, 1983), *The Wine of Youth: Selected Stories of John Fante* (1985), *The Road to Los Angeles* (1985), *1933 Was a Bad Year* (1985), *West of Rome* (1986), *Full of Life* (1952, 1988), *The Brotherhood of the Grape* (1977, 1988), *John Fante & H. L. Mencken: A Personal Correspondence* (1989), *Selected Letters: 1932–1981* (1991), and *The Big Hunger: Stories 1932–1959* (2000). Warmest thanks to Joyce Fante for permission to print a number of previously unpublished letters.

EDITOR'S PREFACE

The selections in this reader represent the legacy of a writer who was almost forgotten in his lifetime. When he died in 1983 at the age of seventy-four, John Fante could not have known that less than two decades later he would be regarded as an important figure in twentieth-century literature, nor that he would also be recognized internationally for his influence on younger generations of writers.

In the present arrangement of stories and excerpts from his novels we can learn much about John Fante, both his life in the world and the life of his imagination. A selection of letters, including material never before published, helps round out the fictional picture.

Fante was often unabashedly autobiographical in his writing. It should be noted, however, that he never hesitated to change the facts to serve his stories, which, after all, were at the heart of his life. Adventurous readers worldwide continue to find the interplay of that life and those stories compelling. Welcome to John Fante's world.

Part One

HOME CONFESSIONS

A KIDNAPING IN THE FAMILY

THERE WAS AN OLD TRUNK in my mother's bedroom. It was the oldest trunk I ever saw. It was one of those trunks with a round lid like a fat man's belly. Away down in this trunk, beneath wedding linen that was never used because it was wedding linen, and silverware that was never used because it was a wedding present, and beneath all kinds of fancy ribbons, buttons, birth certificates, beneath all this was a box containing family pictures. My mother wouldn't permit anyone to open this trunk, and she hid the key. But one day I found the key. I found it hidden under a corner of the rug.

On spring afternoons that year I would come home from school and find my mother working in the kitchen. Her arms would be limp and white like dry clay from toil, her hair thin and dry against her head, and her eyes sunken and large and sad in their sockets.

The picture! I would think. Oh, that picture in the trunk!

When my mother wasn't looking I would steal into her bedroom, lock the door, and open the trunk. There were many pictures down there, and I loved all of them, but there was one alone which my fingers ached to clutch and my eyes longed to see when I found my mother that way—it was a picture of her taken a week before she married my father.

Such a picture!

She sat on the arm of a plush chair in a white dress spilling down to her toes. The sleeves were puffy and frothy: they were very elegant sleeves. There was scarcely any neck to the dress, and at her throat was a cameo on a thin gold chain. Her hat was the biggest hat I ever saw in my life. It went entirely around her shoulders like a white parasol, the brim dipping slightly, and covering most of her hair except a dark mound in back. But I could see the green, heavy eyes, so big that not even that hat could hide them.

I would stare at that strange picture, kissing it and crying over it, happy because once it had been true. And I remember an afternoon when I took it down to the creek bank, set it upon a stone, and prayed to it. And in the kitchen was my mother, imprisoned behind pots and pans: a woman no longer the lovely woman in the picture.

And so it was with me, a kid home from school.

Other times I did other things. I would stand at the dresser mirror with the picture at my ear, facing the round mirror. A sheepishness, a shivering delight would possess me. How unbelievable this grand lady, this queen! And I remember that I would be speechless.

My mother in the kitchen at that moment was not my mother. I wouldn't have it. Here was my mother, the lady in the big hat. Why couldn't I remember anything about her? Why did I have to be so young when I was born? Why couldn't I have been born at the age of fourteen? I couldn't remember a thing. When had my mother changed? What caused the change? How did she grow old? I made up my mind that if I ever saw my mother as beautiful as she was in the picture I would immediately ask her to marry me. She had never refused me anything, and I felt she would not refuse me as a husband. I elaborated on this determination, even discovering a way to dispose of my father: my mother could divorce him. If the Church would not grant a divorce, we could wait and be married as soon as my father died. I searched my catechism and prayer book for a law which stated that mothers could not marry their sons. I was satisfied to find nothing on the subject.

One evening I slipped the picture under my waist and took it to my father. He sat reading the paper on the front porch.

"Look," I said. "Guess who?"

He looked at it through a haze of cigar smoke. His indifference annoyed me. He examined it as though it were a bug, or something; a piece of stale cake, or something. His eyes slid up and down the picture three times, then crosswise three times. Turning it over, he examined the back. The composition interested him more than the subject, and I had hoped his eyes would pop and that he would shout with excitement.

"It's Mamma!" I said. "Don't you recognize her?"

He looked at me wearily. "Put it back where you found it," he said, picking up his newspaper.

"But it's Mamma!"

"Good God!" he said. "I know who it is! I'm the man who married her."

"But look!"

"Go away," he said.

"But, Papa! Look!"

"Go away. I'm reading."

I wanted to hit him. I was embarrassed and sad. Something happened at that moment and the picture was never so wonderful again. It became another picture—just a picture. I seldom looked at it again, and after that evening I never opened my mother's trunk and burrowed for treasure at the bottom.

Before her marriage my mother was Maria Scarpi. She was the daughter of Giuseppe and Stella Scarpi. They were peasants from Naples. Giuseppe Scarpi—he was a shoemaker. He and his wife came to Denver from Italy. My mother, Maria Scarpi, was born there in Denver. She was the fourth child. With her brothers and sisters she went to the Sisters' school. Then she went to a public high school for three years. But this public high school wasn't like the Sisters' school, and she didn't like it. Her two brothers and four sisters married after completing high school.

But Maria Scarpi would not marry. She told her people marriage did not interest her. What she wanted was to become a nun. This shocked the whole family. Her brothers and sisters thought such an ambition didn't make sense. What about children? What about home, and a nice husband, a fine man like Paul Carnati? And to all these questions the woman who became my mother put her nose in the air and held to her monastic ambitions. She was a rebel, and her brothers and sisters brought all sorts of possible suitors to the house in an effort to persuade her to get over her foolishness. But Maria Scarpi was cold and mean, even refusing to speak to them. Hearing voices downstairs, she would lock herself in the bedroom and stay there until they went away.

Paul Carnati owned a bakery. He made lots of money, he had a lot of good ideas, and he was crazy about my mother. One day he drove up to the Scarpi house in a brand-new buggy with rubber tires and a fine young horse pulling it. This Carnati had so much money that he was actually going to give the horse and buggy to my mother for nothing. My mother wouldn't look at it; she wouldn't even come downstairs, and Paul Carnati went away so angry and insulted he never came back again. He carried his grief further by charging the Scarpi family twice as much for bread, until they had to quit buying from him; and, to top it all off, he furiously married somebody else. Italians called this a spite marriage.

My mother told me of her first meeting with my father. It was in 1910. It was in August of that year, on the feast day of Saint Rocco, the powerful patron saint of all Italians. On that great day the Italians lined the streets of the North Side, and down the middle of the street passed the gaudy parade, with three complete bands and the Sons of Saint Rocco in their red uniforms with white plumes in their hats. The Knights of Columbus were there, and they had a band, and the Sons of Little Italy were there with their band. In fact, everybody who counted was there, including a lot of Americans who didn't count but who came down just to look and laugh, because they thought feast days on the North Side were amusing.

The parade moved down Osage Street to Belmont, and east on Belmont to St. Stephen's Church. My mother stood on the corner of Osage and Belmont, in front of the drugstore, which still stands there, and watched the parade.

She was alone, surrounded by young Italian fellows who had hurried away from the pool-tables in the Star Hall, cues in their hands, hats on the back of their heads. They knew my mother, the young fellows did, they knew all about her. Everybody on the North Side knew Maria Scarpi who wanted to become a nun instead of a wife. She stood with her back to them, detesting them; they were hoodlums, first of the gangster breed which later brought disgrace upon the good name of Italians in Denver.

They pretended they were interested in the parade. But they weren't. It was a bluff. What they were interested in was my mother. Here was a peculiar situation, foreign to hoodlums. What could a man say to a girl about to become a nun? They said nothing, not a word. They merely stood there applauding the parade.

There was a commotion in the rear. Somebody was shoving. Nudging this fellow and that, snarling with importance—he was not a big man, so he snarled twice as hard as necessary—he pushed his way through until, lo, who was this before him? This girl under the great hat? Guido Toscana was gay with white wine, but he saw beauty much clearer that way. Puffing a twisted cigar, he halted. The others ignored him. Who the hell did he think he was? They had never seen him before, although they were sure that like themselves he was an Italian.

My mother felt him near, the brim of her hat touching his shoulder. She moved forward. But not too far. The gutter was an inch from her toes.

"Good day!" said Guido Toscana.

"I don't know you," she said.

"Ho!" he said. "Ho ho! My name is Guido Toscana. What is your name?"

He turned and winked at the young men. Their faces froze. My mother's eyes raced along the faces across the street in search of one of her brothers. A drunken man. And she a girl who wanted to become a nun! O dear God, she prayed, please help me! But apparently even God was enjoying this, or He was too busy watching the parade in honor of His sainted Rocco, for He permitted Guido Toscana other liberties. Filling his cheeks with cigar smoke, my future father leaned over and—poufffff!— squirted smoke under the brim of my future mother's hat. The white pungency stung. She gagged, coughed into a small handkerchief. Toscana laughed uproariously, turning to the young men for approbation. They pretended they had not seen. Ah, thought Guido Toscana, so that's it: the Dagos!

My mother had had enough. Clutching her hat, she pushed him aside, broke through the crowd of Italians, and walked rapidly up the street. The Scarpi house was three blocks away. At the end of the block she turned the corner, glancing over her shoulder.

Her breath leaped. He was following her! He had taken off his hat and, dodging through the crowd, he was waving to her, beckoning her to return. She ran then, those two remaining blocks. He too ran.

"Mamma!" screamed Maria Scarpi. "Mamma! Mamma!"

She ascended the six porch steps in one jump. Mamma Scarpi, big and wide as three ordinary mothers, opened the front door and Maria flew inside. The door slammed, the bolt clicked. Guido Toscana came puffing down the street. All was peaceful and quiet when he reached the house. The shades were down and no smoke came from the chimney. The place looked vacant. But he loitered. He would not go away. Up and down he walked like a sentinel before the Scarpi house. Up and down. Up and down. From behind a curtain upstairs peeped the head of Maria Scarpi. Up and down walked Guido Toscana. Up and down.

Fearless Mamma Scarpi opened the front door and stood behind the screen. In a shrill Italian she yelled: "What do you want, you drunken vagabond? Go away from here! Begone!"

"I wish to speak to the young lady," said Guido Toscana.

"Go away from this house, you drunken pig!"

"I am not drunk. I wish to speak to the young lady."

"On your way before I shout for the police, you drunken pig!"

He tried to smile away his fear of the police.

"A word with the young lady, and I will go."

"Polizia!" screamed Mamma Scarpi. *"Polizia!"*

Guido Toscana winced, closed his eyes, and made grimaces. He held his palms before his face, as though Mamma Scarpi's screams were bottles aimed at his head.

"*Polizia! Polizia! Polizia!*"

There was a movement at the window upstairs. The shade went up with a squeal and a succession of flappings. The window rose and Maria Scarpi's head appeared.

"Mamma!" she called. "Please don't yell. People will think we're crazy!"

To Guido Toscana her voice was that little girl in the throat of Enrico Caruso.

"Don't yell, Mamma! Let's see what he wants."

"Yes," said the great Mamma. "What do you want, you drunken pig?"

He stood under the window, looked up, and spoke in Italian.

"What is your name?"

A sigh.

"My name is Maria Scarpi."

"Will you marry me?"

Mamma Scarpi was too disgusted.

"Get out of this yard!" she yelled. "Back to the drunken pigs—you drunken pig!"

He was not listening. He opened his mouth and began to sing. There was no stopping him. People returning from the parade gaped in amazement. Mamma Scarpi slammed the door and went inside. My mother, not much for sharp wits, a soft-hearted girl who wanted to become a nun and pray for the sins of the world, was transfixed at the window.

She is still transfixed. She still wonders. And this used to annoy me, a kid home from school.

"I didn't know what to do," she would say. "All those people and all— I felt sorry for him."

"What did he sing?"

"That crazy song, the one he sings when he shaves."

I knew that song. Everybody for blocks around knew it. Every time he stood before a mirror lathering his face I thought of him under a window in Denver a year before I was born. The song was *"Mena, Me!"*

Ah, lass, you've hurt me sadly. Oh, sadly.
My heart is bleeding badly. Yes, badly.
My life blood's ebbing slowly,
And I cannot stop the flow.

Mena, me! Let me be!
Give a kiss. One kiss. You must do this!
A little kiss is not amiss.
Mind you, don't get coquettish,
What's a little kiss to you?
See the state you've got me into.
Have a little pity, do!

"What happened after that, Mamma?"

She was sweeping the kitchen floor, stooping to reach the crumbs of coal behind the concave stove legs. I could hear the cracking of her joints as she bent down.

"My brother Joe came home, and he saw your father."

"What did Uncle Joe say?"

"I don't know. I don't remember."

"Yes, you do. What did Uncle Joe say?"

"He laughed."

"Didn't he get sore?"

"No. Not at all."

"I'll bet he was afraid of Papa, wasn't he?"

"Not at all."

"Just the same, I'll bet he was scared to death."

"Have it your own way, then."

"What did Uncle Joe do, if he wasn't sore?"

"He invited your father in."

"Didn't they have a fight, or anything? Didn't Papa lick him, or anything?"

"No. Not at all."

"Did Papa go in?"

"Yes."

"What did you do?"

"I don't remember."

"Yes, you do too."

"It's been so long—I've forgotten."

"No, you haven't. You just won't tell me."

She raised herself, gasping for breath.

"I stayed upstairs in my room for a while, and then Uncle Joe came up and told me to come down. So I did."

"And what happened?"

"Nothing."

"Something *did* happen! What happened?"

"Nothing happened!" she said in exasperation. "Your uncle told me who your father was, and we shook hands. And that's all!"

"Is that all?"

"That's all."

"Didn't anything else happen?"

"Your father courted me, and after a few months we were married. That's all."

But I didn't like it that way. I hated it. I wouldn't have it. I couldn't believe it. I wouldn't believe it.

"No sirree!" I said. "It didn't happen like that."

"But it did! Why should I lie to you? There's nothing to hide."

"Didn't he do anything to you? Didn't he kidnap you, or something?"

"I don't remember being kidnaped."

"But you *were* kidnaped!"

She sat down, the broom between her knees, her two hands clutching it, and her head resting on her hands. She was so tired, and yet the fatigue melted from her face and she smiled vaguely, the ghost-smile of the lady in the picture.

"Yes!" she said. "He did kidnap me! He came one night when I was asleep and took me away."

"Yes!" I said. "Yes!"

"He took me to an outlaw cabin in the mountains!"

"Sure! And he was carrying a gun, wasn't he?"

"Yes! A big gun! With a pearl handle."

"And he was riding a black horse."

"Oh," she said, "I shall never forget that horse. He was a beauty!"

"And you were scared to death, weren't you?"

"Petrified," she said. "Simply petrified."

"You screamed for help, didn't you?"

"I screamed and screamed."

"But he got away, didn't he?"

"Yes, he got away."

"He took you to the outlaw cabin."

"Yes, that's where he took me."

"You were scared, but you liked it, didn't you?"

"I loved it."

"He kept you a prisoner, didn't he?"

"Yes, but he was good to me."

"Were you wearing that white dress? The one in the picture?"

"I certainly was. Why?"

"I just wanted to know," I said. "How long did he keep you prisoner?"

"Three days and nights."

"And on the third night he proposed to you, didn't he?"

Her eyes closed reminiscently.

"I shall never forget it," she said. "He got down on his knees and begged me to marry him."

"You wouldn't marry him at first, would you?"

"Not at first. I should say not! It was a long time before I said yes.

"But finally you did, huh?"

"Yes," she said. "Finally."

This was too much for me. Too much. I threw my arms around her and kissed her, and on my lips was the sharp tang of tears.

—*The Wine of Youth*

THE STILL SMALL VOICES

YOUR BROTHER SHOOK YOU BY THE HAIR until you were awake. It was about two o'clock in the morning.

He whispered, "Wake up. Mama and Papa's started in again."

In the next room you heard the voices of the two. The door was open, but there was no light. The whole house was dark. The bitterness in the voices was the same as on the other nights. The fire in the voice of your father made you and your brother reach for the skins of one another as you lay listening to the inscrutable words of the two, sometimes inaudible English words, but mostly Italian you had never heard.

Your brother Pete, who lay beside you, who was ten, said, "This is a hell of a house."

In the next room your father said, "I'm through, that's all. I'm through."

Your mother said, "And what about the kids?"

Your father said, "Take them and get the hell out."

Your sister in the room beyond theirs began to cry. She called out to you in the darkness of the old house, and you answered, "What?" And your mother and father became quiet so that they could hear what your sister was wanting, and she called out again, her voice weaving through the doors to where you lay, "Go see why Mama and Papa are fighting, Jimmie. Please go see. I'm scared."

And your youngest brother Tommy, who slept in the bed with your sister, shouted to you who were twelve and the oldest, "I ain't scared, Jimmie. She's eight too, and I'm only six."

Your father roared, his voice vibrating the whole house, "If you kids don't shut up, I'll give you something to be scared about."

The brother who slept beside you said, "Tommy is sure a nervy little guy."

Your mother said to your father, "Now you woke up everybody."

Your father said, "Let 'em wake up. See if I give a damn."

Your room was between that of your mother and father and that of your grandmother, and now you heard your grandmother rising from her bed. She would come to your room as she always did when your mother and father quarreled in the night. With every step she took, she moaned a strange "oh oh oh."

The brother beside you said, "Now here comes Grandma to butt in."

The door creaked, and your little grandmother was standing beside the bed, her very dry hand pawing the pillow in search of your head.

She whispered, and she was always crying on nights like this, "Go see, Jimmie, go see. You must make them stop. Your father will kill her."

Braggadocio, you said loud enough for your father to hear, "Aw, Papa's all right."

The house was quiet except for the "oh oh oh" from your grandmother's old bosom.

You said, "See? There ain't no more fighting."

Your father heard. There was the known sound of whining bedsprings, and your father sat up in bed and sputtered rapid angry words at your grandmother. It was that Italian of which you knew nothing. You did not catch a single ascertained word. Your grandmother went slowly on tiptoe back to her room, and her door closed, and the springs in her bed creaked.

Your mother said to your father, "That was a fine thing to say to your own mother."

From the room beyond, your sister said, "Mama, Mama, please don't start again."

Your little brother Tommy said to your sister, "Scaredy cat."

The brother beside you said in a whisper, "What did Papa say to Grandma?"

You said, "I don't know. Go to sleep."

The walls around the room were of lath and cracked plaster, and you could hear your grandmother in her bed. The strange "oh oh ohs" were round sobs that shook the bed now.

The brother beside you said, "Grandma's crying."

You said, "I'm not deaf. I hear her."

Your brother who was six said to his sister, who slept beside him: "Hey Jo, Grandma's crying."

Your sister said, "Well, you'd cry too, I bet, if you was her."

Your brother said, "Aw, how can I be her?"

The brother beside you said, "Listen to Tommy."

Your father asked in the darkness, "Who's crying?"

"Grandma's crying."

Your mother said, "His own mother."

Your brother Tommy said, "Papa, why's Grandma crying?"

Your father said, "You go to sleep, Tommy. It's awful late."

The brother beside you said, "Tommy sure asks questions."

Your mother got out of bed and put on her kimono. You heard her scrape through the room in her raggedy red slippers with the holey toes.

Your father said, "Where you going now?"

Your mother said, "Don't talk to me.' "

The moon was shining through the dining room windows, and you saw your mother pass them by. You heard the creak of the good rocking chair, and you knew your mother had seated herself by the stove. The embers in the stove were going out now, but she would not pour in coal because it made a kind of desecrating noise. The chair purred sweetly as your mother rocked to and fro, and pretty soon all was very quiet, and your mother was asleep in the dining room.

In the yard next door you heard the tumble of boxes, behind the grocery store. It was the neighborhood cats looking for meat scraps.

Your grandmother was asleep now. There were no sounds from her room.

Your father sighed. The springs in his bed whined angrily. Your father was fighting for sleep.

The brother at your side snored in the fresh sleep of boys.

Your little brother Tommy and your sister Josephine were soundless.

And after a little while, you heard your father whisper to your sister.

He called softly, "Jo, Jo . . . Josephine."

She did not answer, and your father got up from his bed and went to the room where she slept.

Your father shook your sister until she woke up.

He whispered to her, "Josephine, will you be Papa's nice little girl and go sleep with Grandma?"

She said, "Oh, I like to sleep with Grandma."

"All right, you go. Just tell Grandma you wanna sleep with her."

Your little brother Tommy was awake now, and he said, "I wanna sleep with somebody. I'm scared to sleep alone."

Your sister said, "Scaredy cat."

Your father said, "You come and sleep with Papa, Tommy—just you and Papa all alone."

And before they went to their different beds, you too were asleep.

—*The Big Hunger*

The Odyssey of a Wop

I

I PICK UP LITTLE BITS OF INFORMATION about my grandfather. My grandmother tells me of him. She tells me that when he lived he was a good fellow whose goodness evoked not admiration but pity. He was known as a good little Wop. Of an evening he liked to sit at a table in a saloon sipping a tumbler of anisette, all by himself. He sat there like a little girl nipping an ice-cream cone. The old boy loved that green stuff, that anisette. It was his passion, and when folks saw him sitting alone it tickled them, for he was a good little Wop.

One night, my grandmother tells me, my grandfather was sitting in the saloon, he and his anisette. A drunken teamster stumbled through the swinging doors, braced himself at the bar, and bellowed:

"All right, everybody! Come an' get 'em! They're on me!"

And there sat my grandfather, not moving, his old tongue coquetting with the anisette. Everyone but he stood at the bar and drank the teamster's liquor. The teamster swung round. He saw my grandfather. He was insulted.

"You too, Wop!" said he. "Come up and drink!"

Silence. My grandfather arose. He staggered across the floor, passed the teamster, and then what did he do but go through the swinging doors and down the snowy street! He heard laughter coming after him from the saloon and his chest burned. He went home to my father.

"*Mamma mia!*" he blubbered. "Tummy Murray, he calla me Wopa."

"*Sangue della Madonna!*"

Bareheaded, my father rushed down the street to the saloon. Tommy Murray was not there. He was in another saloon half a block away, and there my father found him. He drew the teamster aside and spoke under his breath. A fight! Immediately blood and hair began to fly. Chairs were drawn back. The customers applauded. The two men fought for an hour. They rolled over the floor, kicking, cursing, biting. They were in a knot in the middle of the floor, their bodies wrapped around each other. My father's head, chest, and arms buried the teamster's face. The teamster screamed. My father growled. His neck was rigid and trembling. The teamster screamed again, and lay still. My father got to his feet and wiped blood from his open mouth with the back of his hand. On the floor the teamster lay with a loose ear hanging from his head. . . . This is the story my grandmother tells me.

I think about the two men, my father and the teamster, and I picture them struggling on the floor. Boy! *Can* my father fight!

I get an idea. My two brothers are playing in another room. I leave my grandmother and go to them. They are sprawled on the rug, bent over crayons and drawing-paper. They look up and see my face flaming with my idea.

"What's wrong?" one asks.

"I dare you to do something!"

"Do what?"

"I dare you to call me a Wop!"

My youngest brother, barely six, jumps to his feet, and dancing up and down, screams: "Wop! Wop! Wop! Wop!"

I look at him. Pooh! He's too small. It's that other brother, that bigger brother, I want. He's got ears too, he has.

"I bet *you're* afraid to call me Wop."

But he senses the devil in the woodpile.

"Nah," says he. "I don't wanna."

"Wop! Wop! Wop! Wop!" screams the little brother.

"Shut your mouth, you!"

"I won't neither. You're a Wop! Wop! Woppedy Wop!"

My older brother's box of crayons lies on the floor in front of his nose. I put my heel upon the box and grind it into the carpet. He yells, seizing my leg. I back away, and he begins to cry.

"Aw, that was sure dirty," he says.

"I dare you to call me a Wop!"

"Wop!"

I charge, seeking his ear. But my grandmother comes into the room flourishing a razor strop.

—*The Wine of Youth*

H E CAME ALONG, kicking the deep snow. Here was a disgusted man. His name was Svevo Bandini, and he lived three blocks down that street. He was cold and there were holes in his shoes. That morning he had patched the holes on the inside with pieces of cardboard from a macaroni box. The macaroni in that box was not paid for. He had thought of that as he placed the cardboard inside of his shoes.

He hated the snow. He was a bricklayer, and the snow froze the mortar between the brick he laid. He was on his way home, but what was the sense in going home? When he was a boy in Italy, in Abruzzi, he hated the snow too. No sunshine, no work. He was in America now, in the town of Rocklin, Colorado. He had just been in the Imperial Poolhall. In Italy there were mountains, too, like those white mountains a few miles west of him. The mountains were a huge white dress dropped plumb-like to the earth. Twenty years before, when he was twenty years old, he had starved for a full week in the folds of that savage white dress. He had been building a fireplace in a mountain lodge. It was dangerous up there in the winter. He had said the devil with the danger, because he was only twenty then, and he had a girl in Rocklin, and he needed money. But the roof of the lodge had caved beneath the suffocating snow.

It harassed him always, that beautiful snow. He could never understand why he didn't go to California. Yet he stayed in Colorado, in the deep snow, because it was too late now. The beautiful white snow was like the beautiful white wife of Svevo Bandini, so white, so fertile, lying in a white bed in a house up the street. 456 Walnut Street, Rocklin, Colorado.

Svevo Bandini's eyes watered in the cold air. They were brown, they were soft, they were a woman's eyes. At birth he had stolen them from his mother—for after the birth of Svevo Bandini, his mother was never quite the same, always ill, always with sickly eyes after his birth, and then she died and it was Svevo's turn to carry soft brown eyes.

A hundred and fifty pounds was the weight of Svevo Bandini, and he had a son named Arturo who loved to touch his round shoulders and feel for the snakes inside. He was a fine man, Svevo Bandini, all muscles, and he had a wife named Maria who had only to think of the muscle in his loins and her body and her mind melted like the spring snows. She was so white, that Maria, and looking at her was seeing her through a film of olive oil.

Dio cane. Dio cane. It means God is a dog, and Svevo Bandini was saying it to the snow. Why did Svevo lose ten dollars in a poker game tonight at the Imperial Poolhall? He was such a poor man, and he had three children, and the macaroni was not paid for, nor was the house in which the three children and the macaroni were kept. God is a dog.

Svevo Bandini had a wife who never said: give me money for food for the children, but he had a wife with large black eyes, sickly bright from love, and those eyes had a way about them, a sly way of peering into his mouth, into his ears, into his stomach, and into his pockets. Those eyes were so clever in a sad way, for they always knew when the Imperial Poolhall had done a good business. Such eyes for a wife! They saw all he was and all he hoped to be, but they never saw his soul.

That was an odd thing, because Maria Bandini was a woman who looked upon all the living and the dead as souls. Maria knew what a soul was. A soul was an immortal thing she knew about. A soul was an immortal thing she would not argue about. A soul was an immortal thing. Well, whatever it was, a soul was immortal.

Maria had a white rosary, so white you could drop it in the snow and lose it forever, and she prayed for the soul of Svevo Bandini and her children. And because there was no time, she hoped that somewhere in this world someone, a nun in some quiet convent, someone, anyone, found time to pray for the soul of Maria Bandini.

He had a white bed waiting for him, in which his wife lay, warm and waiting, and he was kicking the snow and thinking of something he was going to invent some day. Just an idea he had in his head: a snow plow. He had made a miniature of it out of cigar boxes. He had an idea there. And then he shuddered as you do when cold metal touches your flank, and he was suddenly remembering the many times he had got into the warm bed beside Maria, and the tiny cold cross on her rosary touched his flesh on winter nights like a tittering little cold serpent, and how he withdrew quickly to an even colder part of the bed, and then he thought of the bedroom, of the house that was not paid for, of the white wife endlessly waiting for passion, and he could not endure it, and straightway in his fury he plunged into deeper snow off the sidewalk, letting his anger fight it out with the snow. *Dio cane. Dio cane.*

He had a son named Arturo, and Arturo was fourteen and owned a sled. As he turned into the yard of his house that was not paid for, his feet suddenly raced for the tops of the trees, and he was lying on his back, and Arturo's sled was still in motion, sliding into a clump of snow-weary lilac bushes. *Dio cane!* He had told that boy, that little bastard, to keep his sled out of the front walk. Svevo Bandini felt the snow's cold attacking his hands like frantic ants. He got to his feet, raised his eyes to the sky, shook his fist at God, and nearly collapsed with fury. That Arturo. That little bastard! He dragged the sled from beneath the lilac bush and with systematic fiendishness tore the runners off. Only when the destruction was complete did he remember that the sled had cost seven-fifty. He stood brushing the snow from his clothes, that strange hot feeling in his ankles, where the snow had entered from the tops of his shoes. Seven dollars and fifty cents torn to pieces. *Diavolo!* Let the boy buy another sled. He preferred a new one anyway.

———

The house was not paid for. It was his enemy, that house. It had a voice, and it was always talking to him, parrot-like, forever chattering the same thing. Whenever his feet made the porch floor creak, the house said insolently: you do not own me, Svevo Bandini, and I will never belong to you. Whenever he touched the front doorknob it was the same. For fifteen years that house had heckled him and exasperated him with its idiotic independence. There were times when he wanted to set dynamite under it, and blow it to pieces. Once it had been a challenge, that house so like a woman, taunting him to possess her. But in thirteen years he had wearied and weakened, and the house had gained in its arrogance. Svevo Bandini no longer cared.

The banker who owned that house was one of his worst enemies. The mental image of that banker's face made his heart pound with a hunger to consume itself in violence. Helmer, the banker. The dirt of the earth. Time and again he had been forced to stand before Helmer and say that he had not enough money to feed his family. Helmer, with the neatly parted grey hair, with the soft hands, the banker eyes that looked like oysters when Svevo Bandini said he had no money to pay the installment on his house. He had had to do that many times, and the soft hands of Helmer unnerved him. He could not talk to that kind of a man. He hated Helmer. He would like to break Helmer's neck, to tear out Helmer's heart and jump on it with both feet. Of Helmer he would think and mutter: the day is coming! the day is coming! It was not his house, and he had but to touch the knob to remember it did not belong to him.

Her name was Maria, and the darkness was light before her black eyes. He tiptoed to the corner and a chair there, near the window with the green shade down. When he seated himself both knees clicked. It was like the tinkling of two bells to Maria, and he thought how foolish for a wife to love a man so much. The room was so cold. Funnels of vapor tumbled from his breathing lips. He grunted like a wrestler with his shoelaces. Always trouble with his shoelaces. *Diavolo!* Would he be an old man on his death bed before he ever learned to tie his shoelaces like other men?

"Svevo?"

"Yes."

"Don't break them, Svevo. Turn on the light and I'll untie them. Don't get mad and break them."

God in heaven! Sweet Mother Mary! Wasn't that just like a woman? Get mad? What was there to get mad about? Oh God, he felt like smashing his fist through that window! He gnawed with his fingernails at the knot of his shoe laces. Shoe laces! Why did there have to be shoe laces? Unnh. Unnh. Unnh.

"Svevo."

"Yes."

"I'll do it. Turn on the light."

When the cold has hypnotized your fingers, a knotted thread is as obstinate as barbed wire. With the might of his arm and shoulder he vented his impatience. The lace broke with a cluck sound, and Svevo Bandini almost fell out of the chair. He sighed, and so did his wife.

"Ah, Svevo. You've broken them again."

"Bah," he said. "Do you expect me to go to bed with my shoes on?"

He slept naked, he despised underclothing, but once a year, with the first flurry of snow, he always found long underwear laid out for him on the chair in the corner. Once he had sneered at this protection: that was the year he had almost died of influenza and pneumonia; that was the winter when he had risen from a death bed, delirious with fever, disgusted with pills and syrups, and staggered to the pantry, choked down his throat a half dozen garlic bulbs, and returned to bed to sweat it out with death. Maria believed her prayers had cured him, and thereafter his religion of cures was garlic, but Maria maintained that garlic came from God, and that was too pointless for Svevo Bandini to dispute.

He was a man, and he hated the sight of himself in long underwear. She was Maria, and every blemish on his underwear, every button and every thread, every odor and every touch, made the points of her breasts ache with a joy that came out of the middle of the earth. They had been married fifteen years, and he had a tongue and spoke well and often of this and that, but rarely had he ever said, I love you. She was his wife, and she spoke rarely, but she tired him often with her constant, I love you.

He walked to the bedside, pushed his hands beneath the covers, and groped for that wandering rosary. Then he slipped between the blankets and seized her frantically, his arms pinioned around hers, his legs locked around hers. It was not passion, it was only the cold of a winter night, and she was a small stove of a woman whose sadness and warmth had attracted him from the first. Fifteen winters, night upon night, and a woman warm and welcoming to her body feet like ice, hands and arms like ice; he thought of such love and sighed.

And a little while ago the Imperial Poolhall had taken his last ten dollars. If only this woman had some fault to cast a hiding shadow upon his own weaknesses. Take Teresa DeRenzo. He would have married Teresa DeRenzo, except that she was extravagant, she talked too much, and her breath smelled like a sewer, and she—a strong, muscular woman—liked to pretend watery weakness in his arms: to think of it! And Teresa DeRenzo was taller than he! Well, with a wife like Teresa he could enjoy giving the Imperial Poolhall ten dollars in a poker game. He could think of that breath, that chattering mouth, and he could thank God for a chance to waste his hard-earned money. But not Maria.

"Arturo broke the kitchen window," she said.

"Broke it? How?"

"He pushed Federico's head through it."

"The son of a bitch."

"He didn't mean it. He was only playing."

"And what did you do? Nothing, I suppose."

"I put iodine on Federico's head. A little cut. Nothing serious."

"Nothing serious! Whaddya mean, nothing serious! What'd you do to Arturo?"

"He was mad. He wanted to go to the show."

"And he went."

"Kids like shows."

"The dirty little son of a bitch."

"Svevo, why talk like that? Your own son."

"You've spoiled him. You've spoiled them all."

"He's like you, Svevo. You were a bad boy too."

"I was—like hell! You didn't catch me pushing my brother's head through a window."

"You didn't have any brothers, Svevo. But you pushed your father down the steps and broke his arm."

"Could I help it if my father . . . Oh, forget it."

He wriggled closer and pushed his face into her braided hair. Ever since the birth of August, their third son, his wife's right ear had an odor of chloroform. She had brought it home from the hospital with her ten years ago: or was it his imagination? He had quarreled with her about this for years, for she always denied there was a chloroform odor in her right ear. Even the children had experimented, and they had failed to smell it. Yet it was there, always there, just as it was that night in the ward, when he bent down to kiss her, after she had come out of it, so near death, yet alive.

"What if I did push my father down the steps? What's that got to do with it?"

"Did it spoil you? Are you spoiled?"

"How do I know?"

"You're not spoiled."

What the hell kind of thinking was that? Of course he was spoiled! Teresa DeRenzo had always told him he was vicious and selfish and spoiled. It used to delight him. And that girl—what was her name—Carmela, Carmela Ricci, the friend of Rocco Saccone, she thought he was a devil, and she was wise, she had been through college, the University of Colorado, a college graduate, and she had said he was a wonderful scoundrel, cruel, dangerous, a menace to young women. But Maria—oh Maria, she thought he was an angel, pure as bread. Bah. What did Maria know about it? She had had no college education, why she had not even finished high school.

Not even high school. Her name was Maria Bandini, but before she married him her name was Maria Toscana, and she never finished high school. She was the youngest daughter in a family of two girls and a boy. Tony and Teresa—both high school graduates. But Maria? The family curse was upon her, this lowest of all the Toscanas, this girl who wanted things her own way and refused to graduate from high school. The ignorant Toscana. The one without a high school diploma—almost a diploma, three and one-half years, but still, no diploma. Tony and Teresa had them, and Carmela Ricci, the friend of Rocco, had even gone to the University of Colorado. God was against him. Of them all, why had he fallen in love with this woman at his side, this woman without a high school diploma?

"Christmas will soon be here, Svevo," she said. "Say a prayer. Ask God to make it a happy Christmas."

Her name was Maria, and she was always telling him something he already knew. Didn't he know without being told that Christmas would soon be here? Here it was, the night of December fifth. When a man goes to sleep beside his wife on a Thursday night, is it necessary for her to tell him the next day would be Friday? And that boy Arturo—why was he cursed with a son who played with a sled? *Ah, povera America!* And he should pray for a happy Christmas. Bah.

"Are you warm enough, Svevo?"

There she was, always wanting to know if he was warm enough. She was a little over five feet tall, and he never knew whether she was sleeping or waking, she was that quiet. A wife like a ghost, always content in her little half of the bed, saying the rosary and praying for a merry Christmas. Was it any wonder that he couldn't pay for this house, this mad-house occupied by a wife who was a religious fanatic? A man needed a wife to goad him on, inspire him, and make him work hard. But Maria? *Ah, povera America!*

She slipped from her side of the bed, her toes with sure precision found the slippers on the rug in the darkness, and he knew she was going to the bathroom first, and to inspect the boys afterward, the final inspection before she returned to bed for the rest of the night. A wife who was always slipping out of bed to look at her three sons. Ah, such a life! *Io sono fregato!*

How could a man get any sleep in this house, always in a turmoil, his wife always getting out of bed without a word? Goddamn the Imperial Poolhall! A full house, queens on deuces, and he had lost. *Madonna!* And he should pray for a happy Christmas! With that kind of luck he should even talk to God! *Jesu Christi*, if God really existed, let Him answer—why!

As quietly as she had gone, she was beside him again.

"Federico has a cold," she said.

He too had a cold—in his soul. His son Federico could have a snivel and Maria would rub menthol on his chest, and lie there half the night talking about it, but Svevo Bandini suffered alone—not with an aching body: worse, with an aching soul. Where upon the earth was the pain greater than in your own soul? Did Maria help him? Did she ever ask him if he suffered from the hard times? Did she ever say, Svevo, my beloved, how is your soul these days? Are you happy, Svevo? Is there any chance for work this winter, Svevo? *Dio Maledetto!* And she wanted a merry Christmas! How can you have a merry Christmas when you are alone among three sons and a wife? Holes in your shoes, bad luck at cards, no work, break your neck on a goddamn sled—and you want a merry Christmas! Was he a millionaire? He might have been, if he had married the right kind of woman. Heh: he was too stupid though.

Her name was Maria, and he felt the softness of the bed recede beneath him, and he had to smile for he knew she was coming nearer, and his lips opened a little to receive them—three fingers of a small hand, touching his lips, lifting him to a warm land inside the sun, and then she was blowing her breath faintly into his nostrils from pouted lips.

"Cara sposa," he said. "Dear wife."

Her lips were wet and she rubbed them against his eyes. He laughed softly.

"I'll kill you," he whispered.

She laughed, then listened, poised, listened for a sound of the boys awake in the next room.

"Che sara, sara," she said. "What must be, must be."

Her name was Maria, and she was so patient, waiting for him, touching the muscle at his loins, so patient, kissing him here and there, and then the great heat he loved consumed him and she lay back.

"Ah, Svevo. So wonderful!"

He loved her with such gentle fierceness, so proud of himself, thinking all the time: she is not so foolish, this Maria, she knows what is good. The big bubble they chased toward the sun exploded between them, and he groaned with joyous release, groaned like a man glad he had been able to forget for a little while so many things, and Maria, very quiet in her little half of the bed, listened to the pounding of her heart and wondered how much he had lost at the Imperial Poolhall. A great deal, no doubt; possibly ten dollars, for Maria had no high school diploma but she could read that man's misery in the meter of his passion.

"Svevo," she whispered.

But he was sound asleep.

Bandini, hater of snow. He leaped out of bed at five that morning, like a skyrocket out of bed, making ugly faces at the cold morning, sneering at it: bah, this Colorado, the rear end of God's creation, always frozen, no place for an Italian bricklayer; ah, he was cursed with this life. On the sides of his feet he walked to the chair and snatched his pants and shoved his legs through them, thinking he was losing twelve dollars a day, union scale, eight hours hard work, and all because of that! He jerked the curtain string; it shot up and rattled like a machine gun, and the white naked morning dove into the room, splashing brightly over him. He growled at it. *Sporca chone*: dirty face, he called it. *Sporcaccione ubriaco*: drunken dirty face.

Maria slept with the drowsy awareness of a kitten, and that curtain brought her awake quickly, her eyes in nimble terror.

"Svevo. It's too early."

"Go to sleep. Who's asking you? Go to sleep."

"What time is it?"

"Time for a man to get up. Time for a woman to go to sleep. Shut up."

She had never got used to this early morning rising. Seven was her hour, not counting the times in the hospital, and once, she had stayed in bed until nine, and got a headache because of it, but this man she had married always shot out of bed at five in winter, and at six in summer. She knew his torment in the white prison of winter; she knew that when she arose in two hours he would have shoveled every clod of snow from every path in and around the yard, half a block down the street, under the clothes lines, far down the alley, piling it high, moving it around, cutting it viciously with his flat shovel.

And it was so. When she got up and slipped her feet inside of slippers, the toes aburst like frayed flowers, she looked through the kitchen window and saw where he was, out there in the alley, beyond the high fence. A giant of a man, a dwarfed giant hidden on the other side of a six foot fence, his shovel peering over the top now and then, throwing puffs of snow back to the sky.

But he had not built a fire in the kitchen stove. Oh no, he never built a fire in the kitchen stove. What was he—a woman, that he should build a fire? Sometimes though. Once he had taken them into the mountains for a beefsteak fry, and absolutely no one but himself was permitted to build that fire. But a kitchen stove! What was he—a woman?

It was so cold that morning, so cold. Her jaw chattered and ran away from her. The dark green linoleum might have been a sheet of ice under her feet, the stove itself a block of ice. What a stove that was! A despot, untamed and ill-tempered. She always coaxed it, soothed it, cajoled it, a black bear of a stove subject to fits of rebellion, defying Maria to make him glow; a cantankerous stove that, once warm and pouring sweet heat, suddenly went berserk and got yellow hot and threatened to destroy the very house. Only Maria could handle that black block of sulking iron, and she did it a twig at a time, caressing the shy flame, adding a slab of wood, then another and another, until it purred beneath her care, the iron heating up, the oven expanding and the heat thumping it until it grunted and groaned in content, like an idiot. She was Maria, and the stove loved only her. Let Arturo or August drop a lump of coal into its greedy mouth and it went mad with its own fever, burning and blistering the paint on the walls, turning a frightful yellow, a chunk of hell hissing for Maria, who came frowning and capable, a cloth in her hand as she twitted it here and there, shutting the vents deftly, shaking its bowels until it resumed its stupid normalcy. Maria, with hands no larger than frayed roses, but that black devil was her slave, and she really was very fond of it. She kept it shining and flashily vicious, its nickel plated trade name grinning evilly like a mouth too proud of its beautiful teeth.

When at length the flames rose and it groaned good morning, she put water on for coffee and returned to the window. Svevo was in the chicken yard, panting as he leaned on his shovel. The hens had come out of the shed, clucking as they eyed him, this man who could lift the fallen white heavens off the ground and throw them over the fence. But from the window she saw that the hens did not saunter too close to him. She knew why. They were her hens; they ate from her hands, but they hated him; they remembered him as the one who sometimes came of a Saturday night to kill. This was alright; they were very grateful he had shoveled the snow away so they could scratch the earth, they appreciated it, but they could never trust him as they did the woman who came with corn dripping from her small hands. And spaghetti too, in a dish; they kissed her with their beaks when she brought them spaghetti; but beware of this man.

Their names were Arturo, August, and Federico. They were awake now, their eyes all brown and bathed brightly in the black river of sleep. They were all in one bed, Arturo twelve, August ten, and Federico eight. Italian boys, fooling around, three in a bed, laughing the quick peculiar laugh of obscenity. Arturo, he knew plenty. He was telling them now what he knew, the words coming from his mouth in hot white vapor in the cold room. He knew plenty. He had seen plenty. He knew plenty. You guys don't know what I saw. She was sitting on the porch steps. I was about this far from her. I saw plenty.

Federico, eight years old.

"What'ya see, Arturo?"

"Shut yer mouth, ya little sap. We ain't talkin' to you!"

"I won't tell, Arturo."

"Ah, shut yer mouth. You're too little!"

"I'll tell, then."

They joined forces then, and threw him out of bed. He bumped against the floor, whimpering. The cold air seized him with a sudden fury and pricked him with ten thousand needles. He screamed and tried to get under the covers again, but they were stronger than he and he dashed around the bed and into his mother's room. She was pulling on her cotton stockings. He was screaming with dismay.

"They kicked me out! Arturo did. August did!"

"Snitcher!" yelled from the next room.

He was so beautiful to her, that Federico; his skin was so beautiful to her. She took him into her arms and rubbed her hands into his back, pinching his beautiful little bottom, squeezing him hard, pushing heat into him, and he thought of the odor of her, wondering what it was and how good it was in the morning.

"Sleep in Mamma's bed," she said.

He climbed in quickly, and she clamped the covers around him, shaking him with delight, and he was so glad he was on Mamma's side of the bed, with his head in the nest Mamma's hair made, because he didn't like Papa's pillow; it was kind of sour and strong, but Mamma's smelt sweet and made him warm all over.

"I know somethin' else," Arturo said. "But I ain't telling."

August was ten; he didn't know much. Of course he knew more than his punk brother Federico, but not half so much as the brother beside him, Arturo, who knew plenty about women and stuff.

"What'll ya give me if I tell ya?" Arturo said.

"Give you a milk nickel."

"Milk nickel! What the heck! Who wants a milk nickel in winter?"

"Give it to you next summer."

"Nuts to you. What'll ya give me now?"

"Give you anything I got."

"It's a bet. Whatcha got?"

"Ain't got nothing."

"Okay. I ain't telling nothing, then."

"You ain't got anything to tell."

"Like hell I haven't!"

"Tell me for nothing."

"Nothing doing."

"You're lying, that's why. You're a liar."

"Don't call me a liar!"

"You're a liar if you don't tell. Liar!"

He was Arturo, and he was fourteen. He was a miniature of his father, without the mustache. His upper lip curled with such gentle cruelty. Freckles swarmed over his face like ants over a piece of cake. He was the oldest, and he thought he was pretty tough, and no sap kid brother could call him a liar and get away with it. In five seconds August was writhing. Arturo was under the covers at his brother's feet.

"That's my toe hold," he said.

"Ow! Leggo!"

"Who's a liar!"

"Nobody!"

Their mother was Maria, but they called her Mamma, and she was beside them now, still frightened at the duty of motherhood, still mystified by it. There was August now; it was easy to be his mother. He had yellow hair, and a hundred times a day, out of nowhere at all, there came that thought, that her second son had yellow hair. She could kiss August at will, lean down and taste the yellow hair and press her mouth on his face and eyes. He was a good boy, August was. Of course, she had had a lot of trouble with him. Weak kidneys, Doctor Hewson had said, but that was over now, and the mattress was never wet anymore in the mornings. August would grow up to be a fine man now, never wetting the bed. A hundred nights she had spent on her knees at his side while he slept, her rosary beads clicking in the dark as she prayed God, please Blessed Lord, don't let my son wet the bed anymore. A hundred, two hundred nights. The doctor had called it weak kidneys; she had called it God's will; and Svevo Bandini had called it goddamn carelessness and was in favor of making August sleep in the chicken yard, yellow hair or no yellow hair. There had been all sorts of suggestions for cure. The doctor kept prescribing pills. Svevo was in favor of the razor strap, but she had always tricked him out of the idea; and her own mother, Donna Toscana had insisted that August drink his own urine. But her name was Maria, and so was the Savior's mother, and she had gone to that other Maria over miles and miles of rosary beads. Well, August had stopped, hadn't he? When she slipped her hand under him in the early hours of the morning, wasn't he dry and warm? And why? Maria knew why. Nobody else could explain it. Bandini had said, by God it's about time; the doctor had said it was the pills had done it, and Donna Toscana insisted it would have stopped a long time ago had they followed her suggestion. Even August was amazed and delighted on those mornings when he wakened to find himself dry and clean. He could remember those nights when he woke up to find his mother on her knees beside him, her face against his, the beads ticking, her breath in his nostrils and the whispered little words, Hail Mary, Hail Mary, poured into his nose and eyes until he felt an eerie melancholy as he lay between these two women, a helplessness that choked him and made him determined to please them both. He simply *wouldn't* pee the bed again.

It was easy to be the mother of August. She could play with the yellow hair whenever she pleased because he was filled with the wonder and mystery of her. She had done so much for him, that Maria. She had made him grow up. She had made him feel like a real boy, and no longer could Arturo tease him and hurt him because of his weak kidneys. When she came on whispering feet to his bedside each night he had only to feel the warm fingers caressing his hair, and he was reminded again that she and another Maria had changed him from a sissy to a real guy. No wonder she smelled so good. And Maria never forgot the wonder of that yellow hair. Where it came from God only knew, and she was so proud of it.

Breakfast for three boys and a man. His name was Arturo, but he hated it and wanted to be called John. His last name was Bandini, and he wanted it to be Jones. His mother and father were Italians, but he wanted to be an American. His father was a bricklayer, but he wanted to be a pitcher for the Chicago Cubs. They lived in Rocklin, Colorado, population ten thousand, but he wanted to live in Denver, thirty miles away. His face was freckled, but he wanted it to be clear. He went to a Catholic school, but he wanted to go to a public school. He had a girl named Rosa, but she hated him. He was an altar boy, but he was a devil and hated altar boys. He wanted to be a good boy, but he was afraid to be a good boy because he was afraid his friends would call him a good boy. He was Arturo and he loved his father, but he lived in dread of the day when he would grow up and be able to lick his father. He worshipped his father, but he thought his mother was a sissy and a fool.

Why was his mother unlike other mothers? She was that, and everyday he saw it again. Jack Hawley's mother excited him: she had a way of handing him cookies that made his heart purr. Jim Toland's mother had bright legs. Carl Molla's mother never wore anything but a gingham dress; when she swept the floor of the Molla kitchen he stood on the back porch in an ecstasy, watching Mrs. Molla sweep, his hot eyes gulping the movement of her hips. He was twelve, and the realization that his mother did not excite him made him hate her secretly. Always out of the corner of his eye he watched his mother. He loved his mother, but he hated her.

Why did his mother permit Bandini to boss her? Why was she afraid of him? When they were in bed and he lay awake sweating in hatred, why did his mother let Bandini do that to her? When she left the bathroom and came into the boys' bedroom, why did she smile in the darkness? He could not see her smile, but he knew it was upon her face, that content of the night, so much in love with the darkness and hidden lights warming her face. Then he hated them both, but his hatred of her was greatest. He felt like spitting on her, and long after she had returned to bed the hatred was upon his face, the muscles in his cheeks weary with it.

Breakfast was ready. He could hear his father asking for coffee. Why did his father have to yell all the time? Couldn't he talk in a low voice? Everybody in the neighborhood knew everything that went on in their house on account of his father constantly shouting. The Moreys next door—you never heard a peep out of them, never; quiet, American people. But his father wasn't satisfied with being an Italian, he had to be a noisy Italian.

"Arturo," his mother called. "Breakfast."

As if he didn't know breakfast was ready! As if everybody in Colorado didn't know by this time that the Bandini family was having breakfast!

He hated soap and water, and he could never understand why you had to wash your face every morning. He hated the bathroom because there was no bathtub in it. He hated toothbrushes. He hated the toothpaste his mother bought. He hated the family comb, always clogged with mortar from his father's hair, and he loathed his own hair because it never stayed down. Above all, he hated his own face spotted with freckles like ten thousand pennies poured over a rug. The only thing about the bathroom he liked was the loose floorboard in the corner. Here he hid *Scarlet Crime* and *Terror Tales*.

"Arturo! Your eggs are getting cold."

Eggs. Oh Lord, how he hated eggs.

They were cold, alright; but no colder than the eyes of his father, who glared at him as he sat down. Then he remembered, and a glance told him that his mother had snitched. Oh Jesus! To think that his own mother should rat on him! Bandini nodded to the window with eight panes across the room, one pane gone, the opening covered with a dish towel.

"So you pushed your brother's head through the window?"

It was too much for Federico. All over again he saw it: Arturo angry, Arturo pushing him into the window, the crash of glass. Suddenly Federico began to cry. He had not cried last night, but now he remembered: blood coming out of his hair, his mother washing the wound, telling him to be brave. It was awful. Why hadn't he cried last night? He couldn't remember, but he was crying now, the knuckle of his fist twisting tears out of his eyes.

"Shut up!" Bandini said.

"Let somebody push *your* head through a window," Federico sobbed. "See if *you* don't cry!"

Arturo loathed him. Why did he have to have a little brother? Why had he stood in front of the window? What kind of people were these Wops? Look at his father, there. Look at him smashing eggs with his fork to show how angry he was. Look at the egg yellow on his father's chin! And on his mustache. Oh sure, he was a Dago Wop, so he had to have a mustache, but did he have to pour those eggs through his ears? Couldn't he find his mouth? Oh God, these Italians!

—*Wait Until Spring, Bandini*

THE ODYSSEY OF A WOP

II

FROM THE BEGINNING, I hear my mother use the words Wop and Dago with such vigor as to denote violent distaste. She spits them out. They leap from her lips. To her, they contain the essence of poverty, squalor, filth. If I don't wash my teeth, or hang up my cap, my mother says: "Don't be like that. Don't be a Wop." Thus, as I begin to acquire her values, Wop and Dago to me become synonymous with things evil. But she's consistent.

My father isn't. He's loose with his tongue. His moods create his judgments. I at once notice that to him Wop and Dago are without any distinct meaning, though if one not an Italian slaps them onto him, he's instantly insulted. Christopher Columbus was the greatest Wop who ever lived, says my father. So is Caruso. So is this fellow and that. But his very good friend Peter Ladonna is not only a drunken pig, but a Wop on top of it; and of course all his brothers-in-law are good-for-nothing Wops.

He pretends to hate the Irish. He really doesn't, but he likes to think so, and he warns us children against them. Our grocer's name is O'Neil. Frequently and inadvertently he makes errors when my mother is at his store. She tells my father about short weights in meats, and now and then of a stale egg.

Straightway my father grows tense, his lower lip curling. "This is the last time that Irish bum robs me!" And he goes out, goes to the grocery-store, his heels booming.

Soon he returns. He's smiling. His fists bulge with cigars. "From now on," says he, "everything's gonna be all right."

I don't like the grocer. My mother sends me to his store every day, and instantly he chokes up my breathing with the greeting: "Hello, you little Dago! What'll you have?" So I detest him, and never enter his store if other customers are to be seen, for to be called a Dago before others is a ghastly, almost a physical, humiliation. My stomach expands and contracts, and I feel naked.

I steal recklessly when the grocer's back is turned. I enjoy stealing from him—candy bars, cookies, fruit. When he goes into his refrigerator I lean on his meat scales, hoping to snap a spring; I press my toe into egg baskets. Sometimes I pilfer too much. Then, what a pleasure it is to stand on the curb, my appetite gorged, and heave *his* candy bars, *his* cookies, *his* apples into the high yellow weeds across the street! . . . "Damn you, O'Neil, you can't call me a Dago and get away with it!"

His daughter is of my age. She's cross-eyed. Twice a week she passes our house on her way to her music lesson. Above the street, and high in the branches of an elm tree, I watch her coming down the sidewalk, swinging her violin case. When she is under me, I jeer in sing-song:

Martha's crooooooss-eyed!
Martha's crooooooss-eyed!
Martha's crooooooss-eyed!

—*The Wine of Youth*

CHARGE IT

THE GROCERY BILL—I can never forget it. Like a tireless ghost it haunts me, though boyhood is gone and those days are no more. We lived in a small town in northern Colorado. Our red brick house was my mother's wedding gift from my father. Brick for brick he had built it himself, working evenings and on Sundays.

It took a year to build that house, and on the first anniversary of their marriage my mother and father took possession. I was the first son and the only child not born in the red brick house. In the first year in the new house my brother was born. The following year another brother was born. And then another. And another. And another. My mother gave birth to sons with such rapidity that my bricklaying father was sent spinning into a daze from which he never entirely recovered. There were nine of us.

Next door to the red brick house was Mr. Craik's grocery store. Shortly after moving into the new house my father opened a credit account with Mr. Craik. In the first years he managed to keep the bills paid. But the children grew older and hungrier, more children arrived, and still more, and the grocery bill whizzed into crazy figures. Worse, every time we had a birth in our house, it seemed to bring my father bad luck. His worries and his brood moved up a notch, and his income moved down. He was sure that God had a powerful grudge against him for earlier excesses. Money! When I was twelve my father had so many bills that even I knew he had no intention or opportunity to pay them.

But the grocery bill harassed him. Owing Mr. Craik a hundred dollars, he paid fifty. Owing two hundred, he paid seventy-five. Owing three hundred, he somehow managed to pay a hundred. And so it was with all his debts. There was no mystery about them. There were no hidden motives in their non-payment. No budget could solve them. No planned economy could alter them. It was very simple—his family ate more than he earned. He knew his only escape lay in a streak of good luck. His tireless presumption that such good luck was coming had stalled his desertion and kept him from blowing out his brains. He constantly threatened both, but did neither.

Mr. Craik complained unceasingly. He never really trusted my father. If our family had not lived next door to his store, where he could keep an eye on us, and if he had not felt that ultimately he would receive at least part of the money owed him, he would not have allowed further credit. He sympathized with my mother, and pitied her with that quasi-sympathy and cold pity that businessmen show the poor as a class, and with that frigid apathy toward individual members of it. Now that the bill was so high, he abused my mother and even insulted her. He knew that she herself was honest to the point of childish innocence, but that did not seem relevant when she came to his store to make additional increases on the account. He was a man who dealt in merchandise and not feelings. Money was owed him and he was allowing her additional credit. His demands for money were in vain. Under the circumstances, his attitude was the best he could possibly muster.

It took courage for my mother to go in and face him day after day. She had to coax herself to a pitch of inspired audacity. My father didn't pay much attention to her mortifications at the hands of Mr. Craik. Beyond expressing her dismay at again confronting the grocer she did not tell my father of Mr. Craik's cruelty in detail. It was too humiliating. And so my father was not fully aware of it. He suspected it, but that was the sort of suspicion one hated verifying. He naturally expected some trouble in obtaining additional credit. As his wife, that was her obligation. To his way of thinking, it wasn't *his* fault that there were so many children. He looked upon that part of it as a deliberate conspiracy between her and God. He was merely a man who worked for a living. He loved his children of course—but after all! And so she had to do her part, which he thought was awfully easy, since it had nothing to do with the sweat and toil of his trade.

All afternoon and until an hour before dinner, my mother would wait for the valiant and desperate inspiration so necessary for a trip to the store. She sat with hands in her apron pockets—waiting. But her courage slept from overuse and would not rise.

This winter afternoon was typical. I remember: it was late. From the window she could see me across the street with a gang of neighborhood kids. We were having a snowball fight. She opened the door.

"Arturo!"

I saw her standing at the edge of the porch. She called me because I was the oldest. It was almost darkness. Deep shadows crept fast across the milky snow. The streetlamps burned coldly, a cold glow in a colder haze. An automobile passed, its tire chains clanging dismally.

"Arturo!"

I knew what she wanted. In disgust I snapped my fingers. I just *knew* she wanted me to go to the store. Her voice had that peculiar, desperate tremor that came with grocery-store time. I tried to get out of it by pretending I hadn't heard, but she kept calling until I was ready to scream and the rest of the kids stopped throwing snowballs.

I tossed one more snowball, watched it splatter, and then trudged through the snow and across the icy pavement. Now I could see her plainly. Her jaws quivered from the twilight cold. She stood with folded arms, tapping her toes to keep them warm.

"Whaddya want?" I said.

"It's cold," she said. "Come inside and I'll tell you."

"What *is* it, Ma? I'm in a hurry."

"I want you to go to the store."

"The store? No. I'm not going. I know why you want me to go—because you're afraid on account of the bill. Well, I ain't going."

"Please go," she said. "You're big enough to understand. You know how Mr. Craik is."

I did know. I hated him. He was always asking me if my father was drunk or sober, and what the hell did my father do with his money, and how do you wops live without a cent, and how does it happen your old man never stays home at night? I knew Mr. Craik, and hated him.

"Why can't August go?" I said. "Heck sakes, I do all the work around here."

"But August is too young. He wouldn't know what to buy."

"Well," I said, "I'm not going."

I turned and tramped back to the boys. The snowball fight resumed. She called. I didn't answer. She called again. I shouted that her voice might be drowned out. Now it was darkness, and Mr. Craik's windows bloomed in the night. My mother stood looking at the store door.

———

The grocer was whacking a bone with a cleaver on the chopping-block when she entered. As the door squealed he looked up and saw her—a

small, insignificant figure in an old black coat with a high fur collar, most of the fur having been shed so that white hide-spots appeared in the dark mass. One of her stockings, always the left, hung loose and wrinkled at the ankle. You knew a safety pin supported a garter of worn elastic. The faded gloss from her rayon hose made them a yellowish tan, accentuating the small bones and white skin under them and making her old shoes seem even more damp and ancient. She walked like a woman in a cathedral, fearfully on tiptoe, to that familiar place from which she invariably made her purchases, where the counter met the wall. She smiled, as though at herself for being what she was: a mother, a prolific mother, and not a society lady.

In earlier years she used to greet him with a "howdydo." But now she felt that perhaps he wouldn't like such familiarity, and she stood quietly in her corner, waiting until he was ready to wait on her.

Seeing who it was, he paid no attention, and she tried to be an interested and smiling spectator while he swung his cleaver. He was of middle-height, partly bald, wearing celluloid glasses—a man of forty-five. A thick pencil rested behind one ear and a cigarette behind the other. His white apron hung to his shoe tops, a blue string wound many times around his waist. He was hacking a bone inside a red and juicy rump.

"My!" she said. "It looks good, doesn't it?"

He flipped the steak up and over, swished a square of paper from the roll, spread it over the scales, and tossed the steak upon it. His quick, soft fingers wrapped it expertly. She estimated that it was close to ninety cents, and she wondered who had purchased it.

Mr. Craik heaved the rest of the rump upon his shoulder and disappeared inside the icebox, closing the door behind him. She wondered why butchers always closed icebox doors behind them; and she guessed that, assuming you locked yourself in and couldn't get out, you wouldn't starve to death at least—you could always eat the wieners. It seemed he stayed a long time in the icebox. Then he emerged, clearing his throat, clicked the icebox door shut, padlocked it for the night, and disappeared into the back room.

She supposed he was going to the washroom to wash his hands and that made her wonder if she was out of Gold Dust Cleanser; and then, all at once, she realized she was out of *everything*.

He appeared with a broom and began to sweep the sawdust around the chopping-block. She lifted her eyes to the clock. Ten minutes to six. Poor Mr. Craik! He looked so tired. He was like all men, probably starved for a hot meal, and she thought how nice to be the wife of a grocer; but even if she *were* a grocer's wife she wouldn't allow anything but homemade bread on her table. That made her think again of how much money you could make if you had a little store downtown and sold good homemade bread, the big loaves like the ones she herself baked. She was sure she could handle such a business, and she couldn't help thinking how mad her husband would be if she went out and earned her living like so many of these women were doing nowadays. She could see herself in that little bakery store, with cakes and cookies and loaves of bread in the window, herself behind the counter in a white apron, society ladies from University Hill coming in and saying, "Oh, Mrs. Bandini! You bake such wonderful things!" And of course she would have a delivery route, too, and Frederick and August and Arturo would be the delivery boys, and later their brothers would follow; she wondered how much she would pay them as a start; and since Arturo was the oldest and needed most coaxing she would pay him six dollars a week, and August three, and little Frederick one. They would put their money in a savings bank and after that first store was a success she would . . .

Mr. Craik finished his sweeping and paused to light a cigarette.

She said, "Cold weather we're having, isn't it?"

But he coughed, and she supposed he hadn't heard, for he disappeared into the back room and returned with a dustpan and a paper box. Bending down, he swept the sawdust into the pan and threw it into the box.

"I don't like cold weather at all," she said.

He coughed again, and before she knew it he was carrying the box back to the rear. She heard the splash of running water. He returned, drying his hands on his apron, that nice white apron. She smiled sympathetically, but he wasn't looking in her direction. At the cash register, very loudly he rang up NO SALE. She changed her position, moving her weight from one foot to the other. The big clock ticked away. Now it was exactly six o'clock.

Mr. Craik scooped the coins from the cashbox and laid them on the counter. He tore a slip of paper from the roll and reached for his pencil. Then he leaned over and counted the day's receipts. She coughed. Was it possible he didn't know she was in the store? He wet the pencil on the end of his pink tongue and began to add figures. Patting her hair, she raised her eyebrows and strolled to the front window to look at the fruits and vegetables.

"Strawberries!" she said. "And in the winter too! Are they California strawberries, Mr. Craik?"

He swept the coins into a bank sack and went to the safe, where he squatted and fingered the combination lock. The big clock ticked like the beat of a small hammer. It was ten minutes after six when he closed the safe.

She was no longer facing him. Her feet had tired, and with hands clasped in her lap she sat on a box and stared at the frosted front windows. Mr. Craik took off his apron and threw it over the chopping-block. He threw his cigarette on the floor, stepped on it, and went after his coat in the back room. As he straightened his collar, he spoke to her for the first time.

"Come on, Mrs. Bandini. Make up your mind. I can't hang around here all night long."

At the sound of his voice she lost her balance and nearly fell off the box. She smiled to conceal her embarrassment, but her face was very red and her eyes lowered. Her hands fluttered at her throat like disturbed leaves

"Oh!" she said. "And here I was, waiting for you! I'm awfully sorry. I never thought . . ."

"What'll it be, Mrs. Bandini—shoulder steak?"

She stood at the counter, her lips pursed.

"How much is shoulder steak today?"

"Same price. Same price."

"That's nice. I'll take fifty cents' worth."

He tossed his head grimly.

"Why didn't you tell me before?" he said. "Here I went and put all that meat in the icebox."

"Oh. I'm awfully sorry. Let it go then."

"No," he said. "I'll get it this time. But after this, come early. I got to get home some time tonight."

He brought out a cut of shoulder and stood sharpening his knife.

"Say," he said. "What's Svevo doing these days?"

In twelve years the two men had rarely spoken to one another, but the grocer always referred to her husband by his first name. She always felt that Mr. Craik was afraid of him. It was a belief that secretly made her very proud. Now they talked of Svevo, and she told again the monotonous tale of a bricklayer's misfortunes in the wintertime. She was anxious to get away; it was so painful to give Mr. Craik the same report day after day, year after year.

"Oh, yes!" she said, gathering her packages. "I almost forgot! I want some fruit, too—a dozen apples."

It was a bombshell. Mr. Craik swore under his breath as he whipped a sack open and dropped apples into it.

"Good God!" he said. "This charging business has got to stop, Mrs. Bandini. I tell you it can't go on like this."

"I'll tell him," she said hurriedly. "I'll tell him, Mr. Craik."

"Ach. A lot of good that does. I'm not running a charity."

She gathered her packages and fled for the door.

"I'll tell him, Mr. Craik. I'll tell him. Good night, Mr. Craik. Good night, sir!"

Such a relief to step into the street! How tired she was! Every cell in her body ached. But once more, and for another day, the problem of food was solved. She smiled as she breathed the cold night air, and she hugged her packages lovingly, as though they were life itself.

—*The Big Hunger*

THE ODYSSEY OF A WOP

III

As I GROW OLDER, I find out that Italians use Wop and Dago much more than Americans. My grandmother, whose vocabulary of English is confined to the commonest of nouns, always employs them in discussing contemporary Italians. The words never come forth quietly, unobtrusively. No; they bolt forth. There is a blatant intonation, and then the sense of someone being scathed, stunned.

I enter the parochial school with an awful fear that I will be called Wop. As soon as I find out why people have such things as surnames, I match my own against such typically Italian cognomens as Bianchi, Borello, Pacelli—the names of other students. I am pleasantly relieved by the comparison. After all, I think, people will say I am French. Doesn't my name sound French? Sure! So thereafter, when people ask me my nationality, I tell them I am French. A few boys begin calling me Frenchy. I like that. It feels fine.

Thus I begin to loathe my heritage. I avoid Italian boys and girls who try to be friendly. I thank God for my light skin and hair, and I choose my companions by the Anglo-Saxon ring of their names. If a boy's name is Whitney, Brown, or Smythe, then he's my pal; but I'm always a little breathless when I am with him; he may find me out. At the lunch hour I huddle over my lunch pail, for my mother doesn't wrap my sandwiches in wax paper, and she makes them too large, and the lettuce leaves protrude. Worse, the bread is homemade; not bakery bread, not "American" bread. I make a great fuss because I can't have mayonnaise and other "American" things.

The parish priest is a good friend of my father's. He comes strolling through the school grounds, watching the children at play. He calls to me and asks about my father, and then he tells me I should be proud to be studying about my great countrymen, Columbus, Vespucci, John Cabot.

He speaks in a loud, humorous voice. Students gather around us, listening, and I bite my lips and wish to Jesus he'd shut up and move on.

Occasionally now I hear about a fellow named Dante. But when I find out that he was an Italian I hate him as if he were alive and walking through the classrooms, pointing a finger at me. One day I find his picture in a dictionary. I look at it and tell myself that never have I seen an uglier bastard.

We students are at the blackboard one day, and a soft-eyed Italian girl whom I hate but who insists that I am her beau stands beside me. She twitches and shuffles about uneasily, half on tiptoe, smiling queerly at me. I sneer and turn my back, moving as far away from her as I can. The nun sees the wide space separating us and tells me to move nearer the girl. I do so, and the girl draws away, nearer the student on her other side.

Then I look down at my feet, and there I stand in a wet, spreading spot. I look quickly at the girl, and she hangs her head and looks at me in a way that begs me to take the blame for her. We attract the attention of others, and the classroom becomes alive with titters. Here comes the nun. I think I am in for it again, but she embraces me and murmurs that I should have raised two fingers and of course I would have been allowed to leave the room. But, says she, there's no need for that now; the thing for me to do is go out and get the mop. I do so, and amid the hysteria I nurse my conviction that only a Wop girl, right out of a Wop home, would ever do such a thing as this.

Oh, you Wop! Oh, you Dago! You bother me even when I sleep. I dream of defending myself against tormentors. One day I learn from my mother that my father went to the Argentine in his youth, and lived in Buenos Aires for two years. My mother tells me of his experiences there, and all day I think about them, even to the time I go to sleep. That night I come awake with a jerk. In the darkness I grope my way to my mother's room. My father sleeps at her side, and I awaken her gently, so that he won't be aroused.

I whisper: "Are you sure Papa wasn't *born* in Argentina?"

"No. Your father was born in Italy."

I go back to bed, disconsolate and disgusted.

— *The Wine of Youth*

IT WAS A BAD ONE, the Winter of 1933. Wading home that night through flames of snow, my toes burning, my ears on fire, the snow swirling around me like a flock of angry nuns, I stopped dead in my tracks. The time had come to take stock. Fair weather or foul, certain forces in the world were at work trying to destroy me.

Dominic Molise, I said, hold it. Is everything going according to plan? Examine your condition with care, take an impartial survey of your situation. What goes on here, Dom?

There I was in Roper, Colorado, growing older by the minute. In six months I would be eighteen and graduated from high school. I was sixty-four inches tall and had not grown one centimeter in three years. I was bowlegged and pigeon-toed and my ears protruded like Pinocchio's. My teeth were crooked, and my face was as freckled as a bird's egg.

I was the son of a bricklayer who had not worked in five months. I didn't own an overcoat, I wore three sweaters, and my mother had already begun a series of novenas for the new suit I needed to graduate in June.

Lord, I said, for in those days I was a believer who spoke frankly to his God: Lord, what gives? Is this what you want? Is this why you put me on the earth? I didn't *ask* to be born. I had absolutely nothing to do with it, except that I'm here, asking fair questions, the reasons why, so tell me, give me a sign: is this my reward for trying to be a good Christian, for twelve years of Catholic doctrine and four years of Latin? Have I ever doubted the Transubstantiation, or the Holy Trinity, or the Resurrection? How many masses have I missed on Sundays and holy days of obligation? Lord, you can count them on your fingers.

Are you playing a game with me? Have things gotten out of hand? Have you lost control? Is Lucifer back in power? Be honest with me, for

I'm troubled all the time. Give me a clue. Is life worth while? Will everything turn out right?

We lived on Arapahoe Street, at the foot of the first hills that rose to become the eastern slope of the Rocky Mountains. They shot up like jagged skyscrapers, staring down at our town, a haze of blue and green in summer, sugar white in winter, with peaked turrets shrouded in the clouds. Every winter someone was lost up there, trapped in a canyon or buried in a snowslide. In spring the melting snows turned Roper Creek into a wild river that swept away fences and bridges and flooded the streets, piling mud along Pearl Street and inundating the courthouse basement. Cold country, bad-tempered country, the earth's crust a sheet of ice through April, snow on Easter Sunday, sometimes a sudden snowstorm in May: bad country for a ballplayer, specially for a pitcher who hadn't thrown a ball since October.

But The Arm kept me going, that sweet left arm, the one nearest my heart. The snow couldn't hurt it and the wind couldn't pierce it because I kept it soaked with Sloan's Liniment, a little bottle of it in my pocket at all times, I reeked with it, sometimes sent out of class to wash the pine tartness away, but I walked out proudly without shame, conscious of my destiny, steeled against the sneers of the boys and the tilted nostrils of the girls.

I had a great stride in those days, the gait of a gunslinger, the looseness of the classic lefthander, the left shoulder drooping a little, The Arm dangling limp as a serpent—my arm, my blessed, holy arm that came from God, and if The Lord created me out of a poor bricklayer he hung me with jewels when he hinged that whizzer to my collarbone.

Let it snow then! And let the winters be long and cold with spring a time to dream about, for this was not the end of Dominic Molise after all, only his beginning, and the warm summer sun would find him doing the work of God with his cunning left arm. This snow-swept Arapahoe Street was a place of distinction, a landmark where once he walked on despairing nights, his birthplace, to be so inscribed in the Hall of Fame. A plaque, if you please, a bronze plaque set in concrete on a monument at the corner of Ninth and Arapahoe Streets: Boyhood Neighborhood of Dominic Molise, World's Greatest Southpaw.

God had answered my questions, cleared my doubts, restored my faith, and the world was right again. The wind vanished and the snow drifted down like hushed confetti. Grandma Bettina used to say that snowflakes were the souls in heaven returning to Earth for brief visits. I knew this was not true but it was possible, and I believed it sometimes when the whim amused me.

I held out my hand and many flakes fell upon it, alive and star-shaped for a few seconds, and who could say? Perhaps the soul of Grandpa Giovanni, dead seven years now, and Joe Hardt, our third baseman, killed last summer on his motorcycle, and all of my father's people in the faraway mountains of Abruzzi, great-aunts and uncles I had never known, all vanished from the earth. And the others, the billions who lived a while and went away, the poor soldiers killed in battle, the sailors lost at sea, the victims of plague and earthquake, the rich and the poor, the dead from the beginning of time, none escaping except Jesus Christ, the only one in all the history of man who ever came back, but no one else, and did I believe that?

I had to believe it. Where did my slider come from, and my knuckleball, and where did I get all that control? If I stopped believing I might come apart, lose my rhythm, start walking batters. Hell yes, there were doubts, but I pushed them back. The life of a pitcher was tough enough without losing faith in his God. One flash of doubt might bring a crimp in The Arm, so why muddy the water? Leave things alone. The Arm came from heaven. Believe that. Never mind predestination, and if God is all good how come so much evil, and if he knows everything how come he created people and sent them to hell? Plenty of time for that. Get into the minors, move up to the big time, pitch in the World Series, make the Hall of Fame. *Then* sit back and ask questions, ask what does God look like, and why are babies born crippled, and who made hunger and death.

Through the whispering snow I saw dimly the small houses along Arapahoe. I knew everyone in every house, every cat and dog in the neighborhood. In truth I knew almost everyone of Roper's ten thousand people, and some day they would all be dead. That too was the fate of everyone in the house at the end of the street, the frame house with the sagging front porch, paint-blistered, with the slanting peaked roof, home of bricklayer Peter Molise, where the only bricks were in the chimney, and even that was crumbling.

But when it was time to die the condition of your house didn't matter, and all of us would have to go—Grandma Bettina next, then Papa, then Mama, then myself since I was the oldest, then my brother August, two years younger, then my sister Clara, and finally my little brother Frederick. Somewhere along the way our dog Rex would crawl off and die too.

Why was I thinking these things and making a graveyard of the world? Was I losing my faith after all? Could it be because I was poor?

Impossible. All great ballplayers came from poor folks. Who ever heard of a rich rookie becoming a Ty Cobb or a Babe Ruth! Was it a girl? There were no girls in my life, except Dorothy Parrish, who hardly knew I existed, a mere gnat in her life.

Oh, God, help me! And I walked faster, my thoughts pursuing me, and I began to run, my frozen shoes squealing like mice, but running didn't help, the thoughts to the left and right and behind me. But as I ran, The Arm, that good left arm, took hold of the situation and spoke soothingly: ease up, Kid, it's loneliness, you're all alone in the world; your father, your mother, your faith, they can't help you, nobody helps anybody, you only help yourself, and that's why I'm here, because we are inseparable, and we'll take care of everything.

Oh, Arm! Strong and faithful arm, talk sweetly to me now. Tell me of my future, the crowds cheering, the pitch sliding across at the knees, the batters coming up and going down, fame and fortune and victory, we shall have it all. And one day we shall die and lie side by side in a grave, Dom Molise and his beautiful arm, the sports world shocked, in mourning, the telegram to my family from the President of the United States, the flags at half-mast at every ball park in the nation, fans weeping unashamed, Damon Runyon's four-part biography in the *Saturday Evening Post*: Triumph over Adversity, the Life of Dominic Molise.

Under an elm tree I stopped to cry, the bitterness of my approaching death too much to bear; one so young, so talented, cut down in the prime of his life. Oh God, be merciful: don't take me too fast! Spare me a few years, look kindly upon my youth. By nineteen I shall be ready for the big time. Give me those years and ten more, a total of twelve, no more and no less, I don't care if it's with the Phillies or the Cubs, only give me those years and you can strike me down at twenty-nine, which is plenty of time, my sweet Lord, figuring thirty games a year, that's three hundred and sixty games, a lot of baseball, a lot of pitches to emblazon the name of Dom Molise among the immortals.

— *1933 Was a Bad Year*

The Odyssey of a Wop

IV

URING A BALL GAME ON THE SCHOOL GROUNDS, a boy who plays on the opposing team begins to ridicule my playing. It is the ninth inning, and I ignore his taunts. We are losing the game, but if I can knock out a hit our chances of winning are pretty strong. I am determined to come through, and I face the pitcher confidently. The tormentor sees me at the plate.

"Ho! Ho!" he shouts. "Look who's up! The Wop's up. Let's get rid of the Wop!"

This is the first time anyone at school has ever flung the word at me, and I am so angry that I strike out foolishly. We fight after the game, this boy and I, and I make him take it back.

Now school days become fighting days. Nearly every afternoon at 3:15 a crowd gathers to watch me make some guy take it back. This is fun; I am getting somewhere now, so come on, you guys, I dare you to call me a Wop! When at length there are no more boys who challenge me, insults come to me by hearsay, and I seek out the culprits. I strut down the corridors. The smaller boys admire me. "Here he comes!" they say, and they gaze and gaze. My two younger brothers attend the same school, and the smallest, a little squirt seven years old, brings his friends to me and asks me to roll up my sleeve and show them my muscles. Here you are, boys. Look me over.

My brother brings home furious accounts of my battles. My father listens avidly, and I stand by, to clear up any doubtful details. Sadly happy days! My father gives me pointers: how to hold my fist, how to guard my head. My mother, too shocked to hear more, presses her temples and squeezes her eyes and leaves the room.

I am nervous when I bring friends to my house; the place looks so Italian. Here hangs a picture of Victor Emmanuel, and over there is one of the cathedral of Milan, and next to it one of St. Peter's, and on the buffet stands a wine pitcher of medieval design; it's forever brimming, forever red and brilliant with wine. These things are heirlooms belonging to my father, and no matter who may come to our house, he likes to stand under them and brag.

So I begin to shout to him. I tell him to cut out being a Wop and be an American once in a while. Immediately he gets his razor strop and whales hell out of me, clouting me from room to room and finally out the back door. I go into the woodshed and pull down my pants and stretch my neck to examine the blue slices across my rump. A Wop, that's what my father is! Nowhere is there an American father who beats his son this way. Well, he's not going to get away with it; some day I'll get even with him.

I begin to think that my grandmother is hopelessly a Wop. She's a small, stocky peasant who walks with her wrists crisscrossed over her belly, a simple old lady fond of boys. She comes into the room and tries to talk to my friends. She speaks English with a bad accent, her vowels rolling out like hoops. When, in her simple way, she confronts a friend of mine and says, her old eyes smiling: "You lika go the Seester scola?" my heart roars. *Mannaggia*! I'm disgraced; now they all know that I'm an Italian.

My grandmother has taught me to speak her native tongue. By seven, I know it pretty well, and I always address her in it. But when friends are with me, when I am twelve and thirteen, I pretend ignorance of what she says, and smirk stiffly; my friends daren't know that I can speak any language but English. Sometimes this infuriates her. She bristles, the loose skin at her throat knits hard, and she blasphemes with a mighty blasphemy.

—*The Wine of Youth*

I WENT BACK TO THE BEDROOM and lay down. The kitchen light went out and the floor creaked with his steps as he walked into the bedroom next to ours. There was a boom when his shoe hit the floor, and then another. I heard the tinkle of coins and nails as he pulled off his pants then the twang of bed springs as his weight descended at my mother's side.

I pictured them lying there in the darkness of different worlds, sharing the same manger, like a burro and a hen. Man and wife, side by side, in two nests of a sagging mattress, yet separated by the remains of their dead marriage. It had me writhing. Well, all right! So my mother wasn't much any more, with aching teeth that had to come out and hair streaked with grey that wouldn't stay in. She owned no rouge or lipstick, and her rear would look ridiculously small on one of those bar stools at the Onyx, but she would never leave the mark of her mouth on another man's face. She did what had to be done, submissive to the will of God—the laundry, the cleaning, the cooking, the raising of her family. All in all, it was enough to drive a man out of the house and you couldn't blame my father for running for his life. But those women! Those big-assed, loafing women! They knew he had a wife and family, yet they smeared their lipstick on him, and he was as bad as they for allowing it.

Sleep would not come as I twisted and groped, and my hand came upon something under August's pillow. I drew it carefully from under the weight of his head. It was a large brown envelope. For months I had been searching for that mysterious envelope, knowing he kept it hidden, his most secret possession.

He slept deeply with his mouth open and I sat up and drew out the contents of the envelope. They were glossy photographs of Carole Lombard, a varied collection, curiously luminous in that cold clear light. They showed her in bathing suits and evening gowns, in wide hats and pirate costumes, on horseback and in speed boats, on tiptoe in lingerie.

Then I found the real reason for August's secrecy. Some of the portraits were signed in his own handwriting. "For my darling August, adoringly—Carole." "To August, with undying love—Carole." "For Augie, passionate memories of Malibu nights—Carole." "Dear August: do with me what you will. I am yours body and soul. Your Carole."

You were supposed to laugh at such things, for they made you out a fool. I looked at him with his open mouth, his breath puffing steam into the frigid air. The autographs were not funny. He had written sad things, intimate things, too sacred for anyone else to see. He was fifteen, and I had got used to treating him as though he was no more than five or six. Yet there he was, only two years younger than myself, dreaming of Carole Lombard as fiercely as I dreamed of baseball. Tenderness filled me. I bent over and kissed his cold forehead. Then I put the pictures back into the envelope and slipped it under his pillow.

I lay there in the white night watching my breath escape in misty plumes. Dreamers, we were a house full of dreamers. Grandma dreamed of her home in faroff Abruzzi. My father dreamed of being free of debt and laying brick side by side with his son. My mother dreamed of her heavenly reward with a cheerful husband who didn't run away. My sister Clara dreamed of becoming a nun, and my little brother Frederick could hardly wait to grow up and become a cowboy. Closing my eyes I could hear the buzz of dreams through the house, and then I fell asleep.

All at once I felt myself lifted awake out of the depth of sleep and feeling a presence close by. It was not a dream. Someone was in the bedroom besides my brother and myself. I opened my eyes.

The room was glacier cold, my breath funneling carbon monoxide into the frozen air. At the bedside stood a woman so near I could have reached out and touched her. Her gown was a flowing blue velvet, and her slender waist was cinched with a golden cord that matched her yellow hair. Her feet were in blue sandals with golden thongs. She looked down on me and smiled. For a moment I thought it was Carole Lombard. Her hand held a luminous globe, the planet earth, the land bodies in gold, the oceans and rivers a bright blue.

Suddenly it came to me who she was, and the shock pushed me trembling under the blankets. She was the Virgin Mary. She had to be. The bed throbbed with the beat of my heart and I was afraid to look again.

I shook my brother. "Augie."

"What?" He rolled away from me.

I shook him again and crawled closer.

"Somebody's here," I whispered.

He bolted to a sitting position, suddenly wide awake and afraid. "Where?" he said. "I don't see anybody."

I sat up and looked at the place where she had stood. She was gone. I pointed. "She was right there. I saw her plain as day."

"Who?"

"The Blessed Virgin."

"Oh, shit!" he said, sinking back in disgust and pulling the covers over his head.

— *1933 Was a Bad Year*

ARTURO BANDINI WAS PRETTY SURE that he wouldn't go to hell when he died. The way to hell was the committing of mortal sin. He had committed many, he believed, but the Confessional had saved him. He always got to Confession on time—that is, before he died. And he knocked on wood whenever he thought of it—he always would get there on time—before he died. So Arturo was pretty sure he wouldn't go to hell when he died. For two reasons. The Confessional, and the fact that he was a fast runner.

But Purgatory, that midway place between Hell and Heaven, disturbed him. In explicit terms the Catechism stated the requirements for Heaven: a soul had to be absolutely clean, without the slightest blemish of sin. If the soul at death was not clean enough for Heaven, and not befouled enough for Hell, there remained that middle region, that Purgatory where the soul burned and burned until it was purged of its blemishes.

In Purgatory there was one consolation: soon or late you were a cinch for Heaven. But when Arturo realized that his stay in Purgatory might be seventy million trillion billion years, burning and burning and burning, there was little consolation in ultimate Heaven. After all, a hundred years was a long time. And a hundred and fifty million years was incredible.

No: Arturo was sure he would never go straight to Heaven. Much as he dreaded the prospect, he knew that he was in for a long session in Purgatory. But wasn't there something a man could do to lessen the Purgatory ordeal of fire? In his Catechism he found the answer to this problem.

The way to shorten the awful period in Purgatory, the Catechism stated, was by good works, by prayer, by fasting and abstinence, and by piling up indulgences. Good works were out, as far as he was concerned. He had never visited the sick, because he knew no such people. He had never clothed the naked because he had never seen any naked people. He had never buried the dead because they had undertakers for that. He had never given alms to the poor because he had none to give; besides, "alms" always sounded to him like a loaf of bread, and where could he get loaves of bread? He had never harbored the injured because—well, he didn't know—it sounded like something people did on seacoast towns, going out and rescuing sailors injured in shipwrecks. He had never instructed the ignorant because after all, he was ignorant himself, otherwise he wouldn't be forced to go to this lousy school. He had never enlightened the darkness because that was a tough one he never did understand. He had never comforted the afflicted because it sounded dangerous and he knew none of them anyway: most cases of measles and smallpox had quarantine signs on the doors.

As for the ten commandments he broke practically all of them, and yet he was sure that not all of these infringements were mortal sins. Sometimes he carried a rabbit's foot, which was superstition, and therefore a sin against the first commandment. But was it a mortal sin? That always bothered him. A mortal sin was a serious offense. A venial sin was a slight offense. Sometimes, playing baseball, he crossed bats with a fellow-player: this was supposed to be a sure way to get a two-base hit. And yet he knew it was superstition. Was it a sin? And was it a mortal sin or a venial sin? One Sunday he had deliberately missed mass to listen to the broadcast of the world series, and particularly to hear of his god, Jimmy Foxx of the Athletics. Walking home after the game it suddenly occurred to him that he had broken the first commandment: thou shalt not have strange gods before me. Well, he had committed a mortal sin in missing mass, but was it another mortal sin to prefer Jimmy Foxx to God Almighty during the world series? He had gone to Confession, and there the matter grew more complicated. Father Andrew had said, "If you think it's a mortal sin, my son, then it is a mortal sin." Well, heck. At first he had thought it was only a venial sin, but he had to admit that, after considering the offense for three days before Confession, it had indeed become a mortal sin.

The third commandment. It was no use even thinking about that, for Arturo said "God damn it" on an average of four times a day. Nor was that counting the variations: God damn this and God damn that. And so, going to Confession each week, he was forced to make wide generalizations after a futile examination of his conscience for accuracy. The best he could do was confess to the priest, "I took the name of the Lord in vain about sixty-eight or seventy times." Sixty-eight mortal sins in one week, from the second commandment alone. Wow! Sometimes, kneeling in the cold church awaiting Confessional, he listened in alarm to the beat of his heart, wondering if it would stop and he drop dead before he got those things off his chest. It exasperated him, that wild beating of his heart. It compelled him not to run but often to walk, and very slowly, to Confessional, lest he overdo the organ and drop in the street.

"Honor thy father and thy mother." Of course he honored his father and his mother! Of course. But there was a catch in it: the Catechism went on to say that any disobedience of thy father and thy mother was dishonor. Once more he was out of luck. For though he did indeed honor his mother and father, he was rarely obedient. Venial sins? Mortal sins? The classifications pestered him. The number of sins against that commandment exhausted him; he would count them to the hundreds as he examined his days hour by hour. Finally he came to the conclusion that they were only venial sins, not serious enough to merit Hell. Even so, he was very careful not to analyze this conclusion too deeply.

He had never killed a man, and for a long time he was sure that he would never sin against the fifth commandment. But one day the class in Catechism took up the study of the fifth commandment, and he discovered to his disgust that it was practically impossible to avoid sins against it. Killing a man was not the only thing: the by-products of the commandment included cruelty, injury, fighting, and all forms of viciousness to man, bird, beast, and insect alike.

Goodnight, what was the use? He enjoyed killing bluebottle flies. He got a big kick out of killing muskrats, and birds. He loved to fight. He hated those chickens. He had had a lot of dogs in his life, and he had been severe and often harsh with them. And what of the prairie dogs he had killed, the pigeons, the pheasants, the jackrabbits? Well, the only thing to do was to make the best of it. Worse, it was a sin to even think of killing or injuring a human being. That sealed his doom. No matter how he tried, he could not resist expressing the wish of violent death against some people: like Sister Mary Corita, and Craik the grocer, and the freshmen at the university, who beat the kids off with clubs and forbade them to sneak into the big games at the stadium. He realized that, if he wasn't actually a murderer, he was the equivalent in the eyes of God.

One sin against that fifth commandment that always seethed in his conscience was an incident the summer before, when he and Paulie Hood, another Catholic boy, had captured a rat alive and crucified it to a small cross with tacks, and mounted it on an anthill. It was a ghastly and horrible thing that he never forgot. But the awful part of it was, they had done this evil thing on Good Friday, and right after saying the Stations of the Cross! He had confessed that sin shamefully, weeping as he told it, with true contrition, but he knew it had piled up many years in Purgatory, and it was almost six months before he even dared kill another rat.

Thou shalt not commit adultery; thou shalt not think about Rosa Pinelli, Joan Crawford, Norma Shearer, and Clara Bow. Oh gosh, oh Rosa, oh the sins, the sins, the sins. It began when he was four, no sin then because he was ignorant. It began when he sat in a hammock one day when he was four, rocking back and forth, and the next day he came back to the hammock between the plum tree and the apple tree in the back yard, rocking back and forth.

What did he know about adultery, evil thoughts, evil actions? Nothing. It was fun in the hammock. Then he learned to read, and the first of many things he read were the commandments. When he was eight he made his first Confession, and when he was nine he had to take the commandments apart and find out what they meant.

Adultery. They didn't talk about it in the fourth grade Catechism class. Sister Mary Anna skipped it and spent most of the time talking about Honor thy Father and Mother and Thou Shalt Not Steal. And so it was, for vague reasons he never could understand, that to him adultery always has had something to do with bank robbery. From his eighth year to his tenth, examining his conscience before Confession, he would pass over "Thou shalt not commit adultery" because he had never robbed a bank.

The man who told him about adultery wasn't Father Andrew, and it wasn't one of the nuns, but Art Montgomery at the Standard Station on the corner of Arapahoe and Twelfth. From that day on his loins were a thousand angry hornets buzzing in a nest. The nuns never talked about adultery. They only talked about evil thoughts, evil words, evil actions. That Catechism! Every secret of his heart, every sly delight in his mind was already known to that Catechism. He could not beat it, no matter how cautiously he tiptoed through the pinpoints of its code. He couldn't go to the movies anymore because he only went to the movies to see the shapes of his heroines. He liked "love" pictures. He liked following girls up the stairs. He liked girls' arms, legs, hands, feet, their shoes and stockings and dresses, their smell and their presence. After his twelfth year the only things in life that mattered were baseball and girls, only he called them women. He liked the sound of the word. Women, women, women. He said it over and over because it was a secret sensation. Even at Mass, when there were fifty or a hundred of them around him, he reveled in the secrecy of his delights.

And it was all a sin—the whole thing had the sticky sensation of evil. Even the sound of some words was a sin. Ripple. Supple. Nipple. All sins. Carnal. The flesh. Scarlet. Lips. All sins. When he said the Hail Mary. Hail Mary full of grace, the Lord is with thee and blessed art thou among women, and blessed is the fruit of thy womb. The word shook him like thunder. Fruit of thy womb. Another sin was born.

Every week he staggered into the church of a Saturday afternoon, weighted down by the sins of adultery. Fear drove him there, fear that he would die and then live on forever in eternal torture. He did not dare lie to his confessor. Fear tore his sins out by the roots. He would confess it all fast, gushing with his uncleanliness, trembling to be pure. I committed a bad action I mean two bad actions and I thought about a girl's legs and about touching her in a bad place and I went to the show and thought bad things and I was walking along and a girl was getting out of a car and it was bad and I listened to a bad joke and laughed and a bunch of us kids were watching a couple of dogs and I said something bad, it was my fault, they didn't say anything, I did, I did it all, I made them laugh with a bad idea and I tore a picture out of a magazine and she was naked and I knew it was bad but did it anyway. I thought a bad thing about Sister Mary Agnes; it was bad and I kept on thinking. I also thought bad things about some girls who were laying on the grass and one of them had her dress up high and I kept on looking and knowing it was bad. But I'm sorry. It was my fault, all my fault, and I'm sorry, sorry.

He would leave the Confessional, and say his penance, his teeth gritted, his fist tightened, his neck rigid, vowing with body and soul to be clean forevermore. A sweetness would at last pervade him, a soothing lull him, a breeze cool him, a loveliness caress him. He would walk out of the church in a dream, and in a dream he would walk, and if no one was looking he'd kiss a tree, eat a blade of grass, blow kisses at the sky, touch the cold stones of the church wall with fingers of magic, the peace in his heart like nothing save a chocolate malted, a three-base hit, a shining window to be broken, the hypnosis of that moment that comes before sleep.

No, he wouldn't go to Hell when he died. He was a fast runner, always getting to Confession on time. But Purgatory awaited him. Not for him the direct, pure route to eternal bliss. He would get there the hard way, by detour.

—*Wait Until Spring, Bandini*

MY FATHER'S GOD

U PON THE DEATH OF OLD FATHER AMBROSE, the Bishop of Denver assigned a new priest to St. Catherine's parish. He was Father
Bruno Ramponi, a young Dominican from Boston. Father Ramponi's picture appeared on the front page of the Boulder *Herald*. Actually there were
two pictures—one of a swarthy, short-necked prelate bulging inside a
black suit and reversed collar, the other an action shot of Father Ramponi
in football gear leaping with outstretched hands for a forward pass. Our
new pastor was famous. He had been a football star, an All-American half-
back from Boston College.

My father studied the pictures at the supper table.

"A Sicilian," he decided. "Look how black he is."

"How can he be a Sicilian?" my mother asked. "The paper says he was
born in Boston."

"I don't care where he was born. I know a Sicilian when I see one." His
brows quivered like caterpillars as he studied the face of Father Ramponi.
"I don't want any trouble with this priest," he brooded.

It was an ominous reminder of the many futile years Father Ambrose
had tried to bring my father back to the church. "The glorious return to
divine grace," Father Ambrose had called it. "The prodigal son falling
into the arms of his heavenly father." On the job or in the street, at band
concerts and in the pool hall, the old pastor constantly swooped down on
my father with these pious objurgations which only served to drive him
deeper among the heathens, so that the priest's death brought a gasp of
relief.

But in Father Ramponi he sensed a renewal of the tedious struggle for
his soul, for it was only a question of time before the new priest discovered
that my father never attended Mass. Not that my mother and we four kids
didn't make up for his absences. He insisted that it had to be that way,
and every Sunday, through rain, sleet and snow he watched us trek off to

St. Catherine's ten blocks away, his conscience vicariously soothed, his own cop-out veiled in righteous paternalism.

The day after the announcement of Father Ramponi's appointment, St. Catherine's school droned like an agitated beehive with rumors about our new priest. Gathered in clusters along the halls, the nuns whispered breathlessly. On the playground the boys set aside the usual touchball game to crowd into the lavatory and relate wild reports. The older boys did all the talking, cigarettes dangling from their lips, while second graders like myself listened with bulging eyes.

It was said that Father Ramponi was so powerful that he could bring down a bull with one punch, that he was structured like a gorilla, and that his nose had been kicked in on an historic Saturday afternoon when he had torn apart the Notre Dame line. We younger kids stiffened in fear and awe. After the gentle Father Ambrose, the thought of being hauled before Father Ramponi for discipline was too ghastly to contemplate. When the first bell rang we rushed to our classrooms, dreading the sudden, unexpected appearance of Father Ramponi in the halls.

At 11:30, in the midst of arithmetic, the classroom door opened and our principal, Sister Mary Justinus, entered. Her cheeks shone like apples. Her eyes glittered with excitement.

"The class will please rise," she announced.

We got to our feet and caught sight of him in the hall. This was it. The awesome Father Ramponi was about to make his debut before the Second Grade class.

"Children," Sister Justinus fluttered, "I want you to say 'Good morning,' to your new pastor, Father Bruno Ramponi." She raised her hands like a symphony conductor and brought them down briskly as we chanted, "Good morning, Father," and the priest stepped into the room.

He moved forward to stand before us with massive hands clasped at his waist, a grin kneading his broken face. All the rumors about him were true—a bull of a man with dark skin and wide, crushed nostrils out of which black hairs flared. His jaw was as square as a brickbat, his short neck like a creosoted telephone pole. From out of his coat sleeves small bouquets of black hair burst over his wrists.

"Please be seated," he smiled.

The moment he uttered those three words the myth of his ferocity vanished. For his voice was small and sibilant, surprisingly sweet and uncertain, a mighty lion with the roar of a kitten. The whole class breathed a sigh of deliverance as we sat down.

For twenty seconds he stood there lost for words, his large face oozing perspiration. With the uncanny intuition of children we were on to him, knowing somehow that this colossus of the gridiron would never loose his terrible wrath upon us, that he was as docile as a cow and harmless as a butterfly.

Drawing a handkerchief from his pocket, he dabbed at his moist neck and we grew uneasy and embarrassed waiting for him to say more, but he was locked to the spot, his tongue bolted down.

Finally Sister Justinus came to his rescue, breaking the silence with a brisk slap of her hands. "Now children, I want each of you to rise and give Father your name so that he can greet you personally."

One at a time we stood and pronounced our names, and in each instance Father Ramponi nodded and said," "How do you do, Tom," or "How do you do, Mary," or "How do you do, Patrick."

At my turn I rose and spoke my name.

"Paisan," the priest grinned.

I managed a smile.

"Tell your folks I'll be around to meet them soon."

Even though he told most of the students the same thing, I sat there in a state of shock. There were some things I could tell my father and others I preferred to delete, but there was one thing I didn't dare tell him—that a priest was coming to visit him.

With my mother it didn't matter, and upon hearing that Father Ramponi was coming she lifted her eyes to heaven and moaned.

"Oh, my God," she said. "Whatever you do, don't tell your father. We might lose him for good."

It was our secret, my mother's and mine, and we paid the price, specially Mamma. All that was required of me was to keep the front yard clean, raking the October leaves and sweeping the front porch every day. She took on the rest of the house alone, and in the days that followed she washed the walls and ceilings, she washed the windows, she laundered and ironed the curtains, she waxed the linoleum, she dragged the frazzled rugs out to the back yard, flung them over the clothesline and beat them with a broom.

Every evening, home from work, my father strode through the house and paused, the smell of ammonia in his nostrils as he looked around and found some small new change. The gas heater in the living room polished and shining, its chrome gleaming like a band of dazzling silver, the furniture luminous as dark mirrors, the broken rocker repaired, the worn needlepoint replaced with a piece of blue wool from an old coat.

He crossed the linoleum that sparkled like a sheet of ice. "What's happening?" he asked. "What's going on around here?"

"House cleaning," my mother said, her face careworn, her hair coming loose from the bun in back, her bones aching. He frowned at her curiously.

"Take it easy. What's the good of a clean house if you end up in the hospital?"

Days passed and November showed up, bringing the first snow of winter. But Father Ramponi did not visit us. I saw him almost every day at school, and he always tossed a word or two my way, but he made no mention of the visit.

The snow fell steadily. The streets disappeared. The windows frosted. My mother strung clotheslines around the stove in the living room, in order to dry the washing. The cold weather confined the little ones indoors. Crayons were crushed underfoot, toys kicked beneath the furniture. My brother spilled a bottle of ink on the linoleum, my sister drew a pumpkin face with black crayon on the best wall in the front room. Then she melted the crayon against the side of the hot stove. Mama threw up her hands in defeat. If Father Ramponi ever visited us, he would have to take us for what we were—just plain, stupid peasants.

The snow was my father's deadly enemy, burying his job in desolate white mounds, engulfing brick, cement and scaffolding, robbing him of his livelihood and sending him home with an unopened lunch pail. He became a prisoner in his own house.

Nor was he the loving husband a woman could enjoy through long winter days. He insisted on taking command of a ship that was already on course through rough waters. Lounging in the kitchen he watched my mother's every move as she prepared meals, finding fault with everything. More salt, too much pepper, turn up the oven, turn down the oven, watch the potatoes, add some onion, where's the oregano, fry some garlic, and finally, "Let me do that!"

She flung down her apron and stalked out of the kitchen to join us in the living room, her arms folded, her eyes blazing. Oh God! If Father Ramponi didn't arrive soon she would be driven to the rectory to see him herself.

Our house on Sunday morning was chaos. I can still see my frantic mother dashing from bedroom to bedroom in her pink slip, her braided hair piled atop her head, as she got us dressed for ten o'clock Mass. She polished our shoes, fashioned knots in our neckties, sewed buttons, patched holes, prepared breakfast, ironed pleats in my sister's dress, raced from one of us to the other, picking up a shoe on the way, a toy. Armed with a washcloth, she inspected our ears and the backs of our necks, scraping away dirt, my sister screaming, "You're cruel, cruel!"

Lastly, in the final moments before we departed, she slapped talcum powder over her face and came out to the front room where my oblivious father sprawled reading the Denver *Post*. She turned her back for him to button up her dress.

"Fix me."

Chewing a cigar, he squinted as the curling smoke blurred his eyes and he worked the buttons through the holes with blunt fingers. It was the only contribution he made to those hectic mornings.

"Why don't you come to Mass with us?" she often asked.

"What for?"

"To worship God. To set an example for your children."

"God sees my family at church. That's enough. He knows I sent them."

"Wouldn't it be better if God saw you there too?"

"God's everywhere, so why do I have to see Him in a church? He's right here too, in this house, this room. He's in my hand. Look." He opened and closed his fist. "He's right in there. In my eyes, my·mouth, my ears, my blood. So what's the sense of walking eight blocks through the snow, when all I got to do is sit right here with God in my own house."

We children stood listening enthralled at this great and refreshing piece of theology, our collars pinching, our eyes moving to the window as the silent snow drifted down, shivering at the thought of plowing through the drifts to the cold church.

"Papa's right," I said. "God is everywhere. It says so in the catechism."

We looked imploringly at my mother as she put on her wool coat with the rabbit fur collar, and there was a sob in my sister's voice as she begged, "Can't we all just kneel down here and pray for a while? God won't mind."

"You see!" my mother glared at my father.

"Nobody prays here but me," he said. "The rest of you get going."

"It's not fair!" I yelled. "Who're *you*?"

"I'll tell you who I am," he said threateningly. "I'm the owner of this house. I come and go as I please. I can throw you out any time I feel like it. Now get going!" He rose in a towering fury and pointed at the door, and we filed out like humble serfs, heads bowed, trudging through snow a foot deep. God, it was cold! And so unfair. I clenched my fists and longed for the day I would become a man and knock my father's brains out.

In the seventh week of his pastorate Father Ramponi finally visited our house. He came in the darkness of evening, through a roaring storm, his arrival presaged by the heavy pounding of his overshoes on the front porch as he kicked off the clinging snow. It shook the house.

My father sat at the dining room table drinking wine and I sat across from him, doing my homework. We both stared as the wine in the carafe tossed like a small red sea. Mamma and Grandma came startled from the kitchen. We heard the rap of knuckles on the front door.

"Come in!" my father shouted.

Father Ramponi loomed in the doorway, hat in hand, so tall he barely made it through the door. Had the President of the United States entered, we could not have been more surprised.

"Good evening," he smiled.

"Whaddya say there," Papa said, too astonished for amenities as Father Ramponi walked deeper into the house. All atwitter, my mother's face tingled with excitement as she hurried to take the priest's overcoat. He laid it across her arms like a massive black rug, so large that it dragged over the floor as she hauled it away to the bedroom.

By now the rest of us were on our feet, staring at the towering priest. Everything shrank proportionately, the room, the furniture, and the members of our family. Suddenly we were a tribe of pygmies confronted by a giant explorer from the outside world.

As they shook hands, Father Ramponi lowered a friendly paw on Papa's shoulder and spoke in his high, gentle voice.

"They tell me you're the finest stonemason in Colorado. Is it true?"

My father's face blossomed like a sunflower.

"That's the truth, Father."

"Fine, fine. I like a man who's not ashamed of his worth."

Reeling with flattery, Papa turned and ordered the room cleared. "Everybody out!"

With grand pretensions of authority Mamma herded us into the living room, which didn't in the least add to the privacy since the two rooms were separated by French doors, only there weren't any doors, just the hinges. The doors were out in the garage, for reasons nobody ever questioned.

We kids flung ourselves on the floor near the stove and Mamma settled into the rocking chair. Presently Grandma appeared, a black shawl around her shoulders, the rosary twined in her fingers, and she too found a chair. No more than four feet away, Papa and Father Ramponi had the entire dining room to themselves.

Those were the days of Prohibition and Papa's routine with guests never changed. Every caller was invited down into the earthen cellar where four fifty-gallon barrels of wine were stored—a hundred gallons matured, and a hundred in the fermentation process.

Through the trapdoor in the pantry he and Father Ramponi disappeared into the cellar. We listened to them down there under the house, their voices muffled, their laughter rumbling in the ground. Patiently we waited for them to reappear, like an audience expecting the return of the players to the stage.

As they came back Papa carried a fresh pitcher of wine, the beaded foam still bubbling. They sat at the table beneath light pouring down from a green metal shade. Papa filled two tumblers with wine and Father Ramponi lit a cigarette.

Raising his glass, the priest proposed a toast. "To Florence, city of your birth."

Pleased but dubious, my father shook his head. "I come from Abruzzi, Father. From Torcelli Peligna."

It surprised Father Ramponi. "Is that so? Now where did I get the idea you were a Florentine?"

"Never been there in my life."

"Maybe your relatives came from there."

"Maybe," Papa shrugged.

"You *look* like a Florentine."

"You think so?"

"A true Florentine, a craftsman in the tradition of that great city." He drained his tumbler.

We watched Papa expand with a sense of importance. It was as if Father Ramponi had sprinkled him with a holy water of magic powers. From that moment he was Father Ramponi's pigeon, eating corn from the good priest's hand. Then the subject matter changed quickly, and the real reason for the priest's visit became apparent.

"Nick," he said with a new familiarity, his voice softer than ever. "Why is it that I never find you at Mass on Sunday morning?"

Mamma and Grandma nodded at one another smugly. My father was a long time answering, kneading a kink in his neck, smiling as he sensed a trap.

"I been thinking about that," he said.

"Thinking about it?"

"About going."

"You should. As an example to your children."

There was an uncomfortable silence. My father put the tip of his fingernail in the wine glass and twirled it absently. "We'll talk about it some other time," he said.

"Come to the rectory tomorrow," Father Ramponi suggested.

"I'm gonna be pretty busy tomorrow."

"How about the day after tomorrow?"

"I'm pretty busy, Father."

"In this wretched weather?"

"Lots of figuring to do. Getting ready for Spring."

"Shall we make it next week?"

Papa frowned, rubbed his chin. "Too far ahead. You never know, one day to the next."

The priest sighed, lifted his hands. "Then I leave it entirely up to you. When would it be most convenient?"

My father found a cigar butt in the ashtray and went to a lot of trouble scraping and lighting it. "Let me think about it, Father." He produced clouds of smoke that hid his face. Then, to everyone's surprise, he said, "Let's make it tomorrow."

Mamma's gulp of delight sounded like a shout.

Father Ramponi rose and offered his hand. He was smiling in triumph and my father shook hands and squinted at him skeptically. Having committed himself, he seemed to regret it.

"Two o'clock tomorrow?" Father Ramponi asked.

"Not possible," Papa said.

"Three, then? Four?"

"Can't make it."

"Would you prefer to come in the morning?"

"How can I come in the morning? You don't understand, Father! I got things to do, people to see. I'm a busy man. All the time. Day and night!"

The priest did not press it. "I leave it up to you. Come when you can."

Papa nodded bleakly. "We'll see. I can't promise anything. I'll do the best I can."

———

The very next day my father began a series of talks at the rectory with Father Ramponi. The meetings left him in a somber mood, and a brooding calm settled over our house. We tiptoed around him, we talked in whispers. During meals he was completely silent, tearing bread and holding it uneaten in his hand. Even my little sister felt his melancholy.

"Are you sick, Papa?" she asked.

"Shhh!" Mamma said.

My father exhaled a sigh and stared, his forkful of macaroni dangling limply in mid-air.

Every day he wore his Sunday clothes with a white shirt and a necktie. So intent was his concentration that he stopped talking altogether and merely gestured when he had some request. A wave of his hand could clear the room. A nod at his feet summoned his slippers. A flat stare and talking ceased among us. Moving furtively in the background, my mother and grandmother watched him with sympathetic, adoring eyes. The man of the house was in crisis, grappling with the devil, and the decision was in doubt. Every night at bedtime we left him alone in the dining room, seated under the light, sipping wine and writing on a jumbo school tablet with a stubby pencil.

A week of this, and suddenly the saturnine atmosphere of our home was shattered and my father was himself again. We awoke to hear him in the front yard, shoveling snow. Mamma called him to breakfast. He bounded into the house with scarlet cheeks and purple ears, his eyes snow-bright as he slapped his hands hungrily and sat down before his scrambled eggs. One mouthful and he scowled.

"Can't you even fry eggs?" he said.

We were happy again. Papa was complaining like his old self.

As I prepared for school, my mother followed me into the living room and brought my mackinaw from the closet. She buttoned me up while my father stood watching. He had a bulky envelope in his hand.

"Give this to Father Ramponi," he said, handing it to me. I said okay and folded it to the size of my pocket.

"Not like that," he said, taking it from me. He opened the mackinaw and stuffed the envelope under my T-shirt. "Guard it with your life," he warned.

"What the heck is it?"

"Never mind. Just give it to Father Ramponi."

"Tell him," Mamma said. "So he'll know how important it is."

"You talk too much!" he snapped.

"It's your father's confession," Mamma said.

I suddenly felt it there against my flesh, and sucked in my stomach. It was incredible, impossible, sacrilegious.

"You can't *write* your confession!" I wailed. "You have to *tell* it. In the confessional!"

"Who says so?"

"It's the rule. Everybody knows that!"

"He won't get me in that confession box."

"It's the rule!" I cried, ready to burst into tears. "Mamma! Tell him, please! He doesn't understand!"

"That shows how much you know," Papa said. "He told me to write it: so what do you think of that!"

I searched my mother's face for the truth. She smiled. "Father Ramponi said it was all right this way."

I looked at my father accusingly.

"Why can't you be like everybody else?"

"No, sir. You can't get me in that box!"

Dazed and angry and disgusted, I walked out into the cold morning, my lunch pail rigid in one hand, my books in the other, my father's cold envelope freezing my stomach. Who the hell did he think he was? Why didn't he take his damned confession to the priest himself? Why should I be forced to walk the streets with it? They weren't *my* sins, they were his, so let him carry them to the priest.

The frozen air took my breath and whirled it into ostrich plumes and I walked afraid, like a glass vial, fearful of spilling my burden. I knew my father had not been to confession for thirty years, not since he was a boy of my age.

All of this wickedness, every human being he had injured, every sin against God's commandments were congealed in a block of ice burning against my stomach as I crossed town, under dripping maple trees, around grey mounds of mud-splattered snow, my toes picking their way with the delicacy of bird's feet, across the town, the awful responsibility of my burden hurting my flesh, too sacred, too heavy for my life.

As I reached St. Catherine's Father Ramponi drove up and parked in front of the stone steps leading to the main entrance. I waited for him to step out, pulling the envelope from under my shirt as the bell sounded and stragglers raced up the stairs.

"Oh, yes," he smiled, taking the envelope. "Thank you." He seemed in a great hurry and at a loss as to what to do with the envelope. Opening the car door, he tossed the envelope on the seat and dashed away, taking the stairs three at a time.

I watched in dismay as he disappeared. How could he do such a thing?

That document was no trifling thing. It was my father's confession, a matter sacred to God, and there it lay on the car seat, cast aside like a rag.

What if someone came by and filched it—one of the older boys? The school was full of thieves who stole anything not nailed down. Suddenly I was in a panic as I imagined the confession being passed around, being read in the lavatory, touching off raucous laughter spilling into the halls, the streets, as the whole town laughed at my father's sins.

Guard it with your life, my father had warned, and guard it I did. For three hours I posted myself beside Father Ramponi's car, my feet numbed with cold, my ears burning like ice cubes as I stayed out of school and scorned the wrath of Sister Justinus.

At last the noon bell sounded and the students burst from the doors and down the stairs. I concealed myself as Father Ramponi appeared. He slid under the steering wheel and drove away, and the minuscule pinching pain in my stomach vanished at last.

That night Father Ramponi made his second visit to our house. It was very late and Papa was turning out the lights when the priest knocked. Papa welcomed him and they came into the dining room. Through the open bedroom door I saw them as I lay beside my sleeping brother. Father Ramponi stood huge as a black bear under the green lampshade. Then my father noticed the open bedroom door and he closed it, and I was in darkness save for a ribbon of light under the threshold. I slipped out of bed and peered through the keyhole.

Papa had seated himself before the wine, but Father Ramponi was still on his feet. He drew the envelope from his overcoat and tossed it on the table.

"You deceived me," he said quietly.

My father lifted the envelope and tested it in his fist. "It's all there, Father. I didn't forget a thing."

"It's long enough. God knows."

"Some things I wrote, they were very hard, but it's all there, over thirty years, the bad things in a man's life."

"But you wrote it in Italian . . ."

"What's wrong with that?"

Father Ramponi sank gloomily into a chair, his hands thrust deeply into his overcoat pockets. "I don't speak Italian," he sighed. "Or read it. Or write it. Or understand it."

My father stared.

"Bruno Ramponi, and you don't speak Italian? That's terrible."

The priest sank deeper in his chair and covered one eye. "It simply never entered my mind that you'd make your confession in Italian."

"The pope speaks Italian," my father said. "The cardinals, they speak Italian. The saints speak Italian. Even God speaks Italian. But you, Father Bruno Ramponi, don't speak Italian."

A moan from the priest. He pushed the envelope toward my father. "Burn it."

"Burn it?"

"Burn it. Now."

It was an order, angry and incontrovertible. My father rose and took the envelope into the kitchen. I heard the lid of the stove open, then close, and then he returned to the dining room where Father Ramponi now stood and draped a purple stole around his neck.

"Please kneel for penance and absolution," he said.

My father's joints cracked like sticks as he knelt on the linoleum. He clasped his hands together and lowered his eyes. Father Ramponi made the sign of the cross over him and murmured a Latin prayer. Then he touched my father's shoulder.

"As a penance, I want you to say The Lord's Prayer once a day until Christmas."

My father lifted his eyes.

"Until Christmas, Father? That's sixty days."

"You can say it in Italian."

It pleased my father and he lowered his eyes. Father Ramponi absolved and blessed him, and the little ceremony was concluded. My father got to his feet.

"Thank you, Father. How about a glass of wine?"

The priest declined. They moved toward the front door. Suddenly my father laughed. "I feel good," he said. "Real good, Father."

"Next time I'll expect you to come to the church for your confession."

"We'll see, Father."

"And I'll expect you at Mass Sunday."

"I'll try and make it, Father."

They said good night and the door closed. I heard Father Ramponi's car drive away. My father returned to the dining room. Through the keyhole I watched him pour a glass of wine. He raised it heavenward and drank. Then he turned out the light and all was darkness.

—*The Wine of Youth*

Part Two

DAYS OF FEVER

THE ODYSSEY OF A WOP

V

WHEN I FINISH IN THE PAROCHIAL SCHOOL my people decide to send me to a Jesuit academy in another city. My father comes with me on the first day. Chiseled into the stone coping that skirts the roof of the main building of the academy is the Latin inscription: *Religioni et Bonis Artibus*. My father and I stand at a distance, and he reads it aloud and tells me what it means.

I look up at him in amazement. Is this man my father? Why, look at him! Listen to him! He reads with an Italian inflection! He's wearing an Italian mustache. I have never realized it until this moment, but he looks exactly like a Wop. His suit hangs carelessly in wrinkles upon him. Why the deuce doesn't he buy a new one? And look at his tie! It's crooked. And his shoes: they need a shine. And, for the Lord's sake, will you look at his pants! They're not even buttoned in front. And oh, damn, damn, damn, you can see those dirty old suspenders that he won't throw away. Say, Mister, are you really my father? You there, why, you're such a little guy, such a runt, such an old-looking fellow! You look exactly like one of those immigrants carrying a blanket. You can't be my father! Why, I thought . . . I've always thought . . .

I'm crying now, the first time I've ever cried for any reason excepting a licking, and I'm glad he's not crying too. I'm glad he's as tough as he is, and we say good-by quickly, and I go down the path quickly, and I do not turn to look back, for I know he's standing there and looking at me.

I enter the administration building and stand in line with strange boys who also wait to register for the autumn term. Some Italian boys stand among them. I am away from home, and I sense the Italians. We look at one another and our eyes meet in an irresistible amalgamation, a suffusive consanguinity; I look away.

A burly Jesuit rises from his chair behind the desk and introduces himself to me. Such a voice for a man! There are a dozen thunderstorms in his chest. He asks my name, and writes it down on a little card.

"Nationality?" he roars.

"American."

"Your father's name?"

I whisper it: "Guido."

"How's that? Spell it out. Talk louder."

I cough. I touch my lips with the back of my hand and spell out the name.

"Ha!" shouts the registrar. "And still they come! Another Wop! Well, young man, you'll be at home here! Yes, sir! Lots of Wops here! We've even got Kikes! And, you know, this place reeks with shanty Irish!"

Dio! How I hate that priest!

He continues: "Where was your father born?"

"Buenos Aires, Argentina."

"Your mother?"

At last I can shout with the gusto of truth.

"Denver!" Aye, just like a conductor.

Casually, by way of conversation, he asks: "You speak Italian?"

"Nah! Not a word."

"Too bad," he says.

"You're nuts," I think.

VI

That semester I wait on table to defray my tuition fee. Trouble ahead; the chef and his assistants in the kitchen are all Italians. They know at once that I am of the breed. I ignore the chef's friendly overtures, loathing him from the first. He understands why, and we become enemies. Every word he uses has a knife in it. His remarks cut me to pieces. After two months I can stand it no longer in the kitchen, and so I write a long letter to my mother; I am losing weight, I write; if you don't let me quit this job, I'll get sick and flunk my tests. She telegraphs me some money and tells me to quit at once; oh, I feel so sorry for you, my boy; I didn't dream it would be so hard on you.

I decide to work just one more evening, to wait on table for just one more meal. That evening, after the meal, when the kitchen is deserted save for the cook and his assistants, I remove my apron and take my stand across the kitchen from him, staring at him. This is my moment. Two months I have waited for this moment. There is a knife stuck into the chopping block. I pick it up, still staring. I want to hurt the cook, square things up.

He sees me, and he says: "Get out of here, Wop!"

An assistant shouts: "Look out, he's got a knife!"

"You won't throw it, Wop," the cook says. I am not thinking of throwing it, but since he says I won't, I do. It goes over his head and strikes the wall and drops with a clatter to the floor. He picks it up and chases me out of the kitchen. I run, thanking God I didn't hit him.

―――

That year the football team is made up of Irish and Italian boys. The linemen are Irish, and we in the backfield are four Italians. We have a good team and win a lot of games, and my teammates are excellent players who are unselfish and work together as one man. But I hate my three fellow-players in the backfield; because of our nationality we seem ridiculous. The team makes a captain of me, and I call signals and see to it my fellow-Italians in the backfield do as little scoring as possible. I hog the play.

The school journal and the town's sport pages begin to refer to us as the Wop Wonders. I think it an insult. Late one afternoon, at the close of an important game, a number of students leave the main grandstand and group themselves at one end of the field, to improvise some yells. They give three big ones for the Wop Wonders. It sickens me. I can feel my stomach move; and after that game I turn in my suit and quit the team.

I am a bad Latinist. Disliking the language, I do not study, and therefore I flunk my examinations regularly. Now a student comes to me and tells me that it is possible to drop Latin from my curriculum if I follow his suggestion, which is that I fail deliberately in the next few examinations, fail hopelessly. If I do this, the student says, the Jesuits will bow to my stupidity and allow me to abandon the language.

This is an agreeable suggestion. I follow it out. But it backtracks, for the Jesuits are wise fellows. They see what I'm doing, and they laugh and tell me that I am not clever enough to fool them, and that I must keep on studying Latin, even if it takes me twenty years to pass. Worse, they double my assignments and I spend my recreation time with Latin syntax. Before examinations in my junior year the Jesuit who instructs me calls me to his room and says:

"It is a mystery to me that a thoroughbred Italian like yourself should have any trouble with Latin. The language is in your blood and, believe me, you're a darned poor Wop."

Abbastanza! I go upstairs and lock my door and sit down with my book in front of me, my Latin book, and I study like a wild man, tearing crazily into the stuff until, lo, what is this? What am I studying here? Sure enough, it's a lot like the Italian my grandmother taught me so long ago—this Latin, it isn't so hard, after all. I pass the examination, I pass it with such an incredibly fine grade that my instructor thinks there is knavery somewhere.

Two weeks before graduation I get sick and go to the infirmary and am quarantined there. I lie in bed and feed my grudges. I bite my thumbs and ponder old grievances. I am running a high fever, and I can't sleep. I think about the principal. He was my close friend during my first two years at the school, but in my third year, last year, he was transferred to another school. I lie in bed thinking of the day we met again in this, the last year. We met again on his return that September, in the principal's room. He said hello to the boys, this fellow and that, and then he turned to me, and said:

"And you, the Wop! So you're still with us."

Coming from the mouth of the priest, the word had a lumpish sound that shook me all over. I felt the eyes of everyone, and I heard a giggle. So that's how it is! I lie in bed thinking of the priest and now of the fellow who giggled.

All of a sudden I jump out of bed, tear the fly-leaf from a book, find a pencil, and write a note to the priest. I write: "Dear Father: I haven't forgotten your insult. You called me a Wop last September. If you don't apologize right away there's going to be trouble." I call the brother in charge of the infirmary and tell him to deliver the note to the priest.

After a while I hear the priest's footsteps rising on the stairs. He comes to the door of my room, opens it, looks at me for a long time, not speaking, but only looking querulously. I wait for him to come in and apologize, for this is a grand moment for me. But he closes the door quietly and walks away. I am astonished. A double insult!

I am well again on the night of graduation. On the platform the principal makes a speech and then begins to distribute the diplomas. We're supposed to say: "Thank you," when he gives them to us. So thank you, and thank you, and thank you, everyone says in his turn. But when he gives me mine, I look squarely at him, just stand there and look, and I don't say anything, and from that day we never speak to each other again.

The following September I enroll at the university.
"Where was your father born?" asks the registrar.
"Buenos Aires, Argentina."
Sure, that's it. The same theme, with variations.

—The Wine of Youth

DURING MY SECOND YEAR at the university I fell in love with a girl who worked in a clothing store. Her name was Agnes, and I wanted to marry her. She moved to North Platte, Nebraska, for a better job, and I quit the university to be near her. I hitchhiked from Boulder to North Platte and arrived dusty and broke and triumphant at the rooming house where Agnes lived. We sat on the porch swing and she was not glad to see me.

"I don't want to marry you," she said. "I don't want to see you any more. That's why I'm here, so we don't see each other."

"I'll get a job," I insisted. "We'll have a family."

"Oh for Christ's sake."

"Don't you want a family? Don't you like kids?"

She got quickly to her feet. "Go home, Arturo. Please go home. Don't think about me any more. Go back to school. Learn something." She was crying.

"I can lay brick," I said, moving to her. She threw her arms around me, and planted a wet kiss on my cheek, then pushed me away.

"Go home, Arturo. Please." She went inside and closed the door.

I walked down to the railroad tracks and swung aboard a freight train bound for Denver. From there I took another freight to Boulder and home. The next day I went to the job where my father was laying brick.

"I want to talk to you," I said. He came down from the scaffold and we walked to a pile of lumber.

"What's the matter?" he said.

"I quit school."

"Why?"

"I'm not cut out for it."

His face twisted bitterly. "What are you going to do now?"

"I don't know. I haven't figured it out."
"Jesus, you're crazy."

———————

I became a bum in my home town. I loafed around. I took a job pulling weeds, but it was hard and I quit. Another job, washing windows. I barely got through it. I looked all over Boulder for work, but the streets were full of young, unemployed men. The only job in town was delivering newspapers. It paid fifty cents a day. I turned it down. I leaned against walls in the pool halls. I stayed away from home. I was ashamed to eat the food my father and mother provided. I always waited until my father walked out. My mother tried to cheer me. She made me pecan pie and ravioli.

"Don't worry," she said. "You wait and see. Something will happen. It's in my prayers."

I went to the library. I looked at the magazines, at the pictures in them. One day I went to the bookshelves, and pulled out a book. It was *Winesburg, Ohio.* I sat at a long mahogany table and began to read. All at once my world turned over. The sky fell in. The book held me. The tears came. My heart beat fast. I read until my eyes burned. I took the book home. I read another Anderson. I read and I read, and I was heartsick and lonely and in love with a book, many books, until it came naturally, and I sat there with a pencil and a long tablet, and tried to write, until I felt I could not go on because the words would not come as they did in Anderson, they only came like drops of blood from my heart.

—Dreams from Bunker Hill

The Odyssey of a Wop

TIME PASSES, and so do school days. I am sitting on a wall along the plaza in Los Angeles, watching a Mexican *fiesta* across the street. A man comes along and lifts himself to the wall beside me, and asks if I have a cigarette. I have, and, lighting the cigarette, he makes conversation with me, and we talk of casual things until the *fiesta* is over. Then we get down from the wall and, still talking, go walking through the Los Angeles Tenderloin. This man needs a shave and his clothes do not fit him; it's plain that he's a bum. He tells one lie upon another, and not one is well told. But I am lonesome in this town, and a willing listener.

We step into a restaurant for coffee. Now he becomes intimate. He has bummed his way from Chicago to Los Angeles, and has come in search of his sister; he has her address, but she is not at it, and for two weeks he has been looking for her in vain. He talks on and on about this sister, seeming to gyrate like a buzzard over her, hinting to me that I should ask some questions about her. He wants me to touch off the fuse that will release his feelings.

So I ask: "Is she married?"

And then he rips into her, hammer and tongs. Even if he does find her, he will not live with her. What kind of a sister is she to let him walk these streets without a dime in his pocket, and she married to a man who has plenty of money and can give him a job? He thinks she has deliberately given him a false address so that he will not find her, and when he gets his hands on her he's going to wring her neck. In the end, after he has completely demolished her; he does exactly what I think he is going to do.

He asks: "Have you got a sister?"

I tell him yes, and he waits for my opinion of her; but he doesn't get it.

We meet again a week later.

He has found his sister. Now he begins to praise her. She has induced her husband to give him a job, and tomorrow he goes to work as a waiter in his brother-in-law's restaurant. He tells me the address, but I do not think more of it beyond the fact that it must be somewhere in the Italian quarter.

And so it is, and by a strange coincidence I know his brother-in-law, Rocco Saccone, an old friend of my people and a *paesano* of my father's. I am in Rocco's place one night a fortnight later. Rocco and I are speaking in Italian when the man I have met on the plaza steps out of the kitchen, an apron over his legs. Rocco calls him and he comes over, and Rocco introduces him as his brother-in-law from Chicago. We shake hands.

"We've met before," I say, but the plaza man doesn't seem to want this known, for he lets go my hand quickly and goes behind the counter, pretending to be busy with something back there. Oh, he's bluffing; you can see that.

In a loud voice, Rocco says to me: "That man is a skunk. He's ashamed of his own flesh and blood." He turns to the plaza man. "Ain't you?"

"Oh, yeah?" the plaza man sneers.

"How do you mean—he's ashamed? How do you mean?"

"Ashamed of being an Italian," Rocco says.

"Oh, yeah?" from the plaza man.

"That's all he knows," Rocco says. "Oh, yeah? That's all he knows. Oh, yeah? Oh, yeah? Oh, yeah? That's all he knows."

"Oh, yeah?" the plaza man says again.

"Yah," Rocco says, his face blue. *"Animale codardo!"*

The plaza man looks at me with peaked eyebrows, and he doesn't know it, he standing there with his black, liquid eyes, he doesn't know that he's as good as a god in his waiter's apron; for he is indeed a god, a miracle worker; no, he doesn't know; no one knows; just the same, he is that—he, of all people. Standing there and looking at him, I feel like my grandfather and my father and the Jesuit cook and Rocco; I seem to have come home, and I am surprised that this return, which I have somehow always expected, should come so quietly, without trumpets and thunder.

"If I were you, I'd get rid of him," I say to Rocco.

"Oh, yeah?" the plaza man says again.

I'd like to paste him. But that won't do any good. There's no sense in hammering your own corpse.

—The Wine of Youth

M Y FIRST DAY IN LOS ANGELES I took a job washing dishes at Clifton's Cafeteria. After a few days I was promoted to busboy and was sacked for "socializing with the public," in this case a girl carrying a volume of Edna St. Vincent Millay who invited me to her table for coffee and a talk on poetry.

Next day I found another dishwashing job at a saloon on the corner of Fifth and Main. My room was upstairs for four dollars a week, shared by another dishwasher. His name was Hernandez and he was crazy. He was the first writer I ever met, a tall, laughing Mexican sitting on the bed with a typewriter in his lap, guffawing at every line he wrote. His project was a book called *Fun and Profit in Dishwashing*. It was as mad as Hernandez himself. I used to fall asleep listening to him read the manuscript, convulsing with pleasure. One of his chapters was "The Mystery of Hot Water," another, "Clean Hands Make Clean Minds."

But the job was exhausting, the floor always submerged from leaking pipes, and the food inedible. I quit to work in the garment district pushing dress racks and running errands for everyone. I had a dozen bosses who kept me rushing after coffee, sandwiches, newspapers and a hundred other trifles. One of them owned an independent cab service and offered me a job driving at night. I accepted though I knew nothing of the huge, complicated city. For eight hours I cruised downtown Los Angeles that first night without catching a single fare. My boss assured me that things would improve when the dry spell ended, and to pray for rain.

The following night I had my first customers, a black man and his girl. The man asked to be driven to Ninety-sixth and Central Avenue. As I consulted a map of the city he said, "You mean to tell me you don't know where Ninety-sixth and Central is?" I told him I was new in town. "I'll show you the way," he said. "Down one block and turn left."

For two hours I followed his directions, all the way to San Bernardino, where I was told to stop in a tractless, houseless wasteland without street lights or sidewalks. I felt the barrel of a pistol in my ear as he ordered me out of the car. His girlfriend searched me and took all I possessed, nine dollars. They drove off, leaving me there in a place resembling Death Valley.

As daylight pulsed in the east, a police car came up silently and found me walking toward what appeared to be the lights of a distant city. I spent three hours in the San Bernardino Police Station being grilled mercilessly by two detectives who suspected me of being AWOL or draft-dodging. The 4-F status of my draft card did not impress them. They fingerprinted me and ran a check. At noon they released me, without breakfast or even coffee, and ordered me out of town. They were bad guys: they wouldn't even give me directions.

I got out on the street and began to ask passers-by. Nobody seemed to know how to get out of San Bernardino, so I finally found it myself. I thumbed for an hour before a truck stopped. The driver wasn't going to Los Angeles but to Wilmington. Good enough. Anything was better than San Bernardino. When I told him of being robbed and arrested he laughed. "Lotsa luck," he said as he let me off on Wilmington Boulevard.

Wilmington was paranoid, a seaport town in the midst of war. It did not seem to have been laid out so much as dumped out. Big trucks hogged the streets, roaring through crowded intersections where soldiers, sailors and civilians ignored traffic signals in the middle of honking claxons and cursing drivers. I moved with the flow of people, aimlessly following a surge down Avalon Boulevard. I was tired, dirty and dazed, tumbled like a cork along a street of oil derricks, factories, lumberyards, piles of girders and steel pipe, row upon row of army tanks and trucks, pool halls, poker palaces, used-car lots, and even an amusement park with a merry-go-round and a Ferris wheel. The laughter of women in bars flooded the streets. Hustlers leaned in doorways, drunks sat on the curb, smiling cops cruised in bemused attention. Where was I? Liverpool? Singapore? Marseilles? I thought of my father, how he would have loved this singular place—the gambling, the bars, the buildings shooting up on every empty piece of land.

Hunger. I smelled the tomato sauce, the pizza coming from an Italian restaurant. I turned the corner and moved down the alley to the rear of the place. As I knocked on the black screen door a cloud of flies whined away and I saw the face of an Italian woman peering out, a plump woman in her forties, round as a meatball. I'll work for something to eat, I said. She was startled, frowning. I'm hungry, I said. She opened the door and pointed to three overloaded garbage cans, motioning me to take them outside. I rolled them out among the ecstatic flies. She worked swiftly at a butcher's table with half a loaf of French bread split down the middle, hollowed out and filled with pastrami and cream cheese. I thanked her and said I was looking for a job. Experienced dishwasher, I said. She opened the door and invited me out. I went away down the alley to a trailer park where a black hose curled like a snake through uncut lawn, and I sat on a trailer hitch eating the sandwich and drinking warm water from the hose.

Down in the harbor a mile away I came to the Toyo Fish Company. There was a sign:

WANTED: MACHINE OPERATORS, LABORERS.

Me, laborer. No hod carrier, me. No stonemason. No bricklayer. I could hear the old man: learn a trade, be something special. Oh shit, Papa. I'm not twenty yet, give me time.

The man's name was Coletti. Dark, maybe Sicilian. Foreman of the labor gang. Paisan, I smiled. He didn't like it. I'm looking for a job. No jobs, he said. But the sign outside said . . . Maybe tomorrow, he said.

I walked out into the street, heading for town, up Avalon Boulevard. But where, and why? I found a bus bench. I would call Virgil collect and ask him to send money. No, he'd tell Mama, which was okay, but the old man would find out. He'd laugh. I warned him, he'd say, he wouldn't listen to his father.

I rose and walked again, my feet aching. I met another bum like myself. He wore a long overcoat in that hot late afternoon, the pockets stuffed with junk.

"Hey, where can I get something to eat?"

"They's lots of restaurants," he said.

"I'm broke."

"So am I."

"Where do you eat?"

"Holy Ghost Mission."

"Where's that?"

"Follow me."

Holy Ghost Mission was on Banning Street between two pawnshops. It had once been a store. A crowd of thirty men, all as neatly dressed and clean-shaven as myself, crowded the door. Some sat on the sidewalk, their backs against the storefront. At seven o'clock the door opened and Mr. Atwater, a black man, told us to come inside. There was a podium where Mrs. Atwater stood, holding a guitar. We took our seats on long benches, were given hymn books, and Mrs. Atwater led us in songs. Then Mr. Atwater stood before us and talked about the mercy of God, the importance of faith, and the evils of drink. He was a big, soft-voiced man with a short white beard, a good and gentle man.

After the sermon we were led behind a partition to the dining area, long tables and benches, and two black ladies served us large bowls of beef stew, a hunk of bread and an apple. Everything was free, and it happened every night at seven o'clock. I sighed with relief. I had it made.

That night I slept in a used-car lot on Avalon, an old Cadillac with a velour back seat, comfortable and long enough. At eight o'clock the next morning I was back at the Toyo Fish Company standing in front of Mr. Coletti's desk. He looked up from some papers.

"Nothing today," he said.

"Tomorrow?"

"You never know."

I felt encouraged. I liked Coletti. We were on talking terms, getting acquainted. Every morning I left my Cadillac and trudged down to Toyo for a brief conversation with him. There were never harsh words. Sometimes he glanced at my clothes, the gray suit I had worn since my first day in Los Angeles, rumpled now and soiled and misshapen. "Nothing doing today," he'd say. "Things are still slow." Then one day he let me in on a production matter. "No fish," he said. "We're waiting for the boats." I felt cheered. I had been given confidential information. The job was coming. I had to hold out. Now I need not look for other jobs. God knew I had tried.

Why had I been rejected? Was it my clothes? Was it my face? I studied it in store windows, the dark stubble beard, the gauntness, the aspect of defeat. Did I repel people? Did I give off some mysterious antagonism, some anger at the world? A time came when I became afraid to approach bosses and employers. Only Coletti and Mr. Atwater accepted me, gave me hope and food. I walked the streets. I found the public library and read for hours, then dropped down to the Holy Ghost Mission for my supper. I thought of begging, for I had seen panhandlers scrounging coins and it looked easy. But I lacked courage. I was too ashamed. Even those heady days when I made my way in Los Angeles washing dishes seemed impossible now.

After a month in Wilmington, Coletti came through.

"You start tomorrow. Be here at seven."

I wanted to kiss his hand, but I only said, "Thank you."

I walked away with my chest bursting in joy and pain, past the docks where stevedores loaded ships and men steered forklifts, laughing and kidding as they worked, and I laughed too, for I was one of them, I had a job, I belonged to the human race again. At the Holy Ghost Mission I sang with a full throat, and I cried when Mr. Atwater spoke of the mercy of God. When they passed out the gleaming red Washington apples I held mine like a holy goblet, too sacred to devour.

An old lady with a few teeth like fangs sat next to me. I smiled and said, "Would you like another apple?" She nodded with a smile and accepted my apple and put it in her paper sack. I felt ennobled. I had given something instead of taking.

It was time to sleep now, to retire and prepare for my first day on the job. As I entered my Cadillac and stretched out, the used-car manager pounced on me and ordered me out of the car. He raised a jackhandle as if to smash my skull. "Get the fuck outa here, you bum. Next time I'll call the cops."

When you are a drifter you take note of places to bed down—abandoned buildings, open basements, sheds. I had such a place filed away in my mind—a hideaway beneath a bridge over the Tucker River, which wasn't a river at all except when it rained.

On the way to Tucker Bridge I stopped at the Catalina Steamship Terminal to pick up some cigarettes. The terminal was without doubt the best source of cigarettes in the harbor. It supplied the top brands—Pall Mall, Tareyton and Chesterfield—in king sizes and in ample quantities. This was the best hour to go there and stock up, for the *Catalina* had just returned from the island and the passengers had departed. I was not disappointed. Every sand-filled ashtray was crammed with lovely butts, and I went from one to another, selecting my favorite brands and stuffing them into my coat pockets. It had been a good day for me. The new job, an excellent meal at Holy Ghost, and enough cigarettes to get through the following day.

A butter moon lit the harbor as I trudged through weeds and sand to the entrance of Tucker Bridge. The stream was no more than a trickle of sewer water through white sand. Someone had dragged a skiff beneath the bridge and covered it with a tarp. I rolled the canvas up and shaped it into a mattress. How beautiful it was under that bridge! Yellow moonbeams flooded both openings, and the water laughed as the tide splashed the pilings with its ebb and flow.

I lay on my back and thought of the future. Any hopes for writing would have to be postponed. What mattered now was just staying alive. From that day forward I resolved never to be poor again. I would work hard for Coletti and the Toyo Fish Company. I would hoard every penny. I would jingle coins in my pocket and store away dollars in the bank. I would cover my body, my life, with money. I would be impregnable. I would not be hurt again. I was still a young man. On December 8, a month from now, I would be twenty years old. There was plenty of time. I had everything going at last in my favor. I smiled as I said the Lord's Prayer.

Something bit me and I wakened. Something on my leg. I sat up. Something stung my hand, the small finger. I flicked my hand. I looked. A beast, an animal, a thing, clinging to my finger. It was a brown thing. It was a crab. It hung on. I beat it against the boat. It fell away. I sat up. They were all over me. They were on my legs, under my pants, they were biting, crawling. I felt them at my scrotum. I pulled one out of my hair. I jumped up and screamed. They fell from my clothes. They made a sound of clicking. I jumped up and down. I screamed in fear. I ran out from under the bridge and tore off my clothes in the daylight. I saw the traffic. I pulled off my pants, my shirt, my shorts. I was naked, on fire, rubbing sand into little bleeding holes in my body, running like crazy, flinging myself in weeds and sand, howling like a dog.

I heard a siren. I saw the spinning red light. I saw the police car roaring down, churning up sand. Two cops with batons rushed at me. "My clothes!" I said, grabbing at them—a shirt, my coat, my pants—the cops scrambling after me as I crawled on hands and knees. They picked me up by the armpits and staggered toward the police car. They opened the door and tossed me inside, the clothes in my arms. I covered my groin with the clothes and began to shake out of control as the car roared away and my teeth chattered as I kept dying and trying to stay alive.

They took me to the emergency room of the hospital, slamming to a stop in the driveway.

"Put your pants on," the older cop said.

I fumbled with the bundle of sand-laden clothes, teeth clicking, hands shaking the loose sand on the seat and the carpet. The old cop was furious. "Watch it with that sand!" He unfolded a blanket and opened the door. He threw the blanket over me as I got out.

They marched me into the side door of the emergency room and the old cop snatched away the blanket. He threw it on the floor in disgust. The medic stared as I stood clutching my clothes.

"Got a beauty this time, Doc." The old cop smiled.

The medic was a blond guy of about thirty in a blue smock. A fingernail gently scraped the flesh at my shoulder. The dirty skin was as greenish gray as a mackerel.

"You ever had a bath before?" the medic asked.

"I used to bathe all the time."

"Put your clothes on the chair and follow me."

I spilled my rags on the chair and went down the hall with him to a shower. He handed me a bar of soap and a towel. I got under the hot water. It was as close to heaven as I had ever been. It stopped the shaking and I began to see the pink of my flesh. I toweled off and walked back to the emergency room. The cops were still there, smoking and talking to the doctor. I lay on the table and he dabbed the wounds with a yellowish antiseptic as the old cop began to question me: name, address, draft status.

Quietly he asked, "How long you been doing this?"

I looked at him. "Doing what?"

"Indecent exposure."

I sat up.

"Never!"

I was shaking again as I told about the crab attack. They were amused but not convinced. I thrust out my arms, my legs, to show the gouged flesh. The cops were not impressed.

"Could be self-inflicted," the old cop said, turning to the doctor. "What do you think, Doc?"

My gut hardened and my eyes devoured the medic. He had been rather friendly and dispassionate, a professional but not a cop. I screamed at him.

"Tell them!"

He looked from me to the two cops, then turned back to swabbing the wounds. "I don't believe they're self-inflicted," he said. "But I don't think he was attacked by crabs either."

I felt the grief in my chest, the turmoil to break into tears. God almighty, don't make me cry. God keep me a man like my father!

Suddenly the old cop jumped away.

"Jesus Christ!" he said, looking down at the floor. Crawling toward him, skittering across the gleaming tile floor, was a crab. Another was moving frantically toward the crack in the door. A third crawled out of the leg of my pants, his feelers moving as he checked the strange territory. I cried then. I sat up and held my knees and cried because everybody was so fucking rotten, and the only ones coming to my rescue were the little beasties who had caused all the trouble in the first place, the crabs.

My outburst chilled the cops. They backed out of the room and returned to the squad car. Through the window I saw them sitting in the front seat, heads back, caps pulled over their eyes.

The medic washed his hands. He looked disturbed as he dried them on a towel. "Let's have a look at those crab bites again," he suggested, murmuring to himself as he probed here and there.

"I think I'll give you a tetanus shot," he said. "You ever had one?" I told him yes, a couple of years ago. Turning me over on my stomach, he jabbed a hypodermic into my butt. It hurt and I sat up.

"Is that all?"

"Not quite. I'm giving you penicillin too."

I took it in the arm.

"Okay. You can get dressed."

I picked up my sand-laden pants. They were obscene and disgusting as I held them in the air.

"If the cops don't mind, I'd just as soon have their blanket."

"I'll fix that," the medic said.

He walked down the hall and returned with a pair of Levi's, a gray sweatshirt, shorts and socks. They were old but clean. I thanked him and got dressed as he chased the crabs around with a rag saturated in chloroform.

We said so long and I walked out to the police car and was driven to the Wilmington Substation of the L.A.P.D. I was booked on a charge of vagrancy. They put me in a holding cell with four other criminals, and around noon the police van hauled us to Lincoln Heights Jail in Los Angeles.

I thought of the Toyo Fish Company and all that it had promised, and how beautiful it was, rotting away there on the dock, all tin and stinking enchantingly of fish and bilge and scum and tar, and I thought fondly of Coletti, who believed in me, and I wondered if I was really as old as I felt. I looked at the other prisoners in the van. They had been arrested for brawling—their eyes blackened, some with bandaged heads and knuckles. What a sad bunch we were, riding off in the warm sunshine.

We ended our journey in the drunk tank at Lincoln Heights, an oversized cell where tired, waiting men slumped on wooden benches, shriveled in their clothes.

The next morning fifty of us were marched before the judge in Sunrise Court. When my name was called I stepped forward and pleaded guilty to the charge of vagrancy. There wasn't much choice. Had I pleaded innocent without the necessary bail, the court would have confined me for two months while I waited for a trial date and the assignment of a public defender. The judge fined me ten dollars or five days.

The fourth morning of my term I woke to see an old acquaintance, brought in during the night. It was Crazy Hernandez, the dishwashing writer, sitting on his bunk smoking a cigarette. He leaped at me like a beloved friend, dancing me around the cell. Hernandez was charged with marijuana possession. Not only was he charged with it, he was actually smoking it, the joint concealed in his cupped hands. That explained his enthusiasm at our reunion. Taking advantage of his euphoria, I asked him to loan me some money.

"All I got!" He pulled off his shoe, dug a bill from inside, and slapped it into my hand. A dollar. "There's more where that came from!" he boasted. It was not so. I saw the inside of the shoe and there was nothing more within.

Oh, that Hernandez! He would never know what his dollar meant to me the morning I was sprung—a ride on the Big Red Car back to the harbor, no hitchhiking, no dread of being snatched again by the cops, a ride back to the Toyo Fish Company and my friend Coletti.

He was studying some papers at his desk.

I said, "Hi, Mr. Coletti."

"I thought you wanted to work."

"I was sick, in the hospital."

"You look sick now."

"I'm okay."

—*The Brotherhood of the Grape*

WE LIVED IN AN APARTMENT HOUSE next door to a place where a lot of Filipinos lived. The Filipino influx was seasonal. They came south for the fishing season and went back north for the fruit and lettuce seasons around Salinas. There was one family of Filipinos in our house, directly below us. It was a two story pink stucco place with big slabs of stucco wiped from the walls by earthquakes. Every night the stucco absorbed the fog like a blotter. In the mornings the walls were a damp red instead of pink. I liked the red best.

The stairs squealed like a nest of mice. Our apartment was the last on the second floor. As soon as I touched the door knob I felt low. Home always did that to me. Even when my father was alive and we lived in a real house I didn't like it. I always wanted to get away from it, or change it. I used to wonder what home would be like if it was different, but I never could figure out what to do to make it different.

I opened the door. It was dark, the darkness smelling of home, the place where I lived. I turned on the lights. My mother was lying on the divan and the light was waking her up. She rubbed her eyes and got up to her elbows. Every time I saw her half awake it made me think of the times when I was a kid and used to go to her bed in the mornings and smell her asleep until I grew older and couldn't go to her in the mornings because it reminded me too much that she was my mother. It was a salty oily odor. I couldn't even think about her getting older. It burned me up. She sat up and smiled at me, her hair mussed from sleep. Everything she did reminded me of the days when I lived in a real house.

"I thought you'd never get here," she said.

I said, "Where's Mona?"

My mother said she was at church and I said, "My own sister reduced to the superstition of prayer! My own flesh and blood. A nun, a god-lover! What barbarism!"

"Don't start that again," she said. "You're nothing but a boy who's read too many books."

"That's what you think," I said. "It's quite evident that you have a fixation complex."

Her face whitened.

"A what?"

I said, "Forget it. No use talking to yokels, clodhoppers and imbeciles. The intelligent man makes certain reservations as to the choice of his listeners."

She pushed back her hair with long fingers like Miss Hopkins's but they were worn with knobs and wrinkles at the joints, and she wore a wedding ring.

"Are you aware of the fact," I said, "that a wedding ring is not only vulgarly phallic but also the vestigial remains of a primitive savagery anomalous to this age of so-called enlightenment and intelligence?"

She said, "What?"

"Never mind. The feminine mind would not grasp it, even if I explained."

I told her to laugh if she felt like it but some day she would change her tune, and I took my new books and magazines to my private study, which was the clothes closet. There was no electric light in it, so I used candles. There was a feeling in the air that someone or something had been in the study while I was away. I looked around, and I was right, for my sister's little pink sweater hung from one of the clothes hooks.

I lifted it off the hook and said to it, "What do you mean by hanging there? By what authority? Don't you realize you have invaded the sanctity of the house of love?" I opened the door and threw the sweater on the divan.

"No clothes allowed in this room!" I yelled.

My mother came in a hurry. I closed the door and flipped the lock. I could hear her footsteps. The door knob rattled. I started unwrapping the package. The pictures in *Artists and Models* were honeys. I picked my favorite. She was lying on a white rug, holding a red rose to her cheek. I set the picture between the candles on the floor and got down on my knees. "Chloe," I said, "I worship you. Thy teeth are like a flock of sheep on Mount Gilead, and thy cheeks are comely. I am thy humble servant, and I bringeth love everlasting."

"Arturo!" my mother said. "Open up."

"What do you want?"

"What're you doing?"

"Reading. Perusing! Am I denied even that in my own home?"

She rattled the buttons of the sweater against the door. "I don't know what to do with this," she said. "You've got to let me have this clothes closet."

"Impossible."

"What're you doing?"

"Reading."

"Reading what?"

"Literature!"

She wouldn't go away. I could see her toes under the door crack. I couldn't talk to the girl with her standing out there. I put the magazine aside and waited for her to go away. She wouldn't. She didn't even move. Five minutes passed. The candle spluttered. The smoke was filling the place again. She hadn't moved an inch. Finally I set the magazine on the floor and covered it with a box. I felt like yelling at my mother. She could at least move, make a noise, lift her foot, whistle. I picked up a fiction book and stuck my finger in it, as if marking the place. When I opened the door she glared at my face. I had a feeling she knew all about me. She put her hands on her hips and sniffed at the air. Her eyes looked everywhere, the corners, the ceiling, the floor.

"What on earth are you doing in there?"

"Reading! Improving my mind. Do you forbid even that?"

"There's something awfully strange about this," she said. "Are you reading those nasty picture books again?"

"I'll have no Methodists, prudes, or pruriency in my house. I'm sick of this polecat wowserism. The awful truth is that my own mother is a smut hound of the worst type."

"They make me sick," she said.

I said, "Don't blame the pictures. You're a Christian, an Epworth Leaguer, a Bible-Belter. You're frustrated by your brummagem Christianity. You're at heart a scoundrel and a jackass, a bounder and an ass."

She pushed me aside and walked into the closet. Inside was the odor of burning wax and brief passions spent on the floor. She knew what the darkness held. Then she ran out.

"God in heaven!" she said. "Let me out of here." She pushed me aside and slammed the door. I heard her banging pots and pans in the kitchen. Then the kitchen door slammed. I locked the door and went back to the picture and lit the candles. After a while my mother knocked and told me supper was ready. I told her I had eaten. She hovered at the door. She was getting annoyed again. I could feel it coming on. There was a chair at the door. I heard her drag it into position and sit down. I knew she sat with folded arms, looking at her shoes, her feet straight out in that characteristic way she had of sitting and waiting. I closed the magazine and waited. If she could stand it I could too. Her toe beat a tap on the carpet. The chair squeaked. The beat increased. All at once she jumped up and started hammering the door. I opened it in a hurry.

"Come out of there!" she screamed.

I got out as fast as I could. She smiled, tired but relieved. She had small teeth. One below was out of line like a soldier out of step. She wasn't more than five three but she looked tall when she had on high heels. Her aged showed most in her skin. She was forty-five. Her skin sagged some under the ears. I was glad her hair wasn't grey. I always looked for grey hairs but didn't find any. I pushed her and tickled her and she laughed and fell into the chair. Then I went to the divan and stretched out and slept awhile.

—*The Road to Los Angeles*

THEY WENT TO BED. I had the divan and they had the bedroom. When their door closed I got out the magazines and piled into bed. I was glad to be able to look at the girls under the lights of the big room. It was a lot better than that smelly closet. I talked to them about an hour, went into the mountains with Elaine, and to the South Seas with Rosa, and finally in a group meeting with all of them spread around me, I told them I played no favorites and that each in her turn would get her chance. But after a while I got awfully tired of it, for I got to feeling more and more like an idiot until I began to hate the idea that they were only pictures, flat and single-faced and so alike in color and smile. And they all smiled like whores. It all got very hateful and I thought, Look at yourself! Sitting here and talking to a lot of prostitutes. A fine superman you turned out to be! What if Nietzsche could see you now? And Schopenhauer—what would he think? And Spengler! Oh, would Spengler roar at you! You fool, you idiot, you swine, you beast, you rat, you filthy, contemptible, disgusting little swine! Suddenly I grabbed the pictures up in a batch and tore them to pieces and threw them down the bowl in the bathroom. Then I crawled back to bed and kicked the covers off. I hated myself so much that I sat up in bed thinking the worst possible things about myself. Finally I was so despicable there was nothing left to do but sleep. It was hours before I dozed off. The fog was thinning in the east and the west was black and grey. It must have been three o'clock. From the bedroom I heard my mother's soft snores. By then I was ready to commit suicide, and so thinking I fell asleep.

—*The Road to Los Angeles*

WHEN I WOKE UP IT was around noon and they were gone somewhere. I got out the picture of an old girl of mine I called Marcella and we went to Egypt and made love in a slave-driven boat on the Nile. I drank wine from her sandals and milk from her breasts and then we had the slaves paddle us to the river bank and I fed her hearts of hummingbirds seasoned in sweetened pigeon milk. When it was over I felt like the devil. I felt like hitting myself in the nose, knocking myself unconscious. I wanted to cut myself, to feel my bones cracking. I tore the picture of Marcella to pieces and got rid of it and then I went to the medicine cabinet and got a razor blade, and before I knew it I slit my arm below the elbow, but not deeply so that it was only blood and no pain. I sucked the slit but there was still no pain, so I got some salt and rubbed it in and felt it bite my flesh, hurting me and making me come out of it and feel alive again, and I rubbed it until I couldn't stand it any longer. Then I bandaged my arm.

They had left a note for me on the table. It said they had gone to Uncle Frank's and that there was food in the pantry for my breakfast. I decided to eat at Jim's Place, because I still had some money. I crossed the schoolyard which was across the street from the apartment and went over to Jim's. I ordered ham and eggs. While I ate Jim talked.

He said, "You read a lot. Did you ever try writing a book?"

That did it. From then on I wanted to be a writer. "I'm writing a book right now," I said.

He wanted to know what kind of a book.

I said, "My prose is not for sale. I write for posterity."

He said, "I didn't know that. What do you write? Stories? Or plain fiction?"

"Both. I'm ambidextrous."

"Oh. I didn't know that."

I went over to the other side of the place and bought a pencil and a notebook. He wanted to know what I was writing now. I said, "Nothing. Merely taking random notes for a future work on foreign trade. The subject interests me curiously, a sort of dynamic hobby I've picked up."

When I left he was staring at me with his mouth open. I took it easy down to the harbor. It was June down there, the best time of all. The mackerel were running off the south coast and the canneries were going full blast, night and day, and all the time at that time of the year there was a stink in the air of putrefaction and fish oil. Some people considered it a stink and some got sick from it, but it was not a stink to me, except the fish smell which was bad, but to me it was great. I liked it down there. It wasn't one smell but a lot of them weaving in and out, so every step you took brought a different odor. It made me dreamy and I did a lot of thinking about far-away places, the mystery of what the bottom of the sea contained, and all the books I'd read came alive at once and I saw better people out of books, like Philip Carey, Eugene Witla, and the fellows Dreiser made.

I liked the odor of bilge water from old tankers, the odor of crude oil in barrels bound for distant places, the odor of oil on the water turned slimy and yellow and gold, the odor of rotting lumber and the refuse of the sea blackened by oil and tar, of decayed fruit, of little Japanese fishing sloops, of banana boats and old rope, of tugboats and scrap iron and the brooding mysterious smell of the sea at low tide.

I stopped at the white bridge that crossed the channel to the left of the Pacific Coast Fisheries on the Wilmington side. A tanker was unloading at the gasoline docks. Up the street Jap fishermen were repairing their nets, stretched for blocks along the water's edge. At the American-Hawaiian stevedores were loading a ship for Honolulu. They worked in their bare backs. They looked like something great to write about. I flattened the new notebook against the rail, dipped the pencil on my tongue and started to write a treatise on the stevedore: "A Psychological Interpretation of the Stevedore Today and Yesterday, by Arturo Gabriel Bandini."

It turned out a tough subject. I tried four or five times but gave up. Anyhow, the subject took years of research; there wasn't any need for prose yet. The first thing to do was get my facts together. Maybe it would take two years, three, even four; in fact it was the job of a lifetime, a magnum opus. It was too tough. I gave it up. I figured philosophy was easier.

"A Moral and Philosophical Dissertation on Man and Woman, by Arturo Gabriel Bandini." Evil is for the weak man, so why be weak. It is better to be strong than to be weak, for to be weak is to lack strength. Be strong, my brothers, for I say unless ye be strong the forces of evil shall get ye. All strength is a form of power. All lack of strength is a form of evil. All evil is a form of weakness. Be strong, lest ye be weak. Avoid weakness that ye might become strong. Weakness eateth the heart of woman. Strength feedeth the heart of man. Do ye wish to become females? Aye, then grow weak. Do ye wish to become men? Aye, aye. Then grow strong. Down with Evil! Up with Strength! Oh Zarathustra, endow thy women with plenty of weakness! Oh Zarathustra, endow thy men with plenty of strength! Down with woman! Hail Man!

Then I got tired of the whole thing. I decided maybe I wasn't a writer after all but a painter. Maybe my genius lay in art. I turned a page in the book and figured on doing some sketching just for the practice, but I couldn't find anything worth drawing, only ships and stevedores and docks, and they didn't interest me. I drew cats-on-the-fence, faces, triangles and squares. Then I got the idea I wasn't an artist or a writer but an architect, for my father had been a carpenter and maybe the building trade was more in keeping with my heritage. I drew a few houses. They were about the same, square places with a chimney out of which smoke poured. I put the notebook away.

It was hot on the bridge, the heat stinging the back of my neck. I crawled through the rail to some jagged rocks tumbled about at the edge of the water. They were big rocks, black as coal from immersions at high tide, some of them big as a house. Under the bridge they were scattered in crazy disorder like a field of icebergs, and yet they looked contented and undisturbed.

I crawled under the bridge and I had a feeling I was the only one who had ever done it. The small harbor waves lapped at the rocks and left little pools of green water here and there. Some of the rocks were draped in moss, and others had pretty spots of bird dung. The ponderous odor of the sea came up. Under the girders it was so cold and so dark I couldn't see much. From above I heard the traffic pounding, horns honking, men yelling, and big trucks battering the timber crosspieces. It was such a terrible din that it hammered my ears and when I yelled my voice went out a few feet and rushed back as if fastened to a rubber band. I crawled along the stones until I got out of the range of the sunlight. It was a strange place. For a while I was scared. Farther on there was a great stone, bigger than the rest, its crest ringed with the white dung of gulls. It was the king of all those stones with a crown of white. I started for it.

All of a sudden everything at my feet began to move. It was the quick slimy moving of things that crawled. I caught my breath, hung on, and tried to fix my gaze. They were crabs! The stones were alive and swarming with them. I was so scared I couldn't move and the noise from above was nothing compared to the thunder of my heart.

I leaned against a stone and put my face in my hands until I wasn't afraid. When I took my hands away I could see through the blackness and it was grey and cold, like a world under the earth, a grey, solitary place. For the first time I got a good look at the things living down there. The big crabs were the size of house bricks, silent and cruel as they held forth on top the large stones, their menacing antennae moving sensuously like the arms of a hula dancer, their little eyes mean and ugly. There were a lot more of the smaller crabs, about the size of my hand, and they swam around in the little black pools at the base of the rocks, crawling over one another, pulling one another into the lapping blackness as they fought for positions on the stones. They were having a good time.

There was a nest of even smaller crabs at my feet, each the size of a dollar, a big chunk of squirming legs jumbled together. One of them grabbed my pants cuff. I pulled him off and held him while he clawed helplessly and tried to bite me. I had him though and he was helpless. I pulled back my arm and threw him against a stone. He crackled, smashed to death, stuck for a moment upon the stone, then falling with blood and water exuding. I picked up the smashed shell and tasted the yellow fluid coming from it, which was salty as sea water and I didn't like it. I threw him out to deep water. He floated until a jack smelt swam around him and examined him, and then began to bite him viciously and finally dragged him out of sight, the smelt slithering away. My hands were bloody and sticky and the smell of the sea was on them. All at once I felt a swelling in me to kill these crabs, every one of them.

The small ones didn't interest me, it was the big ones I wanted to kill and kill. The big fellows were strong and ferocious with powerful incisors. They were worthy adversaries for the great Bandini, the conquering Arturo. I looked around but couldn't find a switch or a stick. On the bank against the concrete there was a pile of stones. I rolled up my sleeves and started throwing them at the largest crab I could see, one asleep on a stone twenty feet away. The stones landed all around him, within an inch of him, sparks and chips flying, but he didn't even open his eyes to find out what was going on. I threw about twenty times before I got him. It was a triumph. The stone crushed his back with the sound of a breaking soda cracker. It went clear through him, pinning him to the stone. Then he fell into the water, the foamy green bubbles at the edge swallowing him. I watched him disappear and shook my fist at him, waving angry farewells as he floated to the bottom. Goodbye, goodbye! We will doubtless meet again in another world; you will not forget me, Crab. You will remember me forever and forever as your conqueror!

Killing them with stones was too tough. The stones were so sharp they cut my fingers when I heaved them. I washed the blood and slime off my hands and made my way to the edge again. Then I climbed onto the bridge and walked down the street to a ship chandler's shop three blocks away, where they sold guns and ammunition.

I told the white-faced clerk I wanted to buy an air gun. He showed me a high powered one and I laid the money down and bought it without questions. I spent the rest of the ten on ammunition—BB shot. I was anxious to get back to the battlefield so I told white face not to wrap the ammunition but give it to me like that. He thought that was strange and he looked me over while I scooped the cylinders off the counter and left the shop as fast as I could but not running. When I got outside I started to run, and then I sensed somebody was watching me and I looked around, and sure enough white face was standing in the door and peering after me through the hot afternoon air. I slowed down to a fast walk until I got to the corner and then I started to run again.

I shot crabs all that afternoon, until my shoulder hurt behind the gun and my eyes ached behind the gunsight. I was Dictator Bandini, Ironman of Crabland. This was another Blood Purge for the good of the Fatherland. They had tried to unseat me, those damned crabs, they had had the guts to try to foment a revolution, and I was getting revenge. To think of it! It infuriated me. These goddamned crabs had actually questioned the might of Superman Bandini! What had got into them to be so stupidly presumptuous? Well, they were going to get a lesson they would never forget. This was going to be the last revolution they'd ever attempt, by Christ. I gnashed my teeth when I thought of it—a nation of revolting crabs. What guts! God, I was mad.

I pumped shot until my shoulder ached and a blister rose on my trigger finger. I killed over five hundred and wounded twice as many. They were alive to the attack, insanely angry and frightened as the dead and wounded dropped from the ranks. The siege was on. They swarmed toward me. Others came out of the sea, still others from behind rocks, moving in vast numbers across the plain of stones toward death who sat on a high rock out of their reach.

I gathered some of the wounded into a pool and had a military conference and decided to court-martial them. I drew them out of the pool one at a time, sitting each over the mouth of the rifle and pulling the trigger. There was one crab, bright colored and full of life who reminded me of a woman: doubtless a princess among the renegades, a brave crabess seriously injured, one of her legs shot away, an arm dangling pitifully. It broke my heart. I had another conference and decided that, due to the extreme urgency of the situation, there must not be any sexual discrimination. Even the princess had to die. It was unpleasant but it had to be done.

With a sad heart I knelt among the dead and dying and invoked God in a prayer, asking that he forgive me for this most beastly of the crimes of a superman—the execution of a woman. And yet, after all, duty was duty, the old order must be preserved, revolution must be stamped out, the regime had to go on, the renegades must perish. For some time I talked to the princess in private, formally extending to her the apologies of the Bandini government, and abiding by her last request—it was that I permit her to hear La Paloma—I whistled it to her with great feeling so that I was crying when finished. I raised my gun to her beautiful face and pulled the trigger. She died instantly, gloriously, a flaming mass of shell and yellowed blood.

Out of sheer reverence and admiration I ordered a stone placed where she had fallen, this ravishing heroine of one of the world's unforgettable revolutions, who had perished during the bloody June days of the Bandini government. History was written that day. I made the sign of the cross over the stone, kissed it reverently, even with a touch of passion, and held my head low in a momentary cessation of attack. It was an ironic moment. For in a flash I realized I had loved that woman. But, on Bandini! The attack began again. Shortly after, I shot down another woman. She was not so seriously injured, she suffered from shock. Taken prisoner, she offered herself to me body and soul. She begged me to spare her life. I laughed fiendishly. She was an exquisite creature, reddish and pink, and only a foregone conclusion as to my destiny made me accept her touching offer. There beneath the bridge in the darkness I ravaged her while she pleaded for mercy. Still laughing I took her out and shot her to pieces, apologizing for my brutality.

The slaughter finally stopped when my head ached from eye strain. Before leaving I took another last look around. The miniature cliffs were smeared with blood. It was a triumph, a very great victory for me. I went among the dead and spoke to them consolingly, for even though they were my enemies I was for all that a man of nobility and I respected them and admired them for the valiant struggle they had offered my legions. "Death has arrived for you," I said. "Goodbye, dear enemies. You were brave in fighting and braver in death, and Führer Bandini has not forgotten. He overtly praises, even in death." To others I said, "Goodbye, thou coward. I spit on thee in disgust. Thy cowardice is repugnant to the Führer. He hateth cowards as he hateth the plague. He will not be reconciled. May the tides of the sea wash thy cowardly crime from the earth, thou knave."

I climbed back to the road just as the six o'clock whistles were blowing, and started for home. There were some kids playing ball in an empty lot up the street, and I gave them the gun and ammunition in exchange for a pocket knife which one kid claimed was worth three dollars, but he didn't fool me, because I knew the knife wasn't worth more than fifty cents. I wanted to get rid of the gun though, so I made the deal. The kids figured I was a sap, but I let them.

—*The Road to Los Angeles*

ONE NIGHT MY UNCLE DROPPED IN. He gave my mother some money. He could only stay a moment. He said he had good news for me. I wanted to know what he meant. A job, he said. At last he had found me a job. I told him this was not good news, necessarily, because I didn't know what kind of a job he got me. To this he told me to shut up, and then he told me about the job.

He said, "Take this down and tell him I sent you."

He handed me the note he had already written.

"I talked to him today," he said. "Everything is set. Do what you're told, keep your fool mouth shut, and he'll keep you on steady."

"He ought to," I said. "Any paranoiac can do cannery work."

"We'll see about that," my uncle said.

Next morning I took the bus for the harbor. It was only seven blocks from our house, but since I was going to work I thought it best not to tire myself by walking too much. The Soyo Fish Company bulged from the channel like a black dead whale. Steam spouted from pipes and windows.

At the front office sat a girl. This was a strange office. At a desk with no papers or pencils upon it, sat this girl. She was an ugly girl with a hook nose who wore glasses and a yellow skirt. She sat at the desk doing absolutely nothing, no telephone, not even a pencil before her.

"Hello," I said.

"That's not necessary," she said. "Who do you want?"

I told her I wanted to see a man named Shorty Naylor. I had a note for him. She wanted to know what the note was about. I gave it to her and she read it. "For pity's sakes," she said. Then she told me to wait a minute. She got up and went out. At the door she turned around and said, "Don't touch anything, please." I told her I wouldn't. But when I looked about I saw nothing to touch. In the corner on the floor was a full tin of sardines, unopened. It was all I could see in the room, except for the desk and chair. She's a maniac, I thought; she's dementia praecox.

As I waited I could feel something. A stench in the air all at once began to suck at my stomach. It pulled my stomach toward my throat. Leaning back, I felt the sucking. I began to feel afraid. It was like an elevator going down too fast.

Then the girl returned. She was alone. But no—she wasn't alone. Behind her, and unseen until she stepped out of the way, was a little man. This man was Shorty Naylor. He was much smaller than I was. He was very thin. His collarbones stuck out. He had no teeth worth mentioning in his mouth, only one or two which were worse than nothing. His eyes were like aged oysters on a sheet of newspaper. Tobacco juice caked the corners of his mouth like dry chocolate. His was the look of a rat in waiting. It seemed he had never been out in the sun, his face was so grey. He didn't look at my face but at my belly. I wondered what he saw there. I looked down. There was nothing, merely a belly, no larger than ever and not worth observation. He took the note from my hands. His fingernails were gnawed to stumps. He read the note bitterly, much annoyed, crushed it, and stuck it in his pocket.

"The pay is twenty-five cents an hour," he said.

"That's preposterous and nefarious."

"Anyway, that's what it is."

The girl was sitting on the desk watching us. She was smiling at Shorty. It was as if there was some joke. I couldn't see anything funny. I lifted my shoulders. Shorty was ready to go back through the door from which he had come.

"The pay is of little consequence," I said. "The facts in the case make the matter different. I am a writer. I interpret the American scene. My purpose here is not the gathering of money but the gathering of material for my forthcoming book on California fisheries. My income of course is much larger than what I shall make here. But that, I suppose, is a matter of no great consequence at the moment, none at all."

"No," he said. "The pay is twenty-five cents an hour."

"It doesn't matter. Five cents or twenty-five. Under the circumstances, it doesn't matter in the least. Not at all. I am, as I say, a writer. I interpret the American scene. I am here to gather material for my new work."

"Oh for Christ's sake!" the girl said, turning her back. "For the love of God get him out of here."

"I don't like Americans in my crew," Shorty said. "They don't work hard like the other boys."

"Ah," I said. "That's where you're wrong, sir. My patriotism is universal. I swear allegiance to no flag."

"Jesus," the girl said.

But she was ugly. Nothing she could possibly say would ever disturb me. She was too ugly.

"Americans can't stand the pace," Shorty said. "Soon as they get a bellyful they quit."

"Interesting, Mr. Naylor." I folded my arms and settled back on my heels. "Extremely interesting what you say there. A fascinating sociological aspect of the canning situation. My book will go into that with great detail and footnotes. I'll quote you there. Yes, indeed."

The girl said something unprintable. Shorty scraped a bit of pocket sediment from a plug of tobacco and bit off a hunk. It was a large bite, filling his mouth. He was scarcely listening to me, I could tell by the scrupulous way he chewed the tobacco. The girl had seated herself at the desk, her hands folded before her. We both turned and looked at one another. She put her fingers to her nose and pressed them. But the gesture didn't disturb me. She was far too ugly.

"Do you want the job?" Shorty said.

"Yes, under the circumstances. Yes."

"Remember: the work is hard, and don't expect no favors from me either. If it wasn't for your uncle I wouldn't hire you, but that's as far as it goes. I don't like you Americans. You're lazy. When you get tired you quit. You fool around too much."

"I agree with you perfectly, Mr. Naylor. I agree with you thoroughly. Laziness, if I may be permitted to make an aside, laziness is the outstanding characteristic of the American scene. Do you follow me?"

"You don't have to call me Mister. Call me Shorty. That's my name."

"Certainly, sir! But by all means, certainly! And Shorty, I would say, is a most colorful sobriquet—a typical Americanism. We writers are constantly coming upon it."

This failed to please him or impress him. His lip curled. At the desk the girl was mumbling. "Don't call me sir, neither," Shorty said. "I don't like none of that high-toned crap."

"Take him out of here," the girl said.

But I was not in the least disturbed by the remarks from one so ugly. It amused me. What an ugly face she had! It was too amusing for words. I laughed and patted Shorty on the back. I was short, but I towered over this small man. I felt great—like a giant.

"Very amusing, Shorty. I love your native sense of humor. Very amusing. Very amusing indeed." And I laughed again. "Very amusing. Ho, ho, ho. How very amusing."

"I don't see nothing funny," he said.

"But it is! If you follow me."

"The hell with it. You follow me."

"Oh, I follow you, all right. I follow."

"No," he said. "I mean, you follow me now. I'll put you in the labeling crew."

As we walked through the back door the girl turned to watch us go. "And stay out of here!" she said. But I paid no attention at all. She was far too ugly.

We were inside the cannery works. The corrugated iron building was like a dark hot dungeon. Water dripped from the girders. Lumps of brown and white steam hung bloated in the air. The green floor was slippery from fish oil. We walked across a long room where Mexican and Japanese women stood before tables gutting mackerel with fish knives. The women were wrapped in heavy oil-skins, their feet cased in rubber boots ankle-deep in fish guts.

The stench was too much. All at once I was sick like the sickness from hot water and mustard. Another ten steps across the room and I felt it coming up, my breakfast, and I bent over to let it go. My insides rushed out in a chunk. Shorty laughed. He pounded my back and roared. Then the others started. The boss was laughing at something, and so did they. I hated it. The women looked up from their work to see, and they laughed. What fun! On company time, too! See the boss laughing! Something must be taking place. Then we will laugh too. Work was stopped in the cutting room. Everybody was laughing. Everybody but Arturo Bandini.

Arturo Bandini was not laughing. He was puking his guts out on the floor. I hated every one of them, and I vowed revenge, staggering away, wanting to be out of sight somewhere. Shorty took me by the arm and led me toward another door. I leaned against the wall and got my breath. But the stench charged again. The walls spun, the women laughed, and Shorty laughed, and Arturo Bandini the great writer was heaving again. How he heaved! The women would go home tonight and talk about it at their houses. That new fellow! You should have seen him! And I hated them and even stopped heaving for a moment to pause and delight over the fact that this was the greatest hatred of all my life.

"Feel better?" Shorty said.

"Of course," I said. "It was nothing. The idiosyncrasies of an artistic stomach. A mere nothing. Something I ate, if you will."

"That's right!"

We walked into the room beyond. The women were still laughing on company time. At the door Shorty Naylor turned around and put a scowl on his face. Nothing more. He merely scowled. All the women stopped laughing. The show was over. They went back to work.

Now we were in the room where the cans were labeled. The crew was made up of Mexican and Filipino boys. They fed the machines from flat conveyor lines. Twenty or more of them, my age and more, all of them pausing to see who I was and realizing that a new man was about to go to work.

"You stand and watch," Shorty said. "Pitch in when you see how they do it."

"It looks very simple," I said. "I'm ready right now."

"No. Wait a few minutes."

And he left.

I stood watching. This was very simple. But my stomach would have nothing to do with it. In a moment I was letting go again. Again the laughter. But these boys weren't like the women. They really thought it was funny to see Arturo Bandini having such a time of it.

That first morning had no beginning and no end. Between vomitings I stood at the can dump and convulsed. And I told them who I was. Arturo Bandini, the writer. Haven't you heard of me? You will! Don't worry. You will! My book on California fisheries. It is going to be the standard work on the subject. I spoke fast, between vomitings.

"I'm not here permanently. I'm gathering material for a book on California Fisheries. I'm Bandini, the writer. This isn't essential, this job. I may give my wages to charity: the Salvation Army."

And I heaved again. Now there was nothing in my stomach except that which never came out. I bent over and choked, a famous writer with my arms around my waist, squirming and choking. But nothing would come. Somebody stopped laughing long enough to yell that I should drink water. Hey writer! Dreenk water! So I found a hydrant and drank water. It came out in a stream while I raced for the door. And they laughed. Oh that writer! What a writer he was! See him write!

"You get over it," they laughed.

"Go home," they said. "Go write book. You writer. You too good for feesh cannery. Go home and write book about puke."

Shrieks of laughter.

I walked outside and stretched out on a pile of fish nets hot in the sun between two buildings away from the main road that skirted the channel. Over the hum from the machinery I could hear them laughing. I didn't care, not at all. I felt like sleeping. But the fish nets were bad, rich with the smell of mackerel and salt. In a moment the flies discovered me. That made it worse. Soon all the flies in Los Angeles Harbor had got news of me. I crawled off the nets to a patch of sand. It was wonderful. I stretched my arms and let my fingers find cool spots in the sand. Nothing ever felt so good. Even little particles of sand my breath blew were sweet in my nose and mouth. A tiny sandbug stopped on a hill to investigate the commotion. Ordinarily I would have killed him without hesitating. He looked into my eyes, paused, and came forward. He began to climb my chin.

"Go ahead," I said. "I don't mind. You can go into my mouth if you want to."

He passed my chin and I felt him tickle my lips. I had to look at him cross-eyed to see him.

"Come ahead," I said. "I'm not going to hurt you. This is a holiday."

He climbed toward my nostrils. Then I went to sleep.

A whistle woke me up. It was twelve o'clock, noon. The workers filed out of the buildings, Mexicans, Filipinos, and Japanese. The Japanese were too busy to look anywhere other than straight ahead. They hurried by. But the Mexicans and Filipinos saw me stretched out, and they laughed again, for there he was, that great writer, all flattened out like a drunkard.

It had got all over the cannery by this time that a great personality was in their midst, none other than that immortal Arturo Bandini, the writer, and there he lay, no doubt composing something for the ages, this great writer who made fish his specialty, who worked for a mere twenty-five cents an hour because he was so democratic, that great writer. So great he was indeed, that—well, there he sprawled, flat on his belly in the sun, puking his guts out, too sick to stand the smell he was going to write a book about. A book on California fisheries! Oh, what a writer! A book on California puke! Oh, what a writer he is!

Laughter.

Thirty minutes passed. The whistle blew again. They streamed back from the lunch counters. I rolled over and saw them pass, blurred in shape, a bilious dream. The bright sun was sickening. I buried my face in my arm. They were still enjoying it, but not so much as before, because the great writer was beginning to bore them. Lifting my head I saw them out of sticky eyes as the stream moved by. They were munching apples, licking ice-cream bars, eating chocolate covered candy from noisy packages. The nausea returned. My stomach grumbled, kicked, rebelled.

Hey writer! Hey writer! Hey writer!

I heard them gather around me, the laughter and the cackling. Hey writer! The voices were shattered echoes. The dust from their feet rolled in lazy clouds. Then louder than ever a mouth against my ear, and a shout. Heeey writer! Arms grabbed me, lifted me up and turned me over. Before it happened I knew what they were going to do. This was their idea of a really funny episode. They were going to stick a fish down my waist. I knew it without even seeing the fish. I lay on my back. The mid-day sun smeared my face. I felt fingers at my shirt and the rip of cloth. Of course! just as I thought! They were going to stick that fish down my waist. But I never even saw the fish. I kept my eyes closed. Then something cold and clammy pressed my chest and was pushed down to my belt: that fish! The fools. I knew it a long time before they did it. I just knew they were going to do that. But I didn't feel like caring. One fish more or less didn't matter now.

———

Time passed. Maybe a half hour. I reached into my shirt and felt the fish against my skin. I ran my fingers along the surface, feeling his fins and tail. Now I felt better. I pulled the fish out, held him up, and looked at him. A mackerel, a foot long. I held my breath so I would not smell him. Then I put him in my mouth and bit off his head. I was sorry he was already dead. I threw him aside and got to my feet. There were some big flies making a feast of my face and the wet spot on my shirt where the fish had lain. A bold fly landed on my arm and stubbornly refused to move, even though I warned him by shaking my arm. This made me insanely angry with him. I slapped him, killing him on my arm. But I was still so furious with him that I put him in my mouth and chewed him to bits and spat him out. Then I got the fish again, placed him on a level spot in the sand, and jumped on him until he burst open. The whiteness of my face was a thing I could feel, like plaster. Every time I moved a hundred flies dispersed. The flies were such idiotic fools. I stood still, killing them, but even the dead among them taught the living nothing. They still insisted on annoying me. For some time I stood patiently and quietly, scarcely breathing, watching the flies move into a position where I could kill them.

The nausea was past. I had forgotten that part of it. What I hated was the laughter, the flies, and the dead fish. Again I wished that fish had been alive. He would have been taught a lesson not soon forgotten. I didn't know what would happen next. I would get even with them. Bandini never forgets. He will find a way. You shall pay for this—all of you.

—*The Road to Los Angeles*

T HE DAY AFTER I DESTROYED THE WOMEN I wished I had not destroyed them. When I was busy and tired I did not think of them, but Sunday was a day of rest, and I would loaf around with nothing to do, and Helen and Marie and Ruby and the Little Girl would whisper to me frantically, asking me why I had been so hasty to destroy them, asking me if I did not now regret it. And I did regret it.

Now I had to be satisfied with their memories. But their memories were not good enough. They escaped me. They were unlike the reality. I could not hold them and look at them as I did the pictures. Now I went around all the time wishing I had not destroyed them, and I called myself a dirty stinking Christian for having done it. I thought about making another collection, but that was not so easy. It had taken a long time to gather those others. I couldn't at will go about finding women to equal the Little Girl, and probably never again would there ever in my life be another woman like Marie. They could never be duplicated. There was another thing that prevented me from making another collection. I was too tired. I used to sit around with a book of Spengler or Schopenhauer and always as I read I kept calling myself a fake and a fool, because what I really wanted were those women who were no more.

Now the closet was different, filled with Mona's dresses and the disgusting odor of fumigation. Some nights I thought I could not bear it. I walked up and down the grey carpet thinking how horrible grey carpets were, and biting my fingernails. I couldn't read anything. I didn't feel like reading a book by a great man, and I used to wonder if they were so great after all. After all, were they as great as Hazel or Marie, or the Little Girl? Could Nietzsche compare with the golden hair of Jean? Some nights I didn't think so at all. Was Spengler as great as Hazel's fingernails? Sometimes yes, sometimes no. There was a time and place for everything, but as far as I was concerned I would rather have the beauty of Hazel's finger-nails to ten million volumes by Oswald Spengler.

I wanted the privacy of my study again. I used to look at that closet door and say it was a tombstone through which I could never enter again. Mona's dresses! It sickened me. And yet I could not tell my mother or Mona to please move the dresses elsewhere. I couldn't walk up to my mother and say, "Please move those dresses." The words would not come. I hated it. I thought I was becoming a Babbitt, a moral coward.

One night my mother and Mona were not at home. Just for old time's sake I decided to pay my study a visit. A little sentimental journey into the land of yesterday. I closed the door and stood in the darkness and thought of the many times when this little room was my very own, with no part of my sister disturbing it. But it could never be the same again.

In the darkness I put out my hand and felt her dresses hanging from the clothes-hooks. They were like the shrouds of ghosts, like the robes of millions and millions of dead nuns from the beginning of the world. They seemed to challenge me: they seemed to be there only to harass me and destroy the peaceful fantasy of my women who had never been. A bitter-ness went through me, and it was painful to even remember the other times. By now I had almost forgotten the features of those others.

I twisted my fist into the folds of a dress to keep from crying out. Now the closet had an unmistakable odor of rosaries and incense, of white lilies at funerals, of carpetry in the churches of my boyhood, of wax and tall, dark windows, of old women in black kneeling at mass.

It was the darkness of the confessional, with a kid of twelve named Arturo Bandini kneeling before a priest and telling him he had done something awful, and the priest telling him nothing was too awful for the confessional, and the kid saying he wasn't sure it was a sin, what he had done, but still he was sure nobody else ever did a thing like that because, father, it's certainly funny, I mean, I don't know how to tell it; and the priest finally wheedling it out of him, that first sin of love, and warning him never to do it again.

I wanted to bump my head against the closet wall and hurt myself so much that I would be senseless. Why didn't I throw those dresses out? Why did they have to remind me of Sister Mary Justin, and Sister Mary Leo, and Sister Mary Corita? I guess I was paying the rent in this apart-ment; I guess I could throw them out. And I couldn't understand why. Something forbade it.

I felt weaker than ever before, because when I was strong I would not have hesitated a moment; I would have bundled those dresses up and heaved them out the window and spat after them. But the desire was gone. It seemed silly to get angry and start heaving dresses about. It was dead and drifted away.

I stood there, and I found my thumb in my mouth. It seemed amazing that it should be there. Imagine. Me eighteen years old, and still sucking my thumb! Then I said to myself, if you're so brave and fearless, why don't you *bite* your thumb? I dare you to bite it! You're a coward if you don't. And I said, oh! Is that so? Well, I'm not either a coward. And I'll prove it!

I bit my thumb until I tasted blood. I felt my teeth against the pliant skin, refusing to penetrate, and I turned my thumb slowly until the teeth cut through the skin. The pain hesitated, moved to my knuckles, up my arm, then to my shoulder and eyes.

I grabbed the first dress I touched and tore it to pieces. Look how strong you are! Tear it to bits! Rip it until there is nothing left! And I ripped it with my hands and teeth and made grunts like a mad dog, rolling over the floor, pulling the dress across my knees and raging at it, smearing my bloody thumb over it, cursing it and laughing at it as it gave way under my strength and tore apart.

Then I started to cry. The pain in my thumb was nothing. It was a loneliness that really ached. I wanted to pray. I had not said a prayer in two years—not since the day I quit high school and began so much reading. But now I wanted to pray again, I was sure it would help, that it would make me feel better, because when I was a kid prayer used to do that for me.

I got down on my knees, closed my eyes and tried to think of prayer-words. Prayer-words were a different kind of word. I never realized it until that moment. Then I knew the difference. But there were no words. I had to pray, to say some things; there was a prayer in me like an egg. But there were no words.

Surely not those old prayers!

Not the Lord's Prayer, about Our Father who art in Heaven, hallowed be Thy name, Thy kingdom come. . . . I didn't believe that anymore. There wasn't any such thing as heaven; there might be a hell, it seemed very possible, but there wasn't any such thing as heaven. Not the Act of Contrition, about O my God, I am heartily sorry for having offended Thee, and I detest all my sins. . . . Because the only thing I was sorry about was the loss of my women, and that was something which God emphatically opposed. Or did He? Surely, He must be against that. If I were God I would certainly be against it. God could hardly be in favor of my women. No. Then He was against them.

There was Nietzsche, Friedrich Nietzsche.

I tried him.

I prayed, "Oh dearly beloved Friedrich!"

No good. It sounded like I was a homosexual.

I tried again.

"Oh dear Mr. Nietzsche."

Worse. Because I got to thinking about Nietzsche's pictures in the frontispieces of his books. They made him look like a Forty-niner, with a sloppy mustache, and I detested Forty-niners. Besides, Nietzsche was dead. He had been dead for years. He was an immortal writer, and his words burned across the pages of his books, and he was a great modern influence, but for all that he was dead and I knew it.

Then I tried Spengler.

I said, "My dear Spengler."

Awful.

I said, "Hello there, Spengler."

Awful.

I said, "Listen, Spengler!"

Worse.

I said, "Well, Oswald, as I was saying. . . ."

Brrr. And still worse.

There were my women. They were dead too; maybe I could find something in them. One at a time I tried them out, but it was unsuccessful because as soon as I thought of them it made me wildly passionate. How could a man be passionate and be in prayer? That was scandalous.

After I had thought of so many people without avail I was weary of the whole idea and about to abandon it, when all of a sudden I had a good idea, and the idea was that I should not pray to God or others, but to myself.

"Arturo, my man. My beloved Arturo. It seems you suffer so much, and so unjustly. But you are brave, Arturo. You remind me of a mighty warrior, with the scars of a million conquests. What courage is yours! What nobility! What beauty! Ah, Arturo, how beautiful you really are! I love you so, my Arturo, my great and mighty god. So weep now, Arturo. Let your tears run down, for yours is a life of struggle, a bitter battle to the

very end, and nobody knows it but you, no one but you, a beautiful warrior who fights alone, unflinching, a great hero the likes of which the
world has never known."

I sat back on my heels and cried until my sides ached from it. I opened
my mouth and wailed, and it felt ah so good, so sweet to cry, so that soon
I was laughing with pleasure, laughing and crying, the tears spilling
down my face and washing my hands. I could have gone on for hours.

Footsteps in the living room made me stop. The steps were Mona's. I
stood up and wiped my eyes, but I knew they were red. Stuffing the torn
skirt under my shirt I walked out of the closet. I coughed a little, clearing
my throat, to show I was at ease with everything.

Mona didn't know anyone was in the apartment. The lights were out
and everything, and she thought the place was deserted. She looked at me
in surprise, as if she had never seen me before. I walked a few feet, this
way and that, coughing and humming a tune, but still she watched, saying nothing but keeping her eyes glued to me.

'Well," I said. "You critic of life—say something."

Her eyes were on my hand.

"Your finger. It's all . . ."

"It's my finger," I said. "You God-intoxicated nun."

I locked the bathroom door behind me and threw the tattered dress
down the air shaft. Then I bandaged my finger. I stood at the mirror and
looked at myself. I loved my own face. I thought I was a very handsome
person. I had a good straight nose and a wonderful mouth, with lips red-
der than a woman's, for all her paint and whatnot. My eyes were big and
clear, my jaw protruded slightly, a strong jaw, a jaw denoting character
and self-discipline. Yes, it was a fine face. A man of judgment would have
found much in it to interest him.

In the medicine cabinet I came upon my mother's wedding ring,
where she usually left it after washing her hands. I held the ring in the
palm of my hand and looked at it in amazement. To think that this ring,
this piece of mere metal, had sealed the connubial bond which was to pro-
duce me! That was an incredible thing. Little did my father know, when
he bought this ring, that it would symbolize the union of man and
woman out of which would arrive one of the world's greatest men. How
strange it was to be standing in that bathroom and realizing all these
things! Little did this piece of stupid metal know its own significance.
And yet someday it would become a collector's item of incalculable value.
I could see the museum, with people milling about the Bandini heir-

looms, the shouting of the auctioneer, and finally a Morgan or a Rocke-feller of tomorrow raising his price to twelve million dollars for that ring, simply because it was worn by the mother of Arturo Bandini, the greatest writer the world had ever known.

—*The Road to Los Angeles*

ONE NIGHT I WAS SITTING ON THE BED in my hotel room on Bunker Hill, down in the very middle of Los Angeles. It was an important night in my life, because I had to make a decision about the hotel. Either I paid up or I got out: that was what the note said, the note the landlady had put under my door. A great problem, deserving acute attention. I solved it by turning out the lights and going to bed.

In the morning I awoke, decided that I should do more physical exercise, and began at once. I did several bending exercises. Then I washed my teeth, tasted blood, saw pink on the toothbrush, remembered the advertisements, and decided to go out and get some coffee.

I went to the restaurant where I always went to the restaurant and I sat down on the stool before the long counter and ordered coffee. It tasted pretty much like coffee, but it wasn't worth the nickel. Sitting there I smoked a couple of cigarets, read the box scores of the American League games, scrupulously avoided the box scores of National League games, and noted with satisfaction that Joe DiMaggio was still a credit to the Italian people, because he was leading the league in batting.

A great hitter, that DiMaggio. I walked out of the restaurant, stood before an imaginary pitcher, and swatted a home run over the fence. Then I walked down the street toward Angel's Flight, wondering what I would do that day. But there was nothing to do, and so I decided to walk around the town.

I walked down Olive Street past a dirty yellow apartment house that was still wet like a blotter from last night's fog, and I thought of my friends Ethie and Carl, who were from Detroit and had lived there, and I remembered the night Carl hit Ethie because she was going to have a baby, and he didn't want a baby. But they had the baby and that's all there was to that. And I remembered the inside of that apartment, how it smelled of mice and dust, and the old women who sat in the lobby on hot afternoons, and the old woman with the pretty legs. Then there was the elevator man, a broken man from Milwaukee, who seemed to sneer every time you called your floor, as though you were such a fool for choosing that particular floor, the elevator man who always had a tray of sandwiches in the elevator, and a pulp magazine.

Then I went down the hill on Olive Street, past the horrible frame houses reeking with murder stories, and on down Olive to the Philharmonic Auditorium, and I remembered how I'd gone there with Helen to listen to the Don Cossack Choral Group, and how I got bored and we had a fight because of it, and I remembered what Helen wore that day—a white dress, and how it made me sing at the loins when I touched it. Oh that Helen—but not here.

And so I was down on Fifth and Olive, where the big street cars chewed your ears with their noise, and the smell of gasoline made the sight of the palm trees seem sad, and the black pavement still wet from the fog of the night before.

So now I was in front of the Biltmore Hotel, walking along the line of yellow cabs, with all the cab drivers asleep except the driver near the main door, and I wondered about these fellows and their fund of information, and I remembered the time Ross and I got an address from one of them, how he leered salaciously and then took us to Temple Street, of all places, and whom did we see but two very unattractive ones, and Ross went all the way, but I sat in the parlor and played the phonograph and was scared and lonely.

I was passing the doorman of the Biltmore, and I hated him at once, with his yellow braids and six feet of height and all that dignity, and now a black automobile drove to the curb, and a man got out. He looked rich; and then a woman got out, and she was beautiful, her fur was silver fox, and she was a song across the sidewalk and inside the swinging doors, and I thought oh boy for a little of that, just a day and a night of that, and she was a dream as I walked along, her perfume still in the wet morning air.

Then a great deal of time passed as I stood in front of a pipe shop and looked, and the whole world faded except that window and I stood and smoked them all, and saw myself a great author with that natty Italian briar, and a cane, stepping out of a big black car, and she was there too, proud as hell of me, the lady in the silver fox fur. We registered and then we had cocktails and then we danced awhile, and then we had another cocktail and I recited some lines from Sanskrit, and the world was so wonderful, because every two minutes some gorgeous one gazed at me, the great author, and nothing would do but I had to autograph her menu, and the silver fox girl was very jealous.

Los Angeles, give me some of you! Los Angeles come to me the way I came to you, my feet over your streets, you pretty town I loved you so much, you sad flower in the sand, you pretty town.

A day and another day and the day before, and the library with the big boys in the shelves, old Dreiser, old Mencken, all the boys down there, and I went to see them, Hya Dreiser, Hya Mencken, Hya, hya: there's a place for me, too, and it begins with B, in the B shelf, Arturo Bandini, make way for Arturo Bandini, his slot for his book, and I sat at the table and just looked at the place where my book would be, right there close to Arnold Bennett; not much that Arnold Bennett, but I'd be there to sort of bolster up the B's, old Arturo Bandini, one of the boys, until some girl came along, some scent of perfume through the fiction room, some click of high heels to break up the monotony of my fame. Gala day, gala dream!

But the landlady, the white-haired landlady kept writing those notes: she was from Bridgeport, Connecticut, her husband had died and she was all alone in the world and she didn't trust anybody, she couldn't afford to, she told me so, and she told me I'd have to pay. It was mounting like the national debt, I'd have to pay or leave, every cent of it—five weeks over-due, twenty dollars, and if I didn't she'd hold my trunks; only I didn't have any trunks, I only had a suitcase and it was cardboard without even a strap, because the strap was around my belly holding up my pants, and that wasn't much of a job, because there wasn't much left of my pants.

"I just got a letter from my agent," I told her. "My agent in New York. He says I sold another one; he doesn't say where, but he says he's got one sold. So don't worry Mrs. Hargraves, don't you fret, I'll have it in a day or so."

But she couldn't believe a liar like me. It wasn't really a lie; it was a wish, not a lie, and maybe it wasn't even a wish, maybe it was a fact, and the only way to find out was watch the mailman, watch him closely, check his mail as he laid it on the desk in the lobby, ask him point blank if he had anything for Bandini. But I didn't have to ask after six months at that hotel. He saw me coming and he always nodded yes or no before I asked: no, three million times; yes, once. One day a beautiful letter came. Oh, I got a lot of letters, but this was the only beautiful letter, and it came in the morning, and it said (he was talking about *The Little Dog Laughed*) he had read *The Little Dog Laughed* and liked it; he said, Mr. Bandini, if ever

I saw a genius, you are it. His name was Leonardo, a great Italian critic, only he was not known as a critic, he was just a man in West Virginia, but he was great and he was a critic, and he died. He was dead when my air-mail letter got to West Virginia, and his sister sent my letter back. She wrote a beautiful letter too, she was a pretty good critic too, telling me Leonardo had died of consumption but he was happy to the end, and one of the last things he did was sit up in bed and write me about *The Little Dog Laughed*: a dream out of life, but very important; Leonardo, dead now, a saint in heaven, equal to any apostle of the twelve.

Everybody in the hotel read *The Little Dog Laughed*, everybody: a story to make you die holding the page, and it wasn't about a dog, either: a clever story, screaming poetry. And the great editor, none but J.C. Hack-muth with his name signed like Chinese said in a letter: a great story and I'm proud to print it. Mrs. Hargraves read it and I was a different man in her eyes thereafter. I got to stay on in that hotel, not shoved out in the cold, only often it was in the heat, on account of *The Little Dog Laughed*. Mrs. Grainger in 345, a Christian Scientist (wonderful hips, but kinda old) from Battle Creek, Michigan, sitting in the lobby waiting to die, and *The Little Dog Laughed* brought her back to the earth, and that look in her eyes made me know it was right and I was right, but I was hoping she would ask about my finances, how I was getting along, and then I thought why not ask her to lend you a five spot, but I didn't and I walked away snapping my fingers in disgust.

The hotel was called the Alta Loma. It was built on a hillside in reverse, there on the crest of Bunker Hill, built against the decline of the hill, so that the main floor was on the level with the street but the tenth floor was downstairs ten levels. If you had room 862, you got in the elevator and went down eight floors, and if you wanted to go down in the truck room, you didn't go down but up to the attic, one floor above the main floor.

Oh for a Mexican girl! I used to think of her all the time, my Mexican girl. I didn't have one, but the streets were full of them, the Plaza and Chinatown were afire with them, and in my fashion they were mine, this one and that one, and some day when another check came it would be a fact. Meanwhile it was free and they were Aztec princesses and Mayan princesses, the peon girls in the Grand Central Market, in the Church of Our Lady, and I even went to Mass to look at them. That was sacrilegious conduct but it was better than not going to Mass at all, so that when I wrote home to Colorado to my mother I could write with truth. Dear Mother: I went to Mass last Sunday. Down in the Grand Central Market I bumped into the princesses accidentally on purpose. It gave me a chance to speak to them, and I smiled and said excuse me. Those beautiful girls, so happy when you acted like a gentleman and all of that, just to touch them and carry the memory of it back to my room, where dust gathered upon my typewriter and Pedro the mouse sat in his hole, his black eyes watching me through that time of dream and reverie.

Pedro the mouse, a good mouse but never domesticated, refusing to be petted or house-broken. I saw him the first time I walked into my room, and that was during my hey-day, when *The Little Dog Laughed* was in the current August issue. It was five months ago, the day I got to town by bus from Colorado with a hundred and fifty dollars in my pocket and big plans in my head. I had a philosophy in those days. I was a lover of man and beast alike, and Pedro was no exception; but cheese got expensive, Pedro called all his friends, the room swarmed with them, and I had to quit it and feed them bread. They didn't like bread. I had spoiled them and they went elsewhere, all but Pedro the ascetic who was content to eat the pages of an old Gideon Bible.

Ah, that first day! Mrs. Hargraves opened the door to my room, and there it was, with a red carpet on the floor, pictures of the English country-side on the walls, and a shower adjoining. The room was down on the sixth floor, room 678, up near the front of the hill, so that my window was on a level with the green hillside and there was no need for a key, for the window was always open. Through that window I saw my first palm tree, not six feet away, and sure enough I thought of Palm Sunday and Egypt and Cleopatra, but the palm was blackish at its branches, stained by carbon monoxide coming out of the Third Street Tunnel, its crusted trunk choked with dust and sand that blew in from the Mojave and Santa Ana deserts.

Dear Mother, I used to write home to Colorado, Dear Mother, things are definitely looking up. A big editor was in town and I had lunch with him and we have signed a contract for a number of short stories, but I won't try to bore you with all the details, dear mother, because I know you're not interested in writing, and I know Papa isn't, but it levels down to a swell contract, only it doesn't begin for a couple of months. So send me ten dollars, mother, send me five, mother dear, because the editor (I'd tell you his name only I know you're not interested in such things) is all set to start me out on the biggest project he's got.

Dear Mother, and Dear Hackmuth, the great editor—they got most of my mail, practically all of my mail. Old Hackmuth with his scowl and his hair parted in the middle, great Hackmuth with a pen like a sword, his picture was on my wall autographed with his signature that looked Chinese. Hya Hackmuth, I used to say, Jesus how you can write! Then the lean days came, and Hackmuth got big letters from me. My God, Mr. Hackmuth, something's wrong with me: the old zip is gone and I can't write anymore. Do you think, Mr. Hackmuth, that the climate here has anything to do with it? Please advise. Do you think, Mr. Hackmuth, that I write as well as William Faulkner? Please advise. Do you think, Mr. Hackmuth, that sex has anything to do with it, because, Mr. Hackmuth, because, because, and I told Hackmuth everything. I told him about the blonde girl I met in the park. I told him how I worked it, how the blonde girl tumbled. I told him the whole story, only it wasn't true, it was a crazy lie—but it was something. It was writing, keeping in touch with the great, and he always answered. Oh boy, he was swell! He answered right off, a great man responding to the problems of a man of talent. Nobody got that many letters from Hackmuth, nobody but me, and I used to take them out and read them over, and kiss them. I'd stand before Hackmuth's picture crying out of both eyes, telling him he picked a good one this time, a great one, a Bandini, Arturo Bandini, me.

The lean days of determination. That was the word for it, determination: Arturo Bandini in front of his typewriter two full days in succession, determined to succeed; but it didn't work, the longest siege of hard and fast determination in his life, and not one line done, only two words written over and over across the page, up and down, the same words: palm tree, palm tree, palm tree, a battle to the death between the palm tree and me, and the palm tree won: see it out there swaying in the blue air, creaking sweetly in the blue air. The palm tree won after two fighting days, and I crawled out of the window and sat at the foot of the tree. Time passed, a moment or two, and I slept, little brown ants carousing in the hair on my legs.

—*Ask the Dust*

I WAS TWENTY THEN. What the hell, I used to say, take your time, Bandini. You got ten years to write a book, so take it easy, get out and learn about life, walk the streets. That's your trouble: your ignorance of life. Why, my God, man, do you realize you've never had any experience with a woman? Oh yes I have, oh I've had plenty. Oh no you haven't. You need a woman, you need a bath, you need a good swift kick, you need money. They say it's a dollar, they say it's two dollars in the swell places, but down on the Plaza it's a dollar; swell, only you haven't got a dollar, and another thing, you coward, even if you had a dollar you wouldn't go, because you had a chance to go once in Denver and you didn't. No, you coward, you were afraid, and you're still afraid, and you're glad you haven't got a dollar.

Afraid of a woman! Ha, great writer this! How can he write about women, when he's never had a woman? Oh you lousy fake, you phony, no wonder you can't write! No wonder there wasn't a woman in *The Little Dog Laughed*. No wonder it wasn't a love story, you fool, you dirty little schoolboy.

To write a love story, to learn about life.

Money arrived in the mail. Not a check from the mighty Hackmuth, not an acceptance from *The Atlantic Monthly* or *The Saturday Evening Post*. Only ten dollars, only a fortune. My mother sent it: some dime insurance policies, Arturo, I had them taken up for their cash value, and this is your share. But it was ten dollars; one manuscript or another, at least something had been sold.

Put it in your pocket, Arturo. Wash your face, comb your hair, put some stuff on to make you smell good while you stare into the mirror looking for grey hairs; because you're worried, Arturo, you're worried, and that brings grey hair. But there was none, not a strand. Yeah, but what of that left eye? It looked discolored. Careful, Arturo Bandini: don't strain your eyesight, remember what happened to Tarkington, remember what happened to James Joyce.

Not bad, standing in the middle of the room, talking to Hackmuth's picture, not bad, Hackmuth, you'll get a story out of this. How do I look, Hackmuth? Do you sometimes wonder, Herr Hackmuth, what I look like? Do you sometimes say to yourself, I wonder if he's handsome, that Bandini fellow, author of that brilliant *Little Dog Laughed*?

Once in Denver there was another night like this, only I was not an author in Denver, but I stood in a room like this and made these plans, and it was disastrous because all the time in that place I thought about the Blessed Virgin and *thou shalt not commit adultery* and the hard-working girl shook her head sadly and had to give it up, but that was a long time ago and tonight it will be changed.

I climbed out the window and scaled the incline to the top of Bunker Hill. A night for my nose, a feast for my nose, smelling the stars, smelling the flowers, smelling the desert, and the dust asleep, across the top of Bunker Hill. The city spread out like a Christmas tree, red and green and blue. Hello, old houses, beautiful hamburgers singing in cheap cafes, Bing Crosby singing too. She'll treat me gently. Not those girls of my childhood, those girls of my boyhood, those girls of my university days. They frightened me, they were diffident, they refused me; but not my princess, because she will understand. She, too, has been scorned.

Bandini, walking along, not tall but solid, proud of his muscles, squeezing his fist to revel in the hard delight of his biceps, absurdly fearless Bandini, fearing nothing but the unknown in a world of mysterious wonder. Are the dead restored? The books say no, the night shouts yes. I am twenty, I have reached the age of reason, I am about to wander the streets below, seeking a woman. Is my soul already smirched, should I turn back, does an angel watch over me, do the prayers of my mother allay my fears, do the prayers of my mother annoy me?

Ten dollars: it will pay the rent for two and a half weeks, it will buy me three pairs of shoes, two pair of pants, or one thousand postage stamps to send material to the editors; indeed! But you haven't any material, your talent is dubious, your talent is pitiful, you haven't any talent, and stop lying to yourself day after day because you know *The Little Dog Laughed* is no good, and it will always be no good.

So you walk along Bunker Hill, and you shake your fist at the sky, and I know what you're thinking, Bandini. The thoughts of your father before you, lash across your back, hot fire in your skull, that you are not to blame: this is your thought, that you were born poor, son of miseried peasants, driven because you were poor, fled from your Colorado town because you were poor, rambling the gutters of Los Angeles because you are poor, hoping to write a book to get rich, because those who hated you back there in Colorado will not hate you if you write a book. You are a coward, Bandini, a traitor to your soul, a feeble liar before your weeping Christ. This is why you write, this is why it would be better if you died.

Yes, it's true: but I have seen houses in Bel-Air with cool lawns and green swimming pools. I have wanted women whose very shoes are worth all I have ever possessed. I have seen golf clubs on Sixth Street in the Spalding window that make me hungry just to grip them. I have grieved for a necktie like a holy man for indulgences. I have admired hats in Robinson's the way critics gasp at Michelangelo.

I took the steps down Angel's Flight to Hill Street: a hundred and forty steps, with tight fists, frightened of no man, but scared of the Third Street Tunnel, scared to walk through it—claustrophobia. Scared of high places too, and of blood, and of earthquakes; otherwise, quite fearless, excepting death, except the fear I'll scream in a crowd, except the fear of appendicitis, except the fear of heart trouble, even that, sitting in his room holding the clock and pressing his jugular vein, counting out his heartbeats, listening to the weird purr and whirr of his stomach. Otherwise, quite fearless.

Here is an idea with money: these steps, the city below, the stars within throwing distance: boy meets girl idea, good setup, big money idea. Girl lives in that grey apartment house, boy is a wanderer. Boy—he's me. Girl's hungry. Rich Pasadena girl hates money. Deliberately left Pasadena millions 'cause of ennui, weariness with money. Beautiful girl, gorgeous. Great story, pathological conflict. Girl with money phobia: Freudian setup. Another guy loves her, rich guy. I'm poor. I meet rival. Beat him to death with caustic wit and also lick him with fists. Girl impressed, falls for me. Offers me millions. I marry her on condition she'll stay poor. Agrees. But ending happy: girl tricks me with huge trust fund day we get married. I'm indignant but I forgive her 'cause I love her. Good idea, but something missing: *Collier's* story.

Dearest Mother, thanks for the ten dollar bill. My agent announces the sale of another story, this time to a great magazine in London, but it seems they do not pay until publication, and so your little sum will come in handy for various odds and ends.

I went to the burlesque show. I had the best seat possible, a dollar and ten cents, right under a chorus of forty frayed bottoms: some day all of these will be mine: I will own a yacht and we will go on South Sea Cruises. On warm afternoons they will dance for me on the sun deck. But mine will be beautiful women, selections from the cream of society, rivals for the joys of my stateroom. Well, this is good for me, this is experience, I am here for a reason, these moments run into pages, the seamy side of life.

Then Lola Linton came on, slithering like a satin snake amid the tumult of whistling and pounding feet, Lola Linton lascivious, slithering and looting my body, and when she was through, my teeth ached from my clamped jaws and I hated the dirty lowbrow swine around me, shouting their share of a sick joy that belonged to me.

If Mamma sold the policies things must be tough for the Old Man and I shouldn't be here. When I was a kid pictures of Lola Lintons used to come my way, and I used to get so impatient with the slow crawl of time and boyhood, longing for this very moment, and here I am, and I have not changed nor have the Lola Lintons, but I fashioned myself rich and I am poor.

Main Street after the show, midnight: neon tubes and a light fog, honky-tonks and all night picture houses. Secondhand stores and Filipino dance halls, cocktails 15¢, continuous entertainment, but I had seen them all, so many times, spent so much Colorado money in them. It left me lonely like a thirsty man holding a cup, and I walked toward the Mexican Quarter with a feeling of sickness without pain. Here was the Church of Our Lady, very old, the adobe blackened with age. For sentimental reasons I will go inside. For sentimental reasons only. I have not read Lenin, but I have heard him quoted, religion is the opium of the people. Talking to myself on the church steps: yeah, the opium of the people. Myself, I am an atheist: I have read *The Anti-Christ* and I regard it as a capital piece of work. I believe in the transvaluation of values, Sir. The Church must go, it is the haven of the booboisie, of boobs and bounders and all brummagem mountebanks.

I pulled the huge door open and it gave a little cry like weeping. Above the altar sputtered the blood-red eternal light, illuminating in crimson shadow the quiet of almost two thousand years. It was like death, but I could remember screaming infants at baptism too. I knelt. This was habit, this kneeling. I sat down. Better to kneel, for the sharp bite at the knees was a distraction from the awful quiet. A prayer. Sure, one prayer: for sentimental reasons. Almighty God, I am sorry I am now an atheist, but have You read Nietzsche? Ah, such a book! Almighty God, I will play fair in this. I will make You a proposition. Make a great writer out of me, and I will return to the Church. And please, dear God, one more favor: make my mother happy. I don't care about the Old Man; he's got his wine and his health, but my mother worries so. Amen.

I closed the weeping door and stood on the steps, the fog like a huge white animal everywhere, the Plaza like our courthouse back home, snowbound in white silence. But all sounds traveled swift and sure through the heaviness, and the sound I heard was the click of high heels. A girl appeared. She wore an old green coat, her face molded in a green scarf tied under the chin. On the stairs stood Bandini.

"Hello, honey," she said, smiling, as though Bandini were her husband, or her lover. Then she came to the first step and looked up at him. "How about it, honey? Want me to show you a good time?"

Bold lover, bold and brazen Bandini.

"Nah," he said. "No thanks. Not tonight."

He hurried away, leaving her looking after him, speaking words he lost in flight. He walked half a block. He was pleased. At least she had asked him. At least she had identified him as a man. He whistled a tune from sheer pleasure. Man about town has universal experience. Noted writer tells of night with woman of the streets. Arturo Bandini, famous writer, reveals experience with Los Angeles prostitute. Critics acclaim book finest written.

Bandini (being interviewed prior to departure for Sweden): "My advice to all young writers is quite simple. I would caution them never to evade a new experience. I would urge them to live life in the raw, to grapple with it bravely, to attack it with naked fists."

Reporter: "Mr. Bandini, how did you come to write this book which won you the Nobel Award?"

Bandini: "The book is based on a true experience which happened to me one night in Los Angeles. Every word of that book is true. I lived that book, I experienced it."

Enough. I saw it all. I turned and walked back toward the church. The fog was impenetrable. The girl was gone. I walked on: perhaps I could catch up with her. At the corner I saw her again. She stood talking to a tall Mexican. They walked, crossed the street and entered the Plaza. I followed. My God, a Mexican! Women like that should draw the color line. I hated him, the Spick, the Greaser. They walked under the banana trees in the Plaza, their feet echoing in the fog. I heard the Mexican laugh.

Then the girl laughed. They crossed the street and walked down an alley that was the entrance to Chinatown. The oriental neon signs made the fog pinkish. At a rooming house next door to a chop suey restaurant they turned and climbed the stairs. Across the street upstairs a dance was in progress. Along the little street on both sides yellow cabs were parked. I leaned against the front fender of the cab in front of the rooming house and waited. I lit a cigaret and waited. Until hell freezes over, I will wait. Until God strikes me dead, I will wait.

A half hour passed. There were sounds on the steps. The door opened. The Mexican appeared. He stood in the fog, lit a cigaret, and yawned. Then he smiled absently, shrugged, and walked away, the fog swooping upon him. Go ahead and smile. You stinking Greaser—what have you got to smile about? You come from a bashed and a busted race, and just because you went to the room with one of our white girls, you smile. Do you think you would have had a chance, had I accepted on the church steps?

A moment later the steps sounded to the click of her heels, and the girl stepped into the fog. The same girl, the same green coat, the same scarf. She saw me and smiled. "Hello, honey. Wanna have a good time?"

Easy now, Bandini.

"Oh," I said. "Maybe. And maybe not. Whatcha got?"

"Come up and see, honey."

Stop sniggering, Arturo. Be suave.

"I might come up," I said. "And then, I might not."

"Aw honey, come on." The thin bones of her face, the odor of sour wine from her mouth, the awful hypocrisy of her sweetness, the hunger for money in her eyes.

Bandini speaking: "What's the price these days?"

She took my arm, pulled me toward the door, but gently.

"You come on up, honey. We'll talk about it up there."

"I'm really not very hot," said Bandini. "I—I just came from a wild party."

Hail Mary full of grace, walking up the stairs, I can't go through with it. I've got to get out of it. The halls smelling of cockroaches, a yellow light at the ceiling, you're too aesthetic for all this, the girl holding my arm, there's something wrong with you, Arturo Bandini, you're a misanthrope, your whole life is doomed to celibacy, you should have been a priest, Father O'Leary talking that afternoon, telling us the joys of denial, and my own mother's money too, Oh Mary conceived without sin, pray for us who have recourse to thee—until we got to the top of the stairs and walked down a dusty dark hall to a room at the end, where she turned out the light and we were inside.

A room smaller than mine, carpetless, without pictures, a bed, a table, a wash-stand. She took off her coat. There was a blue print dress underneath. She was bare-legged. She took off the scarf. She was not a real blonde. Black hair grew at the roots. Her nose was crooked slightly. Bandini on the bed, put himself there with an air of casualness, like a man who knew how to sit on a bed.

Bandini: "Nice place you got here."

My God I got to get out of here, this is terrible.

The girl sat beside me, put her arms around me, pushed her breasts against me, kissed me, flecked my teeth with a cold tongue. I jumped to my feet. Oh think fast, my mind, dear mind of mine please get me out of this and it will never happen again. From now on I will return to my Church. Beginning this day my life shall run like sweet water.

The girl lay back, her hands behind her neck, her legs over the bed. I shall smell lilacs in Connecticut, no doubt, before I die, and see the clean white small reticent churches of my youth, the pasture bars I broke to run away.

"Look," I said. "I want to talk to you."

She crossed her legs.

"I'm a writer," I said. "I'm gathering material for a book."

"I knew you were a writer," she said. "Or a business man, or something. You look spiritual, honey."

"I'm a writer, see. I like you and all that. You're okay, I like you. But I want to talk to you, first."

She sat up.

"Haven't you any money, honey?"

Money—ho. And I pulled it out, a small thick roll of dollar bills. Sure I got money, plenty of money, this is a drop in the bucket, money is no object, money means nothing to me.

"What do you charge?"

"It's two dollars, honey."

Then give her three, peel it off easily, like it was nothing at all, smile and hand it to her because money is no object, there's more where this came from, at this moment Mamma sits by the window holding her rosary, waiting for the Old Man to come home, but there's money, there's always money.

She took the money and slipped it under the pillow. She was grateful and her smile was different now. The writer wanted to talk. How were conditions these days? How did she like this kind of life? Oh, come on honey, let's not talk, let's get down to business. No, I want to talk to you, this is important, new book, material. I do this often. How did you ever get into this racket. Oh honey, Chrissakes, you going to ask me that too? But money is no object, I tell you. But my time is valuable, honey. Then here's a couple more bucks. That makes five, my God, five bucks and I'm not out of here yet, how I hate you, you filthy. But you're cleaner than me because you've got no mind to sell, just that poor flesh.

She was overwhelmed, she would do anything. I could have it any way I wanted it, and she tried to pull me to her, but no, let's wait awhile. I tell you I want to talk to you, I tell you money is no object, here's three more, that makes eight dollars, but it doesn't matter. You just keep that eight bucks and buy yourself something nice. And then I snapped my fingers like a man remembering something, something important, an engagement.

"Say!" I said. "That reminds me. What time is it?"

Her chin was at my neck, stroking it. "Don't you worry about the time, honey. You can stay all night."

A man of importance, ah yes, now I remembered, my publisher, he was getting in tonight by plane. Out at Burbank, away out in Burbank. Have to grab a cab and taxi out there, have to hurry. Goodbye, goodbye, you keep that eight bucks, you buy yourself something nice, goodbye, good-bye, running down the stairs, running away, the welcome fog in the door-way below, you keep that eight bucks, oh sweet fog I see you and I'm coming, you clean air, you wonderful world, I'm coming to you, goodbye, yelling up the stairs, I'll see you again, you keep that eight dollars and buy yourself something nice. Eight dollars pouring out of my eyes, Oh Jesus kill me dead and ship my body home, kill me dead and make me die like a pagan fool with no priest to absolve me, no extreme unction, eight dollars, eight dollars. . . .

———————

The lean days, blue skies with never a cloud, a sea of blue day after day, the sun floating through it. The days of plenty—plenty of worries, plenty of oranges. Eat them in bed, eat them for lunch, push them down for din-ner. Oranges, five cents a dozen. Sunshine in the sky, sun juice in my stomach. Down at the Japanese market he saw me coming, that bullet-faced smiling Japanese, and he reached for a paper sack. A generous man, he gave me fifteen, sometimes twenty for a nickel.

"You like banana?" Sure, so he gave me a couple of bananas. A pleasant innovation, orange juice and bananas. "You like apple?" Sure, so he gave me some apples. Here was something new: oranges and apples. "You like peaches?" Indeed, and I carried the brown sack back to my room. An interesting innovation, peaches and oranges. My teeth tore them to pulp, the juices skewering and whimpering at the bottom of my stomach. It was so sad down there in my stomach. There was much weeping, and little gloomy clouds of gas pinched my heart.

My plight drove me to the typewriter. I sat before it, overwhelmed with grief for Arturo Bandini. Sometimes an idea floated harmlessly through the room. It was like a small white bird. It meant no ill-will. It only wanted to help me, dear little bird. But I would strike at it, hammer it out across the keyboard, and it would die on my hands.

What could be the matter with me? When I was a boy I had prayed to St. Teresa for a new fountain pen. My prayer was answered. Anyway, I did get a new fountain pen. Now I prayed to St. Teresa again. Please, sweet and lovely saint, gimme an idea. But she has deserted me, all the gods have deserted me, and like Huysmans I stand alone, my fists clenched, tears in my eyes. If someone only loved me, even a bug, even a mouse, but that too belonged to the past; even Pedro had forsaken me now that the best I could offer him was orange peel.

I thought of home, of spaghetti swimming in rich tomato sauce, smothered in Parmesan cheese, of Mamma's lemon pies, of lamb roasts and hot bread, and I was so miserable that I deliberately sank my fingernails into the flesh of my arm until a spot of blood appeared. It gave me great satisfaction. I was God's most miserable creature, forced even to torturing myself. Surely upon this earth no grief was greater than mine.

—Ask the Dust

DOWN ON SPRING STREET, in a bar across the street from the secondhand store. With my last nickel I went there for a cup of coffee. An old style place, sawdust on the floor, crudely drawn nudes smeared across the walls. It was a saloon where old men gathered, where the beer was cheap and smelled sour, where the past remained unaltered.

I sat at one of the tables against the wall. I remember that I sat with my head in my hands. I heard her voice without looking up. I remember that she said, "Can I get you something?" and I said something about coffee with cream. I sat there until the cup was before me, a long time I sat like that, thinking of the hopelessness of my fate.

It was very bad coffee. When the cream mixed with it I realized it was not cream at all, for it turned a greyish color, and the taste was that of boiled rags. This was my last nickel, and it made me angry. I looked around for the girl who had waited on me. She was five or six tables away, serving beers from a tray. Her back was to me, and I saw the tight smoothness of her shoulders under a white smock, the faint trace of muscle in her arms, and the black hair so thick and glossy, falling to her shoulders.

At last she turned around and I waved to her. She was only faintly attentive, widening her eyes in an expression of bored aloofness. Except for the contour of her face and the brilliance of her teeth, she was not beautiful. But at that moment she turned to smile at one of her old customers, and I saw a streak of white under her lips. Her nose was Mayan, flat, with large nostrils. Her lips were heavily rouged, with the thickness of a negress' lips. She was a racial type, and as such she was beautiful, but she was too strange for me. Her eyes were at a high slant, her skin was dark but not black, and as she walked her breasts moved in a way that showed their firmness.

She ignored me after that first glance. She went on to the bar, where she ordered more beer and waited for the thin bartender to draw it. As she waited she whistled, looked at me vaguely and went on whistling. I had stopped waving, but I made it plain I wanted her to come to my table. Suddenly she opened her mouth to the ceiling and laughed in a most mysterious fashion, so that even the bartender wondered at her laughter. Then she danced away, swinging the tray gracefully, picking her way through the tables to a group far down in the rear of the saloon. The bartender followed her with his eyes, still confused at her laughter. But I understood her laughter. It was for me. She was laughing at me. There was something about my appearance, my face, my posture, something about me sitting there that had amused her, and as I thought of it I clenched my fists and considered myself with angry humiliation. I touched my hair: it was combed. I fumbled with my collar and tie: they were clean and in place. I stretched myself to the range of the bar mirror, where I saw what was certainly a worried and sallow face, but not a funny face, and I was very angry.

I began to sneer, watched her closely and sneered. She did not approach my table. She moved near it, even to the table adjacent, but she did not venture beyond that. Each time I saw the dark face, the black large eyes flashing their laughter, I set my lips to a curl that meant I was sneering. It became a game. The coffee cooled, grew cold, a scum of milk gathered over the surface, but I did not touch it. The girl moved like a dancer, her strong silk legs gathering bits of sawdust as her tattered shoes glided over the marble floor.

Those shoes, they were huaraches, the leather thongs wrapped several times around her ankles. They were desperately ragged huaraches; the woven leather had become unraveled. When I saw them I was very grateful, for it was a defect about her that deserved criticism. She was tall and straight-shouldered, a girl of perhaps twenty, faultless in her way, except for her tattered huaraches. And so I fastened my stare on them, watched them intently and deliberately, even turning in my chair and twisting my neck to glare at them, sneering and chuckling to myself. Plainly I was getting as much enjoyment out of this as she got from my face, or whatever it was that amused her. This had a powerful effect upon her. Gradually her pirouetting and dancing subsided and she merely hurried back and forth, and at length she was making her way stealthily. She was embarrassed, and once I saw her glance down quickly and examine her feet, so that in a few minutes she no longer laughed; instead, there was a grimness in her face, and finally she was glancing at me with bitter hatred.

Now I was exultant, strangely happy. I felt relaxed. The world was full of uproariously amusing people. Now the thin bartender looked in my direction and I winked a comradely greeting. He tossed his head in an acknowledging nod. I sighed and sat back, at ease with life.

She had not collected the nickel for the coffee. She would have to do so, unless I left it on the table and walked out. But I wasn't going to walk out. I waited. A half hour passed. When she hurried to the bar for more beer, she no longer waited at the rail in plain sight. She walked around to the back of the bar. She didn't look at me anymore, but I knew she knew I watched her.

Finally she walked straight for my table. She walked proudly, her chin tilted, her hands hanging at her sides. I wanted to stare, but I couldn't keep it up. I looked away, smiling all the while.

"Do you want anything else?" she asked.

Her white smock smelled of starch.

"You call this stuff coffee?" I said.

Suddenly she laughed again. It was a shriek, a mad laugh like the clatter of dishes and it was over as quickly as it began. I looked at her feet again. I could feel something inside her retreating. I wanted to hurt her.

"Maybe this isn't coffee at all," I said. "Maybe it's just water after they boiled your filthy shoes in it." I looked up to her black blazing eyes. "Maybe you don't know any better. Maybe you're just naturally careless. But if I were a girl I wouldn't be seen in a Main Street alley with those shoes."

I was panting when I finished. Her thick lips trembled and the fists in her pocket were writhing under the starched stiffness.

"I hate you," she said.

I felt her hatred. I could smell it, even hear it coming out of her, but I sneered again. "I hope so," I said. "Because there must be something pretty fine about a guy who rates your hatred."

Then she said a strange thing; I remember it clearly. "I hope you die of heart failure," she said. "Right there in that chair."

It gave her keen satisfaction, even though I laughed. She walked away smiling. She stood at the bar again, waiting for more beer, and her eyes were fastened on me, brilliant with her strange wish, and I was uncomfortable but still laughing. Now she was dancing again, gliding from table to table with her tray, and every time I looked at her she smiled her wish, until it had a mysterious effect on me, and I became conscious of my inner organism, of the beat of my heart and the flutter of my stomach. I felt that she would not come back to my table again, and I remember that I was glad of it, and that a strange restlessness came over me, so that I was anxious to get away from that place, and away from the range of her persistent smile. Before I left I did something that pleased me very much. I took the five cents from my pocket and placed it on the table. Then I spilled half the coffee over it. She would have to mop up the mess with her towel. The brown ugliness spread everywhere over the table, and as I got up to leave it was trickling to the floor. At the door I paused to look at her once more. She smiled the same smile. I nodded at the spilled coffee. Then I tossed my fingers in a salute of farewell and walked into the street. Once more I had a good feeling. Once more it was as before, the world was full of amusing things.

I don't remember what I did after I left her. Maybe I went up to Benny Cohen's room over the Grand Central Market. He had a wooden leg with a little door in it. Inside the door were marijuana cigarets. He sold them for fifteen cents apiece. He also sold newspapers, the *Examiner* and the *Times*. He had a room piled high with copies of *The New Masses*. Maybe he saddened me as always with his grim horrible vision of the world tomorrow. Maybe he poked his stained fingers under my nose and cursed me for betraying the proletariat from which I came. Maybe, as always, he sent me trembling out of his room and down the dusty stairs to the fog-dimmed street, my fingers itching for the throat of an imperialist. Maybe, and maybe not; I don't remember.

But I remember that night in my room, the lights of the St. Paul Hotel throwing red and green blobs across my bed as I lay and shuddered and dreamed of the anger of that girl, of the way she danced from table to table, and the black glance of her eyes. That I remember, even to forgetting I was poor and without an idea for a story.

———

I looked for her early the next morning. Eight o'clock, and I was down on Spring Street. I had a copy of *The Little Dog Laughed* in my pocket. She would think differently about me if she read that story. I had it autographed, right there in my back pocket, ready to present at the slightest notice. But the place was closed at that early hour. It was called the Columbia Buffet. I pushed my nose against the window and looked inside. The chairs were piled upon the tables, and an old man in rubber boots was swabbing the floor. I walked down the street a block or two, the wet air already bluish from monoxide gas. A fine idea came into my head.

I took out the magazine and erased the autograph. In its place I wrote, "To a Mayan Princess, from a worthless Gringo." This seemed right, exactly the correct spirit. I walked back to the Columbia Buffet and pounded the front window. The old man opened the door with wet hands, sweat seeping from his hair.

I said, "What's the name of that girl who works here?"

"You mean Camilla?"

"The one who worked here last night."

"That's her," he said. "Camilla Lopez."

"Will you give this to her?" I said. "Just give it to her. Tell her a fellow came by and said for you to give it to her."

He wiped his dripping hands on his apron and took the magazine. "Take good care of it," I said. "It's valuable."

The old man closed the door. Through the glass I saw him limp back to his mop and bucket. He placed the magazine on the bar and resumed his work. A little breeze flipped the pages of the magazine. As I walked away I was afraid he would forget all about it. When I reached the Civic Center I realized I had made a bad mistake: the inscription on the story would never impress that kind of a girl. I hurried back to the Columbia Buffet and banged the window with my knuckles. I heard the old man grumbling and swearing as he fumbled with the lock. He wiped the sweat from his old eyes and saw me again.

"Could I have that magazine?" I said. "I want to write something in it."

The old man couldn't understand any of this. He shook his head with a sigh and told me to come inside. "Go get it yourself, goddamnit," he said. "I got work to do."

I flattened the magazine on the bar and erased the inscription to the Mayan Princess. In place of it I wrote:

Dear Ragged Shoes,

You may not know it, but last night you insulted the author of this story. Can you read? If so, invest fifteen minutes of your time and treat yourself to a masterpiece. And next time, be careful. Not everyone who comes into this dive is a bum.

Arturo Bandini

I handed the magazine to the old man, but he did not lift his eyes from his work. "Give this to Miss Lopez," I said. "And see to it that she gets it personally."

The old man dropped the mop handle, smeared the sweat from his wrinkled face, and pointed at the front door. "You get out of here!" he said.

I laid the magazine on the bar again and strolled away leisurely. At the door I turned and waved.

I wasn't starving. I still had some old oranges under the bed. That night I ate three or four and with the darkness I walked down Bunker Hill to the downtown district. Across the street from the Columbia Buffet I stood in a shadowed doorway and watched Camilla Lopez. She was the same, dressed in the same white smock. I trembled when I saw her and a strange hot feeling was in my throat. But after a few minutes the strangeness was gone and I stood in the darkness until my feet ached.

When I saw a policeman strolling toward me I walked away. It was a hot night. Sand from the Mojave had blown across the city. Tiny brown grains of sand clung to my fingertips whenever I touched anything, and when I got back to my room I found the mechanism of my new typewriter glutted with sand. It was in my ears and in my hair. When I took off my clothes it fell like powder to the floor. It was even between the sheets of my bed. Lying in the darkness, the red light from the St. Paul Hotel flashing on and off across my bed was bluish now, a ghastly color jumping into the room and out again.

I couldn't eat any oranges the next morning. The thought of them made me wince. By noon, after an aimless walk downtown, I was sick with self-pity, unable to control my grief. When I got back to my room I threw myself on the bed and wept from deep inside my chest. I let it flow from every part of me, and after I could not cry anymore I felt fine again. I felt truthful and clean. I sat down and wrote my mother an honest letter. I told her I had been lying to her for weeks; and please send some money, because I wanted to come home.

As I wrote Hellfrick entered. He was wearing pants and no bathrobe, and at first I didn't recognize him. Without a word he put fifteen cents on the table. "I'm an honest man, kid," he said. "I'm as honest as the day is long." And he walked out.

I brushed the coins into my hand, jumped out the window and ran down the street to the grocery store. The little Japanese had his sack ready at the orange bin. He was amazed to see me pass him by and enter the staples department. I bought two dozen cookies. Sitting on the bed I swallowed them as fast as I could, washing them down with gulps of water. I felt fine again. My stomach was full, and I still had a nickel left. I tore up the letter to my mother and lay down to wait for the night. That nickel meant I could go back to the Columbia Buffet. I waited, heavy with food, heavy with desire.

———————

She saw me as I entered. She was glad to see me; I knew she was, because I could tell by the way her eyes widened. Her face brightened and that tight feeling caught my throat. All at once I was so happy, sure of myself, clean and conscious of my youth. I sat at that same first table. Tonight there was music in the saloon, a piano and a violin; two fat women with hard masculine faces and short haircuts. Their song was *Over the Waves*. Ta de da da, and I watched Camilla dancing with her beer tray. Her hair was so black, so deep and clustered, like grapes hiding her neck. This was a sacred place, this saloon. Everything here was holy, the chairs, the tables, that rag in her hand, that sawdust under her feet. She was a Mayan princess and this was her castle. I watched the tattered huaraches glide across the floor, and I wanted those huaraches. I would like them to hold in my hands against my chest when I fell asleep. I would like to hold them and breathe the odor of them.

She did not venture near my table, but I was glad. Don't come right away, Camilla; let me sit here awhile and accustom myself to this rare excitement; leave me alone while my mind travels the infinite loveliness of your splendid glory; just leave awhile to myself, to hunger and dream with eyes awake.

She came finally, carrying a cup of coffee in her tray. The same coffee, the same chipped, brownish mug. She came with her eyes blacker and wider than ever, walking toward me on soft feet, smiling mysteriously, until I thought I would faint from the pounding of my heart. As she stood beside me, I sensed the slight odor of her perspiration mingled with the tart cleanliness of her starched smock. It overwhelmed me, made me stupid, and I breathed through my lips to avoid it. She smiled to let me know she did not object to the spilled coffee of the other evening; more than that, I seemed to feel she had rather liked the whole thing, she was glad about it, grateful for it.

"I didn't know you had freckles," she said.

"They don't mean anything," I said.

"I'm sorry about the coffee," she said. "Everybody orders beer. We don't get many calls for coffee."

"That's exactly why you don't get many calls for it. Because it's so lousy. I'd drink beer too, if I could afford it."

She pointed at my hand with a pencil. "You bite your fingernails," she said. "You shouldn't do that."

I shoved my hands in my pockets.

"Who are you to tell me what to do?"

"Do you want some beer?" she said. "I'll get you some. You don't have to pay for it."

"You don't have to get me anything. I'll drink this alleged coffee and get out of here."

She walked to the bar and ordered a beer. I watched her pay for it from a handful of coins she dug out of her smock. She carried the beer to me and placed it under my nose. It hurt me.

"Take it away," I said. "Get it out of here. I want coffee, not beer."

Someone in the rear called her name and she hurried away. The backs of her knees appeared as she bent over the table and gathered empty beer mugs. I moved in my chair, my feet kicking something under the table. It was a spittoon. She was at the bar again, nodding at me, smiling, making a motion indicating I should drink the beer. I felt devilish, vicious. I got her attention and poured the beer into the spittoon. Her white teeth took hold of her lower lip and her face lost blood. Her eyes blazed. A pleasantness pervaded me, a satisfaction. I sat back and smiled to the ceiling.

She disappeared behind a thin partition which served as a kitchen. She reappeared, smiling. Her hands were behind her back, concealing something. Now the old man I had seen that morning stepped from behind the partition. He grinned expectantly. Camilla waved to me. The worst was about to happen: I could feel it coming. From behind her back she revealed the little magazine containing *The Little Dog Laughed*. She waved it in the air, but she was out of view, and her performance was only for the old man and myself. He watched with big eyes. My mouth went dry as I saw her wet her fingers and flip the pages to the place where the story was printed. Her lips twisted as she clamped the magazine between her knees and ripped away the pages. She held them over her head, waving them and smiling. The old man shook his head approvingly. The smile on her face changed to determination as she tore the pages into little pieces, and these into smaller pieces. With a gesture of finality, she let the pieces fall through her fingers and trickle to the spittoon at her feet. I tried to smile. She slapped her hands together with an air of boredom, like one slapping the dust from her palms. Then she put one hand on her hip, tilted her shoulder, and swaggered away. The old man stood there for some time. Only he had seen her. Now that the show was over, he disappeared behind the partition.

I sat smiling wretchedly, my heart weeping for *The Little Dog Laughed*, for every well-turned phrase, for the little flecks of poetry through it, my first story, the best thing I could show for my whole life. It was the record of all that was good in me, approved and printed by the great J. C. Hackmuth, and she had torn it up and thrown it into a spittoon.

After a while I pushed back my chair and got up to leave. Standing at the bar, she watched me go. There was pity for me upon her face, a tiny smile of regret for what she had done, but I kept my eyes away from her and walked into the street, glad for the hideous din of street cars and the queer noises of the city pounding my ears and burying me in an avalanche of banging and screeching. I put my hands in my pockets and slumped away.

Fifty feet from the saloon I heard someone calling. I turned around. It was she, running on soft feet, coins jingling in her pockets.

"Young fellow!" she called. "Oh kid!"

I waited and she came out of breath, speaking quickly and softly. "I'm sorry," she said. "I didn't mean anything—honest."

"It's okay," I said. "I didn't mind."

She kept glancing toward the saloon. "I have to get back," she said. "They'll miss me. Come back tomorrow night, will you? Please! I can be nice. I'm awfully sorry about tonight. Please come, please!" She squeezed my arm. "Will you come?"

"Maybe."

She smiled. "Forgive me?"

"Sure."

I stood in the middle of the sidewalk and watched her hurry back. After a few steps she turned, blew a kiss and called, "Tomorrow night. Don't forget!"

"Camilla!" I said. "Wait. Just a minute!"

We ran toward each other, meeting halfway.

"Hurry!" she said. "They'll fire me."

I glanced at her feet. She sensed it coming and I felt her recoiling from me. Now a good feeling rushed through me, a coolness, a newness like new skin. I spoke slowly.

"Those huaraches—do you have to wear them, Camilla? Do you have to emphasize the fact that you always were and always will be a filthy little Greaser?"

She looked at me in horror, her lips open. Clasping both hands against her mouth, she rushed inside the saloon. I heard her moaning. "Oh, oh, oh."

I tossed my shoulders and swaggered away, whistling with pleasure. In the gutter I saw a long cigaret butt. I picked it up without shame, lit it as I stood with one foot in the gutter, puffed it and exhaled toward the stars. I was an American, and goddamn proud of it. This great city, these mighty pavements and proud buildings, they were the voice of my America. From sand and cactus we Americans had carved an empire. Camilla's people had had their chance. They had failed. We Americans had turned the trick. Thank God for my country. Thank God I had been born an American!

—Ask the Dust

THE NAME ON THE MAILBOX was Vera Rivken, and that was her full name. It was down on the Long Beach Pike, across the street from the Ferris Wheel and the Roller Coaster. Downstairs a pool hall, upstairs a few single apartments. No mistaking that flight of stairs; it possessed her odor. The banister was warped and bent, and the grey wallpaint was swollen, with puffed places that cracked open when I pushed them with my thumb.

When I knocked, she opened the door. "So soon?" she said.

Take her in your arms, Bandini. Don't grimace at her kiss, break away gently, with a smile, say something. "You look wonderful," I said. No chance to speak, she was over me again, clinging like a wet vine, her tongue like a frightened snake's head, searching my mouth. Oh great Italian Lover Bandini, reciprocate! Oh Jewish girl, if you would be so kind, if you would approach these matters more slowly! So I was free again, wandering to the window, saying something about the sea and the view beyond. "Nice view," I said. But she was taking off my coat, leading me to a chair in the corner, taking off my shoes. "Be comfortable, she said. Then she was gone, and I sat with my teeth gritted, looking at a room like ten million California rooms, a bit of wood here and a bit of rag there, the furniture, with cobwebs in the ceiling and dust in the corners, her room, and everybody's room, Los Angeles, Long Beach, San Diego, a few boards of plaster and stucco to keep the sun out.

She was in a little white hole called the kitchen, scattering pans and rattling glasses, and I sat and wondered why she could be one thing when I was alone in my room and something else the moment I was with her. I looked for incense, that saccharine smell, it had to come from somewhere, but there was no incense burner in the room, nothing in the room but dirty blue overstuffed furniture, a table with a few books scattered over it, and a mirror over the paneling of a Murphy bed. Then she came out of the kitchen with a glass of milk in her hand. "Here," she offered. "A cool drink."

But it wasn't cool at all, it was almost hot, and there was a yellowish scum on the top, and sipping it I tasted her lips and the strong food she ate, a taste of rye bread and Camembert cheese. "It's good," I said, "delicious."

She was sitting at my feet, her hands on my knees, staring at me with the eyes of hunger, tremendous eyes so large I might have lost myself in them. She was dressed as I saw her the first time, the same clothes, and the place was so desolate I knew she had no others, but I had come before she had had a chance to powder or rouge and now I saw the sculpture of age under her eyes and through her cheeks. I wondered that I had missed these things that night, and then I remembered that I had not missed them at all, I had seen them even through rouge and powder, but in the two days of reverie and dream about her they had concealed themselves, and now I was here, and I knew I should not have come.

We talked, she and I. She asked about my work and it was a pretense, she was not interested in my work. And when I answered it was a pretense. I was not interested in my work either. There was only one thing that interested us, and she knew it, for I had made it plain by my coming.

But where were all the words, and where were all the little lusts I had brought with me? And where were those reveries, and where was my desire, and what had happened to my courage, and why did I sit and laugh so loudly at things not amusing? So come, Bandini—find your heart's desire, take your passion the way it says in the books. Two people in a room; one of them a woman; the other, Arturo Bandini, who is neither fish, fowl, nor good red herring.

Another long silence, the woman's head on my lap, my fingers playing in the dark nest, sorting out strands of grey hair. Awake, Arturo! Camilla Lopez should see you now, she with the big black eyes, your true love, your Mayan princess. Oh Jesus, Arturo, you're marvelous! Maybe you did write *The Little Dog Laughed*, but you'll never write Casanova's Memoirs. What are you doing, sitting here? Dreaming of some great masterpiece? Oh you fool, Bandini!

She looked up at me, saw me there with eyes closed, and she didn't know my thoughts. But maybe she did. Maybe that was why she said, "You're tired. You must take a nap." Maybe that was why she pulled down the Murphy bed and insisted that I lie upon it, she beside me, her head in my arms. Maybe, studying my face, that was why she asked, "You love somebody else?"

I said, "Yes. I'm in love with a girl in Los Angeles."

She touched my face.

"I know," she said. "I understand."

"No you don't."

Then I wanted to tell her why I had come, it was right there at the tip of my tongue, springing to be told, but I knew I would never speak of that now. She lay beside me and we watched the emptiness of the ceiling, and I played with the idea of telling her. I said, "There's something I want to tell you. Maybe you can help me out." But I got no farther than that. No, I could not say it to her; but I lay there hoping she would somehow find out for herself, and when she kept asking me what it was that bothered me I knew she was handling it wrong, and I shook my head and made impatient faces. "Don't talk about it," I said. "It's something I can't tell you."

"Tell me about her," she said.

I couldn't do that, be with one woman and speak of the wonders of another. Maybe that was why she asked, "Is she beautiful?" I answered that she was. Maybe that was why she asked, "Does she love you?" I said she didn't love me. Then my heart pounded in my throat, because she was coming nearer and nearer to what I wanted her to ask, and I waited while she stroked my forehead.

"And why doesn't she love you?"

There it was. I could have answered and it would have been in the clear, but I said, "She just doesn't love me, that's all."

"Is it because she loves somebody else?"

"I don't know. Maybe."

Maybe this and maybe that, questions, questions, wise, wounded woman, groping in the dark, searching for the passion of Arturo Bandini, a game of hot and cold, with Bandini eager to give it away. "What is her name?"

"Camilla," I said.

She sat up, touched my mouth.

"I'm so lonely," she said. "Pretend that I am she."

"Yes," I said. "That's it. That's your name. It's Camilla."

I opened my arms and she sank against my chest.

"My name is Camilla," she said.

"You're beautiful," I said. "You're a Mayan princess."

"I am Princess Camilla."

"All of this land and this sea belongs to you. All of California. There is no California, no Los Angeles, no dusty streets, no cheap hotels, no stinking newspapers, no broken, uprooted people from the East, no fancy boulevards. This is your beautiful land with the desert and the mountains and the sea. You're a princess, and you reign over it all."

"I am Princess Camilla," she sobbed. "There are no Americans, and no California. Only deserts and mountains and the sea, and I reign over it all."

"Then I come."

"Then you come."

"I'm myself. I'm Arturo Bandini. I'm the greatest writer the world ever had."

"Ah yes," she choked. "Of course! Arturo Bandini, the genius of the earth." She buried her face in my shoulder and her warm tears fell on my throat. I held her closer. "Kiss me, Arturo."

But I didn't kiss her. I wasn't through. It had to be my way or nothing. "I'm a conqueror," I said. "I'm like Cortez, only I'm an Italian."

I felt it now. It was real and satisfying, and joy broke through me, the blue sky through the window was a ceiling, and the whole living world was a small thing in the palm of my hand. I shivered with delight.

"Camilla, I love you so much!"

There were no scars, and no desiccated place. She was Camilla, complete and lovely. She belonged to me, and so did the world. And I was glad for her tears, they thrilled me and lifted me, and I possessed her. Then I slept, serenely weary, remembering vaguely through the mist of drowsiness that she was sobbing, but I didn't care. She wasn't Camilla anymore. She was Vera Rivken, and I was in her apartment and I would get up and leave just as soon as I had some sleep.

She was gone when I woke up. The room was eloquent with her departure. A window open, curtains blowing gently. A closet door ajar, a coat-hanger on the knob. The half-empty glass of milk where I had left it on the arm of the chair. Little things accusing Arturo Bandini, but my eyes felt cool after sleep and I was anxious to go and never come back. Down in the street there was music from a merry-go-round. I stood at the window. Below two women passed, and I looked down upon their heads.

Before leaving I stood at the door and took one last look around the room. Mark it well, for this was the place. Here too history was made. I laughed. Arturo Bandini, suave fellow, sophisticated; you should hear him on the subject of women. But the room seemed so poor, pleading for warmth and joy. Vera Rivken's room. She had been nice to Arturo Bandini, and she was poor. I took the small roll from my pocket, peeled off two one dollar bills, and laid them on the table. Then I walked down the stairs, my lungs full of air, elated, my muscles so much stronger than ever before.

But there was a tinge of darkness in the back of my mind. I walked down the street, past the Ferris Wheel and canvassed concessions, and it seemed to come stronger; some disturbance of peace, something vague and nameless seeping into my mind. At a hamburger stand I stopped and ordered coffee. It crept upon me—the restlessness, the loneliness. What was the matter? I felt my pulse. It was good. I blew on the coffee and drank it: good coffee. I searched, felt the fingers of my mind reaching out but not quite touching whatever it was back there that bothered me. Then it came to me like crashing and thunder, like death and destruction. I got up from the counter and walked away in fear, walking fast down the boardwalk, passing people who seemed strange and ghostly: the world seemed a myth, a transparent plane, and all things upon it were here for only a little while; all of us, Bandini, and Hackmuth and Camilla and Vera, all of us were here for a little while, and then we were somewhere else; we were not alive at all; we approached living, but we never achieved it. We are going to die. Everybody was going to die. Even you, Arturo, even you must die.

I knew what it was that swept over me. It was a great white cross pointing into my brain and telling me I was a stupid man, because I was going to die, and there was nothing I could do about it. *Mea culpa, mea culpa, mea maxima culpa.* A mortal sin, Arturo. Thou shalt not commit adultery. There it was, persistent to the end, assuring me that there was no escape from what I had done. I was a Catholic. This was a mortal sin against Vera Rivken.

At the end of the row of concessions the sand beach began. Beyond were dunes. I waded through the sand to a place where the dunes hid the boardwalk. This needed thinking out. I didn't kneel; I sat down and watched the breakers eating the shore. This is bad, Arturo. You have read Nietzsche, you have read Voltaire, you should know better. But reasoning wouldn't help. I could reason myself out of it, but that was not my blood. It was my blood that kept me alive, it was my blood pouring through me, telling me it was wrong. I sat there and gave myself over to my blood, let it carry me swimming back to the deep sea of my beginnings. Vera Rivken, Arturo Bandini. It was not meant that way: it was never meant that way. I was wrong. I had committed a mortal sin. I could figure it mathematically, philosophically, psychologically: I could prove it a dozen ways, but I was wrong, for there was no denying the warm even rhythm of my guilt.

Sick in my soul I tried to face the ordeal of seeking forgiveness. From whom? What God, what Christ? They were myths I once believed, and now they were beliefs I felt were myths. This is the sea, and this is Arturo, and the sea is real, and Arturo believes it real. Then I turn from the sea, and everywhere I look there is land; I walk on and on, and still the land goes stretching away to the horizons. A year, five years, ten years, and I have not seen the sea. I say unto myself, but what has happened to the sea? And I answer, the sea is back there, back in the reservoir of memory. The sea is a myth. There never was a sea. But there *was* a sea! I tell you I was born on the seashore! I bathed in the waters of the sea! It gave me food and it gave me peace, and its fascinating distances fed my dreams! No, Arturo, there never was a sea. You dream and you wish, but you go on through the wasteland. You will never see the sea again. It was a myth you once believed. But, I have to smile, for the salt of the sea is in my blood, and there may be ten thousand roads over the land, but they shall never confuse me, for my heart's blood will ever return to its beautiful source.

Then what shall I do? Shall I lift my mouth to the sky, stumbling and burbling with a tongue that is afraid? Shall I open my chest and beat it like a loud drum, seeking the attention of my Christ? Or is it not better and more reasonable that I cover myself and go on? There will be confusions, and there will be hunger; there will be loneliness with only my tears like wet consoling little birds, tumbling to sweeten my dry lips. But there shall be consolation, and there shall be beauty like the love of some dead girl. There shall be some laughter, a restrained laughter, and quiet waiting in the night, a soft fear of the night like the lavish, taunting kiss of death. Then it will be night, and the sweet oils from the shores of my sea, poured upon my senses by the captains I deserted in the dreamy impetuousness of my youth. But I shall be forgiven for that, and for other things, for Vera Rivken, and for the ceaseless flapping of the wings of Voltaire, for pausing to listen and watch that fascinating bird, for all things there shall be forgiveness when I return to my homeland by the sea.

I got up and plodded through the deep sand toward the boardwalk. It was the full ripeness of evening, with the sun a defiant red ball as it sank beyond the sea. There was something breathless about the sky, a strange tension. Far to the south sea gulls in a black mass roved the coast. I stopped to pour sand from my shoes, balanced on one leg as I leaned against a stone bench.

Suddenly I felt a rumble, then a roar.

The stone bench fell away from me and thumped into the sand. I looked at the row of concessions: they were shaking and cracking. I looked beyond to the Long Beach skyline; the tall buildings were swaying. Under me the sand gave way; I staggered, found safer footing. It happened again.

It was an earthquake.

Now there were screams. Then dust. Then crumbling and roaring. I turned round and round in a circle. I had done this. I had done this. I stood with my mouth open, paralyzed, looking about me. I ran a few steps toward the sea. Then I ran back.

You did it, Arturo. This is the wrath of God. You did it.

The rumbling continued. Like a carpet over oil, the sea and land heaved. Dust rose. Somewhere I heard a booming of debris. I heard screams, and then a siren. People running out of doors. Great clouds of dust.

You did it, Arturo. Up in that room on that bed you did it.

Now the lamp posts were falling. Buildings cracked like crushed crackers. Screams, men shouting, women screaming. Hundreds of people rushing from buildings, hurrying out of danger. A woman lying on the sidewalk, beating it. A little boy crying. Glass splintering and shattering. Fire bells. Sirens. Horns. Madness.

Now the big shake was over. Now there were tremors. Deep in the earth the rumbling continued. Chimneys toppled, bricks fell and a grey dust settled over all. Still the temblors. Men and women running toward an empty lot away from buildings.

I hurried to the lot. An old woman wept among the white faces. Two men carrying a body. An old dog crawling on his belly, dragging his hind legs. Several bodies in the corner of the lot, beside a shed, blood-soaked sheets covering them. An ambulance. Two high school girls, arms locked, laughing. I looked down the street. The building fronts were down. Beds hung from walls. Bathrooms were exposed. The street was piled with three feet of debris. Men were shouting orders. Each temblor brought more tumbling debris. They stepped aside, waited, then plunged in again.

I had to go. I walked to the shed, the earth quivering under me. I opened the shed door, felt like fainting. Inside were bodies in a row, sheets over them, blood oozing through. Blood and death. I walked off and sat down. Still the temblors, one after another.

Where was Vera Rivken? I got up and walked to the street. It had been roped off. Marines with bayonets patrolled the roped area. Far down the street I saw the building where Vera lived. Hanging from the wall, like a man crucified, was the bed. The floor was gone and only one wall stood erect. I walked back to the lot. Somebody had built a bonfire in the middle of the lot. Faces reddened in the blaze. I studied them, found nobody I knew. I didn't find Vera Rivken. A group of old men were talking. The tall one with the beard said it was the end of the world; he had predicted it a week before. A woman with dirt smeared over her hair broke into the group. "Charlie's dead," she said. Then she wailed. "Poor Charlie's dead. We shouldn't have to come! I told him we shouldn't a come!" An old man seized her by the shoulders, swung her around. "What the hell you sayin'?" he said. She fainted in his arms.

I went off and sat on the curbing. Repent, repent before it's too late. I said a prayer but it was dust in my mouth. No prayers. But there would be some changes made in my life. There would be decency and gentleness from now on. This was the turning point. This was for me, a warning to Arturo Bandini.

Around the bonfire the people were singing hymns. They were in a circle, a huge woman leading them. Lift up thine eyes to Jesus, for Jesus is coming soon. Everybody was singing. A kid with a monogram on his sweater handed me a hymn book. I walked over. The woman in the circle swung her arms with wild fervor, and the song tumbled with the smoke toward the sky. The temblors kept coming. I turned away. Jesus, these Protestants! In my church we didn't sing cheap hymns. With us it was Handel and Palestrina.

It was dark now. A few stars appeared. The temblors were ceaseless, coming every few seconds. A wind rose from the sea and it grew cold. People huddled in groups. From everywhere sirens sounded. Above, airplanes droned, and detachments of sailors and marines poured through the streets. Stretcher-bearers dashed into ruined buildings. Two ambulances backed toward the shed. I got up and walked away. The Red Cross had moved in. There was an emergency headquarters at one corner of the lot. They were handing out big tins of coffee. I stood in line. The man ahead of me was talking.

"It's worse in Los Angeles," he said. "Thousands dead."

Thousands. That meant Camilla. The Columbia Buffet would be the first to tumble. It was so old, the brick walls so cracked and feeble. Sure, she was dead. She worked from four until eleven. She had been caught in the midst of it. She was dead and I was alive. Good. I pictured her dead: she would lie still in this manner; her eyes closed like this, her hands clasped like that. She was dead and I was alive. We didn't understand one another, but she had been good to me, in her fashion. I would remember her a long time. I was probably the only man on earth who would remember her. I could think of so many charming things about her; her huaraches, her shame for her people, her absurd little Ford.

All sorts of rumors circulated through the lot. A tidal wave was coming. A tidal wave wasn't coming. All of California had been struck. Only Long Beach had been struck. Los Angeles was a mass of ruins. They hadn't felt it in Los Angeles. Some said the dead numbered fifty thousand. This was the worst quake since San Francisco. This was much worse than the San Francisco quake. But in spite of it all, everybody was orderly. Everybody was frightened, but it was not a panic. Here and there people smiled: they were brave people. They were a long way from home, but they brought their bravery with them. They were tough people. They weren't afraid of anything.

The marines set up a radio in the middle of the lot, with big loudspeakers yawning into the crowd. The reports came through constantly, outlining the catastrophe. The deep voice bellowed instructions. It was the law and everybody accepted it gladly. Nobody was to enter or leave Long Beach until further notice. The city was under martial law. There wasn't going to be a tidal wave. The danger was definitely over. The people were not to be alarmed by the temblors, which were to be expected, now that the earth was settling once more.

The Red Cross passed out blankets, food, and lots of coffee. All night we sat around the loudspeaker, listening to developments. Then the report came that the damage in Los Angeles was negligible. A long list of the dead was broadcast. But there was no Camilla Lopez on the list. All night I swallowed coffee and smoked cigarets, listening to the names of the dead. There was no Camilla; not even a Lopez.

—*Ask the Dust*

Part Three

A TIME OF DREAM AND REVERIE

MY FIRST COLLISION WITH FAME was hardly memorable. I was a busboy at Marx's Deli. The year was 1934. The place was Third and Hill, Los Angeles. I was twenty-one years old, living in a world bounded on the west by Bunker Hill, on the east by Los Angeles Street, on the south by Pershing Square, and on the north by Civic Center. I was a busboy nonpareil, with great verve and style for the profession, and though I was dreadfully underpaid (one dollar a day plus meals) I attracted considerable attention as I whirled from table to table, balancing a tray on one hand, and eliciting smiles from my customers. I had something else beside a waiter's skill to offer my patrons, for I was also a writer. This phenomenon became known one day after a drunken photographer from the *Los Angeles Times* sat at the bar, snapped several pictures of me serving a customer as she looked up at me with admiring eyes. Next day there was a feature story attached to the *Times* photograph. It told of the struggle and success of young Arturo Bandini, an ambitious, hard-working kid from Colorado, who had crashed through the difficult magazine world with the sale of his first story to *The American Phoenix*, edited, of course, by the most renowned personage in American literature, none other than Heinrich Muller. Good old Muller! How I loved that man! Indeed, my first literary efforts were letters to him, asking his advice, sending him suggestions for stories I might write, and finally sending him stories too, many stories, a story a week, until even Heinrich Muller, curmudgeon of the literary world, the tiger in his lair, seemed to give up the struggle and condescended to drop me a letter with two lines in it, and then a second letter with four lines, and finally a two-page letter of twenty-four lines and then, wonder of wonders, a check for $150, payment in full for my first acceptance.

I was in rags the day that check arrived. My nondescript Colorado clothes hung from me in shreds, and my first thought was a new wardrobe. I had to be frugal but in good taste, and so I descended Bunker Hill to Second and Broadway, and the Goodwill store. I made my way to the better quality section and found an excellent blue business suit with a white pinstripe. The pants were too long and so were the sleeves, and the whole thing was ten dollars. For another dollar I had the suit altered, and while this was being taken care of, I buzzed around in the shirt department. Shirts were fifty cents apiece, of excellent quality and all manner of styles. Next I purchased a pair of shoes—fine thick-soled oxfords of pure leather, shoes that would carry me over the streets of Los Angeles for months to come. I bought other things too, several pairs of shorts and T-shirts, a dozen pairs of socks, a few neckties and finally an irresistible glorious fedora. I set it jauntily at the side of my head and walked out of the dressing room and paid my bill. Twenty bucks. It was the first time in my life that I had bought clothing for myself. As I studied my reflection in a long mirror I could not help remembering that in all my Colorado years my people had been too poor to buy me a suit of clothes, even for the graduation exercises in high school. Well, I was on my way now, nothing could stop me. Heinrich Muller, the roaring tiger of the literary world, would lead me to the top of the heap. I walked out of the Goodwill and up Third Street, a new man. My boss, Abe Marx, was standing in front of the deli as I approached.

"Good God, Bandini!" he exclaimed. "You've been to the Goodwill or something?"

"Goodwill, my ass," I snorted. "This is straight from Bullock's, you boob."

A couple of days later Abe Marx handed me a business card. It read:

Gustave Du Mont, Ph.D.
LITERARY AGENT
Preparation and Editing
of books, plays, scenarios, and stories
Expert editorial supervision
513 Third Street, Los Angeles
No triflers

I slipped the card into the pocket of my new suit. I took the elevator to the fifth floor. Du Mont's office was down the corridor. I entered.

The reception room lurched like an earthquake. I caught my breath and looked around. The place was full of cats. Cats on the chairs, on the valances, on the typewriter. Cats on the bookcases, in the bookcases. The stench was overpowering. The cats came to their feet and swirled around me, pressing my legs, rolling playfully over my shoes. On the floor and on the surface of the furniture a film of cat fur heaved and eddied like a pool of water. I crossed to an open window and looked down the fire escape. Cats were ascending and descending. A huge grey creature climbed toward me, the head of a salmon in his mouth. He brushed past me and leaped into the room.

By now the whir of cat fur enveloped the air. An inner office door opened. Standing there was Gustave Du Mont, a small aged man with eyes like cherries. He waved his arms and rushed among the cats shrieking,

"Out! Out! Go, everybody! Time to go home!"

The cats simply glided off at their leisure, some ending up at his feet some playfully pawing his pants. They were his masters. Du Mont sighed, threw up his hands, and said,

"What can I do for you?"

"I'm from the deli downstairs. You left your card."

"Enter."

I stepped into his office and he closed the door. We were in a small room in the presence of three cats lolling atop a bookcase. They were elite felines, huge Persians, licking their paws with regal aplomb. I stared at them. Du Mont seemed to understand.

"My favorites," he smiled. He opened a desk drawer and drew out a fifth of Scotch.

"How about some lunch, young man?"

"No thanks, Dr. Du Mont. What did you want to see me about?"

Du Mont uncorked the bottle, took a swig from it and gasped.

"I read your story. You're a good writer. You shouldn't be slinging hash. You belong in more amenable surroundings." Du Mont took another swig. "You want a job?"

I looked at all those cats. "Maybe. What you got in mind?"

"I need an editor."

I smelled the pungency of all those cats. "I'm not sure I could take it."

"You mean the cats? I'll take care of that."

I thought a minute. "Well . . . what is it you want me to edit?"

He hit the bottle again. "Novels, short stories, whatever comes in."

I hesitated. "Can I see the stuff?"

His fist came down on a pile of manuscripts. "Help yourself."

I lifted off the top manuscript. It was a short story, written by a certain Jennifer Lovelace, entitled *Passion at Dawn*. I groaned.

Du Mont took another swig. "It's awful," he said. "They're all awful. I can't read them anymore. It's the worst writing I ever saw. But there's money in it if you've got the stomach. The worse they are the more you charge."

By now the whole front of my new suit was coated with cat fur. My nose itched and I felt a sneeze coming. I choked it back.

"What's the job pay?"

"Five dollars a week."

"Hell, that's only a dollar a day."

"Nothin' to it."

I snatched the bottle and took a swig. It scorched my throat. It tasted like cat piss.

"Ten dollars a week or no deal."

Du Mont shoved out his fist. "Shake," he said. "You start Monday."

—Dreams from Bunker Hill

I WONDERED WHAT HEINRICH MULLER WOULD SAY about my integrity. Integrity! I laughed. Integrity—balls. I was a nothing, a zero. To hell with it. I decided to go shopping for a pair of pants. I still had over a hundred dollars. I would splurge and forget my troubles in profligate spending. What was money anyway?

At the Goodwill I selected and tried on three pairs of pants. Somehow they did very little for me. I looked at myself in the long mirror, and there I was—the cipher, the zero. Shameful in the presence of Heinrich Muller, the lion of literature.

Walking across Third and Hill to Angel's Flight, I climbed aboard the trolley and sat down. The only other passenger was a girl across the aisle reading a book. She was in a plain dress and without stockings. She was rather attractive but not my style. As the trolley lurched into motion she moved to another seat. No ass at all, I thought. An ass, yes, but without the splendor of Jennifer Lovelace's. Without nobility, without the grandeur of a thing of beauty. Just an ass, a plain common ass. It was not my day.

I got off the cable car at the top of Angel's Flight and started down Third Street toward my hotel. Then I decided on a cup of coffee and a cigarette in the small Japanese restaurant a few doors ahead. The coffee erased my gloom and I walked on to my hotel. The landlady sat behind the desk in the lobby. The first thing I noticed was a copy of *The American Phoenix*. It was exactly where I had placed it three weeks ago. Annoyed, I walked boldly to the desk and picked it up.

"You haven't read it, have you?"

She smiled, hostile. "No, I haven't."

"Why not?" I said.

"It bored me. I read the first paragraph and that was enough for me."

I put the magazine under my arm.

"I'm moving out," I said. "Real soon."

"Suit yourself."

I walked away and down the hall. As I turned the key in my door I heard the click of a lock across the hall. The door opened and the girl from the trolley stepped out. She still carried the book. It was Zola's *Nana*. She smiled in greeting.

"Hi!" I said. "I didn't know you lived here."

"I just moved in."

"You work around here?"

"I suppose you'd call it that." She made a sensual glance. "Would you like to see me?"

"When?"

"How about right now?"

I didn't want her. Nothing of her lured me, but I had to be manly. These situations could only be resolved in one way.

"Sure," I said.

She turned on the tiny flame of sensuality in her eyes and pushed open her door.

"What are we waiting for?" she said.

I hesitated. Lord help me, I thought, as I crossed the hall and entered her room.

She followed me inside and closed the door.

"What's your name, honey?"

"Arturo," I said. "Arturo Bandini."

She held out her hands and removed my coat.

"How much?" I asked.

"A fin."

She guided me around to face her and began unbuttoning my shirt. Hanging it over a chair she crossed to the bathroom.

"See you in a minute."

She entered the bathroom and closed the door. I sat on the bed and pulled off my clothes. I was naked when she emerged. I tried to hide my disappointment. She was clean and bathed but somehow impure. Her bottom hung there like an orphan child. We would never make it together. My presence there was insanity. She grasped my rod and led me to the bathroom. She washed and soaped my loins and her fingers kneaded my joint determinedly, but there was no response. I could only think of Jennifer Lovelace and the gallantry of her flanks. Then she toweled me off and we went back to the bedroom and lay on the bed. She spread herself out naked and I lay beside her.

"Go ahead," she said. I traced one finger through her pubic hair.

"Do you mind if I read?" she said. "Hand me my book."

I gave her the book and she opened it to her place and began to read. I lay there and wondered. Good God, what if my mother were to walk in? Or my father? Or Heinrich Muller? Where would it all end? She nodded toward a bowl of apples at the bedside.

"Want an apple?" she asked.

"No thanks."

"Give me one please."

I handed her an apple. And so she read and ate.

"Come on, honey," she coaxed. "Enjoy yourself."

I swung my legs out of bed and stood up.

"What's the matter?" she asked, her voice hostile.

"Don't worry. I'll pay you off."

"Would you like me to suck you?"

"No," I said.

She slammed the book shut.

"Do you know what's the matter with you, sonny? You're queer. That's what's the matter with you. You're a fag. I know your kind."

She grabbed my coat, pants, underwear, shoes and socks, raced to the door and threw it all in the hall. I stepped out and began gathering my things.

"I owe you five bucks," I said.

"No, you don't. You don't owe me a thing."

I groped through my coat pocket for the door key. Down the hall, watching me with her arms folded, was Mrs. Brownell, the landlady. I turned the key and jumped into my room.

I felt relieved, saved, rescued. I went to the window to look at all of the great city spread below me. It was like a view of the whole world. Far to the southwest the sun struck the ocean in bars of heavenly light. A message from God. A sign. The infant Jesus in the manger, the light from the Star of Bethlehem. I fell on my knees.

"Oh blessed Infant Jesus," I prayed. "Thank you for saving me this day. Bless you for the surge of God's goodness that moved me from that room of sin. I swear it now—I will never sin again. For the rest of my life

I will remember your glorious intercession. Thank you, little Son of God. I am your devoted servant forever henceforth."

I made the sign of the cross and got to my feet. How good I felt. How recharged with the feelings of my early boyhood. I had to get in touch with Jennifer Lovelace.

—Dreams from Bunker Hill

I PICKED UP THE PHONE. The caller was Harry Schindler, the movie director. He was an old friend of H. L. Muller. He had obtained my address from Muller, and was anxious to talk to me.

"What about?"

"Have you ever written for pictures?"

"No."

"That's fine," Schindler said. "Would you like a job?"

"Doing what?"

"Writing a screenplay."

"I don't know how."

"Nothing to it," Schindler said. "I'll show you. Meet me at Columbia Pictures tomorrow morning at ten o'clock."

I went back to Mrs. Brownell's living room and sat down. She had obviously overheard the telephone conversation.

"I may have a job in the movies."

"At least you'll be clean," she said. I noticed her derriere. It was still contracted. I ate quickly and went back to my room.

—*Dreams from Bunker Hill*

F RANK EDGINGTON AND I BECAME BUDDIES. He loved the flip side of Hollywood, the bars, the mean streets angling off Hollywood Boulevard to the south. I was glad to tag along as he took in the saloons along El Centro, McCadden Place, Wilcox, and Las Palmas. We drank beer and played the pinball games. Edgington was a pinball addict, a tireless devotee, drinking beer and popping the pinballs. Sometimes we went to the movies. He knew all the fine restaurants, and we ate and drank well. On weekends we toured the Los Angeles basin, the deserts, the foothills, the outlying towns, the harbor. One Saturday we drove to Terminal Island, a strip of white sand in the harbor. The canneries were there and we saw the weatherbeaten beach houses where Filipinos and Japanese lived. It was an enchanting place, lonely, decrepit, picturesque. I saw myself in one of the shacks with my typewriter. I longed for the chance to work there, to write in that lonely, forsaken place, where the sand half covered the streets, and the porches and fences hung limp in the wind. I told Frank I wanted to live there and write there.

"You're crazy," he said. "This is a slum."

"It's beautiful," I said. "It gives me a warm feeling."

At the studio we indulged another of Frank Edgington's obsessions— child games. We played pitch, old maid, Parcheesi, and Chinese checkers. We played for small stakes—five cents a game. When Frank was alone he worked on a short story for the *New Yorker*. When I was alone I sat in my office hungering for Thelma Farber. She was impregnable. Sometimes she even denied me a hello, and I was thoroughly squelched and breathing hard. Harry Schindler ordered his old films and Thelma and I sat in the projection room watching them unroll. I tried to sit next to her and she promptly moved two seats away. She was a bitch, unreasonably hostile. I felt like vermin.

After two weeks I picked up my first paycheck, $600. It was a stagger-ing sum. Three hundred dollars a week for doing nothing! I knocked on Schindler's door and thanked him for the check.

"It's okay," he grinned. "We want you happy. That's the whole idea."

"But I'm not doing anything. I'm going crazy. Give me something to write."

"You're doing fine. I need you in case of emergency. I got to have a backup man, someone with talent. Don't worry about it. You're doing a great job. Keep up the good work. Cash the check and have fun."

"Let me write you a western."

"Not yet," Schindler said. "Just do what you're doing and leave the rest to me."

Suddenly I choked up. I wanted to cry. I turned and walked out, brushed past Thelma and into my office. I sat at my desk crying. I didn't want charity. I wanted to be brilliant on paper, to turn fine phrases and dig up emotional gems for Schindler to see. Choking back my sobs I hur-ried down the hall to Edgington's office, and flung myself into a chair.

"What the hell's the matter?" Edgington asked.

I told him. "They won't let me write," I said. "Schindler won't assign me anything. I'm going crazy."

Edgington threw his pencil across the room in disgust.

"What the hell's the matter with you? There are writers in this studio who go months without scratching out a line. They earn ten times as much as you do, and they laugh all the way to the bank. Your trouble is that you're a fucking peasant. If there's so much you don't like about this town, stop jerking off and go back to that dago village your people came from. You make my ass tired!"

I stared at him gratefully. Then I began to laugh.

"Frank," I said. "You're a wonderful person."

"Go and sin no more."

I went downstairs to Gower Street, up to Sunset, and across Sunset to the Bank of America, where I cashed my check. I walked out with a new sensation, a feeling of bitter joy. Down Sunset half a block was a used car lot. I found a second-hand Plymouth for $300 and drove away. I was a new person, a successful Hollywood writer, without even writing a line. The future was limitless.

—*Dreams from Bunker Hill*

A FEW NIGHTS LATER Edgington invited me to dinner. "Best restaurant in town," he said. We left my car in the studio parking lot and drove off in Frank's Cadillac. He went up Beverly Boulevard to Doheny and pulled into the parking lot of an adjacent restaurant. It was Chasen's. Before we entered Frank straightened my tie.

"This is a high-class joint," he said. "I don't want you to embarrass me."

We walked inside. There was a small outer bar, and beyond that the main dining room. We straddled bar stools and ordered drinks. As usual Frank knew everybody. He shook hands with Dave Chasen and introduced me.

"Nice to know you," Chasen grinned, then turned hastily to welcome a man and two women entering from the street. They stood talking a moment.

Frank nudged me. "Guess who's here," he said.

I turned and studied the man and his two feminine companions.

"Who's he?" I whispered, as the trio moved past and entered the dining room.

"Sinclair Lewis," Frank said.

Startled, I coughed in my drink.

"Are you sure?" I asked.

"Sure I'm sure." He beckoned to Chasen, who joined us again. "Who was the guy with the two women?" Frank asked.

"Sinclair Lewis," Chasen said.

"Good God," I said, "the greatest writer in America!" I leaped off the bar stool and crossed to the curtained door leading to the dining room. Pulling the curtain aside, I saw a waiter ushering Lewis and his friends into a booth.

I couldn't stop myself. All at once I was threading my way between tables toward the greatest author in America. It was a blind, crazy impulse. Suddenly I stood before Lewis's booth. Absorbed in conversation with the women, he did not see me. I smiled at his thinning red hair, his rather freckled face, and his long delicate hands.

"Sinclair Lewis," I said.

He and his friends looked up at me.

"You're the greatest novelist this country ever produced," I spluttered. "All I want is to shake your hand. My name is Arturo Bandini. I write for H. L. Muller, your best friend." I thrust out my hand. "I'm glad to know you, Mr. Lewis."

He fixed me with a bewildered stare, his eyes blue and cold. My hand was out there across the table between us. He did not take it. He only stared, and the women stared too. Slowly I drew my hand away.

"It's nice to know you, Mr. Lewis. Sorry I bothered you." I turned in horror, my guts falling out, as I hurried between the tables and back to the bar, and joined Frank Edgington. I was raging, sick, mortified, humiliated. I snatched Frank's scotch and soda and gulped it down. The bartender and Frank exchanged glances.

"Give me a pencil and paper, please."

The bartender put a notepad and a pencil before me. Breathing hard, the pencil trembling, I wrote:

Dear Sinclair Lewis:

You were once a god, but now you are a swine. I once reverenced you, admired you, and now you are nothing. I came to shake your hand in adoration, you, Lewis, a giant among American writers, and you rejected it. I swear I shall never read another line of yours again. You are an ill-mannered boor. You have betrayed me. I shall tell H. L. Muller about you, and how you have shamed me. I shall tell the world.

Arturo Bandini

P.S. I hope you choke on your steak.

I folded the paper and signaled a waiter. He walked over. I handed him the note.

"Would you please give this to Sinclair Lewis."

He took it and I gave him some money. He entered the dining room. I stood in the doorway watching him approach Lewis's table. He handed Lewis the note. Lewis held it before him for some moments, then leaped to his feet, looking around, calling the waiter back. He stepped out of the booth and the waiter pointed in my direction. Carrying his napkin, Lewis took big strides as he came toward me. I shot out of there, out the front door, and down the street to the parking lot, to Frank's Cadillac, and leaped into the back seat. I could see the street from where I sat, and in a moment Lewis appeared nervously on the sidewalk, still clutching his napkin. He glanced about, agitated.

"Bandini," he called. "Where are you? I'm Sinclair Lewis. Where are you, Bandini?"

I sat motionless. A few moments, and he walked back toward the restaurant. I sat back, exhausted, bewildered, not knowing myself, or my capabilities. I sat with doubts, with shame, with torment, with regret. I lit a cigarette and sucked it greedily. In a little while Frank Edgington walked out of the restaurant and came to the car. He leaned inside and looked at me.

"You okay?"

"Okay," I said.

"What happened?"

"I don't know."

"What was that note you wrote?"

"I don't know."

"You're crazy. You want to eat?"

"Not here. Let's go someplace else."

"It's up to you." He got behind the wheel and started the engine.

—*Dreams from Bunker Hill*

THE BEST THING ABOUT MY COLLABORATION with Velda was the money. After fifteen weeks, a three-hundred-dollar check each week, she telephoned. She had finished the script. She was sending it special delivery. It should arrive the next day. She was very proud of her work. She knew I would like it, that we had achieved a masterpiece.

"Did you change it much?" I asked.

"Here and there. Small changes. But the essence of your version, the main thrust, is still there."

"I'm glad, Velda. Frankly, I was worried."

"You're going to be very pleased, Arturo. There was so little for me to do. I hardly deserve any credit at all."

Next day I sat on the porch of Edgington's house and waited for the mailman. At noon a postal truck drove up and the driver put the large envelope in my hands. I signed the receipt, sat on the porch step, and opened the manuscript.

The title page read *Sin City*, screenplay by Velda van der Zee and Arturo Bandini, from a story by Harry Browne. I was down the first page halfway when my hair began to stiffen. In the middle of the second page I was forced to put the script aside and hang on to the porch banister. My breathing was uneven and there were mysterious shooting pains in my legs and across my stomach. I staggered to my feet and went inside to the kitchen and drank a glass of water. Edgington was sitting at the table eating breakfast. He saw my face and stood up.

"Good God, what's wrong?"

I could not speak. I could only point in the direction of the manuscript. Edgington walked to the front door and looked around.

"What's up?" he said. "Who's out there?"

I came through the house to the porch and pointed at the manuscript. He picked it up.

"What's this?" He looked at the title page. "What's wrong with it?"
"Read it."

He took it to the porch swing and sat down.

"I've been had," I said. "I didn't write it. My name's on it, but I didn't write it."

He began to read. Suddenly he laughed, a short barking laugh. "It's funny," he said. "It's a very funny script."

"You mean it's a comedy?"

"That's what's funny. It's not a comedy." He went back to the script and read in silence, another ten pages. Then, deliberately, he folded the manuscript shut and looked at me.

"Is it still funny?"

He rolled up the script and threw it into an ivy patch beyond the porch.

"It's ghastly," he said.

I rescued the script from the ivy bed. He had read my version more than fifteen weeks ago. He had liked it, praised it.

"What should I do?" I asked.

"How about going back to Colorado and learning to lay brick with your old man?"

"That's no solution."

"The only solution is to get your name off this script. Disown it. Don't be associated with it."

"Maybe I can save it."

"Save it from what? It's dead, man. It's been murdered. Call your agent and tell him to remove your name. Either that or get out of town." He rose and walked back into the kitchen. I opened the screenplay and started to read again. What I read was as follows:

A stagecoach rolls across the Wyoming plain pursued by band of Indians. Stagecoach brought to halt. Indians swarm over it. Two passengers: Reverend Ezra Drew and daughter Priscilla. Indian chief drags Priscilla out, throws her on his horse. Priscilla struggles. Chief mounts, rides off with her. Indians follow.

Indian village. Chief rides up with Priscilla, shoves her into teepee, then enters. Indian chief is Magua, enemy of white man. He seizes girl, handles her roughly, kissing her as she struggles.

Over the hill comes posse, led by Sheriff Lawson. He dismounts, hears girl scream, enters teepee, struggles with Magua, knocks him down, helps girl outside, puts her in saddle of his horse, mounts, and rides off. Posse follows.

Sin City. Posse arrives, Sheriff puts Priscilla down. Posse brings up Reverend Drew. Priscilla runs into his arms. Townspeople gather. Sheriff Lawson leads Priscilla into Sin City Hotel.

That night townfolk gather at hotel. Sheriff comes out with Priscilla and Reverend Drew. Townfolk beg them to stay. Local church recently burned out by hostile Indians of Chief Magua. People urge Reverend Drew to rebuild church. He promises to consider it. Playing banjo, Reverend Drew accompanies daughter in singing of "I Love You, Jesus." Great applause. Holding tambourine, Priscilla moves among townfolk and they drop coins into tambourine. Reverend Drew mounts hotel porch and delivers speech. He and daughter promise to remain and rebuild Sin City church. Citizens repair to big saloon. Once more the Reverend strums banjo and Priscilla sings "Lord Welcome Me." Again she passes tambourine and makes generous collection.

Church being rebuilt. Townspeople help, carrying lumber and building material. Sheriff rides up and puts Priscilla in his buckboard. They ride off. In lovely pine grove Sheriff embraces Priscilla and they kiss.

Evening. Sin City saloon. Priscilla sings "The Lord Is My Shepherd," while saloon patrons listen and admire the lovely young woman. She passes tambourine. A drunk at bar seizes her, tries to kiss her. Sheriff Lawson intervenes, fight develops. Lawson knocks intruder down. Priscilla looks to Sheriff gratefully.

On hillside overlooking town sits the sinister Magua on his horse, watching. He dismounts and slinks to window of saloon as Priscilla addresses bar patrons in little speech. She wants townsfolk to form a church choir where hymns can be sung and offerings made for new church. Townspeople agree and applaud. Outside at window the evil Magua smirks as he listens.

Change comes over Sin City. No more liquor in town saloon. No more gambling. Group of women under Priscilla's direction sing spirited hymns. Work on church proceeds. Day arrives when church is complete, and townfolk gather for first service. Watching from above, Magua observes the happenings below and rides off.

Evening. Women of Sin City prepare barbecue outside church. A square dance in progress, led by Reverend Drew and his banjo.

Priscilla whirls to music, her partner the Sheriff. Meanwhile at Indian village Magua gathers his forces. Indians with painted bodies mount their horses and Magua leads them away.

Square dance. Sheriff leads Priscilla into woods. She lifts face for his kiss. He asks her to marry him. She consents. Suddenly the sound of pounding hoofs and Indian yells. Down the hill come Magua and his bloodthirsty Arapahoes. Riding furiously, they ring the church and townspeople with bloodcurdling shouts and thundering hoofs. Shrieking townfolk retreat to church as Indians continue to circle and fire their rifles. Sheriff and Priscilla rush to safety of new church. Round and round the Indians tighten their noose about the church. Gunfire. Cries of wounded. Indians hurl torches upon church roof. Townsfolk mount gun positions at church windows. Battle rages. Women reload rifles. Priscilla reloads her father's rifle. At that moment he is shot. Priscilla shoots Indian who felled her father. Then she turns and gathers fallen parent in her arms and cries.

Meanwhile the treacherous Magua has dismounted and comes slithering toward church door. He enters unseen and swoops down on Priscilla, cups hand over her mouth, and drags her outside. Throwing her upon back of his horse, he mounts behind her and rides off just as Sheriff Lawson appears in doorway. Taking dead aim, Magua fires rifle at Sheriff and bullet strikes him in shoulder. Lawson staggers but does not go down. Instead he lurches toward Magua, who rides off with the struggling Priscilla.

Wounded but undaunted, Sheriff gropes to his horse, mounts, and rides in pursuit. Over hill and dale he follows fleeing Indian and girl. They come to a creek in the foothills and stop. Bleeding and weak, Lawson rides up, then falls to the ground. Eagerly Magua dismounts with menacing tomahawk. Fierce battle, men rolling and twisting, Priscilla watching in horror. They fall into creek. Magua leaps upon weakened Sheriff and tries to drown him, but Sheriff frees himself.

Too weak to resist further, Sheriff collapses in water. With yell of triumph Magua raises tomahawk to strike. Suddenly the crack of a rifle breaks the stillness. Magua falls into the water. Priscilla, smoking rifle in her hands, dismounts and rushes to Sheriff. She drags him from creek. Weakened but defiant, Sheriff throws arms around her. They rise and stagger away. In the water Magua lies dead.

Back in Sin City church siege goes on. Whites slowly gain upper hand. Launch counter attack. Hand to hand combat. Many Indians retreat. Others captured by townsfolk. A dozen savages being led to city jail. In the distance come Priscilla and Sheriff Lawson. Strapped across their horse is body of dead Magua. Great cheer from townsfolk. Priscilla runs into father's arms.

Epilogue. Bright Sunday morning. Songfest comes from church. Inside Priscilla leads choir in "Oh Gentle Jesus." Church packed with townsfolk listening reverently. In back pews, segregated from others, are a dozen captive Indians, penitent, heads bowed. Sheriff comes to Priscilla's side. She looks up adoringly. Fade out.

So there it was, the whole dirty business. My screenplay, without a line of my work in it, in fact an altogether different story, impossible for me to have concocted. I laughed. It was a joke. Somebody was playing around. It was impossible. I went into the house and sat there smoking cigarettes, suddenly aware of the falling rain, the sweet sound of it on the shingle roof, the sweet smell of it coming through the front door. No question about it, Edgington was right. My only course was to have my name removed from the title. I picked up the telephone and dialed Cyril Korn.

"Yeah?" he barked.

"Hello, Korn. This is me. Have you read the story?"

"I liked it."

"You're crazy."

"It's a great western."

"Take my name off."

"What?"

"Remove my name from this monstrosity. You hear me? I want no part of it."

There was a long silence before Korn spoke again. Then he said:

"Suit yourself, kid. This is good news for Velda. She'll get a solo credit now."

"She can have it." I hung up.

———

The rain came down in sheets, whipping the leaves from the eucalyptus trees, digging little rivers across the yard and into the gutter. I drank a glass of wine. Edgington stepped out of the kitchen. He had heard my conversation with Korn.

"You did right," he said. "It was self preservation. You had no choice. If you'd listened to me this wouldn't have happened."

"What do you mean?"

"You should have joined the Guild. I've been telling you for three months."

The cold rainy wind swept in through the front door, chilling the room. Edgington went to the fireplace and lit the gas logs. He took a tobacco sack from his pocket.

"Here," he said, tossing it to me.

It was marijuana. There were cigarette papers in the sack. I had smoked marijuana only once before, in Boulder, and it made me sick. It was time to get sick again. I rolled a cigarette. We sat looking at one another, drawing down the weed into our lungs. Edgington laughed. I laughed too.

"You're a rotten no-good sonofabitchin' English limey toad," I said.

He nodded agreement. "And you, sir, are a miserable, disagreeable dago dog."

We lapsed into silence, smoking the grass. I picked up the manuscript.

"Let's do something to it," I said.

"Let's burn it."

I took it to the fireplace and dropped it on the flames. The pot was taking over. I took off my shirt.

"Let's be Indians," I said. "Let's burn her at the stake."

"Great," Edgington said, pulling off his shirt.

"Let's take off our pants," I said. We laughed and kicked off our pants. In a moment we were naked, dancing in a circle, making what we thought were Indian cries. From the clouds came a clap of thunder. We laughed and rolled on the floor. Edgington had a beer. I drank a glass of wine. The downpour was ear-shattering. I rushed out and we held hands and danced round and round laughing. I ran into the house, sipped on my wine and ran outside again. Edgington rushed in, took a swig of his beer, and joined me in the rain. We lay on the grass, rolling in the rain, shouting at the thunder. A woman's voice pierced the storm. It was from next door.

"Shame on you, Frank Edgington," she screamed. "Put on some clothes before I call the police."

Frank got to his feet and shoved his bare bottom toward her.

"That's for you, Martha!"

We ran into the house. Standing before the fireplace, dripping wet, we watched the sparks from Velda's screenplay dancing up the chimney. We looked at one another and smiled. Then we performed a fitting climax to the whole crazy ritual. We pissed on the fire.

Now a curious thing happened. I looked at Edgington's sopping hair and rain-soaked body and I did not like him. I did not like him at all. There was something obscene about our nakedness, and the burning screenplay, and the floor wet from rain, and our bodies shivering in the cold, and the insolent smile from Edgington's lips, and I recoiled from him, and blamed him for everything. After all, hadn't he sent me to Cyril Korn, and hadn't Cyril Korn brought me together with Velda van der Zee, and hadn't Edgington sneered and scoffed all the weeks that I had been writing the screenplay? I no longer liked this man. He disgusted me. Similar thoughts must have boiled up in his brain for I noticed the hostile sharpness of his glance. We did not speak. We stood there hating one another. We were on the verge of fighting. I picked up my clothes, walked into the bedroom and slammed the door.

—Dreams from Bunker Hill

I DROVE TO AVALON BOULEVARD and south to Wilmington. It was almost sunset as I passed over the bridge onto the big sandbar known as Terminal Island. The rain had washed the sand from the road and I drove on pavement to the little fishing settlement a mile or so from the canneries. There were six rustic bungalows, all in a row facing the channel waters a hundred yards down the beach. None of the bungalows appeared to be occupied. I drove slowly past them. Each showed a "For Rent" sign on the front porch. Then I noticed a light in the last house. Exactly like the others, the house was dark green and rainsoaked. The light shone through the open front door. I pulled to a stop and ran through the rain to the porch.

In ten minutes I had rented one of the cottages and moved in. It was the center cottage, combination bedroom, living room, and a kitchen and bath. Twenty-five dollars a month. I did some quick calculations and realized that I had enough money to live there for ten years. I had it made.

————

The place was paradise, the South Pacific, Bora Bora. I could hear the sea. It came whispering, saying shshsh, for it was always low tide, the island protected by a breakwater. The nights were wondrous. I lay on my small cot and felt the memory of Velda van der Zee slipping from me. In a few days it had vanished. I listened to the sea and felt my heart restored. Sometimes I heard the bark of seals. I stood in the door and watched them in the shallow water, three or four big fellows playing in the soft tide, barking as if to laugh. The city was far away. I had no thought of writing. My mind was barren as the long shore. I was Robinson Crusoe, lost in a distant world, at peace, breathing good air, salty, satisfying.

When day broke I walked barefoot in the water, in the moist sand, a mile to the cannery settlement, teeming with workers, men and women, emptying the fishing boats, dressing and canning the fish in big corrugated buildings. They were mostly Japanese and Mexican folk from San Pedro. There were two restaurants. The food was good and cheap. Sometimes I walked to the end of the pier, to the ferryboat landing, where the boats took off across the channel to San Pedro. It was twenty-five cents round trip. I felt like a millionaire whenever I plunked down my quarter and sailed for Pedro. I rented a bike and toured the Palos Verdes hills. I found the public library and loaded up on books. Back at my shack I built a fire in the woodstove and sat in the warmth and read Dostoevsky and Flaubert and Dickens and all those famous people. I lacked for nothing. My life was a prayer, a thanksgiving. My loneliness was an enrichment. I found myself bearable, tolerable, even good. Sometimes I wondered what had happened to the writer who had come there. Had I written something and left the place? I touched my typewriter and mused at the action of the keys. It was another life. I had never been here before. I would never leave it.

My landlady was a Japanese woman. She was pregnant. She had a noble kind of walk, small steps, very quiet, her black hair in braids. I learned from her how to bow. We were always bowing. Sometimes we walked on the beach too. We stopped, folded our hands and bowed. Then she went her way and I went mine. One day I found a rowboat flopping along the shore. I got in and rowed away, doing poorly, for I could not manage the oars. But I learned how, and pulled the skiff all the way across the channel to the rocks on the San Pedro side. I bought fishing equipment and bait, and rowed out a hundred yards beyond my house and caught corbina and mackerel, and once a halibut. I brought them home and cooked them and they were ghastly, and I threw them out upon the sand, and watchful seagulls swooped down and carried them away. One day I said, I must write something. I wrote a letter to my mother, but I could not date the letter. I had no memory of time. I went to see the Japanese lady and asked her the date of the month.

"January fourth," she said.

I smiled. I had been there two months, and thought it no more than two weeks.

—Dreams from Bunker Hill

I FOUND A ROOM ON TEMPLE STREET, above a Filipino restaurant. It was two dollars a week without towels, sheets, or pillow cases. I took it, sat on the bed and brooded about my life on the earth. Why was I here? What now? Who did I know? Not even myself. I looked at my hands. They were soft writer's hands, the hands of a writer peasant, not suited for hard work, not equal to making phrases. What could I do? I looked around the room, the wine-stained walls, the carpetless floor, the little window looking out on Figueroa Street. I smelled the cooking from the Filipino restaurant below. Was this the end of Arturo Bandini? Would this be the place where I was to die, on this gray mattress? I could lie here for weeks before anyone discovered me. I got to my knees and prayed:

"What have I done to you, Lord? Why do you punish me? All I ask is the chance to write, to have a friend or two, to cease my running. Bring me peace, oh Lord. Shape me into something worthwhile. Make the typewriter sing. Find the song within me. Be good to me, for I am lonely."

It seemed to hearten me. I went to the typewriter and sat before it. A gray wall loomed up. I pushed back my chair and walked down into the street. I got into my car and drove around.

————

I had trouble sleeping in the little room, even though I bought sheets and blankets. The trouble was, the misery of the day, the fruitlessness of working remained in the room during the night. In the morning it was still there, and I went to the street again. Then I remembered one of Edgington's axioms: "When stuck, hit the road." At sunset I wheeled my car out of the parking lot and hit the streets. Hour after hour I drove around. The city was like a tremendous park, from the foothills to the sea, beautiful in the night, the lamps glowing like white balloons, the streets wide and plentiful and moving off in all directions. It did not matter which way you went, the road always stretched ahead and you found yourself in strange little towns and neighborhoods, and it was soothing and refreshing, but it did not bring story ideas. Moving with the traffic, I wondered how many like myself took to the road merely to escape the city. Day and night the city teemed with traffic and it was impossible to believe that all those people had any rhyme or reason for driving.

———

In February Liberty Films released Velda van der Zee's picture, *Sin City*. I caught it at the Wiltern, on Wilshire, the early evening show. I went prepared to loathe it, and I was pleased to find the theater less than half full. I bought a sack of popcorn and found a seat in the loges. I sat there pleased that my name had been scrubbed from the film, and as the lights darkened, I felt very pleased and relieved that my name would not be among the credits. I laughed loudly when Velda's name appeared, and as the picture unreeled and the stagecoach bounded over the terrain, I laughed again loudly. A hand touched my shoulder. I turned to see a woman frowning.

"You're disturbing me," she said.

"I can't help it," I answered. "It's a very funny picture."

Now the hostile band of Indians appeared, and I guffawed. Several people in the vicinity got up and scattered to different seats.

And so it went. All of my work, all of my thinking, was so remote from the picture, that it was stunning, unbelievable. In only two places did I come upon lines that I might possibly have written, that the director did not delete. The first was in an early scene when the sheriff rode into Sin City at full gallop and brought his horse to a halt at the saloon, shouting "Whoa!" Now I remembered that line: "Whoa!" My line. A little further on the sheriff stalked out of the saloon, mounted his horse, and shouted "Giddyup!" That was my line too: "Giddyup." Whoa and giddyup—my fulfillment as a screenwriter.

It was not a good picture, or an exciting picture, or a mature picture, and as it came to an end and the house lights went on, I saw the weary patrons half asleep in their seats, showing no pleasure at all. I was glad. It proved my integrity. I was a better man for having refused the credit, a better writer. Time would prove it. When Velda van der Zee was a forgotten name in tinsel town, the world would still reckon with Arturo Bandini. I walked out into the night, and God, I felt good and refreshed and restored! Whoa and giddyup! Here we go again. I got into my car and took off in the traffic along Wilshire Boulevard, hell bent for my hotel.

I went up to my room and fell on the bed exhausted. I had been deluding myself. There was no pleasure in seeing *Sin City*. I was really not pleased at Velda's failure. In truth I felt sorry for her, for all writers, for the misery of the craft. I lay in that tiny room and it engulfed me like a tomb.

I got up and went down into the street. Half a block away was a Filipino saloon. I sat at the bar and ordered a glass of Filipino wine. The Filipinos around me laughed and played the dart game. I drank more wine. It was sweet and tinged with peppermint, warm in the stomach, tingling. I drank five more glasses, and stood up to leave. I felt nausea, and my stomach seemed to float into my chest. I got out on the sidewalk, leaned against the lamppost and felt the strength ooze from my knees.

Then everything vanished, and I was in a bed somewhere. It was a white room with big windows and it was daylight. There were tubes in my nose and down my throat and I felt the pain of vomiting. A nurse stood at the bedside and watched me gag and writhe until there was no more of it, only the terrible pain in my stomach and throat. The nurse removed the tubes.

"Where am I?" I asked.

"Georgia Street Hospital," she said.

"What's the matter with me?"

"Poison," she said. "Your friend is here."

I looked toward the door. There stood Helen Brownell. She came quietly to the bedside and sat down. I took her hand and began to sob.

"There now," she soothed. "Everything's all right."

"What's the matter with me?" I choked. "What's going on?"

"Don't you remember?"

"I drank some wine—that's all."

"You drank too much," she said. "You passed out, and the wine made you very ill."

"Who brought me here?"

"The police ambulance."

"How did you find out?"

"My address was in your wallet."

"How long have you been here?"

"Since midnight," she said.

"Can I leave now?"

The nurse stepped up. "Not for a while," she said. "The doctor has to look at you first."

Mrs. Brownell stood up and squeezed my hand. "I must go now."

"I'll see you at the hotel."

She bit her lip. "Perhaps you shouldn't."

"Why not? I love you."

"Don't say that," she answered.

"It's true," I insisted. "I love you more than anybody in the world. I always have. I always will."

Without answering, she turned with a wisp of a smile, and walked out of the room. I felt my stomach heaving, and the nurse held my head as I vomited into a basin.

It was late afternoon when the doctor checked me out and permitted me to leave. When I asked about the charges for my stay he answered that they had been paid.

"By whom?" I said.

"Mrs. Brownell."

I got dressed and walked down the hall to the front door, where I took a trolley to Hill Street. At Third I got off and rode the cable car to the top of Bunker Hill.

—Dreams from Bunker Hill

S O I WAS BACK AGAIN, back to LA, with two suitcases and seventeen dollars. I liked it, the sweep of blue skies, the sun in my face, the endearing streets, tempting, beckoning, the concrete and cobblestones, soft and comforting as old shoes. I picked up my grips and walked along Fifth Street. Purposefully I walked, wondering why I could almost never bring myself to call her Helen. I had to break the habit. I would walk to the top of Bunker Hill and open my arms to her and say, "Helen, I love you."

We would start over again. Maybe we'd buy a little house in Woodland Hills, the Kansas type, with a chickenyard and a dog. Oh, Helen, I've missed you so, and now I know what I want. Maybe she wouldn't like Woodland Hills. Maybe she preferred the hotel. It had aged so well, like an aristocrat, like Helen herself. I would choose a room for writing and we would complete our days together. Oh, Helen. Forgive me for ever leaving you. It will never happen again.

I rode on the trolley to the crest of Bunker Hill, and looked at the hotel in the distance. It was magic, like a castle in a book of fairy tales. I knew she would have me this time. I felt the strength of my years, and I knew I was stronger than she, and that she would melt in my arms. I entered the hotel and lowered my suitcases against the wall. She was not behind the desk. I had to smile as I crossed to the desk and rang the bell. When there was no answer I struck the bell again, harder. The door opened slightly. There stood the man I had seen before, the man who said he was her brother. He did not come forward, and spoke in a whisper.

"Yes?"

"I'm looking for Helen."

"She's not here," he said, and closed the door. I walked around the desk and knocked. He opened the door and stood there crying.

"She's gone. She's dead."

"How?" I said. "When?"

"A week ago. She died of a stroke."

I felt myself weakening, as I staggered toward an armchair at the window. I didn't want to cry. Something deep and abiding had caved in, swallowing me up. I felt my chest heaving. The brother came over and stood beside me, crying.

"I'm sorry," he said.

I got up, hefted my suitcase, and walked out. At the little depot on Angel's Flight I sat on a park bench and let my grief have its way. For two hours I was there, grief-stricken and bewildered. I had thought of many things since knowing her, but never her death. For all her years, she nourished a love in me. Now it was gone. Now that she was dead I could think of her no longer. I had sobbed and whimpered and wept until it was all gone, all of it, and as always I found myself alone in the world.

The manager of the Filipino hotel was glad to see me. It was no surprise when he said that my room was unoccupied. It was my kind of room. I deserved it—the smallest, most uninviting room in Los Angeles. I started up the stairs and pushed open the door to the dreadful hole.

"You forgot something," the manager said. He stood in the doorway holding my portable typewriter. It startled me, not because it was there, but because I had completely forgotten it. He placed it on the table and I thanked him. Closing the door, I opened a suitcase and took out a copy of Knut Hamsun's *Hunger*. It was a treasured piece, constantly with me since the day I stole it from the Boulder library. I had read it so many times that I could recite it. But it did not matter now. Nothing mattered.

I stretched out on the bed and slept. It was twilight when I awakened and turned on the light. I felt better, no longer tired. I went to the typewriter and sat before it. My thought was to write a sentence, a single perfect sentence. If I could write one good sentence I could write two and if I could write two I could write three, and if I could write three I could write forever. But suppose I failed? Suppose I had lost all of my beautiful talent? Suppose it had burned up in the fire of Biff Newhouse smashing my nose or Helen Brownell dead forever? What would happen to me? Would I go to Abe Marx and become a busboy again? I had seventeen dollars in my wallet. Seventeen dollars and the fear of writing. I sat erect before the typewriter and blew on my fingers. Please God, please Knut Hamsun, don't desert me now. I started to write and I wrote:

> *"The time has come," the Walrus said,*
>   *"To talk of many things:*
> *Of shoes—and ships—and sealing wax—*
>   *Of cabbages—and kings—"*

I looked at it and wet my lips. It wasn't mine, but what the hell, a man had to start someplace.

—*Dreams from Bunker Hill*

I T WAS A LARGE HOUSE because we were people with big plans. The first was already there, a mound at her waist, a thing of lambent movement, slithering and squirming like a ball of serpents. In the quiet hours before midnight I lay with my ear to the place and heard the trickling as from a spring, the gurgles and sucks and splashings.

I said, "It certainly behaves like the male of the species."

"Not necessarily."

"No female kicks that much."

But she did not argue, my Joyce. She had the thing within her, and she was remote and disdainful and quite beatified.

Still, I didn't care for the bulge.

"It's unaesthetic," and I suggested she wear something to pack it in.

"And kill it?"

"They make special things. I saw them."

She looked at me with coldness—the ignorant one, the fool who had passed by in the night, a person no more, malefic, absurd.

The house had four bedrooms. It was a pretty house. There was a picket fence around it. There was a tall peaked roof. There was a corridor of rose bushes from the street to the front door. There was a wide terra cotta arch over the front door. There was a solid brass knocker on the door. There was a 37 in the house number, and that was my lucky number. I used to cross the street and look at the whole thing with my mouth open.

My house! Four bedrooms. Space. Two of us lived there now, and one was coming. Eventually there would be seven. It was my dream. At thirty there was still time for a man to raise seven. Joyce was twenty-four. One every other year. One coming, six to go. How beautiful the world! How vast the sky! How rich the dreamer! Naturally we would have to add a room or two.

"Do you have whims? Peculiar tastes? I understand it happens. I been reading up on it."

"Of course not."

She was reading too: Gesell, Arnold: *Infant and Child in the Culture of Today*.

"How is it?"

"Very informative."

She looked through the French windows to the street. It was a busy street, just off Wilshire, where the busses roared, where the traffic sounded like the lowing of cattle, a steady roar sometimes zippered down the middle by the shriek of sirens, yet detached, far away, two hundred feet away.

"Can't we have some new drapes? Do we have to have yellow drapes and green valances?"

"Valance? What's a valance, Mother?"

"For God's sake don't call me that."

"Sorry."

She went back to Gesell, Arnold: *Infant and Child in the Culture of Today*. There was solid reading comfort in pregnancy. The mound made a superb place to prop books, almost chin high, easy to turn pages. She was very pretty, with gray eyes incredibly bright. Something new was added to those eyes. Fearlessness. It was startling. You looked away. I glanced at the windows and found out what valances were because that was the only green at the windows, the skirt on top, ruffled.

"What kind of valance do you want, honey?"

"And please don't honey me. I don't like it."

I left her sitting there, the gray eyes bright with menace, the tight mouth around a cigarette holder, the long white fingers clutching Gesell. I walked out into my front yard and stood among roses and gloated over my house. The rewards of authorship. Me, author, John Fante, composer of three books. First book sold 2300 copies. Second book sold 4800 copies. Third book sold 2100 copies. But they don't ask for royalty statements in the picture business. If you have what they want at the moment they pay you, and pay you well. At that moment I had what they wanted, and every Thursday there came this big check.

A gentleman arrived about the valances. He was queer, with pellucid fingernails and a Paisley scarf under his belted sports coat. He wrung his tapered fingers and there was an intimacy between him and Joyce I could not share. They laughed and chatted over tea and cakes and she was delighted to have the companionship of a cock without spurs. He shuddered at the green valances, squealed in triumph as he tore them down and replaced them with blue. He sent for a truck, and the furniture was hauled away to be re-covered to match the valances.

Blue soothed Joyce. Now she was very happy. She began to wash windows. She waxed floors. She didn't like the washing machine and did the laundry by hand. Twice a week we had someone in to do the heavy work, but Joyce fired the woman.

"I'll do it alone. I don't need help."

She got very tired from so much work. There were ten shirts piled up, carefully ironed. There was a red place on her thumb, a burn. Her hair hung down, she was haggard and indeed very tired. But the bump was firm, right out there, not tired at all.

"I can't go on much longer," she groaned. "This big house and all."

"But why do you do it? You know you mustn't."

"Do you like living in dirty surroundings?"

"Call somebody. We can afford it now."

Ah, she detested me, gritting her teeth, bravely pushing back her fallen hair. She picked up a dustcloth and staggered into the dining room, there to polish the table, taking long desperate strokes, utterly weary, propped on her elbows, gasping for breath.

"Let me help you."

"Don't touch me. Don't you dare!"

She sank into a chair, her hair hanging down, her burnt thumb aching, yet a badge for nobility, her bright weary eyes staring dangerously, the dust rag loose in her hand, a wistful smile on her lips, an expression denoting nostalgia, informing me that her thought was of a happier time, probably San Francisco in the summer of 1940, when her body was slender, when there were no back-breaking chores, when she was free and unmarried, climbing all over Telegraph Hill with her easel and paints, writing tragic love sonnets as she gazed at the Golden Gate.

"You ought to have a maid, all day long."

For those were the fat carnal days for the scribbler, and money was piling up with Thursday coming once a week, bringing my agent full of wit and camaraderie and what was left after he and the government cut up the Paramount check. And yet, there was plenty for us all.

"Go shopping, dear. Buy yourself some things."

God help me. I had forgotten the bulge, and I tried vainly to suck the words back into my mouth. But she did not forget and I had to pretend I wasn't looking when she came sweeping down the stairs, a white balloon of a wife, holding back belches and pacing here and there like a prisoner.

She said, "Stop staring."

She said, "I suppose you spend the whole day looking at slender actresses."

She said, "What are you thinking about?"

She said, "Never again. This is the first and last."

And sometimes I would look up to find her staring at me and shaking her head.

"In God's name, why did I ever marry you?"

I kept quiet, smiling foolishly, because I didn't know why either, but I was very glad and proud that she had.

—Full of Life

A T 9:27 ON THE MORNING of March 18th, in the seventh month of her confinement, Joyce Fante fell through the kitchen floor of our house. The sheer weight of her—she had gained twenty-five pounds and tipped the scale at one hundred and forty-four-plus—the condition of the woodwork, came to a shuddering climax as the termite-infested floor boards collapsed beneath the tearing linoleum and the woman with the big bump sank to the ground three feet below.

I was upstairs in the bathtub at the time, and I remember distinctly the minute events coming before and after the calamity. First there was this fine quiet morning, all decked out in the golden gloss of the sun, there was the placidity of the bath, the mysterious evocations of confined water, the conjuring of faraway things, and then, from somewhere, from everywhere, the quivering of the atmosphere, the ominous portent of chain reaction in fissionable materials. A moment later I heard her scream. It was a theater scream, Barbara Stanwyck trapped by a rapist, and it plucked my spinal column like a giant's fingers.

I jumped out of the tub and opened the door. Down there I could hear Joyce shrieking. My one thought was the child—the precious white melon.

"I'm coming, Joyce. Be brave, darling. I'm coming!"

I had a gun in my room, but in that moment my only thought was her need for me. Even as I dashed downstairs naked and frightened I somehow knew those were my last mortal steps, that we would die together, that we might have lived had I been armed.

At first I didn't see her. Then I found her before the kitchen range, even as she had fallen, snug in the neat cave-in, but cut off as if she were a midget, a slice of ham in one hand, a skillet in the other, with many eggs broken and leaking around her. She was more angry than hurt, melted butter trickling from her hair and mingling with her tears, stringy egg yolk dripping from her elbows.

"Get me out of here, if you please."

I pulled her out. She was surprisingly calm. I stood looking down at the floor.

"Woh hoppen?"

Her fingers probed the mound, searching for life. She went to the telephone and began dialing. "Tell Dr. Stanley to hurry. It's an emergency." She hung up and walked to the stairs.

"How'd it happen?"

She didn't answer. A moment later she was in bed. I buzzed around, trying to get her things. She was white-faced but very calm. Then she closed her eyes. It scared me. I shook her.

"You all right?"

"I think so."

She closed her eyes again. I got scared again. I ran downstairs and got her some brandy. She didn't want any. I asked her not to close her eyes.

"I'm just resting."

"I don't think you ought to close your eyes."

"I'm only resting until the doctor comes."

Dr. Stanley was there in twenty minutes. I took him upstairs and he began to examine her. The fall had caused no injury to herself or the child. He put away his stethoscope. I went downstairs to the front door with him. I thought we should have a man-to-man talk about all this.

"Anything I can do, Doc?"

"No. Not a thing."

There was cold glitter in his eyes. He was getting tired of us. We were taking up a lot of his time.

I went back to the kitchen and stood before the hole in the floor. Fungus and termites had eaten the wood. It crumbled like soft bread in my hands. I crossed the room to the sink and banged my heel against the floor. The blow punctured it, leaving a hole. Apparently the entire floor was rotted. In the breakfast nook I hit the wall with my fist. My knuckles sank through spongy plaster and wood. I climbed the table in the breakfast nook to check the ceiling, but my weight made the table legs sink into the floor. I walked into the dining room and stood before an expanse of a pale green wall, freshly painted, immaculate. I raised my fist to let fly, but inside me there was a great sickness and I was afraid to strike.

My house! Why had this happened to John Fante? What had I done to upset the rhythm of the stars in their courses? I went back to Joyce's hole and stared. I picked up a piece of rotten wood. There I saw them, the little white beasties, crawling in the dead wood, the wood of my house, and I took one between my fingers, his little white legs pawing the air—a termite, an inhuman beast, and I killed it; I, who couldn't bear killing anything, but I had to snuff out his life for what he and his vile breed had done to my house. It was the first termite I had ever killed. All those years I had seen them about, watching them in curious admiration. I was a firm believer in the live-and-let-live philosophy, and this was my thanks, this loathsome treachery. Well, there was something wrong with my thinking, there had to be some change in my relations with insects, the hard reality of the facts had to be reckoned, and I started then and there to kill them, breaking the wood open, squashing them, crushing out their nefarious little lives as they ran panic-stricken through my fingers.

—Full of Life

JOYCE WAS IN THE LIVING ROOM READING, surrounded with books. I could see Papa in the back yard. He sat under a wide lawn umbrella, a wine jug on the steel table beside him, a cigar in his mouth as he stretched his legs and took his ease, studying the house.

"What did he say about the hole in the kitchen?"

"He wants to consider it," Joyce said.

"There's nothing to consider. Just fix the hole."

She closed the book. "Let him think about it. He's full of ideas."

"No matter what he thinks, the hole has to be fixed. It was a mistake to bring him down here. He's old and set in his ways. I predict trouble."

"That's not a very nice way to feel about your own father."

"I can't help it. He's turned into an eccentric."

"You should have thought of that before you asked him. The Fourth Commandment, you know."

"The Fourth Commandment?"

"Honor thy father and thy mother."

I gave her a quick look. She was a picture of enormous placidity, her great tummy sitting proudly on her lap like another person. It gave you the feeling you talked to two people. Behind her reading glasses the gray eyes were clear and beautiful. She sat with a dozen books around her, some on the coffee table, others piled beside her on the divan. She was reading Chesterton and Belloc and Thomas Merton and François Mauriac. There were books by Karl Adam, Fulton Sheen and Evelyn Waugh. I glanced at some of the titles: *The Spirit of Catholicism, The Faith of Our Fathers, The Idea of a University*. Some of these books were mine, out of a dusty box in the garage, but most were new and fresh from the bookstore. It was incredible to find her with such books, for she was a cold materialist; she belonged to a semantic group; nay, she was practically an atheist, with a hard scientific patience for facts.

"What you doing?"

"I'm thinking of making a change." She took off her reading glasses. "If God is all-good, why does He permit crippled children to be born?"

It frightened me at once.

"Is something wrong with the baby?"

"Of course not. I'm asking you a question."

"I don't know the answer."

She smiled with satisfaction.

"But I do."

"That's just wonderful."

"Don't you want to hear it?"

I couldn't take her seriously. It was but another whim of her pregnancy. Here was the same girl who liked chili sauce on her avocado salad. It would pass as soon as her figure returned. It was a whim. It had to be. I liked an atheistic wife. Her position made matters easy for me. It simplified a planned family. We had no scruples about contraceptives. Ours had been a civil marriage. We were not chained by religious tenets. Divorce was there, any time we wanted it. If she became a Catholic there would be all manner of complications. It was hard to be a good Catholic, very hard, and that was why I had left the Church. To be a good Catholic you had to break through the crowd and help Him pack the cross. I was saving the breakthrough for later. If she broke through I might have to follow, for she was my wife. No; this was a whim of hers, a passing fancy. It had to be.

"You'll get over it," I said. "Any calls?"

"Nothing important."

I phoned my secretary at the studio. My calls were routine. Somebody wanted to play golf, and somebody else wanted to play poker. My producer was in New York, and the front office was very quiet. It was a good time to proceed with arrangements about repairing the kitchen. There was lumber to buy, and Papa would probably need a helper. I walked out to the back yard and took a chair under the big umbrella. Papa sat quietly, his feet on the table. His jug was almost empty. He watched his cigar smoke climb into the branches of a small mock orange tree in the center of the yard.

"What do you think, Papa? Will it cost much?"

"My eyes hurt. No good, this country."

"Smog. You'll have to replace some of the joists."

"Did I ever tell you about my Uncle Mingo and the bandits?"

"Sure, lots of times. Will you need a helper on the job?"

"Brave man, my Uncle Mingo. He was an Andrilli, your Grandma's

brother. They hang him right there in Abruzzi. The *carabiniere* . . . Two
bullets in his shoulder. They hang him anyway. His wife standing there,
crying. Sixty-one years ago. I seen it myself. Coletta Andrilli, pretty
woman.

He drank, the jug in both hands, his Adam's apple rising and falling.
He put down the jug and resumed his pleasant thoughts. I told him there
was a lumber yard not far away. If he would compute the materials needed
we could drive over to the lumber yard that very day.

"I'm anxious to get started, Papa."

Papa spoke to his cigar: "He's anxious to get started. I been here two
hours. I'm tired. I don't sleep good on the train, but he wants to get
started."

I apologized. He was right, of course. I had been very thoughtless.
"Certainly, Papa. I don't mean to rush you. Take it easy for a few days. Get
a good rest. The kitchen can wait."

"I'll take care of the kitchen, kid. You take care of the writing."

His face showed fatigue, gray bristles at his chin, the tips of his mouth
turned down, his eyes half open and bloodshot, smarting from the poison
gas in the air.

"Enjoy yourself, Papa. Rest. Anything you want just ask for it. You
need more wine?"

"Don't worry about the wine, kid. I'll take care of the wine."

"I'll order you some Chianti, Papa. Real Chianti. Anything else?"

"Typewrite machine."

"I got a portable upstairs. But you can't type, Papa."

He studied his cigar. "You type. I talk."

It touched me. Only last evening he had left Mama, and now he
wanted to send her a little message. "That's fine, Papa. She'll be very
happy."

"She's dead."

"Who?"

"Coletta Andrilli."

"I thought you wanted to write a letter to Mama."

"What for? I seen her yesterday. Good God, kid."

"Why the typewriter?"

"My Uncle Mingo and the bandits. We write the story. For the little
boy, so he'll know about Uncle Mingo. Make him feel good, proud."

"Not today, Papa. We'll do it, but later."

"Today. Now."

"But why today?"

Fiercely he answered, frightened he answered: "Because I might die any time. Any minute."

"Some other time."

Quick pain smothered his face. Without a word he rose and walked very fast into the house. I saw him hurry through the living room without speaking to Joyce. He clambered up the stairs. As I reached the living room the door of the guest bedroom closed sharply. Joyce peered at me over her reading glasses.

"What did you do to that poor old man?"

"Nothing. He wants me to write a story about his Uncle Mingo."

"You refused, of course."

"I said, later."

"After Dorothy Lamour and the gypsies?"

"Don't be clever."

"It's wrong to treat your father like this. It's a sin. You know very well that you should reverence the aged, specially your parents. It's your sacred obligation before God."

Big and calm, she was. A big white rock, unperturbed as the breakers smashed against her. A tower of ivory, she was, a morning star, a rolling hill, a Boulder Dam.

"What's eating you, anyhow?"

"I can't allow you to abuse your father."

I groped around for an answer, but there was none. It shook me up because she was so sure of herself. She was a woman of infinite tact who rarely lashed out. I thought of apologizing to Papa, but that would trap me into a session with his Uncle Mingo. Not that I hated Uncle Mingo. I didn't hate Uncle Mingo. I vowed again that I would write his story, but I just didn't want to write the goddamn thing at that moment.

"I'm going to the studio."

She had resumed her reading. She looked up.

"What did you say?"

"I'm going to the studio."

"If God is all-good and all-knowing, why does He create certain souls He knows will suffer eternal damnation?"

"I don't know."

"But I do," she smiled.

"Isn't that just ducky."

I walked out to the garage and got into the car. It was twenty minutes to the studio, through heavy crosstown traffic, but I was glad for the snarl of cars and the hooting of busses. Here was the temper of our time. After the baby was born, Joyce would feel it again, the comfort of confusion, the all-excluding necessity of staying alive on the earth. A woman's confinement was a bad time for a man. Creation gave her terrible strength and she got along without him. But it would pass. I saw her slim again, in black lace, starved for my arms. A first child improved their figures, ripened them. I was very happy when I got to the studio. I was reeling with love, savoring the joys to come.

My secretary was on her feet, waiting for me.

"Call your wife. It's urgent."

Even as I dialed, I saw her prostrate in the back of a taxi, a messy scene, the baby half born, Joyce moaning, the cab driver in terror, motorcycle police ripping an opening through Wilshire traffic, sirens shrieking as the cab roared to the hospital.

Joyce answered the phone.

"Your father's gone."

"Where'd he go?"

"Back to San Juan."

"But he can't. He hasn't any money."

"He's walking. Down Wilshire. I couldn't stop him."

"I'll get him."

I hung up, hurried out to the car, and raced toward Wilshire. A mile east of my house, I found him. I found him and wept. He sat on a bench on the boulevard, at a bus stop. His tool kit and roped suitcases were beside him. There on the corner he sat, an old man with his ruined possessions. He sat without hope, weary in a big town, at the edge of a river of automobiles, waves of monoxide gas flooding his tired face. Yes, I wept. I wanted to beat my breast and say, *mea culpa, mea culpa,* for I saw the pathos of the aged, the loneliness of the last years, my Papa, my old Papa, all the way from Abruzzi, a peasant to the end, sitting on the bench, alone in the world. Why, sure, I would write his story! Why, sure, we would put it down about Uncle Mingo, for the baby to read! It was the most important thing a man had to write. I parked the car and wiped my eyes and went to him on the bench.

"Papa. What you doing here?"

"Hello, kid."

I put my hand on his shoulder.

"What was Uncle Mingo like, Papa? Tell me the whole thing from the beginning."

"He had red hair, kid. Big feet. Very strong man."

But he couldn't continue. He began to cry, and I cried too, and we put our arms around one another and cried and cried because we knew the importance of Uncle Mingo and we loved him so much after all these years.

"Come on, Papa. Let's go home. We'll write it down. I'm hot now, Papa. I'll write the whole damn thing."

I tried to help him from the bench, but he pulled away.

"I got no home, kid. Nobody wants me."

"Come on, Papa. We'll get you some wine, then we'll go home and write it."

"A little bottle, maybe."

He took out a blue polka dot bandana and wiped his eyes and sent a blast from his nose. Then he pulled out his pocketbook with the many compartments, and I saw the garlic again, like a snarling little brown flame, and he poked around and his fingers held some coins, sixty or seventy cents, which he offered me.

"A little bottle, for your papa."

"Put it away, Papa. I'll get you the best wine in the world. Save your money, Papa. I got money."

We carried the luggage to the car and he got in beside me. So he had forgiven me, and it was good to be forgiven, and I wanted to show my thanks. We drove to a liquor store with many handsome bottles from everywhere, and he looked about, his sadness vanishing in that shimmer of beautiful bottles. Only a little wine, he insisted, something to wet his lips, maybe a pint of California wine, but the great wide world was on these shelves, and it was for my Papa. Some Cabernet from Chile, and he weakened and we ordered a few bottles; and some Château Lyonnat; and a case of golden Bordeaux, and he smiled and thought it was very foolish and expensive for a man who wanted only a sip or two of California claret. Yes, Joyce was right, and I must honor the aged, pay homage to my Papa, and he almost sobbed to hold that bottle of Chianti wrapped in straw, so we bought a case of that too.

"It's too much," he said, and he wrung his hands, but he got into the spirit of the thing presently, he lit a cigar and a shrewd merchant-prince aspect came over him, and he walked up and down the handsome store, pulling out bottles, reading labels, putting bottles back. He was a man of superb taste, he knew Portuguese brandies, and he did not forget Martell. But there was an exotic side to his nature too, for he liked the Florentine anisette made by the Italian monks, and when he saw the tall golden bottle of Galliano I knew he must have that too, an old man must have Galliano, the bottle is so exquisitely tall, the liqueur as yellow as the Italian sun.

The clerk promised quick delivery to my house, but Papa trusted only himself with the Galliano, and he felt he should bring the Martell too. We drove home and pulled into the garage. He got out carefully, measuring each movement.

Joyce was glad to see us come in together and she kissed us, and her lips on my cheeks were the lips of a nun.

"Bless you, dearest," she said.

It was the first time in her life she ever said such a thing. Papa opened the Galliano, and the Martell, and we got comfortable in the living room. Like an alchemist in some ancient Venetian cellar, he poured himself two ounces of Martell and smiled in blissful content as he floated an ounce of Galliano upon it. He sipped, and such ecstasy seized him I thought he might float gently to the ceiling.

"My Uncle Mingo had red hair," he said. "He lived in a stone house with walls three feet thick. . . ."

Joyce brought a plate of cheeses and salami.

"One time I said, 'Uncle Mingo, what makes you so strong?' Uncle Mingo, he picked me up with one hand, held me straight out, and he said, 'Olive oil.'"

We sampled the Galliano, Joyce and I.

"Uncle Mingo's brother, he was the mayor of Torcelli. We had poor roads in those days. Five thousand people. My cousin Aldo died when he was four. Everybody came to the fiesta. Cheese. Antonio didn't like the priest. Some wheat, but mostly oats. I went up there, and I said, 'Vico, what's going on here?' "That was before we had electric lights . . ."

Darkness came. The phone rang many times, and Joyce tiptoed to answer it. She wouldn't let me move. I had to stay there and listen, get the facts. Papa put the Galliano aside and drank the brandy straight. The doorbell rang; some friends of Joyce. She whisked them past us quietly, to the den.

"Uncle Mingo's sister, Della, she married Giuseppe Marcosa. One day I seen d'Annunzio in town, riding a bicycle. Hot in summer, cold in winter. Big man, Uncle Mingo. Chocolate sometimes, but no coffee. Walls, three feet thick. Maybe two acres. Plenty of rock. Six feet six, maybe. Good man. Strong. Tile roof. When Italo died, whole town was there. I said to myself, they could bring the fish from Bari, but he was no good, that Luigi. How could a man steal his own daughter's dowry? I knew there was trouble . . ."

Joyce left her guests to bring my supper on a tray. Papa wasn't hungry. I gritted my teeth and kept listening. Joyce went back to the den and her friends. Their laughter came through. Papa was half finished with the brandy.

"We didn't get no rain that year. My cousin went to Naples. Oh, we had a few grapes but the crop was poor. Olive country, rock in the soil. No barber shops in Torcelli, you cut your own. It didn't snow till the 19th of January. Uncle Mingo came over to the house, and he was mad . . ."

The doorbell rang again. It was the delivery man from the liquor store. He piled sacks and cases in the hall. Papa staggered into the kitchen and returned with a corkscrew. He opened a bottle of Chianti. For a moment I thought the ordeal was over. He swayed uncertainly, pulling at the bottle, but he came back to the living room and sat down again.

"Let me see now—where was I?"

I would see it through to the end. I would die in that room, chained to that chair, but I would hear it all. "Your Uncle Mingo came to the house, and he was mad."

"Sure he was mad! How much can a man stand? You don't know. You sit here in Los Angeles, with plenty to eat, but what do you know about a man's problems? All those rock, falling on his land. The little boy was sick. My mother went over. Wind blowing all the time. The goat died, and Dino went to Rome to be a priest. The taxes were too high. I was seventeen before I got to Naples. Had trouble with my eyes. Uncle Mingo took off his shoe, and his foot was bleeding. We had olive oil, but the frost ruined the grape. No lights, no gas. Elena, my brother's wife, had a baby. Uncle Mingo got him by the neck, and he said, 'Alfredo, I'll break every bone in your body.' That was the night it rained. They were all afraid of Uncle Mingo. . . ."

He never got to the bandits. Joyce's friends departed in respectful silence; he drank two bottles of Chianti, and he spoke of many things, but I never heard the details of Uncle Mingo and the bandits. Nearing midnight, Joyce tiptoed upstairs. We sat in the small light from a table lamp. Slowly, interminably, he went to sleep. I roused him, but still asleep he climbed the stairs, his arm around my shoulder. I helped him to his room, pulled off his clothes, and covered him up, long underwear and all.

My work was not yet finished. In the morning he would ask for the story. I went to my room and uncovered the portable. I set down the date and wrote it in the form of a letter.

Dear Child to Be Born:

Tonight your Grandpa told me the story of his Uncle Mingo and the bandits. Uncle Mingo was your great-great-uncle. I write this tale because your Grandpa wishes it preserved for the day when you will be able to read and possibly enjoy it . . .

I thought it could be done in twenty minutes. But out of that chaos of jumbled anecdotes something had to emerge. It came, a mood. At four in the morning, my teeth afire from cigarettes, I was still pounding away. To hell with the kid; I could sell this one to the *Saturday Evening Post.* Through the night I heard Papa snore. I heard him rise and groan and make his way to the bathroom. There was much commotion in the hall, and the pattering of many feet. If Papa was not in possession of the bathroom, Joyce was. Out of their rooms these two people kept coming in a steady procession to the bathroom. Once I heard rapid pacing in the hall. It was Joyce, awaiting her turn. Papa emerged in his long underwear. They looked at one another, smiled in somnambulistic understanding, and went their separate ways.

I came downstairs next day at noon. I had it with me, twenty good pages about an Italian bandit, a heroic figure with red hair. I found Papa in the dining room. He had a sheet of drawing paper spread across the table, and he worked closely with a pencil and a ruler.

"Here it is, Papa. Uncle Mingo's story."

I tossed it on the drawing paper. He picked up the sheets and handed them back. "Save it for the boy."

"Don't you want to read it?"

"What I got to read it for? Good God, kid, I lived it."

—*Full of Life*

I THOUGHT IT WAS A WHIM OF HERS, a passing fancy, but now she saw no reason to hide the facts. Since the beginning of pregnancy she had felt the pull of religion, the urgency for change. It had grown stronger with the child. At first she had concealed it, even from herself, but the deception made her miserable and she began to read, searching, the mysterious urge increasing. She had kept it from me, but during my absence up North she had made the decision: she was going to join the Church.

She was so ripe now, so juicy, so huge. The gray eyes devoured you with the child she bore, you felt yourself drowning in their hypnotic depths if you stared too long, and the passion of faith throbbed in them. I often found her staring past me, entranced in some spiritual pipe dream. At noon the Angelus sounded in the steeple of St. Boniface, the parish church. She instantly dropped whatever was at hand, her book, her comb, the dustcloth, and recited the Angelus prayers. It made me uneasy.

"Why are you embarrassed?" she asked. "You're supposed to be a liberal. Prove it, right here in your own home."

At meals she announced that we would now say grace, and I would look at Papa and he would shrug at me, and we would stare foolishly at our plates until grace was said. She was in deadly earnest. She spent hours in her room, smoking cigarettes as she lay on the bed and reflected on the fleeting quality of life. I could not fathom it. Sometimes I thought it was the fear of death in relation to childbirth. One night the old passion returned, and I slipped in beside her and put my arms around her. She was sound asleep. Then she woke, snapped on the bed lamp, got to one elbow, and stared down at me, vapors of warm piety coming from her eyes.

"You should practice self-denial," she smiled. "It will make you very strong."

"Who cares about being strong?"

"Today I read a poem. It went like this":

Take all the pleasures of all the spheres
And multiply each through endless years —
One minute of heaven is worth them all.

I made the most dignified exit possible under the circumstances, and crawled back into my own bed, wondering where it all would end.

Twice a week she went to the rectory of St. Boniface for religious instruction. She read the catechism and a few simple tracts the priest had offered. But these were not enough. She was a rapid, voracious reader, wolfing everything she could find on the subject. She read canon law, Aquinas, à Kempis, St. Augustine, the papal encyclicals, and the *Catholic Encyclopedia.*

One evening as I lolled in the bathtub, she knocked on the door and came in.

"Do you believe in free will?"

I could answer that one, remembering it from my schoolboy catechism.

"Certainly I believe in free will."

"Do idiots have free will? The insane?"

That wasn't in the catechism.

"I don't know about idiots."

She beamed in serenity.

"But I do."

"Hurray for you!"

In four weeks, a few days before entering the hospital, she planned to be baptized. She was having a most absorbing and difficult time selecting a patron saint. She screened them down, and out of hundreds she reduced her choice to one of two: Saint Elizabeth and Saint Anne. I did not wish to become involved in this business, but she was always talking about it.

Finally I said, "What's wrong with Saint Teresa? She's got a big reputation, all over the world."

"Too popular," Joyce said. "Not obscure, not mysterious enough. Besides, she was an awfully plain woman. Personally I lean toward Saint Elizabeth. She was very rich and very beautiful. She wrote well, too. I feel very close to Saint Elizabeth. I think she understands me better that anyone in the world."

"Isn't that just ducky."

She gave me a sweet tolerant smile.

"I'm ready for your scoffs. I've prepared myself."

"I'm not scoffing. I just don't want to become involved. I got plenty of troubles of my own."

"You're in my prayers constantly," she said. "I know how troubled you are. I was that way too, once."

"Oh, stop it."

"But I *do* pray for you. And for the baby. And for world peace."

She was suddenly irresistible, and I made a lunge for her, but all I got was a fat kiss on the cheek as the white balloon poked me in the stomach.

She went shopping for rosaries, a statue of Saint Elizabeth, and a number of crucifixes. She brought little bottles of holy water and attached a bronze font inside the door of her bedroom, within easy reach of her hand, so that she could make the sign of the cross with consecrated water whenever she entered the room. The statue of Saint Elizabeth went on an elaborate knickknack shelf in the corner. She heaped flowers before it, lit candles, and read the saint's works.

I said to Papa, "What do you think about Joyce becoming a Catholic?"

"Good. Fine."

"What's good about it?"

"Is it bad?"

"I like to plan my family."

"Then plan it. Get going. Babies."

"Babies, sure. Lots of babies. But I want them when I want them, Papa. No birth control in the Church, Papa."

"Birth control?"

"You can't stop them from coming. They just keep coming, on and on."

"Is that bad? That's good."

"We're not peasants any more, Papa. We got to stop someplace."

His eyes squinted.

"I don't like that kind of talk."

"A man should be able to say when he wants a baby."

"You heard me, kid. I don't like it."

"Suppose they come, and we got no money?"

"Get money."

"It's rough, Papa."

Up came his fist, the fingers splayed, grabbing my shirt.

"Not *my* grandchildren, understand? You leave them alone. Let them come. They got as much right here as you."

I took his fist away.

"It has nothing to do with rights, Papa. It's a question of economics."

"Cut out reading them books."

"Books—what books? I can't support too many."

"We couldn't afford none either, me and Mama. Not one. But we had four. We did it without money, a few dollars, but never enough money. You want we should use something from the drugstore, and you not even born today, without your sister and brothers, and me and Mama alone in the world? For what?"

Stated that way, it was unanswerable.

"I guess you're basically a religious man, Papa. You really believe."

"Grandchildren. That's what I believe in. And leave them books alone."

Yes, she was in deadly earnest, with the passion of a convert. She liked walking up and down before the statue of Saint Elizabeth, saying the rosary. Through the half-open door I saw her moving back and forth, she and the child, her lips reciting the beads, her eyes catching a view of herself in the mirror as she tried to pull her tummy in and up.

One morning she walked with me out to the garage.

"You know of course that we must get married as soon as possible."

"We're already married. The justice of the peace married us in Reno."

"It was a civil ceremony. As far as I'm concerned, it doesn't count."

"It counts with me."

"I want my marriage sanctified."

"You mean—we've been living in adultery all these years?"

"We'll be married after my baptism. It's a lovely ceremony. We'll be married to the end of our lives." She smiled. "You won't be able to divorce me, ever."

You do not argue with the mother of your coming child. You do the very best you can, and try to keep her happy. You have lost caste in her eyes, you are barely tolerated, the part you have played is little enough, she becomes the star of the show, and you are expected to knuckle under, for that is the way the script is written. Otherwise you might upset her, bringing anguish, and in turn upset the child.

"What do you want me to do, darling? In your own words, tell me exactly what you want me to do."

"Father Gondalfo is coming to see you. He's my instructor. I want you to talk to him."

Two days later Father John Gondalfo came to our house. That afternoon I found him sitting in the living room with Papa and Joyce. Father

Gondalfo was the hard-boiled type. He had been a Marine chaplain in the South Pacific. For over an hour he had been waiting for me. Because of the heat, he had removed his coat, and he sat in a white T-shirt, the black hair of his beefy chest seeping through the weave of the shirt. He had the arms of a wrestler and kept himself in condition by playing handball against the wall of the parish garage. He was a young priest, no more than forty-two, with a dark Sicilian face, a broken nose, and a crew haircut. He looked like a guard or tackle from Santa Clara. The moment I saw him I realized he was, like me, of Italian descent, and the consanguinity quickly established a violent familiarity. He crushed my knuckles in a handshake.

"It's five-thirty, Fante. Where you been?"

I told him, working.

"What time you knock off?"

I told him, a little past four.

"Four? Where you been, the last hour and a half?"

I told him, to Lucey's for a highball.

"Don't you know your wife's pregnant?"

Joyce sat in a big chair, the great mound lolling indolently in her lap, her knees spread slightly to support it. She adored Father John. I sensed Papa's admiration too, as well as a slight hostility toward me.

"What's wrong with drinking here in your own home?" Father John said. "With your wife and this great man who's your father? Ever think of that?"

I marveled at his shoulders, the black intensity of his eyes. "Sure, Father, I drink at home, lots."

"Time you got wise to yourself, Fante."

"Certainly, Father. But . . ."

"Don't argue with me, boy. You think I just come over on the ferry from Hoboken?"

I didn't want to argue with anybody. Looking at Joyce, I saw that she was caught up in the fervor of Father John's vague admonition. At that moment she didn't approve of me at all. Neither did Papa, who sat before a bottle of wine, wetting his lips and nodding sagely at the priest's words.

Father John smacked his mighty hands together, rubbed them hard, and said, "Well, let's get down to business. Fante, your wife intends to join the Holy Roman Catholic Church. Any objections?"

"No objections, Father."

And that was the simple truth. There could be no objections. I might wish it otherwise, I might hope that she postpone her desire for a while, but that was something else again.

"And what about you? Your father here, this great and wonderful man, tells me that he sweated and toiled to give you a fine Catholic education. But now you read books, and, if you please, you write books. Just what do you have against us, Fante? You must be very brilliant indeed. Tell me all about it. I'm listening."

"I don't have anything against the Church, Father. It's just that I want to think . . ."

"Ah, so that's it! The infallibility of the Holy Father. So you want to know if the Bishop of Rome is really infallible in matters of faith and morals. Fante, I shall clear that up for you at once: he is. Now, what else is bothering you?"

I crossed to Papa, took his bottle, and swigged from it. Father John's sudden attack had me rocking on my heels, and I had to get matters quiet in my mind.

"You see, Father. The Blessed Virgin Mary . . ."

"I'll tell you about the Blessed Virgin Mary, Fante. I'll let you have it straight, without equivocation. Mary, the Mother of God, was conceived without sin, and upon her death ascended into heaven. Surely a man of your intelligence can understand that."

"Yes, Father. I will accept that for the moment. But in the mass, at the consecration . . ."

"At the consecration, the bread and wine is changed into the body and blood of Christ. What else is eating you?"

"Well, Father. When a man goes to confession . . ."

"Christ gave his priests the power to forgive sins when he said, 'Receive ye the Holy Ghost. Whose sins you shall forgive, they are forgiven them; and whose sins you shall retain, they are retained.' It's right there in the New Testament. Read it yourself."

"I understand the words, Father. But in the doctrine of original sin . . ."

"Ho! So that's it! By original sin we mean that as children of our first parents we are conceived in sin and remain so until the glorious sacrament of baptism."

"Yes, Father. I know. But the resurrection . . ."

"The resurrection? For heaven's sake, Fante, that's simple enough. Christ our Lord was crucified, and then rose from the dead, which is the promise of immortality for all of his children. Or do you choose to die like a dog, consigned forever to oblivion?"

I sighed and sat down. There was nothing more to say. Papa cleared his throat, a small smile on his lips, as he raised the bottle. There was a curious warmth to his eyes. Ash from his cigar fell in gray disorder across his lap.

"The kid reads too much, Father. I been telling him for years."

So it was "the kid" now.

"But I like to read, Papa. It's part of my trade."

"It's them books, Father. Birth control, he told me himself."

"Birth control?" Father John smiled sadly as he shook his head. "I'll tell you about birth control in the Catholic Church. There ain't any."

"I told him, Father. I said, 'I don't like that stuff.' It's not the girl's fault, Father. She's a Protestant. She don't know no better. But him: he told me. 'I like to control my family,' he told me that, coupla days ago. Me, his own father."

"I did say something like that," I admitted. "But what I meant was this, Father. My income . . ."

"You see?" Papa interrupted. "Nearly four years, they been married. Plenty time for two, a little boy and a little girl. My grandchildren. But are they here, Father? Go upstairs. Look in all the rooms, under the beds, in the closets. You won't find them. Little Nicky and little Philomena. Nicky, he'd be about three now, talking to his Grandpa. The little girl, she'd be just walking. You see them around, Father? Go out in the back yard; look in the garage. No, you won't find them, because they ain't here. And it's *his* fault!" Papa's right forefinger, the one with the broken nail, shot toward me.

"Stop it, Papa."

"I won't stop it. I want to know, because I'm their Grandpa: Where's Nicky? Where's Philomena?"

"How do I know where they are?"

Joyce went over to Papa and sat down beside him. She spoke quietly, holding his big red paw. "There haven't been any others, Papa Fante. Really and truly."

This was not the way to handle him, for he could wallow in sentimentality. Sure enough, he began to get grief-stricken, his chin jerking, his eyes suddenly wet. I tried to appeal to Joyce with my eyes. It was true that I had opposed pregnancy until we could afford it. It was also true that she had been willing to risk it without money. But I had never thought of those times as distinct human entities, or given them names, those unconceived babies, and now in Joyce's face I saw the loss, the small despair, since Papa had stated it in that sentimental fashion.

"I am talking with my blood," Papa continued. "There's two I'll never see, but they're here, someplace, and their Grandpa's not feeling so good, because he can't buy them ice cream cones."

He began to weep, poking his big knuckles into his eyes and pushing the tears away. He took another swig from the bottle and stood up, a mixture of many moods, wiping his mouth, puffing his cigar, crying, savoring the wine, pleased with his role of a despairing grandfather, yet brokenhearted because the babies were not present. Father John put an arm around him, hugging him with rough affection. They grumbled something of a farewell in Italian and Papa staggered upstairs to sleep off the wine, his chin out, his chest out, bravely up the stairs to his room, triumphantly up the stairs.

We were silent a moment. Joyce dabbed her eyes and nose with a handkerchief.

"It's the wine," I explained. "The wine makes him very sentimental."

"And you?" the priest asked.

I shrugged. "I do the best I can."

"I wonder . . ."

He had to leave us. Papa had saddened him. I helped him into his black serge coat and the three of us went outside and across the lawn to his car. We shook hands.

"Watch your language around your father," he cautioned. "He's very sensitive."

"I know."

"I want you back in the Church."

"I'll try, Father."

—Full of Life

PEACE IN MY HOUSE, quiet, a time of great calm. She became another woman again. She was out of the fable now, out of the novels, a tale of motherhood, a woman in waiting. No more breaking of stones or mixing mortar. I never saw her so beautiful. She walked on quiet feet, a different perfume trailing after her. Every morning she went to early Mass. Every afternoon she visited the parish house for instructions. Father Gondalfo was rushing it a little, but it was at her insistence. In the evenings I walked with her to the church. She said the rosary, made the stations of the cross, or simply sat quietly, her hands folded in her lap.

It was a strange time for me. I sat beside her, not able to pray, to articulate a feeling for Christ. But it all came back to me, the memory of the old days when I was a boy and this cool and melancholy place meant so much. From the beginning she had assumed I would return with her. It had seemed the right thing to do. Somehow I would capture the old feeling, the reaching out with the fingers of my soul and grasping the rich fine joy of belief. Somehow I had felt it was always there, that I had but to move toward it with only a murmur of desire and it would cloak me in the vast comfort of God's womb. There was the scent of incense, the creaking of pews, the play of sunlight through stained-glass windows, the cool touch of holy water, the laughter of little candles, the stupendous reaching back into antiquity, the baffling realization that countless millions before me had been here and gone, that other billions would come and go through a million tomorrows. These were my thoughts as I sat beside my wife. These and the gradual realization that I had been wrong, that it was not easy to come back to your church, that the Church changeless was always there, but that I had changed. The drift of years had covered me like a mountain of sand. It was not easy to emerge. It was not easy to call out with a small voice and feel that I was being heard. I sat beside her, and I knew it would be very hard. Nay, I knew it would be almost impossible.

I sat beside her and enjoyed the sensation of a new kind of thinking. For one's thoughts were different here. Outside, beyond the heavy oak doors, you thought of taxes and insurance, of fade-outs and dissolves, you weighed the matter of Manhattans and Martinis, you suspected your agent of treachery, your friend of disloyalty, your neighbor of stupidity. And yet I could sit beside her before the altar, her small hands exquisite in green kid gloves, and I could adore her for the beauty of her effort, the striving of her heart, the mighty force that prompted her to be but a good woman, humble and grateful before God. I could sit beside her, my own lips dry for lack of words, I, the phrasemaker, and the pages of my soul were blank and unlettered, and I turned them one after another, seeking a rhyme, a few scattered words to articulate the fact that in this place I thought not of taxes and insurance, and my agent, my neighbor and friend were somehow disembodied, they assumed a spirituality, a beauty; they were entities and not beings, they were souls and not swine.

Yet, in spite of it all, I was not ready. Born a Catholic, I could not bring myself to return. Perhaps I expected too much; a shudder of joyful recognition, the dazzling splendor of faith reborn. Whatever it was, I could not return. There before me was the road, the signposts clearly marking the direction to peace of soul. I could not take the road. I could not believe that it was so easy. I was sure that beyond the next hill lay trouble.

—Full of Life

S HE LAY IN A SMALL OCEAN OF PAIN, the vapors of her anguish clouding the room. She lay upon sheets wet and writhing with perspiration, her mouth distorted, her teeth clenched, her eyes like balls of white milk. At first she did not see me, but as I closed the door she lifted herself out of the waves of her suffering, her fingers clutching the iron bar across the top of the bed as she pulled herself into a sitting position. The white balloon was like an enormous blister, shimmering with pain, too heavy for the wild strength in her bloodless fingers. She panted in exhaustion, her breath coming in harsh jerks through lips twisted in torment.

Then she knew I was there at the foot of her bed. She saw me with startled eyes. My heart went out to her in pity for the blinding pain. I could not find words of consolation, only the clichés, the adumbrations and traps of futile language, the miserable inadequacies. As I stood there with a dry throat, pain seized her. Her knees came up and an animal cry, scarcely more than a suppressed howl, came from her lips. It had rhythm and could be measured, a thin coiling ribbon of noise drawn through her teeth. When it was over and the pain had spent itself, she sighed gratefully and pushed back a mass of wet disheveled hair, her eyes fixed at the ceiling. Then she remembered I was there.

"Oh, I'm such a coward!" she moaned.

"You're nothing of the kind."

I went to her side. The bed was built like a large crib, with adjustable steel sides. As I bent over to kiss her, I saw her red mouth, the lips thick with the sensuality of pain. I saw the white avid eyes and her suffering overwhelmed me. But there was passion in her mouth, and she clung to me with such ferocity that it took all the strength of my thick wrists to break her arms away. She loved me, she moaned, she loved me, loved me, loved me.

Then the pains took her again, sending her rolling from side to side, her knees up, her fingers pulling at the bar above her, the ribbon of anguish spilling out. As the suffering subsided, the white eyes beat about me like captured birds, and the pain reached me too, and I got a terrible stomach-ache. It nearly doubled me up. I backed into a chair and sat down. She was watching me.

"You're sick," she said. "This whole thing has been too much for you."

"I'm fine."

"Drink this," she panted, and she reached for a glass of water on the bed table. But the pains leaped at her as her hand went out, and she twisted and rolled, pouring out the ribbon of noise from her throat. It doubled me up in agony, but I didn't cry out, I just moaned as a crazy upheaval went on inside me, the pain of green apples.

"Darling," she was saying. "Call the doctor. I *know* you're sick!"

"Me? I feel wonderful."

But I could see my reflection in the wall mirror, and I was white and popeyed and disgusted and enraged with myself.

"Don't worry about me," she gasped. "I'm doing wonderfully. The pains have stopped altogether. Look!" She held out her arms, smiling.

As I turned to see her, the pains were upon her again, and she struggled, her eyes softened now, full of tears, and when it was over again she covered her face with her hands and wept softly.

"Oh, God!" she cried. "I can't stand it much longer."

I would have done anything for her, my two arms, my feet, my hands, my life, all of it I would have given to lessen one pang of her anguish, but there I stood, unable to endure a spasmodic bellyache that finally sent me staggering, doubled up, into the hall.

Coming toward me was Dr. Stanley, and a nurse carrying a trayful of bottles and hypodermics.

They looked at me without speaking. Dr. Stanley took a phial of pills from the nurse's tray and tumbled one into his palm.

"Take this," he said.

I swallowed it in a fast gulp.

"My wife's in bad shape, Doc."

They sailed past me into the room. I waited. My bellyache subsided. In a few minutes they emerged, the doctor rubbing his hands.

"She's coming along beautifully."

"I tell you she's suffering terribly, Doc."

"Nonsense. She's had scopolamine. She won't remember a thing. We're taking her to the delivery room."

When they rolled her out of the room and down the hall, I hung back at first, pressed against the wall, afraid my presence would disturb her. But as she floated past I saw that she was asleep. They must have given her something, for her eyes were closed and her face was transformed into an image of white loveliness. I walked down the corridor at her side. Once she moaned. It was the murmur of one who had achieved ineffable peace after hours in the storm. It brought peace to me too. Now I knew that all was well, that the baby would soon be born, and Joyce would be all right.

I turned back to the waiting room. Papa sat in one of the big chairs, his arms folded, an iron silence holding him.

"Soon now," I said.

"What?" he whispered. "Nothing yet?"

"They've taken her to the delivery room."

"What's wrong with them?"

"They're doing all they can."

This made him growl, and I knew he felt I was conspiring with the hospital to keep the baby from being born. He stared ahead, saying no more.

A new crop of fathers sat in the waiting room, but their words were the same, the old wives' tales out of the mouths of baffled men. I couldn't stay there. Thinking of coffee, I left Papa in the waiting room and took the elevator to the hospital restaurant on the ground floor.

The place was full of nurses, doctors and interns. I sat at the counter and studied the menu. But I didn't want anything. In spite of everything, I was deeply worried. I walked out the side door to the street.

It was a dismal morning, the fog heavy and warm. I lit a cigarette and followed the sidewalk around the hospital grounds. The path was lined with tall eugenia hedges, immaculately clipped, a corridor of green that led to a garden where a fountain sprayed water among big red stones. I walked around the fountain, and the spray kissed my face with cool lips. Through the mist I saw the outline of a Gothic door. It was the hospital chapel. Suddenly, inexplicably, I began to cry, for here was the Thing I sought, the end of the desert, my house upon the earth. Eagerly I ran to the chapel.

Pax vobiscum! It was a small place, with only a crucifix at the main altar. I knelt as a tide of contrition engulfed me, a thundering cataract that roared in my ears. There was no need to pray, to beg forgiveness. My whole being lost itself in the deep drift, like waves returning to the shore. I was there for nearly an hour, and full of laughter as I rose to go. For it was a time for laughter, a time for great joy.

—*Full of Life*

Part Four

"I Must Remember to Face It"

I T WAS JANUARY, cold and dark and raining, and I was tired and wretched, and my windshield wipers weren't working, and I was hung over from a long evening of drinking and talking with a millionaire director who wanted me to write a film about the Tate Murders "in the manner of *Bonnie and Clyde,* with wit and style." There was no money involved. "We'll be partners, fifty-fifty." It was the third offer of that kind I'd had in six months, a very discouraging sign of the times.

Crawling along the Coast Highway at fifteen miles an hour, my head out the window, my face dripping rain, my eyes straining to follow the white line, the vinyl top of my 1967 Porsche (four payments overdue, the finance company hollering) was almost ripped off by the driving torrent as I finally made the turn off the highway toward the ocean.

We lived on Point Dume, a thrust of land jutting into the sea like a tit in a porno movie, the northern tip of the crescent that forms Santa Monica Bay. Point Dume is a community without street lights, a chaotic suburban sprawl so intricately bisected by winding streets and dead end roads that after twenty years of living out there I still got lost in fog or rain, often wandering aimlessly over streets not two blocks from my house.

And as I knew I must that stormy night, I turned off on Bonsall instead of Fernhill and began the slow, hopeless business of trying to find my house, knowing that eventually, provided I didn't run out of gas, I would circle back to the Coast Highway and the bleak light of the telephone booth at the bus stop, where I could phone Harriet to come and show me the way home. In ten minutes she appeared over the hill, the headlights of the station wagon spearing holes in the storm and zooming in on me parked beside the phone booth. She gave the horn a blast, leaped from the car and ran toward me in a white raincoat. Her eyes were wide with concern.

"You're going to need this."

She whipped my .22 pistol from under her coat and thrust it through the window. "There's something terrible in the yard."

"What?"

"God knows."

I didn't want the damned gun. I wouldn't take it. She stomped her foot.

"Take it, Henry! It may save your life."

She shoved it right under my nose.

"What the hell is it?"

"I think it's a bear."

"Where?"

"On the lawn. Under the kitchen window."

"Maybe it's one of the kids."

"With fur?"

"What kind of fur?"

"Bear fur."

"Maybe it's dead."

"It's breathing."

I tried to press the gun back to her. "Listen, I sure as hell don't intend to shoot a sleeping bear with a .22! It'll just wake him up. I'll call the sheriff."

I opened the door but she pushed it closed.

"No. Look at it first. Maybe it's nothing. Maybe it's just a burro."

"Oh, shit. Now it's a burro. Does it have big ears?"

"I didn't notice."

I sighed and started the car. She ran back to the station wagon and wheeled it onto the road. There was no white center line, so I stayed close to her tail lights as the car rolled slowly through cascades of rain.

Our house was on an acre of ground a hundred yards from the cliff and the roaring ocean below. It was a Y-shaped so-called rancho inside a concrete wall that completely circled the acre. A hundred and fifty tall pines grew along the walls so that it was like living in a forest, and the entire layout looked exactly like what it was not—the domicile of a successful writer.

But it was paid for, right down to the last sprinkler head, and I had an overwhelming passion to dump it and get out of the country. Over my dead body, Harriet always challenged, and I often amused myself with wistful reveries of her lying in a pool of blood on the kitchen floor as I dug a grave out by the corral, then grabbing an Al Italia for Rome with seventy thousand bucks in my jeans and a new life on the Piazza Navonne, with a brunette for a change.

But she was very good, my Harriet, she had stuck it out with me for twenty-five years and given me three sons and a daughter, any one of whom, or indeed all four, I would have gladly exchanged for a new Porsche, or even an MG GT '70.

—*West of Rome (My Dog Stupid)*

AND SO MY DAY BEGAN, a thrill a minute in the romantic, exciting, creatively fulfilling life of a writer. First, the grocery list. Varoom! and I roar down the coast highway in my Porsche, seven miles to the Mayfair Market. Scree! I brake to a stop in the parking lot, leap from the car, give my white scarf a couple of twirls and zap! I enter the automatic doors. Pow! The lettuce, potatoes, chard, carrots. Swoosh! The roast, chops, bacon, cheese! Wham! The cake, the cereal, the bread. Zonk! The detergent, the floor wax, the paper towels.

Back to the car again varoom varoom up the highway, roaring past a surf creamy as enzyme detergent, the wild carefree author, filling his days with exquisite sensuality. But the wind in my face brought back the only reality and I choked over an ever-returning memory of Rome, a cup of cappuccino at a little table on the Piazza Navonne, a raven-haired girl at my side, eating watermelon and laughing as she spat the seeds to the pigeons.

Jamie was having breakfast as I carried in the groceries. The dog lay at his feet. By now he was so familiar it seemed he had come with the house.

"I see you two have met," I said.

"Yeah, he's okay."

"Has he tried to screw you yet? Last night he almost scored with Rick."

"He tried, but he's kinda stupid. That's why I like him. I'm sick of smart dogs."

"Jamie wants to keep him," Harriet said.

"No chance."

"Why not?"

"Because I've had it with dogs, and because he belongs to somebody else, and because I don't want him around here." I decided to carry it a step further. "In God's name give a thought to your father. I can't work in this madhouse. I need peace and quiet. If you only knew what a writer goes through to . . ."

He threw up his arms.

"Okay, okay! I've heard that before!"

He pushed back his chair and stormed out the back door, shouting to the dog, "Come on, Stupid!"

The dog rose promptly and followed him out. Stupid. The name suited him perfectly. I picked up the phone and began dialing the County Animal Shelter.

From the yard came the thump of a basketball. That was Jamie, draining off his anger by shooting baskets through the hoop on the garage wall. He was the best kid I had. He didn't smoke pot, he didn't drink booze, he didn't sleep with black women, and he didn't want to become an actor. What more could a father ask? There was something wholesome and refreshing about a son like that.

From childhood he had had an abiding love for animals, had raised chickens, ducks, rabbits, hamsters and guinea pigs. I had seen him kiss guinea pigs on the mouth in gushes of affection at their cuddly warmth, and all of one summer he had slept with two king snakes coiled lovingly at his bosom. Now he was nineteen, with a student deferment from the draft, a math whiz with a bright future. He had an after-school job at the supermarket, saved every cent he earned, and planned for a degree in business administration. Most important, he was my best hope for a happy old age. The others, including Tina, would throw me out the way I was banishing the dog, but my Writers' Guild pension, plus social security and a monthly stipend from Jamie promised serenity in my sunset years. So why muck up my own future? Let him keep the dog. How would he feel ten years from now if he remembered his old man as the heartless bastard who had consigned Stupid to the county gas chamber? No, I didn't want that. I hung up and went out to discuss the matter with him.

"You can keep him if you'll promise to take care of him," I said.

"I don't want him, Dad. You're right. They're too much trouble."

"What'll we do with him?"

"Let's take him down to the beach," Jamie said. "He'll wander off on his own and that'll be the end of it."

"Good idea."

The dog lay half-buried in an ivy bed.

"Come on, Stupid," I said.

He ignored it, but when Jamie called he rose immediately. So far, so good. I walked into the house and told Harriet our plan. She was so relieved that she kissed me. I swore she had seen the last of the dog.

"Now be strong," she said. "Don't chicken out."

"You know me. Iron man. Besides, it's the only humane way of getting rid of him. He'll mosey on down the coast and that'll be the end of it."

I joined Jamie and the dog at the front gate and we started down the road. It was a quarter of a mile to the gate that led to the beach, one-acre tracts on either side of the road, a house on each tract, at least one dog, and usually two at every house. Point Dume was dog country, a canine paradise of Dobermans, German shepherds, Labradors, boxers, Weimaraners, Great Danes and Dalmatians.

All hell broke loose as we moved down the road. The Epsteins' prize boxers, Elwood and Gracie, came roaring out of their driveway and smashed into Stupid before he knew what was happening, sweeping him off his feet. Howls, yawps, and yelps filled the air as fur exploded in a swirl of dust at the side of the road. It looked at if they were tearing Stupid to shreds, but he recovered quickly, his bearish jaws wide as a shovel as he fought back. There was a shriek of pain from Gracie and she ran limping away.

On his back, Elwood's teeth were in the thickness of Stupid's neck, pulling out mouthfuls of fur. Stupid stomped him with his paws and his cavernous mouth sank into the boxer's throat. But he didn't hurt Elwood. He only held him down firmly, pressing his heavy body upon the boxer. Then the carrot flashed, emerging like an orange dagger just as Mrs. Epstein in curlers opened the front door and watched in consternation the intended assault upon her pride and joy. Seizing a dust mop, she rushed to the fight.

"Oh, Elwood!" she wailed. "Poor Elwood!"

She beat the mop against Stupid's back as he tried to ram the dagger home. But it slid off harmlessly to one side and then the other, and sometimes poking the ground, gradually diminishing and finally disappearing. Only then did he disengage himself, his face clouded with bewilderment, the dust mop flailing him. Unhurt but embarrassed, Elwood sprang to his feet and lunged for a parting snap at Stupid's thick hide. Then he ran off to join Gracie at the side of the house.

Jamie and I faced Mrs. Epstein. She was panting, furious, glaring at Stupid.

"What is that filthy thing?"

"An Akita," I said.

"What's *that*?"

"A Japanese dog."

"Bull terriers, and now this. Can't you own a civilized dog?"

"He didn't start it, Mrs. Epstein," Jamie said. "Your dogs attacked him."

"Can you blame them? Look at that horrible beast! He doesn't belong in a nice neighborhood. Did you see what he did to Elwood?"

Tongue out, panting and covered with dust, Stupid sat there staring at Mrs. Epstein.

"I'm going to report him," she said, striding back to the house. Pausing in the doorway, she called her dogs. "Elwood! Gracie! You get in here, this minute!" They raced into the house. She lobbed a vile look in my direction and closed the door.

We bent over Stupid as he licked his paws and cleaned himself after the brawl. A fistful of fur was missing from under his chest, but there were no wounds. I slapped his belly admiringly.

"This guy can fight," I said.

"Think he could take Rocco?"

"I wouldn't go that far," I said. "Still, he routed two boxers. He's got great promise."

"He's a fag, Dad."

"So was Caesar. And Michelangelo."

"Wish we could keep him."

"Your mother would blow a fuse."

We moved on down the road, the canine alarm system preceding us and in full operation: the collie at the Hamer place, the hysterical beagles at the Frawleys, the Borchart Doberman, a score of dogs big and small on both sides of the road protesting the alien in their midst.

They saw him between Jamie and me, each of us gripping his collar, they got a whiff of a beast from foreign parts and they went wild with fear and outrage at his presence, some racing up and down behind chain link fences, others retreating to garages and porches where they cracked their throats with howls that brought women and children to the windows to peer anxiously from behind curtains, wondering what monster rambled over Point Dume.

Tongue out and head high Stupid enjoyed the attention, straining at the collar like a horse impatient to break from the starting gate. As we passed the Bigelow house their fawn-colored Great Dane loped to the fence and cut loose with a few asthmatic bellows. Stupid sneered and flashed a wicked white fang.

Beyond the Bigelows a final challenge awaited us before we reached the iron gates to the beach—a savage antagonist too formidable to think about or whisper his name. And yet we knew he lay in wait just around the bend in the road.

His name was Rommel, and his owner's name was Kunz, an executive with the Rand think-tank in Santa Monica. Rommel. Flown in from Berlin, he was the reigning monarch of Point Dume's canine empire. He was a black and silver German shepherd who lived in the last house on that road, and who took it upon himself to guard the gates leading to the beach below. An awesome dog, a gauleiter with an uncanny instinct for screening out strangers and dropouts (and wagging his tail at anyone in uniform), handsome as Cary Grant and ferocious as Joe Louis, a mighty king among dogs, but in my mind inferior to Rocco, my bull terrier, cut down by an assassin's bullet a year before Rommel made the scene.

Even as we approached the cul de sac Rommel presented himself, the warning system from his minions having already alerted him for whatever intruder, man or beast, came down Cliffside Road.

My heart began to rev up and all at once I knew that my only reason for leading Stupid to the beach was this encounter. I looked at Jamie. His face was flushed, his eyes sparkling. The only one among us, man or beast, who was unaware of the impending menace was Stupid. Apparently his sense of smell was as imperfect as his eyesight, for he swaggered into view without seeing Rommel, his big tongue flapping and a grin on his bearish face.

Slinking toward him with menacing tread, one paw stealthily following another, his tail thrust straight out, his hackles rising, Rommel loosed a blood-chilling growl that silenced the yips and yowls along the road. The king had spoken and an awful silence prevailed. Stupid's ears peaked as his eyes found Rommel thirty yards away. He lunged to break the grip on his collar, dragging us along until we released him. He did not crouch like his Teutonic rival. Instead, he walked into the battle with his head high, the loop of his plumed tail swirling like a flag over his rump.

The thing unfolded like Main Street, Dodge City. Jamie licked his chops. My heart roared. We stopped to watch.

Rommel hit first, driving his teeth deeply into the fur at Stupid's throat. It was like biting into a mattress. Stupid tore himself free, high on his hind legs, the move of a bear, his forepaws keeping the Teuton at bay. They snapped at one another, face to face, as Rommel too rose to his hind legs. My Rocco, a street-fighter, would have disemboweled them both had the tactic been used against him. But Rommel was a stand-up fighter, a stickler for the rules, no biting at the under-belly, no attack except at the throat.

He hit several times, but he could not hang on. Stupid, to my surprise, wasn't biting at all. He snarled, his jaws snapped, he roared to match Rommel's roars, but it was obvious that he wanted to wrestle and not kill. He was the same size as Rommel but his chest was more powerful and his paws slugged like clubs.

After half a dozen charges the combat was a draw and there was a momentary pause as the dogs measured each other. The alert Rommel stood still as a statue as Stupid moved closer and began circling him. Rommel watched this maneuver suspiciously, ears up. By all the rules of a classic dog fight the battle should have ended a draw then and there, both animals retiring with honors unchallenged.

Not Stupid. Circling a second time, he suddenly raised his paws to Rommel's back. *Touché!* It was a fantastic ploy, unprecedented, daring, defiant and so unorthodox that Rommel froze in disbelief. It was as if Stupid would rather frolic than fight and it confused Rommel, a noble dog who believed in fair play.

Then Stupid revealed his uncanny purpose, unsheathing his orange sword and leaping upon Rommel's back, truly a bear now, squeezing Rommel with four powerful legs and endeavoring to sink home the sword. What finesse! What brilliance! My blood sang. God, what a dog!

Snarling in disgust, Rommel thrashed to free himself from the obscene assault, his neck twisting to reach Stupid's throat, his bottom dragged protectingly along the ground. Now he knew that his adversary was a fiendish monster with depraved intent and it put him in a panic of energy to disengage. Finally free, he skulked away, tail down and shielding his privates. Stupid romped after him as Rommel retreated to the lawn and planted himself with lips exposing a mouthful of dripping teeth. There was nausea and disgust in the sound that came from his throat, a shrinking away from this revolting adversary too loathsome to attack.

He was beaten, routed. He had quit.

"My God!" I said, going to my knees and throwing my arms around Stupid's neck. "Oh, my God, Jamie! What have we here?"

Jamie seized his collar.

"Let's get him away before it starts again."

"It'll never start again. Rommel's finished, wiped out. Look at him!"

Rommel was walking up the Kunz driveway toward the garage, tail between his legs.

"Let's go," Jamie said.

"We keep him."

"You can't. You promised mother."

"It's my dog, my house, my decision."

"But he's not yours."

"He will be."

"He's trouble. He's crazy."

"He's a fighter with style. He wins without throwing a punch."

"He's not a fighter, Dad. He's a rapist."

"We keep him."

"Tell me why?"

"I don't have to tell you anything."

We started back, Stupid between us, walking a gauntlet of barking dogs. I knew why I wanted that dog. It was shamelessly clear, but I could not tell the boy. It would have embarrassed me. But I could tell myself and it did not matter. I was tired of defeat and failure. I hungered for victory. I was fifty-five and there were no victories in sight, nor even a battle. Even my enemies were no longer interested in combat. Stupid was victory, the books I had not written, the places I had not seen, the Maserati I had never owned, the women I hungered for, Danielle Darrieux and Gina Lollobrigida and Nadia Grey. He was triumph over ex-pants manufacturers who had slashed my screenplays until blood oozed. He was my dream of great offspring with fine minds in famous universities, scholars with rich gifts for the world. Like my beloved Rocco he would ease the pain and bruises of my interminable days, the poverty of my childhood, the desperation of my youth, the desolation of my future.

He was a dog, not a man, but an animal, and in time he would be my friend, filling my skull with pride and fun and nonsense. He was closer to God than I would ever be, he could neither read nor write, and that was good too. He was a misfit and I was a misfit. I would fight and lose, and he would fight and win. The haughty Great Danes, the proud German shepherds, he would kick the shit out of them all, and fuck them too, and I would have my kicks.

—*West of Rome (My Dog Stupid)*

I NEEDED A DOG. He simplified the circle of my life. He was there in the yard, alive and friendly, taking the place of other dogs who were dead and in the same ground over which he roamed. I could understand that—my dog friends, living and dead, joined together on the same piece of ground. It made sense. My father and mother lay in a graveyard up north and I was still alive on Point Dume, walking the same crust of California earth that held them. I understood that too.

I could walk out into the night with my pipe and look from Stupid to the stars, and there was a connection. I liked that dog. When I was a boy in Colorado I used to sit with my dog and look up at the same stars. He was childhood again, bringing back the pages of my catechism. *Who is God?* God is the creator of heaven and earth and of all things. *Is God everywhere?* God is everywhere. *Does God see us?* God sees us and watches over us. *Why did God make us?* God made us to know him and to love him in this world and to be happy with him in the next.

I could sit on the grass with Stupid and believe every word of it. Sometimes as I sat there he would rise up and put his paws on my shoulders and try to screw me. So he loved me. How else could he express it? Write a poem, gather roses? I whacked him with an elbow, and that brought him down. Rocco had loved me too, and expressed it by biting my shoes or tearing apart something I owned, a shirt, a pair of socks, my hat, or, unhappily, the grips on my golf clubs. But Rocco was an out-going fellow who loved bitches, while Stupid had this problem with females, and it endeared him to me.

He was good for me. A month after he arrived I began a novel. Nothing unusual about that. I began novels all the time, filling the gaps between screen assignments. But they petered out for lack of confidence and discipline, and I abandoned them with a sense of relief.

Screenwriting was easier and brought more bread, a one-dimensional kind of scribbling asking no more of the writer than that he keep his people in motion. The formula was always the same: fightin' and fuckin'. When finished you gave it to other people who tore it to pieces trying to put it on film.

But when you undertook a novel, the responsibility was awesome. Not only were you the writer but the star and all the characters, as well as director, producer and cameraman. If your screenplay didn't come off you could blame a lot of people, from the director down. But if your novel bombed, you suffered alone.

I was fifteen thousand words into my novel, with no symptoms of collapse, when the old urge to ditch my family returned. The pages hummed and I wanted to be alone. Naturally I thought of Rome, and even toyed with the idea of taking Harriet with me. To get there we would first sell the establishment on Point Dume, an impossibility until we got the kids off our backs. As for the dog, I didn't think he'd like Rome, where all dogs on a leash are muzzled by law. But somehow I never pictured Stupid with me in Rome. He was only useful until I could make my move. With the kids gone and the house sold I would be loaded, and free.

The more I planned and dreamed, the less Harriet figured in the project. I didn't think she would care for Rome after all. Separated from friends, isolated by the language barrier and culturally alien she might find it a drag. Besides, she no longer had any particular affection for Italian things. I finally decided that the only solution was for her to rent an apartment in Santa Monica, and then I could take off for the Piazza Navonne and plunge into the new life.

—*West of Rome (My Dog Stupid)*

IT WAS ELEVEN O'CLOCK, still hot and too early for bed. I went to my work room and turned on the light over the desk. I had seventy pages now, around twenty thousand words on yellow pages neatly stacked before me. Not once in the writing had I looked back, relying on instinct. Now I decided to read what I had done.

I got a terrible jolt. I could feel the blow in my gut and kidneys, sheer panic, creeping up my back and riffling the hair on my scalp. It wasn't a novel at all. It was conceived as a novel but the wretched thing was actually a detailed screen treatment, a flat, sterile one-dimensional blueprint of a movie. It had dissolves and camera angles, and even a couple of fade-outs. One chapter began: "Full Establishing Shot—Apartment House—Day."

Twenty-five years ago I would have seized that mass of yellow pages in my two hands and courageously torn it to pieces. Now I didn't have the guts, or, for that matter, the strength in my hands.

So, as it must to all men, death had come to Henry J. Molise. The cop-out was complete. Molise would never write again. Molise, cheered by the critics for the four novels of his youth, now more dead than alive on Point Dume.

Reputed to be insane, suffering from ulcers, no longer attending Writers' Guild meetings, regularly observed at the liquor store and the State Department of Employment. Or walking the beach with a large, idiotic and dangerous dog. Tedious bore at parties, talking of the good old days. Boozes it up every night watching talk shows on T.V. Quarrelled with agent and currently unrepresented. Talks obsessively of Rome. Wanders aimlessly in his yard, chipping balls with a nine iron. Scorned by his four children. Oldest son rejects white race and will marry Negro. Second son on relief trying to become an actor. Third son too young to add to the disintegration of family. Daughter in love with beach bum. Loyal wife tends his personal needs, preparing wholesome meals of custards and soft-boiled eggs, frequently assists him to bathroom.

I lit a pipe, wandered out to the patio, and flopped into a chair. The hot night was very quiet on the surface, but beneath was the violent uproar of the battering tide, the hum of crickets, the twitter of restless birds, the barking of squirrels, the howl of twinkling jet planes, the crackling of pines and the eerie sense of fire in the air.

Again the insoluble and most fundamental question of my life began to haunt me. What the hell was I doing on this small planet? Fifty-five years, for this? It was absurd. How far to Rome? Twelve hours? Naples was nice too. Positano. Ischia. Was this the end of my life, in a Y-shaped house on Point Dume? I couldn't believe it. God was pulling my leg.

Out of the darkness on noiseless paws Stupid appeared. He looked at my dangling leg and at me, considering the possibilities. Then he tried to straddle the leg. I pulled it out from under him. Disappointed, he rested his chin in my lap and I rubbed the back of his ears. I needed help.

—*West of Rome (My Dog Stupid)*

DENNY AND DOMINIC HAD GONE, Jamie was in bed, and Harriet and I sat in the living room watching the eleven o'clock movie. She was sipping sherry while I smoked my pipe and drank hot tea. The grass was in my shirt pocket. Question was, how did I get it down her lungs? She was one of those iron-spined people who would no more trifle with grass than smoke opium. I was no expert with the stuff, though I had taken it half a dozen times in my life. I could wish that I had been fortified by it when I learned of my father's death, for I had gotten sickeningly drunk instead, deepening my grief. In truth, my father had been dead for ten years, and I still grieved over the loss of him. Marijuana might have made a difference. It was supposed to be the sure cure for a world falling apart.

The movie gave me a clue. It was literally a film about the dead. It starred Carole Lombard, who was dead. So were the others in the cast, John Barrymore, Lionel Barrymore, Eugene Pallette and the supporting players. So were the director, the writer, and the producer. There they were, moving on film, now rotting in their graves, poor, lovely, beautiful creatures, and it was very sad, and I told Harriet I thought it was so very sad.

I got up and put some scotch in my tea, and at the commercial I got up and did it again. It's sad, I told her, it's heartbreaking. I said life was sad too, short and sad, and she agreed. I said it made me melancholy and unhappy, and she took my hand and smiled and said, don't be.

I said, "If we could only break out of this trap, go somewhere, do something, forget our troubles for a while."

She said, "It's only eleven-thirty. Do you want to drive in to the Cock 'N' Bull?"

"I don't mean that. I mean finding peace, some euphoria to take us past this moment of crisis."

"Why don't you get drunk?" she said.

I told her I didn't mean getting drunk. I meant total escape, the way the kids did it. Like smoking marijuana.

"Why don't you?" she said. "I'm sure you'll find some in the back bedrooms."

"I have some here," I said, patting my shirt.

"Well," she said. "Smoke it if you like."

"Alone? You don't smoke pot alone. To enjoy it you have to share the pleasure with others."

"No one else is here but me."

"How about you?"

"I don't think so."

"That figures," I sneered.

"I'm sorry."

"Leave it to you, of all people."

"But I don't want any!"

"You, the most abused, tormented person in this house, you, who made all the sacrifices, your whole world crumbling around you. . . ."

"My world isn't crumbling!"

"You, who needs it more than anybody else, and you refuse it."

"I don't need it."

"Perhaps you're right. Better to have will-power, to grit your teeth and hang in there, absorb the punishment. The best steel comes from the hottest forge. Forget it. But I hope you don't mind if I sit here and drink until I vomit. That's about all that's left for an embittered father, unless he goes to a saloon and tries to score with some tramp."

She took my hand again. "Oh, come on now. You wouldn't do a thing like that. Get hold of yourself."

"What a marriage, what a mockery! A man asks to smoke a little pot with his wife, and she chickens out. My God, I'm not asking you to shoot heroin. All I want is for the two of us—man and wife—to join hands in a journey to happyland, where the miseries of life are cast off for a little while."

"I'm afraid it'll make me sick."

"Sick? It's therapeutic! Relaxes the body, purifies the mind, restores the soul."

She was silent awhile, nibbling on a fingernail.

"All right," she relented. "But I know it's going to make me sick."

I put my hand over my heart. "I swear to you on my sacred honor you won't be sick."

"All right, then."

In the half-light from the tube I rolled two joints and gave her one of them. "Smoke it like a cigarette. Inhale deeply. Don't wolf it down fast. Take it slow and easy."

We lit up and smoked in silence. She took several deep drags.

"I don't feel a thing."

"Patience. It takes time. Don't hurry it."

After a couple of drags my cigarette went out, but I did not relight it. She smoked hers down to the fingers before snuffing it out. Then she leaned back with beatific indolence, her eyes half closed as she watched the movie. I asked her how she felt.

"I don't feel a thing," she smiled.

Ten minutes passed.

"I'm proud of my children," she said. "I love them dearly. They live in a terrible world, but they have the courage to face the future, and I'm not going to worry about them any more."

I knew it was time to tell her.

"Did Dominic tell you about his marriage?"

"Dominic, married?"

"He and Katy were married Christmas day."

"I didn't know."

"Katy's pregnant."

"How nice."

I looked at her as she lay back in the big reclining chair. She was crying. She cried for two hours, until the pictureless white eye of the tube stared back, glistening on the beads of tears rolling down her cheeks.

"I'm so happy," she said over and over again. "So happy."

Moving like one spooked and shrouded in cobwebs, she clung to me as we floated back to the bedroom. I eased her to the bed, her neck like a broken doll's, her hands limp as gloves. She pined for affection, cooing and groping for my face, her head on my shoulder, but she was so high she couldn't even kiss me. I lowered her to the pillow, removed the rest of her clothes, and marveled at her whiteness, her nipples sweetly pink and reminding me of the four mouths that had got their sustenance from them. I touched her faintly golden pussy, wondering if she tinted it. Mine, all mine. Suddenly I had to have her and I tore off my clothes and was upon her in a frenzy. It was rape, her helplessness swirling me in an orgiastic delirium and I ravaged her with an evil joy, finding hitherto unviolated crevasses and cracks, the most ecstatic affair I ever had with her, and she slept through the whole thing without memory, recalling none of it when she wakened in the morning.

—*West of Rome (My Dog Stupid)*

I NEVER THOUGHT MUCH ABOUT JAMIE. I really didn't want him born into the world so soon after Tina, who screamed horrifically past all endurance in her infancy, leaving me enraged and frightened. I vowed that three were enough and I pleaded with Harriet, no more for God's sake, are you wearing that diaphragm, are you sure it's in place. It was sheer panic with Tina wailing in another room, and when Harriet knew Jamie was coming she was afraid to tell me until the third month.

I was a real shit about it, busting out of the house and staying away two weeks in Palm Springs with a drunken writer who had six kids and blamed them for his alcoholism. I came home with abortion in mind but it was of course too late, and Harriet despised me and ordered me to get out and never come back. But we made a perilous truce blinded by hate and necessity and the coming child was never mentioned.

It was a hideous ordeal for Harriet. The bigger she got the bigger the monster in me. I drank wine through days and nights, slumped viciously in a chair, punishing her with the blade of my tongue, sneering, drooped in a chair, recoiling from the larger and larger roundness of her waist.

Not only did she manage the pregnancy and three other children, she escaped alive from the coil of my despair. Two weeks before the baby was born I was offered a job in Rome. Harriet was so glad to have me out of that chair and I was so eager to get away that I left without packing a suitcase.

When I returned from Rome Jamie was five months old, and I still detested him because he had the colic and cried even more than Tina. The cry of a child! Give me ground glass and tear out my fingernails, but do not subject me to the cry of a child, for it hurts very deep into my umbilicus, hurts all the way back to the beginning of my life.

Harriet had named him Joseph after her father, but Joseph he was not, nor did he look like a Joseph, Jamie suited him better, and after a while the name clung, and we had it officially changed.

There was never enough time for Jamie. It was always Dominic or Tina who churned up the crises, and sometimes Denny, but never this curly-headed, hazel-eyed kid who smiled at the beginning of each new day and didn't cry like the others that first time we took him to school and who spoke so hesitatingly, so falteringly, because nobody bothered to teach him how. But later we learned that he did cry a little every day, sitting in the schoolyard sandbox by himself, and when his teacher asked him why, he answered that there was something in his eye.

When he was six years old we took him to a neighborhood Fourth of July party where he wandered among a hundred guests, amazed and pleased at what he saw. On the way home Harriet asked if he had enjoyed himself, and he answered with sparkling eyes that a man had spoken to him, a nice man in a large black hat. Harriet asked what the man had said and Jamie fondled the delicious memory and sighed. "He said, 'Get out of my way, kid.'"

That was Jamie, lover of flowers, cactus and trees, spiders, caterpillars, starfish and sea shells, worms and rats and dogs and cats and squirrels, horses and men. We never worried much about Jamie through most of his life. He simply made no demands. He didn't ditch school or get into fights or come home in the Sheriff's car with a deputy lecturing his parents on the seriousness of vandalism, or steal or get drunk or wreck cars or have pot parties on the beach or impregnate chicks or run away from home, or lie or steal or cheat.

He got fine grades, kept himself clean and neatly dressed, ate everything put before him, spent whole days shooting baskets, and always kissed his mother good night. Who paid attention to a kid like that? To fall within my attention span a boy had to do something significant, like wrecking a car, or steal my shotgun to shoot quail out of the pines, or get arrested by the game warden for setting illegal lobster traps, or fall off the cliff and plummet to the sand below, or chew his fingernails waiting for a girl to make her next menstrual period, or be rescued from drowning, or throw parties wrecking furniture and breaking windows. Not Jamie. A freak, dullsville, out of the mainstream, a square.

Then from nowhere came the cruncher, and it appeared that our Jamie was not as unsullied and beautiful as we believed. Maybe he was compelled to it in order to call attention to himself. Possibly that was why he had flunked two major subjects at college and deliberately exposed himself to the curiosity of the draft board. But the complexities of his fabrication were more intricate than we imagined.

To believe it, we had to see it on paper. The letter, addressed to Jamie, was from the Dean's office. It was propped near the telephone where Harriet knew he would see it. Sensing its importance I peered through the envelope's transparency and wondered if I dare open it, thus violating a sacred house rule against reading other people's mail. The moral issue delayed me about ten seconds before I tore the envelope open.

The information for James Molise was crisp and impersonal. For absences totaling forty-two days he was herewith notified that he was no longer a student at City College.

"Sacked. Expelled."

"You shouldn't have opened it," Harriet frowned.

"Forty-two days! What's he up to?"

"It doesn't matter. You had no right to open his mail."

Around dinner time he was home, empty-handed.

"No books? How come?"

His eyes sank into me with a quick worried stare before turning away.

"What of it?" he asked.

I picked up the letter and handed it to him, and he made a point of fingering the torn envelope, his face darkening. He tossed the letter on the table without bothering to read it.

"I've quit school."

"You didn't quit, you were kicked out."

"I quit!" he insisted.

"A screw-up like your brothers. And all the time I thought you'd be the one who'd break the mold."

"Will you please be quiet?" Harriet cut in. "What happened, Jamie? Why did you leave school?"

"I took a job," he said, looking at his hands.

"How many jobs you got?" I asked. "I thought you were working at the supermarket."

"Not any more. I'm working at the Children's Clinic."

"Doing what?"

"Teaching things. Sports, crafts. Whatever has to be done."

I began to see an emerging pattern, a clever maneuver, like Denny's, and it relieved me. He was using his head after all.

"Not bad," I said. "It should get you a deferment with the draft board."

"I'm just a volunteer," he said, a little ashamed. "I don't get paid at the clinic."

"You're working for nothing?"

"I like what I'm doing."

"You're off your rocker. Charity begins at home."

There was no hostility in his greenish eyes, only warmth and sympathy. "I knew you'd say something like that, Dad. That's why I couldn't tell you."

At dinner we learned more of his job with the Children's Clinic. He worked fifty hours a week and was given lunch without charge. To reach the clinic in Culver City he hitch-hiked thirty miles there and back each day, except those times when Denny gave him a ride. He pushed crippled children in wheelchairs, gave them whirlpool baths, and massaged their ailing limbs. Those who could walk or run he taught to kick and throw a ball. Otherwise there was nothing to do, except for cleaning toilets, vacuuming rugs and helping with the laundry.

"We're understaffed," he said. "We need help."

I listened and marveled at how little I understood him and what a mystery he had suddenly become. So now we had another martyr in the family. Dominic immolating himself before the altar of Katy Dann, and now Jamie dedicated to maimed children. How different from their father, who wrote cop-out scenarios for fifteen hundred a week (when employed)! No wonder I understood my dogs and not my children. No wonder I couldn't finish a novel anymore. To write one must love, and to love one must understand. I would never write again until I understood Jamie and Dominic and Denny and Tina, and when I understood and loved them I would love all mankind and my harsh view of the world would soften to the beauty that surrounded me, and it would flow smooth as electricity through my fingers and upon the page.

—*West of Rome (My Dog Stupid)*

P EACE.
What is peace?

She lives in the east wing and I live in the north wing. We have three bedrooms apiece. I mow the lawn. I start a new novel. My style has changed. I don't like it. She makes pottery. She studies the occult. I play golf. I have these nightmares. Some blacks roasting Dominic in a pot. She has nightmares. Jamie courtmartialed, blindfolded, shot. I change bedrooms. She changes bedrooms. We sleep together. She snores. She claims I snore. We shift bedrooms. The novel collapses. I start a new one. What happened to my style? She gives me a Tarot reading. The cards are sinister. She cannot finish the reading. The Tower. The Hanged Man. My cards, Death, Catastrophe, Ruin.

Jamie writes daily, phones weekends. His voice is weak, pathetic. He has a severe cold. He hiked eighteen miles. How's my dog? He's okay. Don't worry about your dog. How's the food up there? Awful. He vomits all the time. Are you warm at night? No. They don't give us enough blankets. They made him crawl through a field on his belly, shooting live ammo over his head. Look, Jamie, do you want me to write the post commander? No. It will only increase the persecution. He has a temperature. Go see the medic. No. Absenteeism will mean doing the whole thing over again.

I mow the lawn. Harriet weeds the flower beds. We call the real estate people. They put up a sign. Hordes of strangers arrive. They troop through the house. They hate the place. The kitchen is old-fashioned. The closets too small. The ceilings need paint. The windows need screens. You hear them sneering as they leave. You see the real estate man agreeing with them. We take down the sign. We are alone again. I hear strange footsteps at night. I put a pistol at my bedside. I give Harriet a pistol. I clean and oil my rifles. The place is an armed fortress. There was a time when every door was open day and night. Not anymore. I check the doors, the windows. Harriet paints Easter eggs. She goes on an egg kick. She puts tiny animals inside the eggs. She makes little scenes inside the eggs, a deer at a waterfall, a rabbit under a bush. The living room fills with strange eggs. Friends congratulate her. She has plans with larger eggs. I play golf. We are a little crazy, unraveled, flaky. Not ashamed to admit it.

Denny writes from New York. He is a waiter, he is at acting school. Send a hundred. Tina phones from New Hampshire. She is pregnant. Rick is a carpenter. They are buying a house. Send a hundred. Jamie phones. Send some cookies. Still has a temperature. Hiked twenty miles today. Sergeant is out to break him. Must get up at four to clean every latrine on the post. I'll take care of everything, I tell him, I'll write to Tunney and Cranston and Reagan. Don't. It'll only make things worse. How's my dog?

Let's have a party, people around, old friends, we should entertain more now. We throw a party, people come. Writers and wives. Knives drawn. Booze. Screenwriters versus television writers. Bad scene. A woman calls me a fascist pig. I hit her. Her husband belts me. Big rumble on the patio. Neighbor calls the Sheriff. A drunken actress runs to the edge of the cliff, threatens to jump. Jump, you bitch! A deputy grabs her. Party breaks up. Broken friendships, broken glasses, spilled booze, vomit on the lawn. In the dining room some beast has pissed against the wall. We vow no more parties.

—*West of Rome (My Dog Stupid)*

THE ONLY CHANGE IN THE CAFÉ ROMA in over a quarter of a century was the clientele. The old men I remembered were planted in the graveyard, replaced by a new generation of old men. Otherwise things were as usual. The long mahogany bar was the same and so were the two dusty, fly-specked Italian and American flags above it. A touch of the modern was displayed above the bar, a blowup of Marlon Brando as the Godfather, four feet square, in a frame of gold filigree.

The same propeller fan droned from the ceiling, spinning slowly enough not to disturb the warm air, with sportive flies landing on the propeller blades, enjoying a spin or two, then jumping off. Green shades over the front windows gave the dark interior an illusion of coolness, as did the fragrance of tap beer. But this aroma was knifed by the gut-slashing pungency of olive oil and rancid parmigiana cheese mixed with the piney tang of fresh sawdust deep on the floor.

Something else had changed: when I was a lad the patrons of the Café Roma spoke only Italian. Now the new breed of old cockers spoke English, the English of the street, but English all the same.

Eight or nine of them were crowded around a green felt table in the rear. The low-hanging lamp lit up five card players seated around the table, the others standing about, watching and kibitzing. My father was one of the spectators. They were a cranky, irascible, bitter gang of Social Security guys, intense, snarling, rather mean old bastards, bitter, but enjoying their cruel wit, their profanity and their companionship. No philosophers here, no aged oracles speaking from the depths of life's experience. Simply old men killing time, waiting for the clock to run down. My father was one of them. It came to me as a shock. I never thought of him that way until I saw him with his own kind. Now he looked even older than the gaffers around him.

I moved to Papa's side and said "Hi." He grunted. The baldheaded dealer never took his eyes off the cards as he spoke to my father.

"Friend of yours, Nick?"

"Nah. This is my kid Henry."

I recognized the dealer: Joe Zarlingo, a retired railroad engineer. Though he had not operated a train in ten years, he still wore striped overalls and an engineer's cap and sported all manner of colored pens and pencils in his bib pocket, as if serving notice that he was a very busy man.

I looked around and said "Hello" to everybody, and two or three answered with preoccupied growls, not bothering to look at me. Some I remembered. Lou Cavallaro, a retired brakeman. Bosco Antrilli, once the super at the telegraph office, the father of Nellie Antrilli, whom I seduced on an anthill in a field south of town in the dead of night (the anthill unseen, Nellie and I fully clothed, then screaming and tearing off our clothes as the outraged ants attacked us). Pete Benedetti, formerly postmaster. The game ended, the chips were drawn in, and the players finally took time to study me while Zarlingo shuffled the cards. They were not impressed.

"Which boy is this one, Nick?" Zarlingo asked.

"Writes books."

Zarlingo looked at me.

"Books, uh? What kind of books?"

"Novels."

"What kind?"

"Take your finger out of your ass and deal the cards," Antrilli said.

"Fuck you, you shit-kicker," Zarlingo fired back.

The profanity embarrassed my father, for in his mind I was still fourteen, the kid he dragged around on his tours, and he wanted to shield me from the vulgarity of his more mature friends. He whispered, "Come on," and drew me away, and I followed him out into the trembling sunshine.

"What you hanging around here for?" he said. "No place for you."

"Come on, Papa. I'm fifty years old. I've heard just about everything. I came to tell you I'm staying in town for a while."

It was like poking a stick into a hornet's nest. He squinted at me with his little hot red eyes. "Suit yourself, but don't do me no favors. I don't need any of you people. I been working since I was eight years old. I was laying stone on the streets of Bari twenty years before you were born, so don't think I can't do it myself."

"Do what?"

"Never mind."

I lifted my palms. "Papa, listen. Don't get sore. Let's get out of this heat and talk it over."

His hands plunged from one pocket to another until he found it—the stub of a black cigar. He struck a wooden match against his thigh and lit up, a cloud of white smoke burying his face.

"Okay. Let's talk business."

"Business?"

I followed him into the Roma to the bar. They had no hard liquor, only beer and wine. The bartender was the youngest man in the place, a kid of around forty-five, with hair down to the small of his back and a hip mustache that curled over his cheeks like quarter moons.

"Frank," Papa said. "This here's my son. Give him a beer." To me he said, "This is Frank Mascarini."

Frank drew me an overflowing stein from the tap. He served my father a decanter of Musso claret from one of the wine barrels beneath the bar. Papa took his decanter and a glass to one of the tables and I followed with the beer and we sat down. He sipped his wine thoughtfully. Whatever was on his mind, he was carefully tooling up to speak it.

Finally he said, "I got a chance to make some real money."

"Glad to hear of it."

He was a poor man but not a pauper. Social Security and checks from Virgil and me took care of him and Mama. They lived frugally but well, for my mother could make a meal from hot water and a bone, and dandelions were free in any empty lot.

"What's the job?"

"A stone smokehouse, up in the mountains."

"Can you handle it?"

He chortled at the foolishness of such a question. "When I was fourteen I built a well in the mountains of Abruzzi. Down through solid rock. Thirty feet deep and ten feet wide. Cold spring water. I did it myself. Carried rock out of the hole, then carried it back. I worked in water up to my ass. It took me three months. I got paid a hundred lira. You know how much that was, in those days? Forty-five cents. Fifteen-cents-a-month wages. Now I got a chance to make fifteen hundred dollars in one month, and you want to know if I can handle it!" This amused him. He laughed. "Of course I can handle it! All I need is a little help."

"Papa, you're a liar. Nobody works for fifteen cents a month."

His fist banged the table.

"I did. And I'll tell you something else. I put away half my wages."

"What'd you do with the other half?"

"Squandered it. Gambled. Got drunk. Slept with some woman."

He quaffed a couple of large mouthfuls of the Musso claret as I studied him. There was no questioning the man's years, especially the eyes. Their sparkle was gone, as if behind a yellowish film and a net of small red veins.

I said, "Papa, I don't think you should take that job."

"Who says so?"

"You're too damned old. You'll have a stroke, or a heart attack. It'll finish you off."

"My mother was ninety-four. My father was eighty-one. All I need is a first-class helper, somebody who knows how to mix mortar and carry stone."

"You got anybody in mind?"

He sipped the claret. "Yep."

"Is he reliable?"

"Hell no, but you take what you can get."

I realized whom he had in mind.

"Papa," I smiled. "You're out of your tree."

"How long can you stay?"

"A day or two."

"We can do it in three weeks."

"Impossible."

"Easy job. Little stone house up at Monte Casino. Ten by ten. No windows. One door. I'll lay up the walls, you mix the mortar, carry the stone. Nice place. Good country. Forest. Big trees. Mountain air. Do you good. Get the fat off."

"Fat? What fat?"

"Fat. Out of shape. I pay ten dollars a day. Board and room. Seven days a week. We'll be outa there in two weeks if you don't waste time or quit on me. You want the job? You got it. But remember who's boss. I do the thinkin'."

"Papa, I want you to listen carefully to what I am about to say. I want you to stay calm, and I want you to be reasonable. My business, as you know, is writing. Your business is building things. All I know how to do is string one word after another, like beads. All you know is piling one rock on another. I don't know how to lay brick or mix mortar. I don't want to know. I have certain things to do. I have a commitment. A commitment is a contract. There's a man in New York, a publisher, who's paying me to write a book. He is waiting for this book. He has been waiting for over a year. He is losing his patience. He sends me angry letters. He telephones and calls me filthy names. He threatens to sue me. You understand what I'm saying, Papa?"

"I'll tell you one thing about Monte Casino," he said. "You'll feel better. You'll get healthy. What are you worrying about? Did I say anything about not writing? Bring some pencils and paper. Ask Mama: she's got lots of paper in the closet. Write any time you want. Write something about the mountains. Write at night, after work. It's quiet up there. You know the owls? You can hear them. And the coyotes. Peace, quiet, purify the mind. You'll write better."

I groaned. "What about Garcia, your old hod carrier?"

"Dead."

"What about Red Griffin?"

"Dead."

"That black man, Campbell."

"Dying."

"There's got to be somebody alive around here besides me! There's got to be!"

"Gone, all gone."

"What about Zarlingo, or Benedetti, or one of these bums at the card table?"

"They're pretty old. Benedetti is eighty."

A sigh, like a sigh coming out of the centuries, spilled from his wine-moist lips. He seemed to crumble, as if his skeletal bones were falling apart beneath the weight of despair, his chin settling on his chest.

"Nobody wants to work for Nick Molise," he said. "I been looking for two weeks, but I can't find nobody. Not even my own son." He fought back a sob.

"Good God, Papa, don't start crying on me."

"Ten, twenty generations of stonemasons, and I'm the last, the end of the line, and nobody gives a damn, not even my own flesh and blood."

It was time for reasonableness, for patience and soft words, for restraint, for goodness and charity and filial generosity. I said I was sorry, Papa. I said there were some things I would not ask him to do, and there were other things he should not ask me to do. I said I was not against carrying a hod or laying stone. I said masonry was an honorable profession, the best record of the nobility and aspiration of mankind. I spoke gratefully of the Acropolis, the Pyramids, of Roman aqueducts and the Aztec ruins. Then I began to be annoyed by this irascible, stubborn old man, and my impatience spilled over and the Molise rashness swept through me, the truculence, the bad temper, the frenzy.

"Frankly, old man," I said, "I hate the building profession. I've hated it from the time I was a little kid and you used to come home with mortar splattered all over your shoes and face. I think painters and bricklayers are drunks, and I think plumbers are thieves. I think carpenters are crooks and I think electricians are highway robbers. I don't like flagstone or marble or granite or brick or tile or sand or cement. I don't care if I ever see another stone fireplace or stone wall or stone steps or just plain stones lying on a field, and if you want the truth stripped clean I don't give a shit about stonemasons either." I took a deep breath. "Something else I don't like is mountains and forests and owls and mountain air and coyotes and bears. I never saw a smokehouse in my life and, God willing, I shall never see one, or build one."

The more I shouted and pounded the table the more he drank, and the more he drank the more the tears busted from his eyes. He pulled a polka-dot kerchief from his pocket, blew his nose, and had another gulp of wine. He was pitiful, wretched, embarrassing, revolting, shameless, stupid, gross, ugly and drunk, the worst father a man ever had, so loathsome I spat my beer in the spittoon and got up to leave.

From the back of the saloon came the bellow of a voice, the roar of a bull speaking like a man.

"Just a minute, wise guy. Just who the hell you think you're talking to?"

I turned. The patrons of the Café Roma were glaring at me with cold amorphous eyes, their faces repelled by the presence of an outsider in their midst. Zarlingo got to his feet. The many pens and pencils in his bib were like battle decorations on a colonel.

"That man's your father," Zarlingo declared, pointing at Papa. "And he's my friend. You show some respect, understand?"

"It's none of your business."

Cavallaro stood up threateningly, pushing back his chair. "You want some help, Nick? You want me to take care of this punk?"

"I'm okay," Papa faltered, his voice trembling. "I'm just fine, boys. Tired, that's all. Very tired. Alone in the world. Trying to do the right thing. You do your best for your family. You feed them, buy them clothes,

send them to school, and then they turn around and throw you out. I
don't know what happened . . . what I done wrong. Maybe 'cause I was
too good. I don't know. God help me. I tried. I tried hard . . ."

I said "Oh, balls!" and walked out.

—*The Brotherhood of the Grape*

HALF A BLOCK FROM MY PARENTS' HOUSE on Pleasant Street I breathed the aroma of Mama's cooking. The ugly scene at the Café Roma vanished in the ambrosial waft of sweet basil, oregano, rosemary and thyme.

Suddenly a figure burst from the front door of the house, dashed down the porch steps, and raced to a pickup at the curb.

"Mario!" I shouted. "Mario, wait!"

He either heard me or he didn't hear me as he started the engine and gunned the noisy truck away without looking at me. I crossed the yard to the porch. My mother stood behind the screen door, her silver hair in a neat pile, her apron fresh and white, her face warmed by happiness and a hot stove. By now Mario's truck was two blocks away and still farting on five cylinders.

"What's he running from?"

"He ate and ran. Ascared of your father."

"He still eats here?"

"When he can. His wife don't cook Italian." She glanced down Pleasant Street. "Where's your father?"

"At the Roma."

"You had a fight?"

"Argument."

"You're not going to the mountains?" There was concern in her voice.

"You knew about that?"

We were still talking through the screen door.

"He said he was going to ask you."

"He asked. I said, no chance."

I stepped into the hot, small parlor that was overpowered by the spices from the kitchen. That parlor! It was hellishly hot. A morgue. Walls bedecked with pictures of the dead, aunts, uncles, cousins, grandparents. In the corner on a pedestal stood a statue of Jesus bleeding profusely. Vigil candles in glass cups were at the Savior's feet. They were a vital part of the household, participating in all that was vital and meaningful, for my mother lit the candles whenever a relative died, or when someone got sick, or when something of value was lost, or when lightning came close to the sky.

Dimly I saw a stack of clothing on the sofa. The stuff looked familiar, like images in an old photograph.

"What's all this?"

"Your work clothes."

"Work clothes? What kind of work?"

"Mountain work." She hid her face.

"No mountains for me."

"Think about it. Make up your own mind."

"No mountains."

I studied the clothes, tumbled the garments about. God knew where she had dug them out, some trunk in the hot, stuffy attic where every-thing eventually mummified—jeans, shirts, a pair of boots, even my base-ball sweater with the big SE emblazoned on the chest. The idea that even my baby clothes might be carefully preserved somewhere made me shud-der. There was something artful about those resurrected garments, a planned arrangement, a spider setting a trap, and I the victim. She sensed my thought and slipped into the kitchen. I found her at the stove, stirring things inside pots. She had prepared a great deal of food.

"Who's going to eat all this?"

"Everybody."

"You invited everybody."

"No, but they'll come anyway."

I dropped into a chair at the kitchen table. She was there right away with a bottle of wine from the refrigerator and a chilled glass. I knew the wine. It had to be the new wine from the vines of Angelo Musso's vine-yard, easily the most important commodity in the house, for without it my father would quickly dry up and fade away.

"Mama, what's this about a divorce?"

"What divorce?"

"You know what divorce. Why do you think I'm here?"

She laughed. "Just talk. We're Catholics, we can't divorce. Didn't you know that?"

"Mario said he kicked you, choked you. You had to have him arrested."

"Mario did it. Papa didn't mean it. He didn't do it on purpose."

She began slicing bread.

"How can he kick you, choke you, but not on purpose?"

"He didn't mean it. He was only playing."

"So he went to jail."

"For a half hour. It was nothing."

"What about the lipstick on his underwear?"

"It was jelly."

"I thought it was jelly."

"Cherry jelly. On his pancakes. He spilled some on his lap."

"And for that you accuse him of infidelity?"

"So I was wrong, for once." She heaved a big sigh. "How many times have I been right the last fifty years?"

I took her hand and smoothed the dry, soft skin.

"You don't have to worry about things like that anymore. He's not young anymore. The fire's out."

"He don't need a fire. He keeps going without it."

"In his mind, that's all."

"It's dirty," she said. "It's a sin."

She busied herself with the dinner, checking the eggplant in the oven, the gnocchi warming in a black iron pot, the veal bubbling in Marsala.

"I couldn't find any heavy socks. You'll need them up there. It may snow, this time of the year."

"I'm not going 'up there.' "

"Not even this last time, for your father?"

"I'm working. I can't leave my book."

That sent her suddenly out of the room toward the bedroom, where I heard her shuffling heavy objects about. She returned with an armful of books, dropping them on the table in front of me. They were my high school textbooks: geometry, American history, English composition, Spanish.

"Take them home," she said. "They're still new."

I thanked her. "Just what I need."

She studied my face, her fingers touching the delicate bones of her cheeks as she returned to the one obsession of her existence. "You didn't get him mad? He won't get into trouble?"

"He'll drink too much, that's all."

"I don't mind the drinking. The boys bring him home."

"The boys?"

"Zarlingo and them. They watch him for me. Thank God you'll be there. They scare me, those mountains."

An angel, a persistent, tiresome angel. No wonder my papa booted her in the ass. I felt strangled, helpless as an infant swaddled and straining in futility. What the hell was I doing here? What was my wife up to? I was having a serious problem with my book. What the hell was it? Had the old man really put up with this crap for half a century? Who said he was impulsive, lacking patience, intolerant? The sun had dropped below the houses beyond the alley and it was cooler now, about ninety-five in the shade, the sky exploding with red and orange clouds.

"As long as I know where he is," she was saying. "As long as he lets me know . . ."

I filled my glass and went out on the front porch, sat in the creaking rocker, and lit a cigarette. Darkness came fast. Down the street a mother stepped out on her porch and called her children to supper. The corner street lamp burst into light and an old dog trotted under it, hurrying home. The white eyes of television sets shone through the windows across the street, cowboys racing across the screens, gunfire crackling in the San Elmo twilight. A lonesome town. All the valley towns were like it, desolate, mystically impermanent, enclaves of human existence, people clustered behind small fences and flimsy stucco walls, barricaded against the darkness, waiting. I rocked back and forth and felt grief seeping into my bones, grief for man and the pain of loneliness in the house of my mother and father, aging, waiting, marking time.

Then my mother came quietly to the screen door and stared at me, as if storing up a remembrance of me, as if she might never see me again. I felt her pulsing back and forth, incorporeal and disembodied, sorrowing and lost as she slipped out of reality and back again, ashamed so little time remained.

"Henry?" Her voice was soft and irresolute. "You mustn't worry about me and your father. You get a little crazy when you're older, but it don't do any harm. Be patient, Henry. You want your supper now?"

The baked eggplant took me back to the childhood of my life when they were a nickel apiece and a great feast, purple globular marvels bulging jolly and generous, rich Arab uncles eager to fill our stomachs, so beautiful I wanted to cry.

The thin slices of veal had me fighting tears again as I washed them down with Joe Musso's magnificent wine from the nearby foothills. And the gnocchi prepared in butter and milk finally did it. I covered my eyes over the plate and wept with joy, sopping my tears with a napkin, gurgling as if in my mother's womb, so sweet and peaceful and filling my mouth with life forever. She saw my wet eyes, for there was no hiding them.

"Something in the air," I said. "Ammonia, maybe? It burns my eyes."

"It's ammonia. I mopped the floor with it."

"That's it. Ammonia."

"Your father hates ammonia. He won't let me use it in the washing machine."

"Really?"

"You know what he likes?"

"Tell me."

"Bubble bath."

She veered to questions about Harriet and my boys. I showed her the snapshots in my wallet, the younger twenty-two, the older twenty-four. She studied the pictures under the kitchen light.

"They don't look like stonemasons."

"No."

"Mario's boys don't care for it either. Virgil's boy wants to play the piano and Stella has all girls. He wants a stonemason so bad, poor man. If we had just one in the family I think he'd quit drinking. All his prayers would be answered."

"He prays?"

"Never. Or goes to mass." Her eyes fixed me searchingly. "Do you go to mass, Henry?"

I had anticipated it. "Every Sunday. Like clockwork."

"And your boys?"

"In the same pew with me and their mother, every Sunday."

She almost sailed through the ceiling straight for celestial bliss, but she suddenly caught herself, her face growing serious. "You're lying, Henry. Your wife never turned Catholic."

"I'm working on it. Takes time."

She sat down, sighing, disappointed, pouring a bit of wine into a glass. "No Catholics. No stonemasons. Dear God, whatever happened?"

She reached for my hand and folded it within her dry, warm palms, her voice compassionate and imploring. "Talk to your father, Henry. Make him go back to Our Lord. There isn't much time. When you're his age you never know from one hour to the next. And what'll I do when he goes, worrying about where he went?"

"Why don't you ask Father Martin to talk to him. That's his business, saving souls."

"He's been here lots of times. All they do is fight. Your father has no respect. It's the old country style. He laughs."

"Then leave him alone."

"I hope he goes first. Nobody can put up with him but me. Worse than a child: iron the sheets but not the pillow cases. Starch the cuffs but not the collars. Shine his shoes, trim his mustache, rub his feet, cut his hair, hot water bottle in his bed. You know what he's got now? A bell, by his bed. Every night it rings for something: bring me a glass of wine, rub my back, make me some soup. When I'm gone you think Stella'll do all that?"

The bell puzzled me.

"Don't you sleep together?"

"He threw me out."

"Why?"

"How should I know? I wouldn't touch him anyway." She raced ahead: "Do you know he takes enemas with warm wine, and eats raw eggs in the morning?"

"Nauseating."

"See what I mean?"

A horn sounded from the street.

"That's Virgil. Tell him about the gnocchi."

I walked out on the porch and saw my brother Virgil sitting in his station wagon under the street lamp. I waved him to come in and he motioned me toward the car.

His old wagon was fender-dented, the wood paneling scraped and peeling. We shook hands through the window. We were more like classmates than brothers. Neither of us liked to think of the other, and in that sense we were nonexistent to one another. But he envied me, my lifestyle, my small success that had taken me away from San Elmo. I wasn't sure he hated me, but I was certain he disliked me.

He was porcine now, his navel packed tight against the steering wheel. At forty-seven he looked ten years older, his hair fast vanishing—full at the temples, bald and glistening over the top. He had not married until thirty-five and now he was the father of four girls and a boy. I could smell them as I thrust my head inside the car, the sour taint of vomit and diapers. All the symbols of family joy were piled helter-skelter in the back of the wagon—playpen, tricycles, toys, diapers, blankets.

My brother Virgil! The genius of the family, destined to be a million-aire, straight out of high school with scholastic awards, honored by the faculty and immediately accepted as a clerk in San Elmo's only independent bank. After nearly thirty years with the same firm he now managed the Loan Department, and the future was dim indeed, for the president's three sons, Stanford-educated, had come upon the scene. I felt pity for the guy, but at the same time I thanked God all that baby litter in the back of his car was long gone from my own life.

"How's everything?"

He smiled in a way that bent his mouth out of shape, a man with toothache of the soul. My mother's melancholy eyes took up most of his large Neapolitan face.

"How's Edith?"

"Three guesses." He smiled feebly, like a man on the gallows.

"Good God, Virgil. Not again!"

He nodded with a great head that wearied his shoulders.

"You should stop, Virgil. You ever hear of a drugstore? Use something."

"I use my cock. You have any other suggestions?"

"What about vasectomy?"

"That's for dogs. I'm a man . . . I think."

"Come on in. Let's have a glass of vino."

"I won't go in there," he scowled. "I'm pissed off at them."

"At Mama? Nobody else is here."

"Mama, Papa, Mario, the whole family. That paranoia in front of the police station. I can't take it anymore. They've destroyed me in this fucking town. Now they're trying to bury me."

I opened the door.

"Come on, Virgil. Mama's fixed a lovely dinner."

"Naturally," he smiled. "Tell me something. How come crazy old ladies cook so well? Same thing with my wife's mother. A real psychopath, but God, what stroganoff!" He looked toward the house, tempted, but suddenly he leaned over and jerked the door shut.

"I won't go in there. I'll starve first!"

The screen door squealed and we looked toward the house as Mama stepped outside. "Come and eat, Virgil. It's all fixed."

"No, thanks, Ma."

"Baked eggplant, Virgil," she coaxed. "I fixed it special the way you like it. And gnocchi in milk and butter, and veal in wine."

"Thank you just the same, Ma."

She was hurt and startled by his refusal and slipped back into the darkness of the house. I stared at him.

"Nice going, you jerk."

"I have my reasons."

"How does she know your reasons? All she's thinking about is your gut."

"What's this new madness? Mario says you're going to work for the old man."

"He's crazy."

"I know that. But is it true?"

"Of course it's not true. What kind of an idiot do you take me for? I'm leaving tomorrow morning."

"Leave town, Henry. Leave before they trap you."

"Nobody traps me. I'm my own man."

"Henry," he smiled patiently. "Please. I've heard all that bullshit before. Get out of here as fast as you can. Tonight. Leave now. I'll drive you to the airport."

"Thanks, Virgil. I'm staying."

"The old man's too old to lay stone. Tell him. Then get the hell out."

"If he wants to lay stone, let him. It's his life."

"And it could be the end of his life."

"You want to talk to him, Virgil? You want to reason with that old bastard? He's down at the Café Roma right now. Go on down there and talk it over."

He threw up his hands.

"God, what a family!"

He started the car and I stepped away and watched it move forward about thirty feet. Then it rolled back to where I stood. A foolish, helpless smile crinkled Virgil's fat face.

"Is the eggplant made with bread crumbs and Romano cheese?"

"It sure is."

Resigned, he turned off the engine. Together we walked into the house.

The kitchen. *La cucina,* the true mother country, this warm cave of the good witch deep in the desolate land of loneliness, with pots of sweet potions bubbling over the fire, a cavern of magic herbs, rosemary and thyme and sage and oregano, balm of lotus that brought sanity to lunatics, peace to the troubled, joy to the joyless, this small twenty-by-twenty world, the altar a kitchen range, the magic circle a checkered tablecloth where the children fed, the old children, lured back to their beginnings, the taste of mother's milk still haunting their memories, fra-

252 / The John Fante Reader

grance in the nostrils, eyes brightening, the wicked world receding as the old mother witch sheltered her brood from the wolves outside.

Beguiled and voracious Virgil filled his cheeks with gnocchi and eggplant and veal, and flooded them down his gullet with the fabulous grape of Joe Musso, spellbound, captivated, mooning over his great mother, enrapturing her with loving glances, even pausing midst his greed to lift her hand and kiss it gratefully. She laughed to see how completely she had woven her spell, and while they stared like haunted lovers I slipped into the parlor and telephoned Harriet in Redondo Beach.

"Is everything all right up there?" she asked.

"Fine, fine. No problems."

"What about the divorce?"

"Forgotten."

"Did you see my mother?"

"No."

"Will you?"

"Maybe tomorrow."

"Promise?"

"No."

I felt my mother's warm breath on my neck and turned to face her, eavesdropping behind me. Not surreptitiously, but brazenly listening.

"Let me talk," she said, drawing the phone from my hand. Then, into it: "Halloo, Harrietta. She'sa me talkin', you modderin-law. How you are, Harrietta. Thassa good. Me? I'ma feela fine."

There it was again, my mother's hypocritical fawning before Harriet, that groveling like a serf before the baroness, so self-debasing that even her powers of speech fell apart. Born in Chicago, knowing only the English language, my mother nonetheless spoke like a Neapolitan immigrant fresh off the boat whenever she and Harriet came together.

I listened, exasperated, tearing my hair. "Harrietta, I'ma gonna aska yo wan beeg favor, si? You tink she'sa all right iffen your husba stay two, three day, maybe wan week? He'sa help his papa, poor ole man, he'sa got the rheumatiz. I tink wan week, maybe ten day, maybe two, tree week, and the job, she'sa finish. Okay, Miss Harrietta? Tank you so much. Godda bless . . ."

I ripped the phone from her. "Home tomorrow, Harriet. Forget all that garbage!"

Mama shoved her mouth into the instrument.

"Please, Harrietta, I hope I donna make trouble in you house, okay? I'm joost try to help his papa. He'sa gotta sore back."

"Home tomorrow!" I yelled, clapping down the receiver.

A clatter of heavy shoes on the front porch, the clumsy movement of bodies. Joe Zarlingo and Lou Cavallaro lurched through the front door carrying my father between them. With calm professionalism, like a nurse, my mother cleared the sofa and fluffed a pillow as the men stretched my father out. He lay there besotted, a smile on his dribbling lips.

"He's smashed," I said, looking down at him.

"I'll get the coffee," Mama said.

Zarlingo and Cavallaro glared at me.

"What brought this on?" I asked.

Zarlingo was shocked. "You got the guts to ask?"

It sickened Cavallaro. "Jesus, man. You ain't even human."

Virgil came from the kitchen, wiping his mouth with a napkin and studying the old man without emotion. Then he moved to the front door, tossed the napkin into a chair, and smiled at me.

"What did I tell you?"

He went through the front door. I stepped out on the front porch and watched him drive away. Another car, a Datsun camper, was parked out there. It was Zarlingo's.

He came from the house with Lou Cavallaro and the two stood silently on either side of me. Zarlingo bit off the tip of a Toscanelli and jabbed it between his teeth.

"You going up to Donner Pass with your father?" he demanded.

"Nope."

"You mean, you want your old man to go up there, haul rock, mix mortar, and build a stone house all by himself?"

"If that's what he wants, I certainly won't stand in his way."

"In other words, you don't give a fuck if your father lives or dies."

"I didn't say that, you did."

"He's a proud man," Cavallaro said. "Don't you understand that by now?"

"Pride goeth before the fall."

Suddenly old Zarlingo hauled off and hit me a loud whack across the cheek with his open palm. It was a stinging smack, surprising, shocking. He seemed more surprised than I at what he had done, and Cavallaro stood there bewildered. I laughed. There was nothing else I could do. I laughed to hide my anger and walked away, down the path to the sidewalk, where I turned to look back, a bloat of rage bulging inside my ribs.

"You creep!" I yelled. "You senile, pathetic old drunk!"

"You punk!" he screamed, charging down the steps toward me. "You better show a little respect."

I thought of standing my ground, even of belting him, but none of it made sense, especially my anger, and I quickly walked away. Over my shoulder I saw him pick up a beer can from the gutter and throw it at me. The can clattered harmlessly past my feet, and that made me laugh again. I continued down the street toward town. My mind clicked into gear: I was leaving that goddamn town. In three or four hours I would be under the covers in my own bed, four hundred miles away, listening to the sigh of the surf, and all of this bad dream would be forgotten. Straight down Pleasant Street I walked to Lincoln, then right on Lincoln to the bus depot.

In the alley the Sacramento bus was breathing hard as it took on a handful of passengers. I bought a ticket and walked back to the bus, but I did not get aboard. I had lost the power to make a decision. The longer I lingered—the driver waiting, watching me through the door—the more momentous the choice became as fear set in, the fear of delivering a fatal blow to my aged parents, the fear of regretting it the rest of my life. I had to stay. Not from choice but duty. And so I turned away and walked home, searching myself for a burst of Christian exhilaration for having done the right thing, building up my reward in heaven.

The Datsun was gone when I reached the house and so were Zarlingo and Cavallaro. In the bedroom my mother sat beside the old man, who lay undressed beneath a sheet in the hot, small room.

"Where'd you go?" my mother said. "I was so worried."

"About what?"

"You're a writer. This town's no place for you at night."

I thought I heard my father sob and moved closer to him. In his sleep he wept, tears spilling from his closed eyes. She blotted his wet lashes with the hem of the sheet.

"Why is he crying?"

"He's dreaming. He wants his mother."

His mother. Dead sixty years.

I choked up and fled to the kitchen, craving wine. I was into the second glass when Mama appeared.

"I changed the sheets, Henry. You sleep in my bed."

———

I was too tired to care. Like all the rooms in that old house, my mother's bedroom was small. The bed was still warm from the heat of the day as I slipped naked beneath a sheet and down into a cradle in the mattress that measured the contours of my mother's body. It was very black down there when I snapped off the bedside lamp. In the pillow my nostrils drew the sweet, earthy odor of my mother's hair, pulling me back to other times, when I was not yet twenty and sought to run away.

Yes, I got away. I made it when I was not yet twenty. The writers drew me away. London, Dreiser, Sherwood Anderson, Thomas Wolfe, Hemingway, Fitzgerald, Silone, Hamsun, Steinbeck. Trapped and barricaded against the darkness and the loneliness of the valley, I used to sit with library books piled on the kitchen table, desolate, listening to the call of the voices in the books, hungering for other towns.

I had come to the limits of shooting pool, playing poker and bullshitting over beers, of driving off with other guys and broads into lonely orchards, clawing clumsily at skirts and panties, clawing in vain. Women were fine but demanding, you hurt easily at nineteen; you thought women were sweet and submissive but find them alley cats; you find comfort in whores who are less deceitful, and if you are lucky you learn to read.

My old man, the son of a bitch, lurching home with a snoutful of vino, yelling turn off the lights, get to bed, what the hell's come over you, for books were a drug and my addiction was alarming, and I was hardly his son at all anymore. Get a job, he demanded, do something with your life. He was right. He must have been. Everybody agreed with him. Even the guys at the poolhall noticed the change. We couldn't talk to one another the old way.

I got a job. I picked almonds. I picked grapes. I worked the hop fields. The rains came, the fields wet and unworkable, thank God, and I was back in the kitchen, reading the sweet books. They thought I was ill—my eyes red and staring, my mother feeling my forehead: You all right, Henry? Maybe you got the flu.

He should see a doctor, my father said. Find out what's wrong. Where you going with your life? Who's gonna take care of your mother when I'm gone? They don't pay wages for reading books. Get out of here! There's a war on. Get in the army. Go to San Francisco. Get on a boat. Support yourself. Be a man. You know what a man is? A man works. He sweats. He digs. He pounds. He builds. He gets a few dollars and puts them away. Listen to who's talking! I sneered.

There was no answer for that street-corner Dago, that low-born Abruzzian wop, the yahoo peasant ginzo, that shit-kicker, that curb crawler. What did *he* know? What had *he* read?

For I was okay. I was on to something. A new feeling of the world beyond San Elmo . . . thrilling, shocking, pumping my adrenaline. Why had I not come upon it before? Where had I been all those years? Trying to carry a hod, mixing mortar? Who was it that had stunted my brain, kept books out of my range, ignored them, despised them? My old man. His ignorance, the frenzy of living under his roof, his rantings, his threats, his greed, his bullying, his gambling. Christmas without money. Graduation without a suit of clothes. Debts, debts. We stopped speaking. One day we passed one another crossing the railroad tracks. He went on a few steps, stopped, and began to laugh. I turned. He pointed at me and began to laugh. He pretended to read a book and laughed. It was not amusement. It was rage and disappointment and contempt.

Then it happened. One night as the rain beat on the slanted kitchen roof a great spirit slipped forever into my life. I held his book in my hands and trembled as he spoke to me of man and the world, of love and wisdom, pain and guilt, and I knew I would never be the same. His name was Fyodor Mikhailovich Dostoyevsky. He knew more of fathers and sons than any man in the world, and of brothers and sisters, priests and rogues, guilt and innocence. Dostoyevsky changed me—*The Idiot, The Possessed, The Brothers Karamazov, The Gambler.* He turned me inside out. I found I could breathe, could see invisible horizons. The hatred for my father melted. I loved my father, poor, suffering, haunted wretch. I loved my mother too, and all my family. It was time to become a man, to leave San Elmo and go out into the world. I wanted to think and feel like Dostoyevsky. I wanted to write.

The week before I left town the draft board summoned me to Sacramento for my physical. I was glad to go. Someone other than myself could make my decisions. The army turned me down. I had asthma. Inflammation of the bronchial tubes.

"That's nothing. I've always had it."

"See your doctor."

I got the needed information from a medical book at the public library. Was asthma fatal? It could be. And so be it. Dostoyevsky had epilepsy, I had asthma. To write well a man must have a fatal ailment. It was the only way to deal with the presence of death.

—The Brotherhood of the Grape

I CARRIED THE LUGGAGE and a sack of tools from the truck to Cabin 7. The accommodations were routine motel decor: a kitchen with a bar, a divan, a rug, a couple of chairs, a TV and a bed.

The bed I did not like. It was a double bed and it meant I would have to sleep with the old man. Fretting, I sat on it and considered the dilemma. I had never slept with my father. I had rarely in my life even touched him, except for a rare handshake over the years, and now I had no desire to sleep with him. I considered his old bones, his old skin, the lonely, ornery oldness of him, the wine-soaked oldness of him and his sodden, sinful friends, the son of a bitch he had been: unreasonable, tyrannical, boorish, profligate Wop who had trapped me on this snafu safari into the mountains, far from wife and home and work, all for his bedizened vanity, to prove to himself he was still a hotshot stonemason.

Then it all began to come back. I was ten years old at a street dance in San Elmo, the night of the Fourth of July. I was in the alley behind the dance, searching trash barrels. In the darkness I saw a man and woman making love against a telephone post, the woman holding up her dress, the man throwing his body at her. I knew what they were doing, but it scared me as I crouched behind a pile of crates. Hand in hand the man and woman walked toward me. The man was my father. The woman was Della Lorenzo, who lived two doors from our house with her husband and two sons, my classmates in school. After that I never played with the Lorenzo kids again. I was ashamed to look into their eyes. I hated my father. I hated Mrs. Lorenzo; she was so common, so frumpy and plain. I hated the Lorenzo house, their yard. I kicked their mongrel dog. I strangled one of their chickens. When Mrs. Lorenzo died of breast cancer the next year I was indifferent. She had it coming. No doubt she was in hell, making a place for my father.

Easter Sunday. I was twelve. We were at the Santucci farm, the entire family. Hordes of Italians from all over the county, long tables sagging with wine, pasta, salad and roast goat, my old man with a goat's head on his plate, eating the brains and the eyes, laughing and showing off before women screaming in horror. Afterward, a softball game. Somebody hit a ball over the hedge in the outfield. I leaped after it and landed on top of my father, hidden in the tall grass, his bare bottom white as a winter moon as he pumped Mrs. Santucci, who was supposed to be my mother's best friend. Astounded, I ran toward the orchard, over the creek, down the pear grove. My father came racing after me. I had the speed of a deer. I knew he would never catch me, but he did. He shook me. He was throwing spit in his rage. "One word to your mother and by God I'll kill you!"

I spent the rest of the long afternoon at my mother's side while she gossiped on the lawn with the other ladies. I would not leave her. I sat on the grass and clutched the hem of her dress and it annoyed her. "Go play with the other kids," she said. "You're bothering me."

No. I would not lie down in the mountain darkness beside that abominable old man, rewarding him with affection and companionship after a lifetime of unrepentant sensuality at the expense of his wife and family. No wonder my poor mother thought of divorce, and Virgil was ashamed of him, and Mario fled from the sight of him, and Stella disapproved of him.

I found an extra blanket in the closet, kicked off my shoes, and curled up on the divan. . . .

It was after one o'clock when my father tumbled into the cabin. He switched on the ugly light in the globed overhead chandelier, left the door open, and marched straight to the bed, where he collapsed. In thirty seconds he was deeply asleep, his breathing heavy, his mouth open. I locked the door, peeled off his clothes, and rolled him under the covers. As I turned off the light and lay down on the divan he began to moan, "Mama mia, mama mia."

Then he was sobbing. Was this any way for a man to fall asleep, calling for his mother? It seemed he would never stop. It tore me to shreds. I knew nothing of his mother. She had been dead for over sixty years, had expired in Italy after he had left and come to America, still visiting him now in his old man's sleep, as if he felt her near in his dreams, like one lost and wandering, crying for her.

I lay there tearing my hair and thinking. Stop it, Father, you are drunk and full of self-pity and you must stop it, you have no right to cry, you are my father and the right to cry belongs to my wife and children, to my mother, for it is obscene that you should cry, it humiliates me, I shall die from your grief, I cannot endure your pain, I should be spared your pain for I have enough of my own. I shall have more too, but I shall never cry before others, I shall be strong and face my last days without tears, old man. I need your life and not your death, your joy and not your dismay.

Then I was crying too, on my feet, crossing to him. I gathered his limp head in my arms (as I had seen my mother do), I wiped his tears with a corner of the sheet, I rocked him like a child, and soon he was no longer crying, and I eased him gently to the pillow and he slept quietly.

—The Brotherhood of the Grape

BACK AT THE SMOKEHOUSE my father seemed invigorated, and the kink in his back was gone as he selected a long-handled sledgehammer and positioned himself before a craggy chunk of granite four feet square. He was about to make little ones out of big ones. I stood aside and watched him swing the sledge powerfully, half a dozen blows until the stone began to break, not in clean sheaths, but twisted, jagged chunks and splinters.

"Fine," he pronounced, breathing hard, "just fine. Bring them to the wall."

I hauled them and he laid them, the big ones and the little ones, the chunks and the splinters. I crushed the rock and he did the wall. We did fine. When tired, he called for wine. He could not straighten up, so he stood like an ape as he drank. When he began to sweat the blotches on his back and under his arms were rose-colored. I thought, what the hell, it's nutritious, it's grape sugar, energy, and drank with him every time. We were doing fine, fine. We were tired and dazed, and I thought I saw a gnome with a red hat in the forest as the sun went over the trees and the smokehouse wall sprouted toward the sky.

We stopped work as darkness fell. We could have worked by moonlight, but that would have been the edge of madness. Sam Ramponi might drive home from Reno and laugh at us. Motel guests would wonder what was going on. We called it a day. We had drunk two gallons. We had pissed three or four. We were spinning. We were spooked. Old Nick laughed to himself. He fell on his face as we went for our supper. I laughed and pulled him to his feet. Ramponi wasn't home. Mrs. Ramponi filled our plates. Maybe it was deer meat. What did I care?

My father fell asleep at the table. I dragged him to the cabin and heaped him into bed. I slept. Suddenly it was morning. No need to dress;

I had slept in my clothes. My mouth was full of Mrs. Ramponi's old tennis shoes and dog hair. I cleansed it with a gargle of wine and we went back to work.

We hurried now. We had to get out of there. I busted the big stones and the old man popped them into the wall. We were at sea, on a raft, hurrying, setting a record. Have a drink, son. It was a race. Have a drink, Papa. No starting line, no finish. But fast. He tossed aside the plumb line. He stopped using the mason's level. He worked by instinct. Sometimes he lowered his head down to the line of the wall and squinted, keeping it plumb. The wall went up and the wine went down. Once I looked up at the sky and asked, "What time is it?" He answered, "There ain't no time," and I laughed. God, he was profound. When the wine was gone Ramponi brought more from Reno. Just in time. In the last moment of the last drop from the last jug. Good wine, from Angelo Musso.

———

Then a peculiar thing happened. My father died. We were working away, swirling in mortar and stone, and all of a sudden I sensed that he had left the world. I sought his face and it was written there. His eyes were open, his hands moved, he splashed mortar, but he was dead, and in death he had nothing to say. Sometimes he drifted off like a specter into the trees to take a piss. How could he be dead, I wondered, and still walk off and pee? A ghost he was, a goner, a stiff. I wanted to ask him if he was well, if by chance he was still alive, but I was too tired and too busy dying myself, and too tired of making phrases. I could see the question on paper, typewritten, with quotation marks, but it was too heavy to verbalize. Besides, what difference did it make? We all had to die someday.

On the fourth day, between large draughts of Angelo Musso, we built the scaffold and had two feet to go. Nick, who was dead, could feel no pain as he strung out the stone. He was not neat anymore, not the fussy, fastidious stonemason of the past, and the wall was splattered and the mortar oozed and made big pies at the base. There below, still alive, I broke slabs and packed them on my shoulder and lifted them to the scaffold, and then one day, I know not which day, I died too.

I must have died bravely and quietly, for I did not remember lamentation and tears. First there was this splintering pain in my lumbar region from swinging the sledge and then it was gone, it seemed to drift off into the forest, as did the other pains—my aching feet, my blistered palms, the throb in my kidneys—one by one they all vanished, and I felt the cessation of the nervous system. When I die again, I thought, and undoubtedly for the last time, I must remember to face it as I did that day in the mountains, succumbing to death as if she were my beloved, smiling as I took her into my arms.

The other deceased person, my friend, my old man, greeted me across the threshold of life with eyes vacant as windowpanes as I hoisted him a massive stone and he wrestled it into a nest of mortar.

Then an ironic thing occurred. Turning from the scaffold, I stepped upon the sharp edge of a hoe and it sprang at me with its handle, a brutal clout between the eyes. I felt no pain at all. The blow knocked me down, but I was beyond pain.

We did not see much of Sam Ramponi except in the morning as he drove off to Reno, sometimes waving, sometimes not. Toward evening on the fifth day he strolled up without a sound and stood close to the construction, his arms folded, staring at my father on the scaffold. No greeting, no sign of recognition from either man. My father returned Ramponi's concerned frown with mournful but defiant eyes. Ramponi could not have known of our demise, but he sensed a change in us, an immateriality, spectral and disembodied. He waved me an uneasy glance and hurried away toward the motel, turning once to look over his shoulder at us, like someone repelled.

Mrs. Ramponi was puzzled and disturbed too. Whereas at first she brought our lunches to the job, she now placed the tray on a tree stump fifty feet from where we worked, and then scurried back to the motel. At breakfast she shrank from serving us, showing a fearsome respect. We usually left by the kitchen door, which she promptly bolted shut as we walked out.

Sunday afternoon, six days from the start, my father laid the final stone and the smokehouse was finished. We were bearded and gray, we were drunk and we stank, for we had worked and slept in the same clothes.

Kneeling beside the creek, we pulled on the jug and gazed with sunken eyes at what we had wrought—a chunky little structure that resembled an Arab bunker in the Sinai. It was crude and it was crooked. The stones appeared to have been thrown into the wall rather than set. The walls waved crazily, convex and concave, bellied in and bellied out, and they were very thick, much thicker than Papa had agreed upon. Mortar oozed from the joints, soiling the walls. Whatever its aesthetic flaws, the building looked indestructible. All that remained for completion were the roof and the placement of the single door, tasks for a carpenter. Molise and son were finished.

The area was in ruins, like a deserted battlefield. It badly needed cleaning up, if only to lend a little dignity to the loony smokehouse. Planks were scattered about, odds and ends of lumber and chunks of stone, tools, empty wine jugs, cement sacks, paper plates and napkins, half-eaten sandwiches, clothing. The more my eyes fell upon the smokehouse the crazier it seemed.

It didn't look like a building at all, but more like a load of stone carelessly dumped there. Tired, drunk and hallucinating, I began to see it as an ancient Indian burial. Then an iceberg. I blinked and looked again. It was a polar bear. Now it was Mount Whitney, now a rocky formation on the moon. A mist settled over the clearing as I rolled up the hoses and gathered the tools. When I looked at the thing again it was a ship moving slowly across a fogbound sea. Disquieting and vague alarms sent me hurrying toward the cabins.

Through the mist Sam Ramponi's Cadillac entered the motel driveway. He pulled up beside me. He was in his working clothes, Reno black silk suit, white shirt, black bow tie.

"How you doin'?" he asked.

"All finished."

He sighed. "Good. How does she look?"

"It's a smokehouse, Sam. There's no denying that."

"It sure ain't no Taj Mahal."

"Couldn't be avoided," I said professionally, echoing my father. "You ordered the wrong stone. Alabaster quartz is for tombstones. It's not suited for walls. Too heavy, too hard to maneuver. All things considered, we did a remarkable job."

His fat eyes fell upon me.

"You can say that again."

"That smokehouse will outlast these mountains. If you'd asked for the Acropolis the old man would have built it. You wanted a smokehouse and that's precisely what you got."

Big as a walrus he was, shrugging his silken shoulders, not putting up an argument. Then he suddenly blurted it out:

"Looks like a shithouse to me."

He pulled a wallet from inside his coat pocket, removed a check, and handed it to me.

"Give it to Nick. Paid in full."

The check confused me. Everything about it seemed wrong. It was written in the amount of fifteen hundred dollars, but not to my father. On the contrary, my father had written the check payable to Sam Ramponi on the Reno Bank and Trust Company. I racked my head trying to make some sense out of the transaction.

"What in the hell's this?" I asked.

"It's your old man's IOU from the poker game."

I laughed. "Absurd. My father hasn't got fifteen hundred. He hasn't got fifteen cents. He hasn't had a bank account for years, and he's *never* had a bank account in Reno."

Sam touched the check with his thick finger. "Isn't that your father's signature?"

"The one he uses when he's drunk, yes."

"Drunk or sober, it's legal tender."

"It's not legal and it's not tender. It's just a bad check."

He turned his palms in a shrug.

"So he wrote a bad check. That's against the law. I don't want to make trouble, Henry. Me and your father, we go back a long ways. He owes me fifteen hundred from the poker game and I owe him for that thing out there. So," he smiled with blameless eyes, "we're even."

He had us, my father and me. Euchred. It was staggering. My God, how long had I been tumbling around in this nightmare? Dragged from the peace and quiet of my home by the sea, tricked into becoming a stone-mason's helper, hauled off into the mountains with three tosspots, to spend six wretched days building a hunchbacked monstrosity?

Oh, the pain! The blisters! The screaming backache, the tortured feet, the dead weight of those stones, the delirium of our exhaustion, our wraithlike deaths! How long, O Lord, how long? Why was I being punished so? I scanned the past. Was it the waitress in Paris? The three Naples hookers? I have paid, O Lord, I have paid and paid like a credit card that revolves and revolves. Close the account, O Lord. Give me a break. Give me peace. I am wiser, I have learned my lesson. There shall be no more transgressions. I shall return to the church, for I am old now, too fucking old.

Ramponi, my tormentor, crook, card cheat. Rage. I lunged at him through the car window, my fingers around his thick neck, my mind searching for cruel, obscene curses—something better than motherfucker. But the fat man, like most fat men, was quicker than a bird, twisting from my grasp, and the best I could get off was, "All right for you, Sam Ramponi! You'll be sorry!"

He stepped on the gas and the car moved fifty feet to the motel office and stopped. I wasn't through. I pursued him, walking grimly as he got out of his Cadillac, ready for my onslaught, waiting, fists doubled, big as a walrus, prepared to fight.

Maybe he could have taken me, maybe not. He was ponderous as a hippo, fat, a pasta man. I was short, runty, and strong as an ox. I had been preparing for this without knowing it. Six days on the rock pile. I was like iron. He was older, over seventy. I was a youth of fifty. He had no chance. Quickness was on my side. A generation separated us.

I took my stance, fists raised. I spoke:

"You cheated my father, Ramponi. Now you have to reckon with his son."

He brought up his fists.

"I didn't cheat. When you play cards with your old man you don't have to cheat. There's no way you can lose."

"You take him for fifteen hundred, and you don't call that cheating?"

"It was three thousand, Henry. I settled for half."

"Who changed the stakes? When I left you were playing for nickels and dimes."

"Your father raised the stakes. He wanted action. He said he'd quit unless we made it a no-limit game."

"You jerk! The man was drunk."

"He was no drunker'n me. We were all drunk."

Then silence. Cold statues we were, facing one another, Greeks in stone. Staring, fearful of movement. Who would strike first—the crucial blow, the first? We began to circle, slowly round and round. It became tedious. Then it became clear. We didn't want to fight. We had one thing in common: cowardice.

But Sam was first to back off. Dropping his hands, he groaned, turned his back, and stepped into the motel office. It gave me a sense of victory. As he disappeared, I put my hands on my hips and sneered. I felt pretty good walking back to our cabin.

The old man was taking a shower. I pulled the phony check from my pocket and studied it. The dilemma was, should I give it to him, or would it be better if I pretended not to know? Besides, it was really none of my business. It was a private transaction, a gambling debt between him and Sam. I should not have accepted the check in the first place. Then a way out occurred to me. I took an envelope from the motel stationery, slipped the check inside, and sealed it. Presently he emerged naked from the bathroom and scrambled quickly into bed.

I handed him the envelope.

"Sam said to give you this."

He sat up and looked at it. The fact that it was sealed reassured him and he tore it open. His lips broke into a false smile as he examined the check.

"Been a long time since I had a real good paycheck," he said.

—The Brotherhood of the Grape

THE LIGHTS WERE OUT and my mother's house was in darkness as I turned into the yard, but I saw that the front door was open and I heard the creak of the rocker on the front porch, then my mother's voice:

"Is he dead?"

There was no anxiety in her voice, no emotion, only a flat acceptance of what had to be.

"No, Mama. I just came from the hospital."

"How is he?"

"Okay," I said, finding a bit of her face in the darkness. "Dr. Maselli's with him." I sat on the top porch stair and leaned against the post.

"It's been coming," she said. "I've known all along. Is it his heart?"

"He's got diabetes."

She rose and kissed a white rosary in her hand.

"His father died of diabetes."

"How old was he?"

"Young. Only eighty. When can we go see him?"

"Maybe tomorrow."

"Are you hungry? I made a meat loaf."

I followed her into the house. The meat loaf was in the open oven. It didn't look appetizing, as if it had been prepared for my father, his supper, and I could not eat it. As I spread peanut butter on a slice of bread my mother came to the door. She was in a gray and blue dress with a black shawl over her hair.

"I'm going to church."

"At this hour? It's closed."

"Not anymore. Father Martin keeps the doors open all night."

"Go in the morning."

"Now. I want to pray."

"I'll call a cab."

"No. I'd like to walk."

She left and I felt the peanut butter sticking to my mouth, and I thought of her walking seven blocks in the night, across the railroad tracks, past the lumberyard and out Pacific Street to the frame church in the Mexican neighborhood. I went after her.

As I caught up with her and fell in step she did not acknowledge I was there, moving instead with other thoughts and quiet determination. How beautiful she seemed in that warm night along a dimly lit street of run-down houses, loving that tyrant husband in the hospital, her face like a dove, sweetly moving, reminding me of an old photograph of her in a large hat at Capitol Park in Sacramento when she was twenty, leaning against a tree and smiling, so precious then, so precious now that I wanted to take her into my arms like a lover and carry her through the church door.

Though it was nearly midnight the church was not deserted. It reminded me of an Italian proverb: "If you see a crowd of women, the church is close at hand." A dozen women knelt in the pews, all wearing shawls, old like my mother, most in prayer before the Virgin's altar. My mother stayed at the back of the church, entering a pew and kneeling to kiss the cross on her rosary. I knelt beside her and listened to the old wooden edifice crack and wheeze after the heat of the day. There was a smell of layers and layers of incense and fresh flowers, like marriages piled on funerals, and leaping shadows on the walls behind tiers of vigil lights.

Peace smoothed my mother's face. She had not been married in this church, but her children had been baptized there and educated by the nuns of this parish. Her faith was nourishing her now, and from the way her lips moved you could see her sucking up the magic of the place.

After an hour of kneeling beside her my bones ached and I sat back with folded hands. Presently she sat back too, the beads in her hands. I was very tired now, and sleepy, and I stretched out on the pew and closed my eyes. Her fingers stroked my hair and she drew my head into her lap and smiled down at me. The beads danced over my eyes as I fell asleep. We were there through the night, starting back to the house in the new day, along streets that asked about my father and why he was not with us.

—*The Brotherhood of the Grape*

I T WAS TEN MINUTES DOWN HIGHWAY 80 to the turnoff to Angelo's place, then half a mile up the hill to the winery. Circling the driveway at the rear of the house, I came upon Joe Zarlingo's Datsun camper. It didn't surprise me. (Later I learned that after telephoning Zarlingo from his hospital room that morning, my father had dressed and calmly walked out of the main hospital entrance, past the reception desk and out the front door, waiting on the hospital steps for Joe and his friends to whisk him away.)

The midday heat grabbed me by the neck as I stepped from the Chevy and crossed to a gathering of men under the grape arbor. The six were at the long picnic table, Angelo at one end, my father at the other.

Drooping majestically, my old man slumped deep in a wicker chair, wistfully drunk, his arms limp over the chair arms. He was like an ancient Roman patrician waiting for the blood to drain from his slitted wrists. Across from one another on benches were the four galoots from the Café Roma—Zarlingo, Cavallaro, Antrilli and Benedetti. They were all bombed but under control, swigging wine from thick tumblers. Jugs of Chianti and trays of food were spread over the long table: salami, sausages, prosciuto, bread and anise cakes. They had feasted long and well beneath the hot vine, and so had swarms of stunned bees, staggering over the food and floundering in puddles of wine, while hundreds droned mournfully among overripe muscats hanging from the vines.

Not a word was spoken as I came among them. It was as if I was of no importance, a nuisance, another bee. I moved quietly behind my father's chair and put my hands on his shoulders, his soft flesh drawing away, his bones so near to the touch.

"It's me, Papa."

He raised his head.

"What time is it?"

"Time for you to go back to the hospital."

"No, sir. Not me."

"You need your insulin."

He shook his head.

"Stop picking on your father," Zarlingo said. "Sit down, have a drink. Be quiet. Enjoy the party."

"I'm taking him back to the hospital."

"That's up to him." He reached out and touched my father's hand. "You wanna go back to the hospital, Nick?"

"No, Joe. It's nice here. Quiet."

The voiceless Angelo made a cackling sound, motioning me to come to his side, beguiling me with a toothless smile. As I moved toward him, he began to write something on a pad with a pencil, writing swiftly, slashing the paper, tearing off the sheet and handing it to me.

It was legible, but it was Italian.

"Can't read it," I said, handing it back.

Benedetti snatched it from my grasp. "Let me see it."

He studied the writing for a moment, then nodded approvingly at the old man. "Right," he said to Angelo. "You are always right, Angelo."

"What does it say?" I asked.

"It says, 'It is better to die of drink than to die of thirst.'"

I looked from him to the old winemaker.

"What's that supposed to mean?" I said, staring at Angelo's crumbling eyes. "I don't understand."

Quickly Angelo was writing again, another swift sentence, passing the sheet to Benedetti, who translated once more:

"It is better to die among friends than to die among doctors."

It brought applause, a clapping of hands, glasses held aloft and drained in a toast, even a wave from my father, who was beyond the point of understanding anything.

Encouraged, Angelo began to write once more. There was only one course left for me. I drew back my father's chair and tried to lift him, my arms around his chest. He fought me, feebly but in anger, squirming back into the chair. The *paisani* stared. They would not help me.

I said, "Please, someone, give me a hand. This man is very sick."

They sat there like tombstones. I began to cry. Not from grief, not anguish for my father, but compassion for myself. How good I was. What a loyal, beautiful son! See me trying to save my father's life. How proud I was of myself. What a decent human being I was!

I wept and pounded the table and the wine danced and spilled and the bees snarled. I tore my hair. I fell on my knees and clung to my father. "Come with me, Papa! You need care. You mustn't die in this wretched place."

His vague glance found me.

"Go home, kid. See what your mother wants."

I got up in shame and disgust and sat on the bench, sobbing. I had this talent for crying. It had brought me many rewards through my life, and some trouble too. When your weaknesses are your strengths, you cry. For crying disconcerts people, they don't know how to handle it; they are expecting violence and suddenly it vanishes in a pool of tears. I cried at my first communion. My tears broke Harriet down and she finally married me. Without tears I could never have seduced a woman, and with them I never failed. It has laid waste the hearts of women who disliked me, and who wanted to kill me afterward for succumbing. I cried through melancholy passages of my own writing. The older I got, the more I wept.

Now Zarlingo was affected, reaching across the table to press my hand. "Take it easy, son," he soothed. "Wipe your eyes, have a drink. Don't worry about your father. He's strong as an ox."

I wiped my face and blew my nose. I forced down the wine. From the highway below came the wail of a siren, drawing closer, louder. I walked out to the driveway and saw a white ambulance streaking a trail of dust as it raced up Angelo's private road. As it slowed I saw two white-clad attendants in the cab. Dr. Maselli was with them. They leaped to the ground.

"Where is he?" the doctor asked.

He followed me into the arbor and moved to my father's side. Lifting the drooped head, he peeled back an eyelid. Removing a hypodermic from his kit, he filled it with a milky substance from a vial and injected it into my father's arm. Angelo and the other brothers gathered around, watching. They moved aside as the attendants came up with a stretcher. They carefully eased my father upon the stretcher and lifted him off the ground. As they carried him toward the ambulance each of his friends murmured farewell.

"*Ciao, Nicola. Buono fortuna.*"

"*Addio, amico mio.*"

"*Corragio, Nick.*"

"*Corragioso, Nicola.*"

My father lay motionless, eyes closed. Even the hot sun failed to disturb his eyelids. Now Angelo came to his side with a straw-wrapped bottle of Chianti and placed it lengthwise beneath his arm. It brought a frown from Dr. Maselli. The stretcher was lifted into the ambulance and the door closed. As the white car drove away my father's friends watched it churning dust toward the highway.

"He's gonna be all right," Zarlingo said.

"Sure he is," Cavallaro agreed. "He'll outlive us all."

"I'll drink to that," said Benedetti.

I got into the rented car and followed the ambulance.

For half an hour I waited on a bench in a hall outside the emergency room of the Auburn Hospital. When Dr. Maselli emerged, coatless, the look of death was upon him.

"He's gone."

"How, Doc? Why?"

"Cerebral hemorrhage. Swift, painless. A man couldn't ask for a better way to die."

As I turned to leave he asked, "Do you want me to tell your mother?"

"I'll tell her."

Down the hall in the pay station I telephoned Stella. She choked at the news and began to cry. We cried together for a long time, in each other's arms over the telephone.

I said, "Will you tell Mama?"

"Oh, God!" she sobbed. "Oh, God."

I hung up and walked out to the car in the parking lot. The waning day refused to cool and I was numb and unequal to the drive home to the agony of my mother and the empty space in the world now that my father was gone. Remembering the saloons along Chop Suey Street I thought of getting smashed, of losing myself in the semidarkness with those lonely old men peeling off their last days in one of those places.

As I started the car a nurse came down the hospital steps into the parking lot. It was Miss Quinlan. She was walking straight toward me carrying a white sweater, moving smoothly on low shoes, erect and clean and handsome, the sun behind her, piercing the space between her thighs. I stepped from the car and stood in her path. She paused and smiled.

"I'm sorry about your father," she said.

My eyes filled. I took her hands.

"Oh, Miss Quinlan, help me! I don't know what to do, where to go. What shall I do, Miss Quinlan? I'm lost. I'm wretched!"

She put her arm around me.

"There, there, Mr. Molise. I know how you must feel, I know. It takes time, my dear man. You must be strong, for your father's sake."

All my life was tumbling around me, and I seized upon her with my hands and with my grief. "Oh, please, Miss Quinlan. Fuck me, please, please. Save me, fuck me!"

She freed herself and looked straight into my eyes, startled, hesitant. "You ask me to do *that?*"

"Oh, yes, Miss Quinlan! I love you, I adore you! Have pity on me."

She took a backward step and studied me.

"Well . . . it's possible, I guess."

"Please, dear, wonderful, beautiful Miss Quinlan!"

"I have to go to the supermarket first."

"May I come with you? I'll push your shopping cart."

"If you like," she smiled.

I smothered her hands with kisses and tears. I tried to fall on my knees but she held me up. "Don't do that, Mr. Molise. Stand up, please."

"Oh, thank you, angel. Thank you, thank you!"

We got in my car and drove to the market, my tears drying fast, Miss Quinlan at my side with her pretty nurse's hat over her blond Nordic braids, her knees like pomegranates under her hose, tight together, prim, so ladylike.

How delicious she looked, walking down the market aisles, selecting purchases, dropping them into the shopping cart. I insisted on buying her a bottle of Scotch and a coconut cake and thick lamb chops, and when we went through the checkout stand I paid for the whole damn thing, just to hear her gasp with gratitude and call me crazy. We got to my car again and I opened the door for her, and her magnificent derriere floated past my eyes like the grace of God, like the Holy Ghost. My old man would have loved it; he would have pinched it for sure.

We drove to her apartment, which was above a garage two blocks from the hospital. I carried the groceries while she unlocked the door. That apartment! It was like entering a hospital emergency room. All white it was, white tile along the sink, a white Formica top to the bar separating the kitchen and the living room, and still more white covering the stainless steel tubular chairs and divan. The sharp odor of Lysol cut across the atmosphere. Everything was closeted, hidden—dishes, pots and pans. Even the toaster on the bar was concealed under something plastic. At Miss Quinlan's instructions I put the sacks of groceries in the kitchen sink.

"You can undress here," she said crisply. "Put your clothes on the sofa."

She disappeared into the bedroom and locked the door. I pulled off my clothes and laid them out on the divan, neatly, in keeping with the austerity of the place.

As I finished, Miss Quinlan came from the bedroom. She was naked and not nearly as attractive as she had been in her nursing costume. Whereas I had conceived her a woman with spacious breasts, they were really almost nonexistent, sorry little dabs of flesh not much larger than a man's. Then I saw the flesh marks of falsies, which didn't disturb her in the least.

"Are we all undressed?" she said cheerfully, but with a professional intonation.

"Okay," I answered, standing up, hiding my precious loins with two hands.

She smiled.

"My goodness, aren't we modest." She gestured toward the bathroom. "This way, please."

I followed her into the bathroom, taking note of her drooping buttocks without the trimness her uniform created. The cleavage wasn't fetching either. Both buttocks just hung there lazily, carelessly, and I began to feel that Miss Quinlan was at least sixty.

I stood by as she filled the washbasin and stirred up a solution of soapsuds. None of this invigorated my sword, or, as my father called it, my *spada*. In fact, it began a sullen regression, and when Miss Quinlan grasped it there was little to seize, and she shook it and called it a shy and naughty boy.

"Prophylaxis!" she exclaimed, scooping soapsuds upon it. "That's the name of the game. Prophylaxis!"

The *spada* began to respond as she manipulated it with both hands. "The dear boy," she crooned. "He's such an angel." She handed me a towel, and as I dried myself Miss Quinlan made a soap and water solution, poured it into a douche bag, hung the bag on a hook, sat on the toilet, and plunged the douche nozzle between her thighs.

She toweled herself off, seized my *spada*, and marched me into the bedroom. By now I was without passion but overwhelmed with curiosity. Where would it all end? Miss Quinlan was a fiend but she was fun too, her flabby old buttocks bouncing as she pulled back the bedspread, kneaded the pillows, and nodded approvingly at the bed of love. On swift bare feet she dashed into the kitchen and returned with a jar of honey I had seen her purchase at the market.

"Jasmine honey!" she exclaimed, unscrewing the lid from the jar. "Taste!" She flecked a bit of it on her index finger and held it out. I opened my mouth to partake of it, but it wasn't for me at all, it was for my *spada*, a tiny dab with which to get acquainted, smack on the tip. With sudden and enormous energy the *spada* came forth, head aflame, and looked around, ready to fight. I felt a moment of shame. What a ghastly way to honor my poor father. But I was caught up in it, I had asked Miss Quinlan for it, and there was no reason to stop now, in spite of my father, my wife, and my two sons.

Seating herself on the edge of the bed, Miss Quinlan spread a thin layer of jasmine honey over my *spada*, from the scabbard to the tip. The golden gleam of it delighted her and with a murmur of desire she partook of the delicacy. The dear Miss Quinlan! She took everything—I felt it all going away and out of me, my sword, my glands, my heart, my lungs and my brains, a banquet for a rather elderly queen—and as the sorcery subsided she lay back on the bed, panting desperately, and I sat pooped in a chair. She had taken everything, and I had nothing to give in return.

And as she remained motionless, her arm covering her eyes, I moved to the bathroom and cleansed my sword with warm water and a washcloth. I saw her lying in the same position as I pulled on my clothes. My eyes scanned the apartment for a last look around. A cold, sterile place, but with a terrible beauty, the beauty of loneliness and two strangers sharing an intimacy, the beauty one felt but did not see. Unforgettable.

I started for the bedroom to say good-bye, but in the doorway I saw something that made me hesitate. Miss Quinlan lay as before, her arm shielding her eyes. But her hair had moved. That lovely pile of Nordic blandness wasn't real after all. It had slipped to the side, over her ear, revealing a white, bald skull. It humbled me. Had I stayed longer I would have burst into tears. How good she was!

"Thank you, Miss Quinlan," I said.

"You're welcome, I'm sure." It was a tired whisper.

She did not move.

"My father thanks you too."

"He was a dear man. I'm so glad I could help."

"Good-bye, Miss Quinlan."

"Good-bye."

—*The Brotherhood of the Grape*

TEN CARS OF MOURNERS FOLLOWED the hearse across town to the cemetery a mile away, behind the high school gym. We had a police escort, a cop on a motorcycle leading us through the deserted little town, everybody having gone to the circus. No traffic at all, only the slow-moving funeral procession over the bridge to Pacific Street. My car followed the hearse, Mama sitting between Virgil and me.

"Didn't Papa look great?" Virgil said. "God, the things they can do nowadays."

"He looked happy," Mama said. "It's the way he used to be, always laughing, always making jokes."

The joke was on Papa, but I held my tongue.

At every intersection the cop brought his Harley to a halt, raised his arm, glanced to the left and the right, blew his whistle, and waved the hearse to proceed. It was twelve blocks to the graveyard and he stopped the procession at all twelve intersections. My mother watched, deeply impressed, her veil lifted, for the escort gave her husband an air of importance, as though he'd been a big man in the town.

We moved slowly through the cemetery gates and past the "new" graveyard to the "old" one, the difference being that the new section was without ornate tombstones or large trees, whereas the old place was a brooding fairyland of grotesque marble figures beneath enormous oaks and sycamores, luxuriantly shaded, the grass moist and very green and uncut, as if to devour the ancient sunken graves. Through the trees we could see Father Martin standing before an opening in the ground, waiting, prayer book in hand.

I helped my mother from the car and she choked back a cry as she moved toward the priest. As I started to follow, Virgil snatched my arm.

"Let's watch it now," he cautioned. "Keep her between us. She might try something."

"Try what?"

"Jumping on the coffin."

The thing was possible, but it didn't happen. Each of us held her by an elbow during the last rites, and though she swayed as she watched the casket descend, the pulleys squealing, she remained composed and without grief. Afterward Father Martin came to her side and took her hands in his and she looked up at him and began to cry. He bent and kissed her on the forehead and that made everybody cry, adults and children alike, and people turned away and tried to hide their misery as they drifted back to their cars.

Harriet joined me and we escorted Mama away through the sycamores. Then, from a distance, we heard it: a voice, mechanical, electronic, pulsing across the land and through the trees as if to make every leaf tremble, a cry of battle, growing louder. We stopped to listen. It was a radio voice, a sportscaster, tense, explosive, profaning the holy cemetery with alien vibrations.

"Bottom of the ninth!" the voice proclaimed. "Two out. Bonds at second, Rader at third, Kingman the batter. The count: two balls and two strikes. Capra in a full windup. Here's the pitch: a ball!"

Through the trees lurched Mario's battered truck, nuts and bolts jangling, the voice strident as it swept down upon us. Joy brightened my mother's face.

"It's Mario!" she exulted. "Oh, Mario! He came after all. I knew he would, I knew it! Oh, thanks be to God!"

The truck skidded around a curve and braked to a stop before us, throwing gravel. The radio's irreverent hysteria seemed to jeer at the peaceful dead, rude, flouting their eternal sleep.

Kingman had struck out. The Giants had lost. Momentarily Mario caved in upon the steering wheel. He snapped off the radio and returned to reality, looking at us.

"Am I too late?"

"No, Mario," Mama said. "There's still time. Hurry, before they cover him up!"

He jumped from the truck and walked quickly toward the grave where two men with shovels were preparing to fill the plot. We watched him look down upon the casket, covering his face with both hands as he began to cry. Then we walked to the car.

My mother got between Harriet and me. She took off her veil, leaned back and sighed. Her face was beautiful, her eyes were warm with a sense of peace. She took my hand.

"I'm so happy," she said.

"He died quickly," I said. "He didn't suffer at all."

She sighed.

"He worried me so, all the time, from the day we were married. I never knew where he was, what he was doing, or who he was with. He wouldn't tell me anything. Every night I wondered if he'd come home again. Now it's over. I don't have to worry anymore. I know where he is. That he's all right." She uttered a little moan. "Oh, God. The things I used to find in his pockets!"

I started the car.

"Let's go home."

"I bought a leg of lamb," she said. "We'll have a nice dinner. The whole family. With new potatoes."

—The Brotherhood of the Grape

Part Five

LETTERS

The following letters, several published here for the first time, trace Fante's personal and artistic development over the course of half a century. In the earliest, Fante is twenty-three years old, living in Long Beach during the depths of the Depression, and struggling to make a way for himself as a writer. During this time and later, Fante wrote often to his mother, who after a two-year estrangement had recently reconciled with Fante's father in Roseville, California. In these letters we get a vivid sense of Fante's youthful ambitions as a writer, as well as of his strong attachments to family. Letters to cherished mentor H. L. Mencken, to friends and fellow writers Carey McWilliams and William Saroyan, and to his editor Pascal Covici reveal both the seriousness and the humor with which the young Fante pressed those ambitions. Fante's ambivalent experiences as a Hollywood scenarist come up in a number of letters from the 1930s and 1940s. By the late 1950s Fante was a well-paid screenwriter living in Italy and France, where he wrote marvelously evocative letters home to his wife, Joyce, and their children. Even in the latest letters selected here, in which an aging, ill, and often discouraged John Fante faces obscurity and death, a brimming life spirit can still be felt.

JUNE 24, 1932

Dear Mother:

I haven't heard from the publishers in the east for over a week now, and I'm getting anxious and worried, for I'm broke again. There is no great cause for you to worry, though. I can always manage somehow, and I want you to be confident in me.

At present I'm staying at the house of Sam Boyd, one of the workers with Ralph at the tango joint. He and his wife have gone on their vacation for the last two weeks. They will return Monday. We'll have to move then, of course. Where to, I can't say. I may move to the apartment of a friend on Obispo Street, which is a pretty good distance from town, but it's very quiet there, and I think I shall like it. If I get a check in the mail from The American Mercury I'll move to a reasonable hotel.

This is a bad season for tourists. The local wiseacres say that it's the worst in the town's history, and I'm not surprised either. From what I see, there are many people on the Pike every day and night, but like everyone they meet, they're simply walking around and not spending a dime. The tango joints have started to cut one another's throats, and the boys in the jernt where Ralph works tell me that their boss may be forced out of the racket. Ralph's sister Genevieve will be out here by July 1st or later. She has been doing some dancing in a chorus on the east coast, from New York to Havana, Cuba, but the show was a flop, most of her money she never got, and now she's in Boulder. Ralph has written her to come out and try Hollywood, where the Fanchon-Maroc vaudeville circuit has its studios. Personally, I think it's damned foolish for the girl to [come] here without any professional contacts whatsoever, especially in the hectic and changing show business, but there, more than anywhere else, is the profession where Lady Luck has much to do with a person's success, and I hope Genevieve the best of it.

My things are scattered about in such a terrible mess that I can't find Josephine's picture. Will look for it later.

Love to all,
Johnnie

{*1932: undated*}

Dear Mr. Mencken,

This person at the typewriter once wrote you some letters from Wilmington, California, last year. I had to. Maybe you'll understand the compulsion when I say that, and it's absolutely true, I was turned from Catholicism and the novitiate a week after I decided to be a priest by reading your *Treatise On The Gods*.

I wrote you. The letter described different mental agonies. I was nineteen, without the gods on my side whom I had got used to, and I floundered about in a sad way. Such floundering is amusing in people past forty, but in me, it was pain. Then your answer came. Courteous and pleasing, it said nothing.

A month later you got and returned a story from me. It was a filthy tale. I was ashamed of my mind.

Then I read in "What I Believe" that each morning you saw in your mail that there were worse asses than yourself in the world, and I thought: Well, Mencken, you scummy, hypocritical son of a so-and-so, that's your reaction to my letter, is it? Well, you're a goddam, cheap word-monger. I was crazy with poverty and worry, I wrote to the man who replaced the God Almighty in my heart, and then he uses my feelings for copy in a paragraph in his credo.

Anyway, what I read taught me blandness. If I'm mistaken about it all, won't you please take my deepest apologies?

Futilely, a man must have a god. You're still mine. Maybe the masochism the Catholics gave me makes me admire you, even after what has transpired. In many ways you're a mighty man.

I'd like you to read the enclosed manuscript. You of all people. It's not great or phenomenal, but it's true to me. I write for a living, though I've never sold in my life. If you buy it, will you send the equivalent by telegraph to John Fante, % Helen Purcell, 212 Quincy St., Long Beach. I've asked the same of another editor on another ms., simply because I'm in severe need, practically starving. If it is not worthy of publication, there is return postage, and I will have gotten the happiness of knowing that you read it, which to me is a very great deal.

Thank you, I'm

John Fante

TUESDAY, JULY 26, 1932

Dear Mr. Mencken,

Many thanks for your judgement on that last story. I respect it, and I am grateful for it. I suppose one is supposed to get discouraged. I'm not.

The enclosed is a last fling before I take a freight for home. In my estimation it is so perfect that it will be rejected. I mean that I'm not conscious of a single flaw, and that means I have missed again.

Will you answer a question for me? In the past thirty days I have written 150,000 words. I know a writer with a reputation does not do that many, but is a man just starting supposed to do that much? I certainly feel the effects, for, being broke throughout, I ate very little and lost a pound a day, or thirty pounds. I try not to be careless, for I write a thing twice in longhand and finally type it; moreover, to test my immunity to other writers who are often imitated, I read all of Hemingway, Dos Passos, and De Maupassant, besides great stacks of H. G. Wells and a chronic dose of

Mencken. This is a lot of reading that ceases to become a pleasure, but a task. It means ten hours of the day and night, including the writing. I'm not bragging here. I just want to know whether a man just beginning to write must necessarily work that hard. I want to know whether you did as much in a similar period of your life. I would like to know from you because you're the only person whom I know whose acumen I respect. I get endless unsolicited advice from people who read a lot and plan to write, but never do it. They give me a pain in the neck.

It is my plan to edit The American Mercury some day. By forty or thereabouts I think I shall be qualified. This means a lot of hard work, so I am going about it very systematically, and barring death or blindness a man can get whole warehouses of work done in twenty years, and I know no earthly reason why the job should not be mine at the end of that time. It amuses me very much to think that the magazine I shall edit regularly rejects my stuff, nor am I suffering from any delusions of grandness. The only hitch in the plan is that should you ever decide to quit the job, the magazine is liable to go on the rocks, so for God's sake stick around for a while longer. Put your rubbers on and button up your overcoat.

Yours with great admiration,
John Fante
423 Lincoln Street
Roseville, Calif.

I have no more stamps, but they will follow. Many thanks for your generosity in the stamp act.

I saw my story ["Altar Boy"] in The American Mercury for this August. Pretty hot stuff. My author's note is incorrect. You will inevitably get letters of protest from Denver Jesuits for it. I never did study for the priesthood, nor did I say so in the note I submitted with reference to my past. But I did plan to study at Florissant, Mo., under the Jesuits. That was a temporary vocation which endured for two years. Various things, however, such as skepticism and too much Voltaire and his counterparts, and a sense of injustice over the ruination of my mother's life (too much rel. [religion]) killed the desire for the cloth.

Otherwise, the note is correct.

AUG. 7, 1932

Dear Mr. Mencken,

Ten trillion thanks for your advice concerning working hours and writing output. I respect it absolutely, and I shall follow it. I am very happy that you like the story, and it would be goofy to quibble over the title you have given it. "Home Sweet Home" is all right. The truth is though, that I didn't really sing that song. I can hum the melody, and I know the lyrics, but together, for me they make a cacophonous concatenation, which is eight syllables, anyhow.

You may do as you please with the following:

I was born in Denver, Colorado, in 1911, in a macaroni factory, which is just the right place for a man of my genealogy to get his first slap, for my people were from the peasantry of Italy. My mother was born in Chicago, so that makes me just as much of an American as is necessary. My father was very happy at my birth. He was so happy that he got drunk and stayed that way for a week. On and off for the last twenty-one years he has continued to celebrate my coming.

I have two younger brothers and a sister. Our family moved to Boulder, Colo., when I was still a little squirt, and I began my schooling there, under the nuns. I returned to Denver for high school, attending Regis College, a Jesuit house. Then I went to the University of Colorado for a year. I quit that place because I was just about to flunk out. I couldn't study there. You see, I'd been four years in a Jesuit boarding school, and you can't imagine the overpowering voluptuousness of everything feminine after four years of confinement. I even fell in love with my English teacher at Colorado, and the hell of it is that she knew it. I made an ass out of myself for real, because I wrote her love letters, unsigned, and she knew their asinine source. One night I thought I'd spill her chastity. I got hold of Sherwood Anderson's "I Want to Know Why," and I went up to her apartment to find out what the kid in that story was puzzled about. Well, sir, that teacher didn't know what the [kid] was puzzled about. No ma'am, she didn't. But I know, of course. That was [the] Jesuitical technique of making love. I was sure a flop with her, but I'm a lot better today, and I'll go back to see her sometime.

My family went to smithereens a couple of years ago, my father beating it in one direction, and my ma and we kids to California. It was awful. We didn't have a kopek when we got there, and I'm not implying here that we ever had any to spare. I had to go to work. Ye gods, how I hated it. The only work I ever did previous to that was play all sorts of ball. But

I got a job, and did a pretty swell job of keeping alive my ma and the kids. I had more than one job, I had twenty-four of them, from hotel clerk to stevedore.

Then my father came back, and the folks went north with him, and I went to Long Beach. I went to the junior college in that town until my money gave out. Money has always been my problem, and the thing I'm trying to do is get enough of it to stop starving. I've done a lot of that, believe me. I'm fundamentally a clever fellow, and I've learned the serenity of honesty. I'm going to do my best to appreciate it the more, but I have a shallow side of me, in the estimate of my friends. I have strong prejudices which I feed. For example, I will not read books written by women or Catholic priests. Though I'm young, I've done a lot of harm. I'm revengeful, and I shall never reach a maximum of tranquility until the injuries and humiliations I've suffered have been compensated. Maybe this is conceited rationalization, but who of human flesh and blood can prove beyond adjectives that I'm right or wrong? Thanks, but I'd rather teach myself, and worship the cherished gods of my own choosing. I have but three, and these'll change soon enough. It's my belief that I can be and do exactly what I want to be and do. Hence, my conviction that I'll edit The American Mercury some day. Yet it's all an elaborately dirty trick, for I might slump over this machine, a corpse, within the next two hours. I have a girl, and I love her, and she loves me, and we both are little pigs for the immense music of Richard Wagner, and so the day is long and good, but tomorrow the sunshine will make me perspire and the bark of a dog will drive me nuts, and sticky flies will drone and land on my face.

I began to write a year or so ago. Altar Boy, in the August issue, is the only worthwhile piece I've ever done. I have read extensively, and I know contemporary literature pretty well. When Gamaliel Bradford died, it nearly broke my heart. When Lytton Strachey died, I went around all that day with a smile on my face. On Nietzsche's anniversary, which is my Christmas, I always get stewed. I would rather write than anything else.

I have other tastes. I'm a pretty good pug, and I can handle my dukes. I could have been a professional baseball player. My biggest diversion though, and the one which I'll have to give up because it's polluting me, is my *Pimp's Anthology: A Collection of Pornography Gathered From Lavatories and Behind the Barns of the United States*. I have contributors all over the Pacific Coast. I have some swell poetry here, but I'll have to throw it all away. It's a kind of pigsty Americana, and now my collection has so begun to annoy me that I wash my hands with soap and water every time I pick up the book. I think this idea came from my reading of Krafft-Ebing and his pals. I know abnormal psychology thoroughly, too thoroughly for a layman. My ken of the stuff often comes upon me with a rush, nauseating me. This is bad, but it's good schooling. When I was a kid I ate too many walnuts one Christmas. I've never been able to crack one since. So with erotic literature. I can't stand it anymore. I'm fed up.

I want to begin a novel, but I can't, for I must live. My novel will be written though, and it'll be one to make me proud.

Thanks again for all the grand things you have done. I hope I can continue to write things that please you, and above all, I'm grateful for your suggestions as to work hours and output.

With Admiration,
John Fante
423 Lincoln St.
Roseville, Calif.

DECEMBER 12, 1932

Dear Mother,

I suppose that as this is being written a letter from you is on its way here. I shall be very glad to get it. I haven't heard from home for nearly two weeks now, and I am anxious to know how all is with the family,

Winter has come at last to Southern California. The rain has been coming down in terrific sheets for the last two days and nights. It has just begun, too, The weather man predicts heavy rains for a long time to come. The rain has brought a very cold wind with it. To be out in this kind of weather for even ten minutes leaves you freezing from stem to stern.

I am well situated here in my new apartment. There is plenty of gas heat, and my bed has plenty of extra blankets. It is the first winter in three years that I don't have to be annoyed by the cold when I am asleep.

I suppose you people in Roseville are in for cold weather too. That snow which covered San Francisco has probably gone inland as far as Roseville. I hope to God all of you are well and warm. I know there is a shortage of blankets there at the house, and I hope you have taken care of that need now, before still colder weather comes.

I have sent my dark suit to the cleaners. It needed some repair. I have decided that I can't afford to buy any clothes at all. Not even a shirt. I'll wait until I get more money. Yesterday in Long Beach I went to the hotel at which I stayed and starved this summer. I got my boxful of old clothes, and I found a good shirt, a half dozen pairs clean sox, a half dozen handkerchiefs, and a pair of brown shoes. Also that pair of britches you bought for me when in Wilmington, at Schwartz's. The pants are shot to hell now, but I can wear them around the apartment here.

I suppose that somewhere in the newspapers you have come across the name Lloyd S. Nix, the former assistant prosecutor of Los Angeles County. Well, I have an appointment with the gentleman next Wednesday at his office, when I am going to discuss some material for magazine articles. I hope everything goes through satisfactorily. If it does, it will mean some good money for me.

I have begun to do some more work on short stories, and I think I'll have another in the mail by Thursday or Friday. The story looks good and if it sells, it'll mean a goodly sized check. In her letter, Grace tells me that everybody at the Campiglias read my story, Home Sweet Home. And everybody liked it.

I think I told you in an earlier letter that I saw Susie on the streets of Long Beach. I don't know about the rest of the relatives. I suppose it's customary to keep in touch with them, but I haven't, and it isn't likely that I shall.

Please let me know about everyone and everything. I shall look forward to a long letter from you.

Best love to all,
Johnnie
932 South Lake Street,
Los Angeles, Calif.

JANUARY 18, 1933

Dear Mother,

Just a short note, written from my Long Beach headquarters. Incidentally, the rain is coming down in a terrific gust here, and it has been raining all night. The air is cold as ice. But they say the farmers need the rain. Well, they can have all of it, every last drop as far as I'm concerned. [. . .]

I am enclosing to you a letter from Alfred A. Knopf, which I wish you would return to me when you write. This letter is a response to one I wrote him. I wrote him last week, and I asked him for some advance royalties on a book I want to write, but which I cannot begin until I get enough money to keep me going for about six months. As you will see by the enclosed letter from Knopf, he is at least interested, and it's possible, though not absolutely certain, that I may be able to squeeze $500 in advance from him on my projected book. The synopsis which he asks for, I have finished. (A synopsis is a brief outline of the book.) Before I send it to him, I am having a Los Angeles lawyer friend go over it with me, so that should Knopf like my synopsis, and offer me a contract, there won't be any mistakes made. However, everything depends on what reaction Knopf takes to my synopsis. He may not like it, and if so, I'll have to try another publisher. However, a letter from him like mine is considered quite a compliment among writers, so my chances may be pretty good. Of course, I'll let you know immediately I hear from Knopf. Be sure to return the letter.

My scenario with M.G.M. is still out there, and I haven't heard a word about It. It was probably rejected. When you don't hear from them immediately it means, as a rule, that they have decided not to take a story. Well, I'm not discouraged. I have plenty of time, and I'm learning every day.

Best of love,
Your son
J. Fante
Write me:
John Fante,
705 Fay Building,
Los Angeles., Calif.

19: FEB: 33
LOS ANGELES

Dear Mother,

Not much to say except that today is hot here in Los Angeles, probably the hottest day of the new year. I am in my room, at work on a short story that doesn't seem to be turning out very well. I worked all yesterday afternoon on it and an hour today, but I can't seem to get the right spirit into it. I know how such things go, however, and the knack of it will come to me soon.

Yesterday I sent you a scissor cut silhouette of myself. I had it done by a fellow downtown. I was simply curious, but I think he did a pretty good job of me.

I am enclosing a letter from Alfred Knopf which I know you will enjoy reading. Incidentally, in response to Knopf's terms, I wrote him and asked him for $75 a month for the next seven months. This will be in the form of an advance loan, and will be deducted from the sale royalties of the book I write. I am having my agent in New York handle the business end of this for me. But whether or not my terms are acceptable to Knopf, I really haven't the slightest idea. These are hard times, and a publisher doesn't like to take chances with people who are as young as me. [...]

Say, Mother. What do you think about me going back to Denver? I have wanted to go there to write my novel, and I have been considering it for some time. I know that I could write a better book in Denver, due to the fact that the scene of the story is laid in Colorado. As you can probably guess, a man can write better about an incident if he is on the ground where it took place, and that's the way I feel about my novel. Let me know what you think about it.

I must make this letter short and sweet. See you later. . . .

{To Carey McWilliams}
{Roseville, California}
{c. summer 1933}

Dear Carey,

Here's where I cut loose. As you see, this is pretty long for a letter, but it has to be. I've got a lot to say. The only reason I can show for writing you rather than anyone else is that I think you'll understand better. I'll put it this way: if I knew Mencken (you know what I think of him) as well as I know you, I should be writing this letter to him. But if a Mencken can't be addressed, and a McWilliams can, then to hell with the Menckens and all hail the McWilliams'. So be it.

You have probably guessed right. I am having trouble with my book. Today I tore up about sixty thousand words, the toil of three months. I was absolutely fed up. I am still. I wish I knew positively what the matter is. I can't put my finger on it. There's something wrong—something changing in me. And I don't know what to call it, nor where to find it. The work I destroyed was not good work. I could see it. I was losing faith in it every day from the beginning. The badness of it all didn't seem to increase, and I didn't rebel by degrees. I tore up that work very deliberately. It was hollow, artificial. I started it with a tricky style, found the thing easy to write, and went ahead. I hammered away day after day, just pouring words. It wasn't good stuff. I knew all along that I was playing a trick. Not a trick on Knopf or anyone. But on myself. I have that feeling about writing. I know when I am honest and when I am cheating. The idea is this: Outwardly, characteristically, everywhere but in print I am something of a charlatan. In my relations with people obviously my intellectual inferiors, I play the wise guy. Needless to say, I don't try any tricks on a fellow like you. I'm smart enough to know that you're smarter. But with others I get away with it. My implication here is not of physical dishonesty. I'm not a thief—but of smartaleckery. A wise kid. The white-haired boy. I practice that nonsense a lot. I usually get away with it. I strut abnormally. I know it's a stupid and dangerous kind of play but I do it anyhow. The result is that in print, I am brutally honest, just the opposite of the wise guy in real life. (As you see, I know myself pretty well.) Now in my book, the wise guy and not my real self is writing. The result horrifies me. I think what I have written is putrid, and the wise guy, the white haired boy, the kid who "made" the Mercury when he was twenty, and such disgusting hooey as that is the guy who is so plain in every sentence of this first novel that I would rather go to jail than have people read the book, because there is no truth in it. I don't mean autobiographical fact. I mean something else. I don't know what you would call it, but it's different from autobiography, yet it's very much like it. It's that feeling you get when you begin to write something you really love, that feeling of being in a stream and floating on and on without stopping. I don't think I have made this very clear, but the best I can say is that when you write a letter, but in this vein that I speak of, you have a very keen satisfaction in what you're doing. You don't worry about plots and dramatic sequences. They come quite naturally. You simply write and write, and lo! By God, there's a story, and a swell story. I know that feeling. If I don't have it, I write like the white haired boy. Fuck him!

Well, I have destroyed my work to date, this novel based on my family life. I think I made a mistake in coming to Roseville and being night and day with my family. My mother was here all the time. It was very annoying. Here's a situation for you. A man sits in a room writing a story about his mother. There are episodes in that story which have to do with the secretest events in that mother's life. And in the room this guy writes. And in the next room sits this guy's mother with a rosary in her hand. And what is she doing, but *praying* for the success of that story. Jesus Christ! If you only knew what that does to a man. It makes him feel that his guts are hanging out. I have had enough of it. I'm moving back to Los Angeles.

I am going to begin again. But I don't want to work day and night on this book. I want something else to do. I still have about 200 bucks coming from Knopf, and I can at least get started again. But I would like to take a rest for two weeks. Just loaf around. Do nothing but walk the streets. See people, talk, have a drink, in short, do everything that *can't* be done on $200.

You see, Carey, I've worked hard. I've written myself dry. I was forcing it, and the result was never satisfying. The dissatisfaction plus the effort has made a physical wreck out of me. I have what may be called a lot of stupid ideas about writing, but it won't do any good to tell me they're stupid. I have to find out for myself. In the meantime Knopf awaits his novel. I'm in a horrible mess. I think I am, I mean. Maybe I am taking it too seriously. I sometimes think I have overestimated my own importance and significance. I really don't know for sure. Perhaps I should be digging ditches. I don't know.

However you feel about this letter, I do hope you'll try to see that it's sincere. I am very glad for the unrequested privilege of writing you, and the way I feel is that soon or late someone will have had to listen.

If I force myself on you, well, I can at least say that I know how to pick the wise listeners, and if you don't mind, I would appreciate some good, old-fashioned paternal advice when I get to town. I have to admit it, but I need so goddamn much of it, and I don't know where to get it, and waxing poetical for a moment, I say that I'd scale the highest mountain to get it.

My trouble is that I have had it too easy in the last three months. I did no physical labor at all. I did nothing more than write my own book. This was too much for me. Too luxurious. Oh, the book was work, but the circumstances were far too serene. I was too cocky. I was a "novelist." Hey! hey!

I should like to know what you think of this that I've written, and what you can suggest. My idea is to get a job when I get to the South. I don't want the money, but the discipline, and if I could afford it, I'd pay my own wages on a job, so that my day of working and writing would balance. I want to go to work on Main street, washing dishes. Any goddamn thing. Then I shall write my book slowly, coming to it fresh each day. It will take longer to write, but I want to do a good piece of work. Something I can be proud of. I could sit down and knock off a bad story in two weeks, but that's not the idea. And it's not the money, either. I want to get that "feeling." I hesitate to call it inspiration because the man who uses the word inspiration is usually a fellow who mouths aspirations, "My Jesus, mercy!" etc.

My deepest thanks for reading this over, Carey. I hope you'll form some sort of a judgement and let me know what it is. More than any other thing, I'm willing to listen to good advice, and can recognize it when it is good. I'll drop in and see you shortly after I get into town. I'll phone and find out when you're not so busy. I'll be on my way there by the time this letter reaches you.

Confidentially,

J. Fante

OCTOBER 27, 1933

Dear Mother,

All goes well with me. My novel is now in its last stages; I'm coming into the home stretch as far as the hard work is concerned and in a month I'll be finished with the first draft, which is the hardest work, by far, of the whole process. After that, the rest is simply a matter of polishing up and re-setting for the publisher. I feel very good about it, despite the fact that I still have a lot of work ahead of me. [. . .]

We had another earthquake last Monday night at eleven o'clock. It was a sudden jolt, very abrupt, and ended quickly. I was in a theater; it was a minute or so after eleven o'clock. The walls shook and the crossbeams creaked. That was all. I got up, though, and left the theater and walked to the park, where I sat down. The quakes still scare the living hell out of me. I don't suppose there's any cure for the fear I have. [. . .]

DECEMBER 3RD, 1933

Dear Mother,

It is beginning to show cold signs in these parts. The nights are often very very cold. Here in my room though it is always warm. I have a gas heater which I keep burning constantly, and if it weren't for that I'd probably have to quit writing because in the mornings my fingers are so stiff from cold that I can't touch a typewriter. Incidentally, I have a very nice room. Papered in brown and with a number of appropriate pictures on the walls it's typically a man's room. I think of all the places I have lived in Los Angeles it is the most satisfying, and as long as I remain here in the future I am going to stay in this hotel. I have four big brown leather chairs here in the room and three fine lamps. A rag-weave carpet covers the floor, that is—of course—when I can see the floor. A stranger walking in here would be sure to think that my carpet was made of typewriter paper. Scattered everywhere, I have to wade in it up to my knees. I never seem to find the right thing when I look for it in this place. Books are piled everywhere, and I hang my clothes on the bed, on door knobs, over chairs, and usually toss them on the floor. There's no hope for me ever being an orderly person. The fellow who cleans my room will tell you that I'm the most disorderly guest that ever lived in this hotel. But he likes me, and he doesn't seem to mind the disorder. He says that a person who throws his stuff around as I do is usually a good fellow, and one who is not likely to raise hell the minute something isn't perfect. [. . .]

Don't be alarmed about the visit of my friend Charles Green. He's really not such a bad fellow and as a co-worker on manuscripts he's a great help to me. As for his hell-raising, there is nothing in it out of the ordinary. I think all writers are that way. At least, I have found them so. Writers like to boast and do sensational things. They talk a lot and make a lot of noise, but at bottom they're really a bunch of overgrown children who will never grow up. I suppose if they ever did grow up they'd stop writing. [. . .]

Love,
Johnnie
note the new address—temporary, of course.
255 Bunker Hill, Los Angeles, Calif.

SUNDAY, JULY 22, 1934

Dearest Mother,

I planned to write this letter last Thursday, and I don't know why I didn't do it. I was so glad to hear that Tommy is not discouraged in his search for a job. He has nothing to fear. If he is persistent, and I know he will be, he will find himself in a successful position before long. Perhaps it would be best for him to stay away from college for a year. He is still so young that one year can't matter so much, and in the meantime he can be earning enough money for his return. I hate to see him lose any time at all, but the situation has got to be faced squarely. I only hope to God I get a good break in this town. If I do, you may be sure that I'll be ever so happy to share it with Tommy and all of you. There are so many excellent institutions down here that Tommy would find it a swell place to finish his education. Above all, there is Loyola University. And I think he ought to have at least one year of Catholic philosophy. I don't mean this as a necessary part of his religious education, but simply as a basis for contrast with other non-Catholic philosophic systems. Pete too would find Loyola University better to his liking than any other school on the Pacific Coast.

And how is Pete getting along? I wish he would write me a letter. I would write him first, but for me letter-writing has come to be a dreadful job which I am constantly putting off. Tell Pete to get busy and let me have at least a short note. Did Josephine get a job at the cannery? I read something about cannery strikes in that region the other day, but I was not sure it concerned the canneries near Roseville. For Jo' s and Tommy's sake, I hope not, although my sympathies lean toward strikers in most of their demands.

I finished a short story today and shall mail it tomorrow. I am deluged with all kinds of work and could keep busy all the time but this weather is hardly suitable for a man who works with his brain. After a couple of hours in the sunshine at the beach it takes a terrific amount of will-power to sit down before a typewriter and mumble and muse over a literary product. Our movie story is coming along nicely. We have had to do some revision and expect to have it ready for submission sometime this week. I shall also have another short story in the mail this week. Last week I sent out an old story which I rewrote. My agent now has it. Incidentally, he wrote me last week about the possibility of selling a story to one of the big national women's magazines. They pay large prices, and it would please me to hit their market. I am very worried about my novel. I haven't had time to go to work on the re-writing, and though Knopf has never complained, I don't like to hold him off too long. Things have been so hard with me though—money and all—that I have been forced to put off the work. I lose nothing by it, but I would love to have the work off my hands so that I could stop worrying and start another book.

I shall write Doctor McAnally immediately after I finish this letter, and thank him for being so good to our family. I know he would appreciate a note from me. Give my best love and encouragement to Papa, and all my love to you and my brothers and sister.

ever your son,
J. Fante
2316 Clyde Avenue
Los Angeles, Calif.

MAY 15, 1935

Dearest Mother,

There just isn't any explanation for my silence. Every hour since I got your last letter I have been telling myself to answer. I was out of town over the weekend though; I wanted to send you a telegram on mother's day but I didn't for two reasons.

In the first place, I didn't have enough money with me. In the second place, every day with me is Mother's Day. There is no sense in a special day for Mothers. The whole idea of a Mother's Day was started by the American Florist's Associations, their idea being to drum up a lot of flower business on that day. The idea of using a man's most sacred feeling toward his mother by making him buy flowers and send telegrams seems ugly to me. I don't want to think about you just one day in the year. I don't anyway. I think of you always, every day. It's best that way.

Ross Wills and I left Los Angeles last Saturday noon for a trip into Death Valley, where we planned to take some notes on a prospective movie scenario. Ross has a new car, and away we went. When we got to Baker, California, we changed our minds about continuing the trip to Death Valley. Instead, we went over to Las Vegas, Nevada, and the Boulder Dam. Ross had just sold a story; he had plenty of money, and we wanted to celebrate. We had a jolly time, though it got rather tiresome after such a long ride. We put up in the best hotel in town, arriving in Las Vegas about midnight Saturday night. I had only two dollars with me, for Ross insisted that the whole affair was to be at his expense. We started out by gambling. I on a small scale, and Ross on a larger one. It goes without saying that my two dollars didn't last long. I was broke before we left the first gambling house, and in that town on the main street there are a dozen such places. Ross lost a huge amount of money; I don't know exactly how much, but it was close to a hundred dollars. We got to bed close to four o'clock. We were flat broke. In the morning Ross had to telephone his girl in Los Angeles for more money. She sent us fifteen dollars. This was in the morning. It was then that I wanted to send you a telegram, and I was going to ask Ross for the money, but before I knew about it, he had gone back into a gambling house and lost all but a dollar of the money. It was barely enough for us to get back to town. If he hadn't had a credit card at the filling stations for gasoline we'd still be out on the desert somewhere. [. . .]

With all my love to you and everyone,

Johnnie

NOVEMBER 3, 1935

Dearest Mother,

I have been so sick the past week that I stayed in my hotel and didn't get to work at all. I start again Monday. The trouble is with my stomach. I have had a number of spells which left me pretty weak. I don't know exactly what the cause is, but I would say it was too much acid in my system. For awhile I thought it might be heart-trouble, but since no one in the family has ever been afflicted that way, and since I've never had any trouble with my heart, I think it must be from the food I am eating. Anyway, I nearly collapsed last Wednesday. The blood left my head and knees and everything began to whirl. I had to grab a chair to keep from falling down. My heart was pounding furiously, the sweat broke out in my face, and all at once I had a terrible fever. The siege hit me so suddenly and so unexpectedly that I got a real scare. For a moment I thought I had been poisoned and that I was about to die, but after awhile the fever left and I was alright except for an unusual palpitation of the heart.

I stayed away from the studio and rested for the most part. Today, Sunday, I am alright again. I hope to get back to work tomorrow. [. . .]

At present I am working on a French Foreign Legion story, a subject which I know nothing about, and it is very hard. I have been working like a dog—and sick as I am—I can't seem to get much done. But I hope for the best.

Love to all—

Johnnie

℅ Ross Wills,

1857 North Wilton Place,

Hollywood

{c. November 1935}

Dearest Mother—

I have just been through three very tough days. My stomach went completely on a rampage, giving me violent gas pains which affected my heart, caused a severe case of high blood pressure and nervousness and sent me to the doctor's office. His analysis was not conclusive, but he's pretty sure I'm suffering from an acid stomach and he's placed me on a strict vegetable diet which excludes almost everything worth eating: no meat, no sugar, no cigarettes, no bread, no milk, no coffee, no salt or pepper—in fact, I can eat only greens, and only those foods which do not contain starch. I have been on the diet for three days and the results are so far excellent although I am fast losing weight. In another week there won't be an ounce of excess weight upon me.

I was very worried at the time the attack hit me. My heart behaved queerly, jumping and kicking and sending queer shooting pains through my chest and down my shoulders and arms. My feet became ice-cold, blood rushed from my head, causing dizziness and a feeling that I was about to lose consciousness; I had no strength and felt as though I was going to die. Naturally I was frightened, which aroused the condition and made matters worse. My breathing was difficult, so that I gasped for air, and the ringing in my ears shut off all sounds. It was truly an unforgettable experience and one I shall profit from. It marks the end of my careless eating habits and the beginning of a more normal, sensible life. I am, in fact, very glad it happened. Except for the discomfort at the time, it has done me no harm. I think I shall be on this rigid diet for at least three months—a long time—but when I gradually leave it I shall be cured, not only of the sickness but also of any carelessness which brought it on in the first place. At present I am taking a medicine after meals, but I believe it will only be for the duration of the bottle.

I suppose the best place for me at a time like this is home with you, but right now I can't afford to come home; I have only a few dollars, not enough for the fare, and I don't know that the trip wouldn't cause me harm. I have become a very nervous individual, and among other causes the condition of my stomach is due to nervousness: that is, nervous indigestion.

Except for the time lost in sickness, I have kept myself busy with my work. Two short stories are now in the mail, and I shall have another ready tomorrow. The longer I stay in this business the more I realize its heartlessness. At times one becomes very discouraged. I suppose that happens to the most courageous, however.

Give my love to everyone, and above all, to yourself.

Johnnie
1327 Lemoyne Street
Los Angeles, Calif.

DEC. 30, 1935

Dearest Mother—

I am feeling much better now. My weight has come down to about 138, reducing me to nothing but bone and muscle and the result is, on the whole, good. I seem to lack the vitality I once had, but that is due to the rigorous diet I am living by. There is one item on the doctor's dictum which I have ignored more or less, and that item is cigarettes. I admit I haven't cut down on them as I am supposed to, but the best I can do is try. I'm not smoking nearly as much as before. The order was to smoke about six a day. My best day was twelve; that's pretty good, though. A person with my nervous temperament must do something, and restraint is not so much hard as it is easily forgotten. I smoke a lot without even knowing about it.

The idea of coming home for awhile still appeals to me very much. When you say in your letter that "we'll manage somehow" it is not enough. Where could you put me? I know how small the house is, too small for another bed. And then too, where would I work? Of course I might stay at a hotel in Roseville, or rent a room near the house; that would be alright, I think.

It has been very cold here for the last twenty-four hours. Rain fell a short time Sunday and today too it appears that more rain is coming. I used to like these murky dull rainy days, but since I have been sick I prefer sun and warmth. [. . .]

I can't imagine what I'll do New Years Eve—that's tomorrow night. I have a girl, you know—Marie is her name, and she has been very valuable to me while I have been sick. When you are sick you get very lonely and starved for the presence of another, particularly at night. Marie has been with me every night, taking very good care of me. Indeed she has been like a wife to me, taking care of my laundry, sewing my sox and keeping my clothes in order. Many times these past months I have been without money and she has assisted me. She wants to marry me and I tell her that some day soon we shall certainly become man and wife, but I'm afraid I am not sincere when I tell Marie that. It would hurt her though, if I didn't. She depends on me in many things; she's a highly excitable girl, easily frightened, and she needs me and has come to look forward to our meetings. We see one another constantly, and have a lot of fun together.

Christmas Eve we wanted to do something different, something unusual. We had only nine dollars between us, so our choice was limited. Yet we had a fine time. We got aboard a Red train and went to a lonely little beach town, a perfectly dead and isolated one-horse town much smaller than Roseville. We walked through the streets and along the shore front until we had seen everything the town had to offer, and then we went to bed in a little hotel. Next morning we had breakfast, went to Mass in the town's little church, and then returned to Los Angeles about noon—so that's how I spent Christmas. I enjoyed it too.

Love to all
Johnnie

{To William Saroyan}
WINTER [FALL?]
1938
[C. JANUARY 1938]

Dearest Darling Willie,

I'm still sorry I didn't meet you that night after the Chink dinner and tackle you in a game of pool. I'm a whizzeroo at that game—or certainly I used to be. Indeed, the game is so thoroughly a part of my blood that hereabouts in this goofy town, whenever an actor starts to blab about his "cue" I feel my reflexes jumping into motion and I start reaching for a billiard stick.

I am now a complete and ungarnished hack. The field is radio. The subject matter is one-act plays. The technique is simple, and even interesting. The one-dimensional limitations of a radio play make for some pretty facile quirks and squeezes. And strange as it may seem, the taboos are less rankling than any other field in American writing—excepting of course the stage and serious literature. You can say hell on the radio. You can say damn, and you can even talk about the brotherhood of man and communism with a small c. Reason: you deal with such morons that they don't understand you. The radio today is a sleeping powder. Turn it on, relax, and soon enough the emanating bilge wafts you to slumber. All the inhibitions I ever had are pouring out of me and into a radio script. I mean of course unaesthetic inhibitions. All the crap and guff and flubdub, all the dullness and tedium, all the mediocre thoughts and ideas I've accumulated over a long, terrible life, are walking from under my fingers and across pages and pages of sheer unpolluted crap. [. . .]

There's dough in radio, Willie. Your kind of dough. Ten page, one-act plays—three to five hundred bucks apiece. It's really a lark. I can turn the stuff out hanging from a four story building by one foot, and writing with the toes of my other foot. I've knocked out four plays, and [am] finishing my fifth, in three weeks. You get authorship credit too. Six million people on a chain hookup like Rudy Vallee's—and they do some goddamn good stuff once in while—Chekhov—Shaw—O'Neill—Joyce—and even the morbid "Mice and Men." And within the concentration of one dimension there is power—and above all—speech—words—pure speech and sound. . . . but all of this is naturally the exception rather than the rule. . . . the average is awful, but no worse than pix. The joke shows are all pretty lousy. I'm talking about drama. (Incidentally, I haven't sold any of my plays yet but I am told by my agent at the Morris office that they are damn fine and will click.)

My wife is in Berkeley. We are too poor to live together. Her people are wealthy but they hate me because I am an Italian. It is a disgusting situation . . . and insoluble. My wife needs a job. She writes too. Her poetry has appeared in the Amer. Mercury and California Arts. You met her. I'm sure you liked her. I wrote her to figure on a phone call from you.

It happens that her aunt Mrs. Maynard Shipley, is the head of the San Francisco WPA. In short, she has a big drag but only inferentially. I wrote her that you'd be glad to do all you could. Since she has split wide open with her family—who DO NOT know we are married—she is strictly on her own—naive, innocent, and terribly sincere. She is a graduate of Stanford, a Chi Omega or something etc.

I wish you'd call her, possibly meet her and put her wise to the best way of getting that 94 bucks a month. Her people are through with her since she has openly defied them about me, and since they believe that she is going to marry me, but do not know we are already married.

I an enclosing a page from my wife's last letter. The explanation is self-evident. I know that both of us can trust you to remain secretive about our marriage—her family would tear her to pieces if they discovered the truth.

I have told her you would call her Friday afternoon or evening. I don't recall your own private phone number or I would spare you the trouble, and she could call you. This is a tremendous favor to ask of you, Willie, but a time and place will arrive when I shall be able to repay you in something akin to what this means to my wife and me.

When you call her, be sure you ask for "Joyce Smart" and thereafter always refer to her by that maiden name. She is at this address, listed in the Berkeley exchange. Chris Runckel,

2312 Rose Street,
Berkeley, Calif.

We hope to be together very soon. My heart is set on it. I'm hopelessly in love with her and it eats me inside to feel my helplessness now. But I know I can count on you.

Johnnie
1851 No. Argyle
Hollywood

{c. early 1940}

Dearest Folks,

Now that you have seen Joyce I doubt there is very much I can add to what she had to give in the way of news. I am well, of course, and the effects of the flu have left me no worse. Down here for almost two months we have had fog and damp, cold weather. Today was a good day, but the past months have been very unpleasant. This sort of weather depresses me. I don't think it has any effect on my work, and yet it might, because I frankly haven't done as much as I should. [. . .]

Joyce seems to think that Pappa looks very well, but since your report conflicts so much with what she has seen I have suggested she go to Dr. McAnally and talk to him. I know of course that Pappa should not be working hard, but at the same time it is a great blessing to know that he is still a strong man for his years. Not many men have the courage and stamina to keep at his pace all these years. It shows he comes from fine stock, and I know I am very proud of him. In fact, I like to brag about the fact that he can still lay brick and stone with the best of them, and I tell all my friends about it. Pappa will still be alive and swallowing big glass-esful of vino when the rest of us have been put under the ground. Some people simply refuse to die: he is one of them.

I miss Joyce very much. I have got so used to having her around at all times that the house has become a deserted building, as though all the furniture were gone and nobody lived there anymore. We get along so very well together, the two of us. When you consider that we are both in the same house constantly from morning to night it is a very unusual and very happy situation. Now that she has gone I do little or nothing more than eat and sleep.

That's about all this time. Give my love to everybody at home.

Johnnie

[Letterhead] Hospital of the Good Samaritan

SATURDAY [I.E., FEBRUARY 3, 1940]

Dear Parents—

Monday night about 11:30 I was driving down a narrow street in Manhattan Beach. I was traveling about 50 miles an hour when I suddenly lost control of the car and crashed into a telephone pole. I was not knocked unconscious, but I was pretty badly shaken, and when I got out of the car I was covered with blood and shaking violently. The car was completely wrecked, my right arm crashed through the windshield. I walked six blocks to a friend's house, and he drove me to a hospital. The doctor went to work at once. He gave me local anaesthetics and proceeded to sew up the cuts in my arm, my legs and my face. Altogether he applied 75 stitches—60 of them in my right arm, where the muscles were torn out to the bone. It took him 3 hours and he did a good job. Joyce got there while he worked on me, and I was put to bed. Next day I decided to call an ambulance and come to a big Los Angeles hospital for x-rays, because I was afraid I had broken some bones. Tuesday afternoon I got to this place, and x-rays were taken which showed a compound fracture of my right cheekbone. I have 2 good doctors, and the cheekbone is set now, and I am getting well fast. I shall be able to leave the hospital Monday, and except for a few scars on my face and arm I shall be as good as new. The car is ruined, and we will be broke after paying hospital bills; but I am very glad to report I am out of danger and shall be home Monday.

I didn't let you know because I wanted to be sure I was out of danger first. Please don't worry because I am as good as new—

Johnnie

SATURDAY *(c. April 1941)*

Dear Mother—

We are down to our last 15 dollars, but at last something good has turned up, and I think I shall start work next Monday or Tuesday. If it happens, I shall make $500 or $750 a week for eight or ten weeks. The job is pretty certain, so my agent tells me, but I am not going to allow myself to believe it until I get my first check. Meantime we are both well, and I have been working hard on another movie idea.

Joyce and I are not sure at all, but it may be that you'll have a grandchild in about 9 months. All we know is that Joyce thinks this is going to happen. It might be a false alarm, and we really won't know for a couple of weeks, so please don't get excited until you hear definitely from me that it is going to happen. Keep this a secret, please.

If I get the job I'll send you some money out of my first check. You'll hear from me soon.

Love from Johnnie

{To Pascal Covici, Viking Press}
MAY 26, 1940
2904 Manhattan Ave,
Manhattan Beach, Calif.

Dear Pasquale—

You are right about a book of short stories now. I hate to agree with you but I've got to be honest and face the facts. [. . .]

The man with the scythe nearly got me again. This time it was the flu. Three weeks ago I came down with it and within six hours my fever jumped to 105 and stayed there four days. The doctor gave me heavy doses of sulfanilamide which beat the fever down but damn near killed me. I lost 22 pounds in two weeks. It might have been easier except for the automobile accident, which left me very weak and susceptible.

And so it goes—

I was going to ask you for another advance to see me over this hump but my wife has forbidden it. Anyway I find myself worse off than ever in my life before, and just as soon as the blitzkrieg is licked I shall go to work for you. I'm chafing to write, mad with the desire.

I love war, chaos, gloomy predictions about the end of this civilization. It is always at times like these that I can sock it to my machine. And when in my forties they offer me the Nobel Award you can be sure I shall gladly accept it.

We face eviction here. If it happens my wife will go North and stay with her mother, but I'll stick it out for a couple of weeks and then move in with a friend in Hollywood. This address is good for another ten days however.

The country has gone hog wild, Pasquale. The patriots have come out from under the damp stones and now we shall have a clear-cut view of democracy with her clothes off. Myself, I am innocent. I had nothing to do with Versailles because I was a little boy. I had less to do with the misery and decay after '29, because I too went hungry and roamed the streets, my head buzzing with the fabrications of the liars who turned me loose from their stinking temples of learning. I feel like a man of God. I held my nose and gritted my teeth. Now I come up for air and smell blood. They can tear this over-rated civilization apart, they can have their fascism and nazism and bolshevism and democracy. I shall type with one hand, the fingers of the other pinching my nostrils. It will be slower, less convenient, but it will be great writing anyway. Hitler. Blah. Mussolini. Blah. The fools. Neither have read "The Little Dog Laughed."

Best regards,
John

{To William Saroyan}
TUESDAY *{c. early 1942}*

Dear Willie—

We are awful proud of you up here, us simple folk. (No MGM salary but good people anyway, those Fante people.) I was talking it over with my boy awhile ago (he had just soiled his britches and lay there in it, reveling in it) and I says to him, I says, "Son, what do you want from William Saroyan?" The boy sort of rolled from right to left and back again before replying. Then he said, "Tell the son of a bitch to send me Phyllis Brooks." By this time his enormous penis had risen and lengthened to the size of a pencil eraser and I knew, knew with the conviction of blood echoing down the years, that here was a lad who would in years to come rival even William Saroyan, old Hollywood Bill.

Tell everybody to kiss my ass, with love.

Jf.

AUGUST 2, 1941

Dear Mother and Father,

Joyce got back Monday morning, and it was very good to have her with me again. The apartment had got so dirty, with dishes piled in the kitchen and soiled clothes draped over every chair.

Joyce has told you I am working. It is truly a wonderful job I have now. Orson Welles, our producer, is the finest guy in Hollywood, and the maker of the best pictures. One of the pictures I am writing is supposed to be based on the true story of how a certain bricklayer in San Francisco met a certain Italian girl. I told Welles this was a true story, and he believed it. In a few days the studio will send you a contract which you are to sign, in which you promise not to sue them for libel. Please sign the papers and don't worry about it. The story I have written (with Norman Foster) promises to be the finest love story ever made in Hollywood. You have nothing to worry about, and when you see the picture I can promise you that it will make you very happy and proud.

All stories we do for Welles for this picture are supposed to be true stories. Well, my story of the Italian bricklayer isn't exactly true, but I had to tell them it was true in order to sell it. I got a thousand dollars for the idea. Please do as I say and sign the papers which RKO sends you. I will take care of the rest. Studios have to be very careful not to be sued for libel, and though there is nothing in the story to offend anybody, they still don't want to take any chances. As soon as I get my check I will send you some money on it.

Meantime, I am making 300 a week, and my salary may be boosted to 400 in a month. The job may last a long time—possibly a year. But I am not sure. Anyhow, I am saving my money for the baby and a chance to write my book without any financial help from anybody.

Joyce is well and getting along fine. Sorry I haven't written until now, but I've been awfully busy these past two weeks.

All my love
Johnnie

{*To his Denver cousin Jo Campiglia*}

DECEMBER 30, 1944

[Letterhead] Paramount Pictures, Inc.
West Coast Studios

Dear Jo—

I was very glad to have your note Christmas. It has certainly been a long time since any exchange of letters between us, but I see no reason why we can't start all over again in the New Year, which I hope will be a pleasant one for you, bringing with it all the things you desire most. [. . .]

It's true that I have not done very much writing for publication since the war, but the cause lies in the war itself and a deep sense I possess of the futility of saying much in these bloody times. I have a story forthcoming in the Woman's Home Companion, and I have finished one-half of a new book. Otherwise, I do nothing except play with my sons and screw my wife, both actions which I regard as very noble and good for my immortal soul. My children are simply gorgeous. Nicky, the older, is not yet three; but he knows his letters and can write out the alphabet, as well as spell a number of words. He has memorized nearly two hundred lines of Mother Goose, speaks with marvelous clarity, and says delightful things. On Christmas, for example, I patted his fanny and said, "What's that?" He pulled away from me, frowned, and said, "If you ask questions like that I won't like you anymore." And my boy Danny is really a big fellow. He is nine months old and weighs 27 pounds, has five teeth and the smile of an angel. They are a source of endless pleasure for us, and my wife is really a genius with a master touch when it comes to directing their little lives.

These grandsons have brought much happiness to my mother and father, who literally worship them and spoil them as fast as we try to undo their sinister tricks with cakes, candy, cookies, and anything their little hearts desire. My father even slips Nick a glass of wine now and then. As for my mother, she stands by transfixed with delight when Nicky climbs into a chair and proceeds to throw every dish out of the refrigerator. She thinks he's simply an angel, even when (and he always does it) he throws the cat down the toilet bowl.

I may sit out the war here at Paramount, where I have been offered a contract. It's big dough—$600 a week—and except for being separated from my family I like the assignment—a Gypsy story for Lamour and de Cordova. I have a ten week guarantee with an option at the end of that period. If all goes well, I plan to move the family down here about February, if we can buy a house. [. . .]

But enough of that . . . Please give my love to everybody and my hope that all of you will be happy in the New Year. But most of all I hope that 1945 brings real Peace on Earth so those brave wonderful kids can come home. . . .

Always with affection,
johnnie

{c. summer 1948}
TUESDAY

Dear Mother and Father,

[. . .] Joyce joined the church a month ago. She was baptized in the Church and went to confession right afterward. Monday four weeks ago we both went to communion and Nuptial mass. We were married after Mass, and have been practicing Catholics ever since. Three weeks ago Sunday Danny was baptized. [. . .]

I wish you could have seen Danny at his baptism. He didn't want to go, but finally agreed if we would let him take his gun. So he was baptized holding a cowboy gun, and he threatened to shoot anybody who hurt him.

Love to you both,
Johnnie

SEPTEMBER 15, 1948

Dear Mother and Father,

It's been weeks since I wrote you. I don't know why, except that we have all been busy down here. [. . .]

I had a letter yesterday from Father Paul Reinert, who at 39 is the acting president of St. Louis University. Joyce wrote him, and this was his answer to her letter. A couple of weeks ago Joyce was very puzzled about some of the Church teachings, and she could find nobody to solve her problem. What she wanted to know was this: If God is all-good, and knows all things, then why did he create some men who are doomed to hell? How can an all-good, all-knowing God create a man who is not going to reach heaven?

This is a very tough question to answer. In fact, it was so tough that Paul couldn't answer it either. But he referred her to some books on the subject. Joyce read these and was satisfied.

I have had a lot of trouble with my work lately. It seems I haven't been able to write anything that gives me any satisfaction. I have tried movies, short stories, and even begun a book. But all of these have turned out badly. Rather than worry too much about it, I spent a lot of time playing golf. But there is no money in golf and I have stopped that and gone back to work again. I have another office now. It is right across the alley from the house, on Wilshire Blvd. The room is small but quiet and I pay $25 a month for it. It is a good place to work. I just got started here this morning, and I feel I will produce something here. I was down at Palm Springs last week for 5 days, working on a movie story with a friend, but we didn't get anything on paper.

Covici was in town two weeks ago. I had a long talk with him and told him my idea for a new book. He listened patiently and when I was finished he said he didn't like it. I was very disappointed. [. . .]

JULY 25, 1952
{*To The Stanley Kramer Company, Inc.*}

1438 North Gower Street
Los Angeles 28, California

Gentlemen:

My attention has been directed to a claim made by one Rena Vale that in 1939 she identified me as being a Communist Party member and described me at that time as being employed by RKO in the Orson Welles unit.

I was employed by RKO in 1939 in the Orson Welles unit. I had heard the name of Rena Vale at that time. I did not meet Rena Vale at that time nor at any time since. I was not a member at any time in my life of any Communist organization nor in any Communist front organization.

I am a Roman Catholic in addition to being an American citizen and it is philosophically and emotionally impossible for me to associate myself with any group that is even remotely identified with Communism or Communist front organizations.

I wish to repeat again—I never have been, am not now and under no circumstances would or could be a member of any Communist of Communist front organization.

I am strongly and unalterably opposed to any ideology foreign to our American form of Government.

Sincerely yours,
John Fante

{To his Malibu friend, television writer Jackson Stanley}

17 JAN 1954

Dear Jack:

I am very happy now. It is 2:00 am and the new day is almost here. It has the promise of 18 hours with my beautiful children and perhaps a couple of hours with my book. But I can tell you, my friend, that the bright moments will be with the children, and the sad, confusing, painful, frightening, even horrible hours will be with the book, and the book is nothing—nothing at all; even if it has importance it is still like nothing compared to the pleasures I shall have today with my kids.

Yours truly,

John Fante

JULY 28, 1957

Honey:

The women of Naples are pigs. They are fat pigs in frumpy dresses, usually black, and stained with tomato sauce, urine, grease, or a baby's bowel movement. Their breasts hang down to their knees, and their asses drip like water-filled balloons to the ground. When they walk, they don't—they shuffle, a sliding flop-flop on wooden or leather sandals out of which can be seen ten dirty toes. But I must explain that they are also wonderful women, each with the face of the mother of God and the twisted, calloused, tender hands of women who have spent a lifetime looking after their children and their men. Those giant flopping breasts, so ludicrous, so monstrous, comfort weeping children, and it is not hard to imagine that they arouse men. It is even possible that in Naples men prefer their women hulking and brutalized, with ponderous stomachs and eyes that have looked at God. I imagine the men want the women to possess a strong smell of sweat and menstruation because it is so close to the animal, it is as close as one can get and still live in a civilization. For, they are civilized, sophisticated, generous, kind, polite, gallant, and terribly brave people.

JULY 29

The Albergo Vesuvio is a wonderful hotel. My room overlooks the Via Carracciolo, a promenade skirting the whole Bay. Vesuvius is to my left when I walk out on the grill balcony of my third floor quarters. Across the street beyond the Via is a cluster of cafes built out on the water. Tonight as I write they are lighted by bright neon signs, and a hundred small boats are clustered beneath the wharf upon which the cafes are built. In the day Neapolitan kids dive into the water from the wharf for coins tossed by tourists. The water is incredibly dirty, with bits of food and slime all through it, but these rugged brown alert boys are healthy and possessed of fierce vitality. [. . .]

The food here is in great quantities, richly seasoned, generously served by polite waiters. Their meat is on the strong side, however, and most of it seems to be veal, although you really can get anything you want, from lamb chops to filet mignon. The great problem is avoiding the bread. It is sinfully good in any form, specially the rolls. They are always served with a small saucer filled with balls of creamy butter. Octopus is a famous delicacy hereabouts. [. . .] It is served right out of a pot, boiled, and comes slithering into your dish with all tentacles squashing about.

The back streets are fascinating—I refer to the poorer sections—no more than alleys, really, but swarming with people. Every door is some kind of shop and out front are stacked piles of vegetables, mountains of fish (tubs of eels swimming and very much alive) octopi, big slabs of tuna, and a hundred pink and yellow and white fish I've never seen before. There are shops that sell shirts, others that sell shoes, others dishes, others clothing, others bread, others milk, others pastry, each a specialty shop, some terribly dirty, others clean. Meat shops hang butchered animals in the front door or outside the front of the shop. Other places sell just eggs. Now and then you run into a basso (small lower floor shop) with a chicken out front, a string tied to one of its legs as it forages for food. And God the cats, and the dogs, and the kids! The kids are often bare-assed naked, all are as dirty as is humanly possible, but they are lovely. Sad to state, the little girls already look rather oddly unhandsome, with tight little faces and great beautiful eyes. You should see how sweetly little five year old girls mind their baby brothers, actually carrying them in their arms—for these children have human dolls to play with, early training for the heavy drudgery of early marriage. The boys are all very good-looking, and extremely uninhibited, wild savages in one respect, yet polite in another.

Having been here a few days, I now know why they wanted me to come. We must make this story contemporary, in order to capture the fabulous richness of the present scene. It means writing a brand new script, retaining only the story line of the previous one. At first, in Rome, talking to Jack Fier, I said I was against this, and meant it, but now that I have been here, I see that we have a tremendous opportunity to turn out something very fine and I don't mind the work. I would say that I won't be able to leave Naples until September 10th, or possibly not until the first of October. This does not mean that I am going to have very much fun, however. [. . .] The work is going to be harder. As time passes, I am going to miss you and the children more and more. By September I shall probably be insanely homesick. [. . .]

This is written July 30, after midnight, so that tomorrow marks the 20th anniversary of the best thing that ever happened to me in my lifetime, or in a thousand lifetimes. Surely you know the day will be spent with a twist in my heart for being so far away from the woman I love.

J.F.

{To his children, c. summer 1957}
TUESDAY

Dear Jimmy and Vicky:

Every time I go to a restaurant around the corner from the hotel, I sit outside under a big umbrella. Across the street I can see a lot of Naples children playing in the alley. They are very poor children, barefooted, wearing ragged shirts and shorts. But they don't mind being poor; in fact, they seem to have a very good time.

The very first day I went to that restaurant, a little girl from across the street came over to my table, smiled, touched her lips with her fingertips, and then held her fingers out for some money. In other words, she was giving me a kiss, and I was to give her a coin. She was about nine years old, this girl. She was rather tall, but very thin. She wore an old blue dress torn at the hem and shoulder. Her hair was black and it straggled down over her face. Her eyes were dark brown. The dress was too short, falling above her knees. Her legs were quite dirty. Her toes were simply black from street dirt. She wasn't really a pretty girl; in fact, her nose looked like it might have been broken at one time, and her teeth were not straight, nor were they clean. But in spite of all that, she seemed to be a very nice little girl. That first day, I gave her a coin. It was a 50 lira coin, a little more than a nickel, not quite as much as a dime. She ran across the street with the coin, and I watched her. She went into a store on the corner, and pretty soon she came out with two doughnuts. Then she crossed to the curbing, and sitting on the curbing was a little boy, a very small boy, only two years old, her little brother.

The next day when I went to the restaurant, the little girl came across the street again, and put out her hand, and I gave her another 50 lira, and she did the very same thing with it—bought doughnuts for herself and her brother. And so, every day I have seen her, and she has come over to my table, and each time I give her 50 lira.

I really wanted to do something extra nice for this sweet child. I know she needs a new dress badly, and I think she must need shoes. So last Sunday I thought I would tell her I wanted to take her to a fine store to buy a few things.

But she didn't come last Sunday. I looked for her, I waited for her, I even crossed the street and went down the alley, where she lives, but I couldn't find her. And she wasn't there this morning either. Now I'm worried. Maybe she's sick. Maybe she moved away. The next time I write to you, I will tell you if I saw her again. I don't even know her name, so I don't know how to find her.

Love from Daddy

[Letterhead] Hotel Prince de Galles
33, Avenue George V
Paris

JUNE 25, 1959

Honey:

I finished my draft of the script late this afternoon. It is being typed and Zanuck will get it tomorrow. I imagine he will read it over the weekend. We will then have a conference and do the final polish. It really can't amount to much work—no more than a day or two. After that I am presumably through with Zanuck's operations, unless he has something else to offer.

I am waiting for the script from DeLaurentiis. It was supposed to have been mailed from Rome Tuesday, meaning I should have received it by yesterday. I imagine it will come tomorrow. As you know, I am supposed to go down to Rome this weekend to talk about the script with DeL.

I am living a very quiet life, but this fucking hotel noise out in the plaza is horrible. I just don't get to sleep at night, not until three or so. Next morning I am half-dead with exhaustion, circles under my eyes, and a bad point of view for the new day.

Last night it was simply unspeakable, sounded like half of Paris was down there pushing furniture around, shouting and laughing. At 28 bucks a night it would seem that the cheapest thing they could provide here is a little quiet, but as you know, everybody over the plaza has to put up with it. I don't think the hotel cares because the guests are all transients and they figure to rob and disquiet them just once anyway.

Bill Saroyan came around with his kids for a moment yesterday afternoon during a lovely rain. His boy Aram is a nice looking lad, as tall as Bill and very amiable. Lucy is quite small with a large mouth and quite a big nose. She resembles Carol. She is really a very sweet child. I wish she had a more pleasing face.

I usually go to dinner with Guido Orlando. He keeps telling stories, wild and preposterous. But he is very good company. I haven't seen Zanuck at all since you left. Dorothy is doing the typing of the script. She still calls me Clang Clang. [Elvis] Presley is still here. Orlando introduced me to him. He is quite a nice kid. Every afternoon at this time (7 pm) the street is jammed with kids carrying his picture, waiting for him to come out and autograph.

Wish I had more news but it's pretty quiet. I'm relieved to be finished though. Saroyan wants to sell me his Carmen-Ghia for 1400 dollars. It only has 12,000 miles on it, a little red job with leather bucket seats. It would cost about 400 to ship it home—but I just don't need it.

Love to all,
jf

{1960}

Honey—

I think this is Tuesday, August 16. Nick and I are finally settled in a wonderful old house where Raphael used to live. It is very close to the Vatican, in old Rome. I am at long last settled down and happy, but the road has been long and hard.

The place at Via Giacinto Pizzana was impossible. There were fleas in the beds. There was no hot water (out of order), and there was a lot of noise. It was far away from everything. The nearest restaurant was a mile away. The rent was 80 thousand lira a month, about $116 a month, plus lights and gas and a cleaning woman.

Now we are at Via Rusticucci 14. We each have a bedroom in this very old house. Across the alley is a great ancient Roman wall over which (or through which, because there is a corridor) the popes used to flee to Castel

San Angelo. Beyond this wall are enormously ancient dwellings of poorer people. The whole area is the property of the Vatican and carefully preserved.

At the moment Nick is off somewhere walking around. It is 4:00 pm of a warmish day. He has walked a great deal. I imagine he is looking for a girl, and I think I shall get one for him myself very soon now. Coletti has a sister-in-law, a 19 year old, who is simply ravishing. I want Nick to meet her. He seems rather restless. The language barrier is of course a terrible burden—bad enough for me too, though I am fast learning to say things and be understood.

The lady who owns this apartment is a sweet old signora named Emelia. Her husband died three months ago. She speaks no English but is utterly charming and very glad to have us. The rent is 50,000 lire a month.

It has certainly been hectic so far. I am way behind in the script, but it can't be helped because really it is a very bad thing they gave me, and I have to think it out carefully.

Life in Rome so far has been a journey through the stomach. God, how we eat! No denying I've gained weight, but I am going to get it off. Nick has put on considerable too. He is wild about the food. In this area of the Vatican there are dozens and dozens of small trattoria, or little cafes where the food is exquisite. We plan to try them all out.

I am reasonably healthy—always a bit tired—sleep comes slowly and doesn't last long. The place is terribly noisy everywhere and one must get used to it. As for all that I have seen, I have not quite reacted to anything. I get the odd feeling of walking through post-cards—a one dimensional contact with the past. None of it moves me with any force. But the sky is always exquisite, dazzling white clouds rolling past. The nights are warm and eerily unreal, almost too perfect. I would say this is a more beautiful city than Paris, but somehow it is not charged with the electricity of Paris. It is useless to try and see everything. I am told it is the job of a lifetime and I believe it.

At last a permanent address! VIA RUSTICUCCI 14, Rome.

All my love—

JF

SEPT. 2, 1960

Honey—

I am here one month today. Over 100 pages finished—none of which anybody likes, I think. It's a most complicated business. I had to cut down a 220 page script, so I cut hard. Now the director thinks I cut too deeply, also that I don't understand Neapolitans. Maybe. But I don't think they are nearly as complicated as Coletti likes to believe, and I do understand them, and I furthermore understand only too well what constitutes a good story. Me worried? Honestly I am not. The whole matter will gradually work out, with compromises.

Giuliano, the grave-digger, is going away to Greece to work for 20th Century-Fox. (Isn't that a mad sentence!) He'll be gone five months, leaving his English girl in Rome. She is 28, a dancer, very cute, and got along wonderfully with Nick. I think something will brew here.

Nick has found out there is (Oh, God) a bowling alley in Rome. He will probably be there tonight. He usually goes to a movie at night, coming in about 2 am, always finding me sound asleep. Herb Tobias is here now and may take Nick to Madrid for a couple of days, just for company. Nick (and this is the last item about him) may also go to Milan to watch some automobile races.

This is a haunted house. I think the ghost is Raphael. He does only one enigmatic deed. In the middle of the night, he flushes the toilet. It seems to happen every night. [. . .]

There are two wonderful female bargains in Rome, both of which I want to use for you. Gloves and sweaters. Send me your size in both. I think I know, but I want to be sure. Also, send me Vicky's sweater and skirt (dress) size. The Frederick's purchase intrigues me, even from 5000 miles. All my love . . .

> your affectionate slave,
> Johnny

{*To his son Dan*}
SUNDAY
SEPT 3, 1960

Dear Danny:

I was very glad to get your letter. Thanks for taking the time to write your beat-up old man. You write a very nice letter, by the way—clean, clear statements, direct and to the point. Maybe you're a writer too, like myself. Think about it [. . .]

I keep working, but that's about all. I don't get into any trouble, or get drunk, or blow my dough. I hate to say it, but I'm stiffening up like all old clods. I see lots of broads I'd like to bed down, but it's just a kind of dreamy notion which quickly passes. I'll take your Mother any day. [. . .]

Lots of love . . .

Dad

{To Carey McWilliams}
OCTOBER 10, 1966

Dear Carey:

The other night on the Mort Sahl show, Mort declared that Carey McWilliams, editor of The Nation knew all the unrevealed truths of the Kennedy assassination and found them so perilous, so calamitous that he refused to publish them.

Can this be true? Certainly I can imagine you not publishing a piece for reasons of libel, or bad taste, but I find it hard to believe that you would stint about the truth. This is a very disturbing business, and it is conceivable that the truth about the assassination could have terrible consequences if, say, LBJ had been a part of the conspiracy to gun down JFK, which of course is one of many current rumors on the subject, and one which I don't believe. But pray tell me—are you silent on the subject for the reason Sahl mentions, or is he just sounding off?

Well, Nick finally did it. After living with half a dozen Afro-American females, he finally took one for his bride. We haven't met the unfortunate young lady, but she seems to be uncommonly bright, a graduate of Univ. of Indiana, with an excellent position at General Motors. [. . .]

Danny lives in the Bronx, is wedded to a sweet maternal Jewish girl who has fattened him so that he looks just like the little pig who built his house of bricks. He drives a cab and is getting ready to go back to school at Hunter College. He is 1A in the Draft, but he has declared himself a Conscientious Objector, and every now and then hoists a picket in peace marches. My children . . . oh, my God!

Our daughter Victoria is a ravishing little thing, seventeen now, a truly great beauty [. . .]. This Summer we had as many as 20 boys around here day and night. They were like mongrel dogs sniffing every tree. But now she has found a steady guy [. . .]. They surf tandem style on every beach from here to San Diego. One of the joys of being a father is to witness your daughter held aloft by some jerk riding an eight foot surf on a tandem board.

Finally there is Jimmy, now almost sixteen, my best hope for an unworried old age. He surfs a lot and smokes a lot, but he gets good grades and stays out of trouble. I couldn't ask for more.

I am suddenly and without explanation writing again. One day two weeks ago I made up my mind to abandon pictures and to my astonishment it was easy. Last week I wrote a 25 page short story—and it was easy. I feel reborn. Now, if my money will only hold out. . . .

Best regards,
John Fante
28981 W. Cliffside Drive
Malibu 3, Calif.

FEB. 1, 1971

Dear Carey:

Remember, in "Roughing It," that crazy letter written to Horace Greeley. Every time Greeley read it he got a different interpretation until the thing made no sense at all . . .

I get the same reaction to your letter regarding my novel. I don't know if you like the book or not. I think you *want* to like it but you have reservations. Which is fine. I feel the same way. Sometimes it sends me into utter despair. But I am sure it will be a very successful book. My Hollywood agent is wild about it and has 15 copies in circulation around town. The story editor at Warner's hated it, but the story editor at Universal is crazy about it, and so is the editor at Bing Crosby's. So who knows about these things. It gets down to the simple truth that one must please one's self above all. And except for an occasional shudder of doubt I am pleased with what I wrote.

My New York agent has always been Elizabeth Otis, and she is of course handling the novel from there. I am writing her today and telling her to contact you by telephone. If it's not too much trouble you can suggest her sending the manuscript to the people you mention in your letter [. . .].

My daughter Vicky is taking unto herself a spouse in two weeks and I shall be present in a tux with striped pants to give the bride away. The orgy is wiping me out, but totally. I never thought it would happen to John Fante, but it will. After that only Jimmy will be at home, though not for long. Then we shall be alone, Joyce and I, and I am sure we shall discover some interesting things about one another.

All the best to you and Iris.

Regards
John Fante

APRIL 21, 1971

Dear Carey:

The rejection by Grove Press is dismal news of course, but I am not discouraged. Somewhere in that publishing jungle my little book will surely find a home. [. . .]

My lawsuit against my neighbor is proceeding to a climax. His lawyers have asked for an account of all medical expenses in connection with the dog bite and my attorney Sam Newman (former screenwriter and a brute of a lawyer) expects a settlement soon.

My oddball son Nick is now a preacher of the gospel. Seems that a Hungarian minister of the Church of Universal Light and a machinist at the factory where Nick works has ordained him for the sum of five bucks. The thing is actually legitimate. Nick is now empowered to perform marriages and baptismal services. He gets a 15% discount on airline tickets and, should he be arrested, is entitled to a private cell in jail. He thinks it's a bargain. Incidentally, his black wife is a pretty good country-and-western singer and has signed a contract to record a couple of songs. My little black and white granddaughter is now three, a very beautiful child. She was here Easter and we hid eggs all over the yard for her to find. She is an aggressive little creature and my fearless dogs run and hide in terror at the sight of her.

Many thanks for your help with the book.

Sincerely,
John Fante

APRIL 25, 1974

Dear Carey:

Many sincere thanks for the two fine, persuasive letters you sent to Peregrine Smith and the U. of Washington Press. I have already heard from Gibbs Smith in Salt Lake City asking for a copy of Ask The Dust, and it is in the mail to him as of yesterday.

Today in the mail I had a letter from The Nation—rather, an empty envelope, dated New York, April 22. The flap was only lightly glued, so I presume it came open and the contents spilled out. I don't know if it was a letter from you or not. Maybe all your girls have dry tongues, which, as you know, can be very painful.

I'll keep you informed on what happens to Ask the Dust. Robert Towne, who wrote the screenplay of The Last Detail, has had it optioned from me for the past three years and is supposed to be writing the screenplay. Would you believe that the option dough he has paid me so far (about $4500) is more than twice the money I got for writing Ask the Dust, and that includes royalties, of which there were absolutely none? The combined revenue I have had from Wait Until Spring Bandini, Ask the Dust and Dago Red (in book form) wouldn't purchase a lawnmower on today's market, and man, what I really need today is a good mower.

Which reminds me. I am growing garlic. I have a small patch which is doing so well I may put the whole place in garlic next Spring. An Italian growing garlic sounds like the most natural combination in the world. A friend of my son Jimmy is living in a tent in the back of my acre, and he is growing pot. My wife has found a secluded place among the trees, quiet and invisible, and she plans to build a gazebo where she can meditate. Lots of action around here, as you can see. Meanwhile I sit in my dirty little room sucking my thumb and trying to write a novel. I've got close to 30 thousand words, and I'm calling it The Brotherhood of the Grape— the story of four old Italian wine drunks from Roseville, a tale revolving around my father and his friends.

Have a nice summer. Love to Iris.

Regards,
John Fante

{To his distant East Coast cousin Mary Rose Fante Cunningham}
SEPTEMBER 17, 1981

Dear Mary Rose:

I am sorry not to have answered your letter of last June, but there have been so many changes in my life that letter writing is now a grave problem, for I lost my eyesight two years ago due to the complications of diabetes, which brought on glaucoma and total blindness. Now my wife assists me in my writing, which is difficult and tedious. I have also survived double amputation of my legs because of gangrene. I live in a wheelchair now, and my activity is curtailed. I hate to inform you of these dreadful circumstances, but frankly there isn't very much beyond my misfortunes that I can speak about.

I am not bitter, but I am discouraged. I have begun a new novel and it progresses with considerable difficulty. The worst result of blindness is its effect upon memory. I forget things. I dictate a sentence and in five minutes I can't remember what it was. In the course of filling out a novel you can see the problems I have to face, but I blunder on. My latest novel, an autobiographical fragment called *Dreams from Bunker Hill* will be published by Black Sparrow Press of Santa Barbara this fall.

My memories of Uncle Mingo are dimmed by the passage of time. I best remember when I was a small boy, my father recalling in glowing praise his heroic Uncle Mingo, who must have lived in Abruzzi in 1880 or thereabouts. My father said that Uncle Mingo was loyal to the king at that time and was hanged by the other side. In *Full of Life* I describe my father telling me this wondrous memory of his uncle. I have no copies of *Full of Life* to send you but if I should come across one shall send it on to you. Eventually all of my works will be republished by Black Sparrow Press, and made available in bookstores. Thank you for your very kind letter.

Sincerely yours,
John Fante

{To his aunt Dorothy Shearer, in Paradise, California}
25 SEPTEMBER 1981

Dear Aunt Dorothy:

How did you arrive in Paradise? Did you spend very much time in purgatory? I wonder if you ran into my father. I am certain that he spent at least 25 years in purgatory, and may be in Heaven at this time. I was very sorry to read of your eye problems, but I hasten to say that I too am now blind, after the ravages of diabetes and glaucoma. I have also lost the use of my legs through double amputation, thus I cannot see nor walk, and spend all of my time either in a wheelchair or in bed. Not that I am complaining. On the contrary I'm whining and angry and annoyed and humiliated by my present station in life, but I do have some of the comforts of the living. I have my dear wife Joyce who is taking down this dictation, as well as my four children—my son Nick, 39, Daniel 37,

Victoria 31, and Jimmy 30. I have a number of grandchildren, some of whom visit me frequently.

As for myself I am twenty-six years old, take 26 units of insulin every day, and spend a lot of time listening to the radio. I also write novels. In the order of their appearance my novels include *Wait Until Spring, Bandini, The Brotherhood of the Grape,* and *Dreams From Bunker Hill.* All of these works are being reprinted by Black Sparrow Press, Santa Barbara. I have a few copies of my own, but I need them in my work.

My sons Nick and Jim are engineers in a technology plant in Santa Monica. Both of them are extremely successful and make a lot of money. My son Dan is bright and courageous and one day he will definitely succeed. My daughter Victoria is divorced and the mother of two boys. She is a moody beautiful girl of great passion and style. All of us adore her.

Finally I must not forget Willy and Ginger, my dogs. They have scads of fleas, but they worship me. I accept them, fleas and all.

Last but not least is the woman who brought all of this on—all of my problems, my travail, my bitterness, my true love, my dear and beautiful wife, who is without shame, a born hussy, who mistreats me, reviles me, and loves me in return. We are truly an odd couple, bumping into one another from time to time, cursing one another, and quarreling day and night—but love we never lack, and the moment our quarreling ceases we are in one another's arms again. It's a hard life, but I can't think of any other that suits me so well.

It was good to learn of Ralph and Arthur. Give them my love. My best to your husband.

Your nephew,
John

John Fante died at the Motion Picture Hospital in Woodland Hills, California on May 8, 1983. He was seventy-four years old.

Bibliography

Fante, John. *Ask the Dust*. New York: Stackpole Sons, 1939. Bantam paperback edition, 1954. Reprint, Santa Barbara: Black Sparrow Press, 1980.

———. *The Big Hunger: Stories 1932–1959*. Ed. Stephen Cooper. Santa Rosa: Black Sparrow Press, 2000.

———. and Rudolph Borchert. *Bravo, Burro!* Illustrated by Marilyn Hirsh. New York: Hawthorn Books, 1970.

———. *The Brotherhood of the Grape*. Boston: Houghton Mifflin, 1977. Reprint, Santa Rosa: Black Sparrow Press, 1988.

———. *Dago Red*. New York: The Viking Press, 1940.

———. *Dreams from Bunker Hill*. Santa Barbara: Black Sparrow Press, 1982.

———. *John Fante & H. L. Mencken: A Personal Correspondence 1930–1952*. Ed. Michael Moreau and consulting ed. Joyce Fante. Santa Rosa: Black Sparrow Press, 1989.

———. *John Fante: Selected Letters 1932–1981*. Ed. Seamus Cooney. Santa Rosa: Black Sparrow Press, 1991.

———. *Full of Life*. Boston: Little, Brown, 1952. Bantam paperback edition, 1953. Reprint, Santa Rosa: Black Sparrow Press, 1988.

———. *1933 Was a Bad Year*. Santa Barbara: Black Sparrow Press, 1991.

———. *Prologue to* Ask the Dust. Santa Rosa: Black Sparrow Press, 1990.

———. *The Road to Los Angeles*. Santa Barbara: Black Sparrow Press, 1985.

———. *Wait Until Spring, Bandini*. New York: Stackpole Sons, 1938. Reprint, Santa Barbara: Black Sparrow Press, 1983.

———. *West of Rome*. Santa Rosa: Black Sparrow Press, 1986.

———. *The Wine of Youth: Selected Stories*. Santa Barbara: Black Sparrow Press, 1983.

SELECTED SECONDARY BIBLIOGRAPHY

Collins, Richard. *John Fante: A Literary Portrait*. Toronto: Guernica, 2000.

Cooper, Stephen. *Full of Life: A Biography of John Fante*. New York: North Point Press, 2000.

———. "John Fante's Eternal City." In *Los Angeles in Fiction*, revised ed. Ed. David Fine. Albuquerque: University of New Mexico Press, 1995. 83–99.

———. "Madness and Writing in the Works of Hamsun, Fante and Bukowski." *Genre* 19 (1998): 19–27.

———. and David Fine, eds. *John Fante: A Critical Gathering*. Madison, N.J.: Fairleigh Dickinson University Press, 1999.

Gordon, Neil. "Shanghaied in Tinseltown." *Salon.com* (May 12, 2000).

Kordich, Catherine J. *John Fante: His Novels and Novellas*. New York: Twayne, 2000.

Ulin, David L. "Back from the Dust." *Los Angeles Times Book Review* (May 14, 1995): 9.